LEICA FORMAT

Also by Daša Drndić in English translation

Trieste (2012)
Belladonna (2017)
E.E.G. (2018)

Daša Drndić

LEICA FORMAT

Translated from the Croatian by
Celia Hawkesworth

MACLEHOSE PRESS
QUERCUS · LONDON

First published in the Croatian language as *Leica format* by Meandar in 2003
First published in Great Britain in 2015 by MacLehose Press
This paperback edition published in 2021 by

MacLehose Press
an imprint of Quercus Publishing Ltd
Carmelite House
50 Victoria Embankment
London EC4Y 0DZ

An Hachette UK company

The authorised representative in the EEA is Hachette Ireland, 8 Castlecourt
Centre, Dublin 15, D15 XTP3, Ireland (email: info@hbgi.ie)

The publication of this book is supported by a grant from
the Ministry of Culture of the Republic of Croatia

A CIP catalogue record for this book is available
from the British Library.

ISBN (MMP) 978 1 84866 587 3
ISBN (Ebook) 978 1 84866 586 6

10 9 8 7 6 5 4 3

Designed and typeset in Minion by Libanus Press, Marlborough
Printed and bound in Great Britain by Clays Ltd, Elcograf S.p.A.

MIX
Paper | Supporting
responsible forestry
FSC® C104740

Papers used by Quercus are from well-managed forests and other responsible sources.

fugues
fugues
fugues
fugues
fugues
fugues
fugues
fugues

Fugue – a medical disorder involving memory loss, long-term amnesia, during which mental capacity is not disturbed. The condition may provoke a headlong departure from familiar surroundings as the result of an insuperable, uncontrolled need to create a new life (in new surroundings). Following recovery, the sufferer does not recall the previous – pathological – state. From the Latin word *fuga* – flight, particularly flight from the homeland, persecution, but also expulsion.

Fugue – a polyphonic musical composition in which themes are repeated successively according to specific rules; an artistic form with a theme and response, which is not the case with these sketches that are in fact junk; they contain no response, because it is debatable whether they pose questions at all, any kind of questions. They are sometimes repeated, repeated according to "specific rules", and they are sometimes also outside them, but they have nothing more to ask.

Fugue – a German architectural term, a joint between stones or tiles; a deliberate gap in the building process to obviate the possibility of the construction developing fissures; a crack, which might be a metaphor for this debris.

It is May 1992. More precisely, it is 14 May, 1992, in the morning. The day is sunny, almost summery. Antonia Host, a forty-two-year-old housewife, mother of two (thirteen and sixteen), is carrying a suitcase, brittle, cracked from lying around, from dust and dry air, from non-travel, from non-departure, from non-arrival anywhere or to anyone. The housewife Antonia Host leaves the courtyard of her building, without locking the door behind her. The washing-up is done, the beds made, the flowers bright and blooming. Antonia Host sings "*Bella ciao*" sotto voce and her hair – freshly dyed, streaked with red and cut in a modern style – billows and sways as she walks. *I have lovely hair*, says Antonia Host. *It is shiny. Bella ciao, bella ciao, bella ciao, ciao, ciao*, sings Antonia Host as she walks. It could not be said that Antonia Host is sad.

Antonia Host catches a train and arrives in the port two hours before the boat leaves for the south of Europe. In a fishermen's tavern she eats grilled calamari and chard with olive oil, drinks a glass of Merlot and a coffee with no milk or sugar. She books a cabin. Travels for two days. Watches the sea. Hums. Arrives in a Mediterranean town. Rents a room. Watches the sea. Hums. Drums her fingers. She keeps tapping with her fingers, rapidly and softly, as though she were drumming on the taut skin of an African tom-tom. She is separated from her life by a thousand kilometres and who knows how many nautical miles. Or maybe nothing separates her from anything.

The Mediterranean town is historically famous; it is an old town full of lifelessness, but its music is alive. It is a town with a lively Academy of Music, known far and wide. The day after she arrives, Antonia Host puts sandals, black, with high heels, onto her bare feet, and in a tight

Shantung dress, also black, knocks on the door of the Director of the Academy. It is a sunny day, even more summery, even warmer than the day in the town that Antonia Host has abandoned, which lies at the foot of an oak forest; this town has pines in abundance. The sky is shamelessly blue, *The sky is indigo blue, the sky is singing*, says Antonia Host, *and my make-up looks good*. Antonia Host has green eyes and an elegant height. Antonia Host breathes deeply and regularly. *I like my red lips and my red hair*, she says. *I like my hips, they are serious hips and they carry a song, and my dress is elegant*, she says.

She presents herself to the Director of the Academy as Lydia Paut.

I graduated from here, years ago, she says. *I am a pianist*, she says. *I'd like to teach. My name is Lydia Paut.* That is what she says.

Start with private lessons. Then we'll see. That is what the Director says, very politely, very obligingly.

As Lydia Paut, Antonia Host becomes popular in the once-fortified town, today it is a sunny town and open on all sides. Lydia Paut, alias Antonia Host, plays in chamber concerts, she also makes solo appearances. She plays in the open air, she plays in stone halls in which her shoulders freeze. The audience is international and select. Two years later, the Director of the Academy (that same man) says: *Dear Lydia, I'd like you to become my deputy.* Antonia Host, or Lydia Paut, says: *I would be delighted.*

Lydia Paut has friends. Lydia Paut has a flat, she has a piano, she has new memories. *My old memories are as wide as sails, they flutter like ghosts, they are white as sheets, and nothing is written on them*, says Lydia Paut when someone asks about her past, although few people ask her anything, that is the way people are. They mind their own business. Lydia Paut learns new languages. Lydia Paut laughs.

Five years pass. Life is good. *Sometimes I walk through the stone streets barefoot*, says Lydia Paut. *The stone exudes the warmth of the sun.*

It is the New Year concert. Lydia Paut plays Liszt. The town breathes ceremoniously, multitudes of small silver lights sparkle. The nights are cold and dry. The waves are wild, but they do not enter the town. After the concert, a fat woman approaches Lydia Paut and says:

You are not Lydia Paut. You are Antonia Host. I know you both. We studied together in this town, long ago.

Lydia Paut (Antonia Host) looks at the fat woman, wide-eyed. *That's not possible*, she says. *I've never seen you before.*

Soon after, Antonia Host, still convinced that she is Lydia Paut, is transported by helicopter (forcibly) to her former town, the autumnal one. Her husband, a well-known public figure in politics and the Church, is waiting for her on the tarmac. Her children, now grown up, are waiting for her as well. *Who are you?* asks Antonia Host. *I don't know you.*

Antonia Host is taken to a psychiatric clinic where her amnesia is treated, her fugue rooted out. *We'll bring you back to life*, they say.

To which life? asks Lydia Paut, then falls silent for ever.

A BRIEF BIOGRAPHY OF ANTONIA HOST

Antonia Host grows up in a fanatically religious Catholic family. Despite the fact that her parents publicly advocate strict morals, they accuse one another manically of infidelity, they accuse one another so much, they shout so much, they utter so many appalling words in the small hours of the night, drunk, that Antonia begins to doubt the legitimacy of her conception. *Divorce is out of the question*, Antonia Host's parents keep saying in response to their friends' and relations' increasingly frequent suggestions. *It would be sacrilegious and blasphemous*, they say. And so Antonia Host's parents stay together "until death does them part", venting their mutual intolerance at their two daughters. Antonia lives immured in a world of prohibitions. With no outings and no company. In silent solitude, in pleated tweed dresses, buttoned up to the chin. With a wardrobe full of white collars and long, crocheted socks, with a weight of mousy-brown plaits down her back and nightmares in her head. Antonia has an older sister, Magdalena, with whom she shares secrets, not that she has any. That is how she lives. But, when Antonia is seventeen, Magdalena dies. Antonia is inconsolable. Antonia becomes reticent, even more reticent that is. Antonia does not listen to the music she once loved. Antonia no longer plays the piano, she no longer practises. When she finishes school, her parents send Antonia to a conservatoire in a town in the south of Europe. In the town in the south of Europe, Antonia shares a flat with the student Lydia Paut. Lydia Paut is a sunny, attractive girl with naturally red hair. Lydia Paut is good. Lydia Paut loves Antonia Host. Thanks to her, Antonia Host acquires friends and happiness. *You are my new sister*, Antonia tells her friend Lydia Paut.

But, but. In the fifth year of her studies, Lydia Paut falls in love with a young dentist. Antonia Host goes to dances and outings with the lovers. And, inevitably, begins to nurture a secret inclination towards her "sister's" fiancé. Which is, given her upbringing, an inadmissible state of affairs, an unforgiveable sin. Tormented by jealousy and unrequited love, Antonia Host returns to the cage of her childhood. Lydia Paut abandons her studies, marries and goes off with her husband to another country, across the ocean. Antonia Host, downcast and withdrawn, graduates, but listlessly, and marries a man to whom she is physically and spiritually indifferent, punishing herself because of her unmanageable longing for "forbidden fruit". Life alongside a man of conservative views, a devout believer, opposed to popular music and contemporary films, opposed to abortion, opposed to independent, employed women, opposed to lesbians and homosexuals, opposed to agnostics and atheists, not to mention communists, opposed to fashion, opposed to dyed hair and make-up, opposed to perfume, opposed to cafés, tobacco, wine and coffee, a man fanatically devoted to a healthy lifestyle that makes even the fittest ill, this life becomes intolerable for Antonia Host. Her student days spent in the town in the south of Europe are transformed in her imagination into a fairy tale, which, through her own carelessness of course, she had let slip from her hands to shatter into tiny pieces, which she then masochistically ground into dust. To make matters worse, Antonia Host's younger daughter, exceptionally musically gifted and her favourite, dies after a lengthy illness. This happens on 10 May, 1992. After the funeral, Antonia Host goes to the hairdresser and says: *Give me red streaks.* Three days later, on 14 May, 1992, Antonia Host takes her battered suitcase of sickly brown plastic, without any explanation abandons her home and – as far as those around her are concerned – vanishes without trace.

Fugues – little friends of our reality, indestructible. Sometimes, to a collection of innocent fugues, we add submissive little fuguettes which, like small faithful dogs, scamper round our heels, elusive fugues tasting of dreams. We unearth fugues that we thought were long since dead out of who knows which storehouses. Our fugues are our beliefs, our common sense, our gods, they are the peace with which we decorate our lives as we decorate Christmas trees, at times excessively. How would we manage otherwise, how? It is warm beneath the fugues, they are a tent over our days. Beside them and with them we stroll into a time of paltry pain. When good people come along, and they adore coming along just to suck us into their lives, plucking us out of our own, we say, *Fine*. And we wait for the germ of a new fugue to bud, to uncoil from our breath like the tone of a mysterious melody and grow and grow until it becomes a symphony into which we plunge. One person winks, embraces his fugue and sets sail. Another frowns, tucks his fugue into his bosom and walks on as though nothing were happening, yet another tells his fugue to get lost, turns his back on it and – is extinguished. These extinguished, fugue-less people mill around everywhere, everywhere. They are mobile suits of armour made of plaster, which move, rigid, over this planet and sometimes howl, like ghosts, singing their resonance, their hollowness. At times of heavy rains, when floods burst, they melt and dissolve into nothing, only then. When droughts come, they crack and send out a chilling sound, ominous. And so it goes on for ever, from one life to another, every day.

This is like a fairy tale, all this.

There are nightmare fairy tales. Fairy tales are home to monsters and nymphs, dwarves and giants; murders, great and small, take place in them; in them deaths are tender, loving, but also cruel and vengeful. In fairy tales, murdered beings come to life, one way or another, while some for ever disappear, they leave, but the story still goes on. The fairy tale gets by without those eliminated (dead, murdered) heroes, because that is how it was conceived, to contain disturbances, here and there. This is like a fairy tale, all this, our lives today. Unfathomable.

This is a state of sickness – similar to the state following the parting of two lovers, a parting imposed by circumstance, not volition. A state of nausea, a state of stasis. This is a life that simply will not "lie down"; it rubs and creaks like socialist shoes. This is a dislocated life like a shadow.

These are stains.

Turning and turning in the widening gyre
The falcon cannot hear the falconer;
Things fall apart; the centre cannot hold;
Mere anarchy is loosed upon the world,
The blood-dimmed tide is loosed, and everywhere
The ceremony of innocence is drowned;
The best lack all conviction, while the worst
Are full of passionate intensity.

I once met a man who collected editions of *The Little Prince*. He didn't collect other books, he only collected *The Little Prince*. He had *The Little Prince* in forty-seven languages, all different formats, with illustrations in colour and illustrations in black and white, *The Little Prince* in hardcover, *The Little Prince* in paperback and *The Little Prince* mutilated, without covers, truncated. Perhaps he has more than forty-seven *Little Prince*s by now, I don't know; the man disappeared from my life long ago and it's unclear why I thought of him just now, during this enforced flight. The man may not even be alive; when I met him he was old and smoked a pipe in a large empty house somewhere in America. There was no furniture in his house (there was some folding furniture, mostly for the garden, as though the man were intending at any minute to go off somewhere, as though he were preparing to leave – or to wait) and the man walked through his rooms, alone. Perhaps he really was waiting for something (or someone) to be returned to him, but that is, I see now, senseless. If the man has died, what has happened to his collection? When I have nothing to do, I ought to investigate that, whether his *Little Prince*s are scattered all over the world, whether they ended up in some North American trashcan and have been recycled into new stories.

Pessoa is often annoying. Like when a dentist pokes around an exposed nerve with a drill, that is how he digs. Pessoa scratches at himself and around himself, madly, pityingly, self-pityingly, rarely crossly, but there again . . .

> I don't know if these feelings are some slow madness
> brought on by hopelessness, if they are recollections
> of some other world in which we've lived – confused,
> jumbled memories, like things glimpsed in dreams,
> absurd as we see them now but not in their origin if

we but knew what that was. I don't know if we once were other beings, whose greater completeness we sense only incompletely today, being mere shadows of what they were, beings that have lost their solidity in our feeble two-dimensional imaginings of them amongst the shadows we inhabit.

Who is saying this,

he or I?

Fernando, said Pessoa's grandmother Dionisia before she died in an asylum, *Fernando, you will be like me, because blood is a traitor. You will drag me after you your whole life. Life is madness and you will fill your pockets with madness until the day of your death.*

One night Alberto Caeiro spoke in Fernando's skull, pale, blond and blue-eyed. *I am your father and your master*, he said. *I shall die of tuberculosis in the village of Ribatejo, in the arms of my big fat aunt. Such is life*, replied Pessoa, *enigmatic. Everything in it is hidden, including you.*

When Alberto Caeiro died, Pessoa did not weep, he made love to Ophelia Quéiroz, the young secretary at the company where he worked. *Here is a poem for you*, said Alvaro de Campos, a decadent futurist and nihilist with whom Pessoa occasionally drank, mostly in a little restaurant called "Pessoa", where Bernardo Soares secretly noted his anxieties on paper napkins or old bus tickets. When he had heard the poem by Alvaro de Campos to the end, Pessoa was deeply moved. *It's a wonderful poem*, he said. *There are many young men who look like girls. They even use anti-wrinkle cream around their eyes. They are delicate and like wearing tight clothes. And jewellery. I shall break off my relationship with*

Ophelia. One day Ophelia came to work in a green dress with yellow flowers, a yellow ribbon in her hair. *I often pass by the same beggar*, said Pessoa to Ophelia. *Then his stench follows me for ages. Farewell, dearest Ophelia. I have written verses for all the people in the world, but only my parrot is able to recite them.*

How do the deaf manage? Who do they talk to, who do they hear, where are their voices? Is it possible that a black hole of silence gapes in the heads of the deaf? Had he been born deaf, Pessoa might not have quadrupled, he would have remained alone. And dumb. Returning from work arm in arm with the demure Ophelia, shivering in her violet winter coat, he would have watched cockroaches mating.

Proust gets on my nerves as well. I only look at his books from the outside, there's no question of my reading him. So I won't quote him.

They say that there's a Japanese man who rears bonsai kittens, midgets. He puts them into jars, inserts a tube into their anal opening and draws its other end out through the neck of the jar, then he feeds them through the tube. The food is not natural, but chemical nourishment that sterilises the little creatures at the same time. Eventually, the kittens take on the shape of the jars. In the jars, they cannot move, they cannot turn round, they cannot clean themselves. The jars are usually square, so in time the kittens become square too.

People could be put into jars as well; and people would also become small, they would become midgets, dwarves, looking through the glass wide-eyed and perhaps just moving their lips. These little mannikins and womannikins, these human freaks could be put on shelves like ornamental people. On the shelves there would be a lot of glass jars with a mass of miniature humanoid creatures that breathe, in fact pant, so the jars would be misted up. There would be silence. Living silence, rhythmic and undulating, human. Human silence.

In an asylum in the south, or perhaps in the north, the inmates sewed up their lips – with surgical thread, silken. Surgical thread is strong. The inmates used a (wide) curved needle for the sewing, and each mouth was sewn with three, at most four, stitches. This was the patients' (silent) protest against the staff, who paid them no attention. In the asylum a still greater soundlessness then reigned, a vast hush that today, like steam, like smoke, gushes from the ceilings and walls of the ruined building in the back of beyond and rises in clouds towards the sky; during black nights (moonless nights), that same soundlessness, that ominous human hush, allegedly mad, returns as a breeze; it falls like downy rain onto the clouded panes of our refuge in never-land and, because it is their only air, in order to survive, the patients fill their by now empty, flaccid lungs with this noxious but odourless breeze, this invisible cobweb of silence. The landscape around the asylum is sealed, petrified, motionless as a drawing. It lies under a lava of silence woven of inaudible footsteps, which rustle softly because they stream out of the asylum in which all the slippers are made of felt.

That landscape, that asylum, that madhouse of our age, has scattered its remnants everywhere, even across the seas. Like excavations, like fossils of our history, they emerge, in one shape or another, they emerge every day and create an immense shudder that incites nausea.

Those jars, for instance.

Those jars in which there are none of the above imagined but nevertheless existent humanoid creations shaped in the silence of literary imaginings, people who for centuries have been making an ominous din, those jars in which one ought long ago to have begun to arrange, conserve and hermetically seal exemplars of polluted humanity, as a punishment; those jars, in a real asylum once called Am Steinhof, and later, for the sake of peace in the soul and forced oblivion, renamed Otto Wagner Spital; those jars, which have been waiting on shelves for half a century and more in the dank cellars of Europe, the dark cellars of Vienna; those jars where children's brains float, no-one knows exactly how many, how many children's brains, some say AROUND 500, others AROUND 600, yet others AROUND 770 brains

> some, for the sake of precision, say 772 children's brains, or 789 children's brains – a trifle, that little difference of 17 cerebral masses

of children from six months to fourteen years of age, allegedly damaged brains, for the most part nameless, removed from the skulls of the euthanised little patients from the children's hospital Spiegelgrund within the complex of Am Steinhof psychiatric clinic, known today as Otto Wagner Spital, with the aim of improving the human race, with the aim of improving the human, deranged, mind. Tidily arranged, labelled like jars of *Konfitüre* in a zealous housewife's larder, these preserved but dead brains of the past ring, reverberate in our todays.

My name is Johann. I was born in Vienna in 1931. I'm a house-painter, I have a family, grown-up children, all healthy. I have grandchildren. I have nightmares. I spent three years in Spiegelgrund as the patient of Dr Heinrich Gross. I was ten years old then. Before the trial, we were taken to the hospital cellar. The jars were hermetically sealed and covered with a thick layer of dust. The brains were preserved, they say. They float in formaldehyde, they say. Formaldehyde has a recognisable smell. I do not believe that the brains have been preserved. Dr Gross and the members of his team dug and poked around those brains and even if they were preserved, what could be done with them today, what? They are after all dead brains, they don't pulsate, they are pale. They are soft cerebral fossils, they are mummified brains, eaten away, perhaps even hollow.

Whenever Gross came into the hospital ward we were unable to breathe, an icy wind froze our breath.

Dr Heinrich Gross, former head of the children's department of Am Steinhof hospital and an inveterate Nazi, is now eighty-six years old. He sits in the dock, looking at the house-painter Johann in surprise. He leans on a walking stick with a silver handle. It is an expensive walking stick. His clothes are too big. *I am a psychiatrist*, says Dr Gross, *I know when someone is fantasising. This man has a vivid imagination, he sees things and people. This man needs treatment.*

On winter nights, they used to leave us half naked on the balconies. We died slowly. I didn't die. They gave us injections and sedatives and on those balconies first we shivered, then we fell asleep, then we caught pneumonia.

Gross does not remember his past. The trial is adjourned because Dr Heinrich Gross has no memory, no-one's memory, not his own nor that of his patients, nor historical memory. He languishes in a false fugue, whether in a fugue of dissembling or dementia is not known and never will be. Without memory, it is impossible to summon up the past. There are proofs, small recollections stored in the skulls of those who no longer exist. These preserved proofs of sixty years earlier float in formaldehyde, but they are not sufficient proofs. The court psychiatrist declares the former S.S. psychiatrist Heinrich Gross, from 1950 to 1998 his respected, highly paid colleague, an active paediatric neurologist, author of dozens of scientific papers about the deformation of the brain, senile, while Judge Karl-Heinz Seewald acquits him. Dr Heinrich Gross will die a natural death, as an innocent, free man.

I am Waltraud Haupl. Here is my sister Annemarie's file from 1943. Annemarie was admitted to Spiegelgrund because of rachitic changes to her bones. Dr Gross included her in his programme of euthanasia of mentally retarded children. The file records a therapeutic starvation diet: white coffee with a piece of bread once a day. My sister died when she was three. She weighed nine kilos. I have not yet received her brain.

I would like you to give it to me. I would like to
bury that brain.

Am Steinhof hospital (Otto Wagner Spital) is situated in a beautiful park, with pavilions in the art nouveau style. Until 1945, the cream of Austrian and German medical practitioners worked and carried out research there. Built in 1907, it was long considered the largest and most advanced hospital in Europe. Some thirty years later, in 1940, it became one of forty centres for carrying out the Nazi programme Aktion T4, for the elimination of physically and mentally handicapped patients of all ages, hypocritically named a programme of euthanasia. The Aktion T4 programme got its name from the Berlin address Tiergartenstrasse 4, location of a magnificent villa, the Führer's headquarters; here the team of monstrous, corrupt-minded, sick people then in power devised a plan for the eradication of pathological human genes, the production of a wholesome human race, the cleansing of what were for them undesirables. But, for the sake of truth, it should be said that theories of eugenics, ideas about the sterilisation and euthanasia of people with defects appeared for the first time in the United States and Sweden in the 1920s. The Nazis "simply" adopted them and put them into practice.

I'm Friedl's mother. We lived in a small town some
hundred kilometres from Vienna. The Russian troops
were already in Austria. It rained terribly hard
towards the end of April 1945, it rained for days. I
wanted to see Friedl; he had been at Spiegelgrund for
two weeks, at Spiegelgrund, they told me to come back

in three weeks, they told me Friedl had pneumonia. I didn't want to come back in three weeks, so I came after two weeks, on the twentieth of April. They were celebrating Hitler's birthday. On the ward they told me to come back the next day. I was soaking. My feet were wet. And my hair was wet. It was windy. I had forgotten my gloves. My umbrella had broken. It was a blue umbrella with yellow dots. I had brown stockings. I said, I want to see Friedl. If you want to see Friedl, look for him yourself, replied the nurse. She wasn't a disagreeable nurse; she had a little piece of cake, some chocolate, stuck at the left corner of her mouth. I found Friedl. He was lying in a bed with bars. The bars had been stripped. Throughout that ward, children were lying in little cages, motionless. Those children did not cry, they drooped. They had half-open eyes, heavy lids. I pushed my hand through the bars, I stroked Friedl's cheek; his cheek was cold. Mama's here, I said. Friedl didn't recognise me. He didn't stir. I went home and came back three days later. It was still raining. I've come for my son, I said to the doctor, I'm taking him home. Spiegelgrund was the best hospital in Austria. No-one in his right mind would doubt Spiegelgrund. They told me, your son isn't here, my heart stopped. The nurse looked at the file. Yes, Friedl died, he died yesterday at twenty past two, the nurse announced. This wasn't the nurse with the bit of chocolate in the corner of her mouth. This was the head nurse, stern. I asked for a document, a diagnosis, a report on my son's death. They didn't give me anything. We're very busy, they said. Then I said, give me his body, I want his body, I want that. The stern head nurse said, he has been buried in the hospital cemetery, talk to the gravediggers. In the hospital

cemetery, I saw a lot of open graves; all the graves
were muddy, sodden with rain, full of water. A truck
arrived loaded with paper sacks. The rain dissolved
the paper, the sacks fell apart, out of the sacks dropped
little limbs, children's, little bare feet, little hands.
Fifty-five years passed. I got my son's file. They took
me to the cellar of Spiegelgrund, today that hospital
is named after Otto Wagner. Otto Wagner was an
architect, they told me. He had never been a Nazi,
that's why they called the hospital after him. They took
me to the cellar. There I found my son's brain. In a jar.
They said, take Friedl. Now you can bury him.

The murder of handicapped children did not stop at the end of World War Two. The last victim of the crazed doctor-experimenters was four-year-old Richard Jenne, killed on the children's ward of Kaufbeuren-Irsee state hospital in Bavaria three weeks after Germany's unconditional surrender.

From 1934 to 1945, with the zealous cooperation of scientists, students, medical staff and Nazi functionaries, German and Austrian doctors throughout Europe forcibly sterilised 375,000 women and men who had been allegedly diagnosed as having so-called congenital psycho-physical deformations. More than 5,000 children and 80,000 adults were killed in psychiatric hospitals. Most of the doctors were never brought to trial; they stayed on as heads of hospitals and wards, they carried on with their scientific discoveries, they were given prizes for their professional dedication and died as respected citizens. In the bliss of general oblivion.

Her name was Živka, I don't know whether she's still alive. *Call me Žile, my nickname, call me Žile*, she kept saying. We called her Žile. She was being treated by my mother, who said they should not be treated at all. My mother's patients came to visit us, and, on public holidays they even came to lunch, sometimes several of them at once. Admittedly, some of her patients didn't come. Some of my mother's patients were quiet, some were not quiet. My mother liked her patients.

Žile cut her hair with nail scissors, short and uneven. She liked to show her underwear, *See how clean it is*, she'd say, *I'm a clean woman*. Žile was fat, but sturdy, she talked a lot, and rapidly, and smelled of baby cream and walnut oil. She used to take flowers regularly to my mother's grave; I don't know whether that's the case now, it's all far away, including my mother's grave. If Žile is dead, then probably only Elsa, who is old and immortal, still brings flowers. Along with the flowers, Žile used to light yellow candles, the candles would blow out at once because it's always windy at my mother's grave, with that north wind. After New Year, exactly three decades ago, we transplanted the fir tree from its pot to beside mother's headstone. The tree was small then, now it's tall. It's remarkable that it managed to grow so bushy; graveyards are generally cramped and crowded, over-occupied. The fir tree waves, as if to say *Come*, or perhaps *Flee*! And it rocks the air, sprinkling it with the scent of the Mediterranean. That's odd. My mother's grave is an inland grave, in which lie a painter, also Mediterranean, and his wife Marija in polished, darkened coffins. Their remains, placed there long ago, have already decayed, just brittle bones and grey dust, devoid of the slightest indication of human form. Those are dislocated facts, outside the context of the former lives of the people in this grave, lives composed like a song, salty and sun-drenched. The little transplanted New Year fir, bought in a clay pot at the huge urban market in Belgrade, has also been relocated, exiled, buried where it doesn't belong. So, here I am now, near the sea, my mother is not, and here, beside the sea, I don't have a single important grave, or any grave I can stroll to.

On fine afternoons the living population pays a visit
to the dead and they decipher their own names on
their stone slabs: like the city of the living, this other
city communicates a history of toil, anger, illusions,
emotions; only here all has become necessary, divorced
from chance, categorized, set in order. And to feel sure
of itself, the living Laudomia has to seek in the Laudo-
mia, for different cities that could have been and were
not, or reasons that are incomplete, contradictory,
disappointing.

Žile wore nylon combinations edged with nylon lace, yellowish, because with time nylon turns yellow. Žile adored everything nylon and plastic; both nylon and plastic were for her cosmic discoveries, magic. Plastic containers of various shapes and sizes, brightly coloured, and the dilemma of which one to choose? She would choose them ALL, they were easy to wash and they were not disagreeably heavy. Nylon clothing is playful, it fits in your hand, and when your hand opens it leaps out, expands without wrinkles, oh, I would like to be that kind of woman, plastic and nylon and shiny, Žile would say.

Žile gave me a present of a nylon tablecloth, burgundy, with a cash-mere pattern that is gradually disappearing, its outlines blurring and merging into a monochrome. Žile would adore bringing small gifts, two oranges for instance, which reminded me of the 1950s, of a cheerful poverty woven of difficult improvisations. That burgundy tablecloth was in fact a tear-proof fabric, it's still on my kitchen table here, far away, a miraculous remnant of a former life of which almost nothing is left, and that fabric is the most ordinary junk, which I absolutely do not need and I don't know why I'm writing about it. What I'm now pining for has evaporated, how and where it's hard to say.

One more thing about Živka, whom we called Žile and who is not remotely essential to this story, just as the story itself is not essential, because it is a secondary story, small, it could be said to be riddled with holes. But lives are in fact built of insignificances, like fishing nets. What there is here, now, is full of illusions, empty squares, which give the impression of little cubes, but they are not cubes because they are made of air. These rickety windows, full of holes through which we put our fingers as we play, puncturing the invisible, are perhaps dreams, old dreams made entirely of breath and sighs, elusive, decayed dreams, because as we poke around them nothing hurts, anywhere, only the net twitches and the eye watches. At every touch, intended or not, that net of our days loses its shape, slides, slips away, moves in our hand to and fro, backwards and forwards and in a circle, without rhythm, without harmony, intractable, resembling the gigantic face of a surprised rubber man. If that web of our lives does not fall apart, it is because of the little knots, hundreds, thousands of tiny taut knots that hold it together, just because of them. In that way it becomes a false magic cloak, now visible, now invisible, with which we cover ourselves, with which we warm our reality. If it is turned upside down, that cloak is transformed into a basket, a little pannier in which we tidy away time, neatly, like freshly washed laundry.

> The smallest basket in the world is seven millimetres across. There are basket museums and miniature museums, which are big because, generally speaking and quite absurdly, museums are large buildings, who knows why.

So, Žile has sailed into this story from some hidden meander, she bobbed up and floated in although she has not turned up in a dream of mine for twenty years, let alone in reality. Živka, known as Žile, who used to address my mother as "sister doctor", is an episode, a small dot in my bloodstream, in my mindstream; along with a multitude of these invisible little knots, with delayed action, she is now fermenting, metastasising, the way an injection of felt silence (from an asylum) acts belatedly.

Žile suffered from trichotillomania. That is when a person pulls out their own hair, compulsively, obsessively: from their heads, leaving little bald white islands; the fuzz on their legs, with tweezers or their fingers – there's no end to it; eyebrows; pubic hair. Maybe people know, I'm not sure, why it is mainly women who do it. Why do men not pluck their hair out like that, or so much? It was her pubic hair that Žile liked plucking the most. *Look how smooth it is*, she said pointing – *It's clean and soft, feel it*, she would show us from the doorway, and then she would bequeath us two moist kisses because she always had a dewy upper lip, even in winter. *I want to watch*, I said once, and Žile said I couldn't. *I pluck myself when I'm alone*, she said, straightening my collar which was like giving me a secret embrace, *I do it when I don't know what I'm doing*, she said, *I do it when I don't know what to do, I won't let you watch, I won't*.

This place here is neither a village nor a town, it let go of its geographic breadth and length, which now roam through space wailing like violin strings. Life in this town is painful, dying, as in the whole country.

For those who pass it without entering, the city is one thing; it is another for those who are trapped by it and never leave. There is the city where you arrive for the first time; and there is another city which you leave never to return. Each deserves a different name.

Calvino's cities are invisible cities, or perhaps they're not; perhaps they're cities we use up in passing, on the hoof, and the flakes of their ruins come off on us, and out of them, these "invisible" cities whose bell towers rend our innards, new cities spring up within us, unhappy, tame and impassive, dangerous cities, sun-filled and lazy cities, which are then decanted out of us into reality and we walk along their streets, kiss on their squares, visit their alleyways, descend into their undergrounds, not knowing where we are or why.

I stand in the rain, in front of a shop window with white goods and other household apparatuses; so-called "white technology" is still a socialist stunt that simply will not vanish from the language. "White technology" is a term that comes from poor countries in which the first electric cookers were always white, in which red, yellow or blue fridges were unimaginable. Now, when even in the former "soc"-countries white technology is no longer necessarily white, it is still called white technology there, while "white technical appliances" sounds silly in English. "White technology" definitely came into these regions from Russia, from the Soviet Union, definitely. I stand in front of the shop window, waiting for someone. That someone is insignificant, I could just as well not wait. The shop window is low-down, the shop is the converted cellar of a five-storey apartment block. It is night. All my small domestic appliances are very old, more than thirty years old; I have old white technology. My vacuum cleaner is old, too. I might like to have an entire new set of white technology in dark blue, including the small appliances – toaster, juicer, coffee grinder, deep-fat fryer, electric carving knife, tin opener, all blue as though I were at sea. I sense a wave of nostalgia for new blue household appliances rising in me, perhaps that's why I'm staring at this shop window, perhaps I'm not waiting for anyone at all.

There's a small park behind me, empty, always empty, it makes me nervous. That's the extent of this constricted nocturnal landscape in the rain.

This town has many constricted parts, a lot of small organs, it has an appendix, but you can get by without an appendix.

When I think about this town, that is, about life in this town, my stomach begins to churn, my jaw clicks like a padlock, it closes up, I turn my eyes away although they never rest on anything anymore, I shake my head, I don't yet rock backwards and forwards, I don't sway, cowering in the corner of my empty white room like people in films, not yet, I don't yet hum, that's the current situation.

We have not grown close, this town and I. Even if we do fuse one day, that doesn't guarantee the birth of a mutual, unconditional, blind love. György Konrád adores his city, although all kinds of horrors happen to him constantly there. In the deadness of his city, he sees his own dying. That fusing with towns is a dangerous and, in its final outcome, senseless affair, an eternal battle which will suck the other in, which will infect the other, do the other to death, an eternal duel, a draining of the spirit, poison, that blindness, that feeble-minded carnival devotion, that perfidious, unequal game in which, employing low punches, protected by the sky and by time, the town usually wins. Even small towns win; they are stronger than people. It happens that they die, but still survive. Towns ought to be small inner organs that function by nourishing each other mutually. With the death of one, several others die out.

I could go away anywhere: I shall carry my town in a suitcase and in the lines of my face, like some kind of character fault, I have grown old in it, I cannot free myself from it, I am incapable of distinguishing it from myself. Motorways bypass it, visitors see the whole of it in just a few hours, and by the end of the following day anything more they could find out about it would be more or less repetition. This town interests only its inhabitants, but not even them greatly: a provincial football match sold out in advance, in the second half of which the home team just staggers over the muddy ground. A neglected, scowling, nervous town, it whines when it has to make a decision, does not have the courage to call things by their proper name, forgets its pledges, befriends the more successful and the stronger, imitating and hating them. It has never been able to get over the fateful accident of being dealt bad cards in the poker of history: it scatters its inhabitants, pays for everything in double time, half the day here is spent simulating life, in a ballet of work, ritual running on the spot.

Whose town is this? Konrád's, or this town here, your town, "my" town?

I've grown tired of its whining self-deceptions, the sly theories it uses to justify its dejection, the obsessions

that it stubbornly imposes as reality; and this stage-
managed running the gauntlet, out of some kind of
spite, this brazen skiving off school, all that under-
hand revenge, the snarling slogans with which they
take their teachers to task: me today, you tomorrow; I
too have long arms, I shall catch you out horribly one
day; I prefer not to have a thing, if it means you do not
have it either; we drink from the same flask, we piss
in the same ditch, if you break away, that will be
the end of you.

When the misunderstandings are eliminated, life in the town becomes simple and linear. The misunderstandings need to be eliminated.

There's a telephone beside my computer. When I'm writing and it rings, I put out my hand to lift the receiver. *Don't pick up the receiver straight away,* says Veronika. *Let it ring at least three times. If you answer imme-diately, people will think, this woman's got nothing to do, she's just waiting for the phone to ring.*

On the inside, this town is shrivelled. Inside it is as dry as obsolete ovaries, like little mummified human heads, stuffed, like the heads with which Conrad's infamous Kurtz decorates the approach to his lair, while his African mistress shoots glances at anyone who approaches him and jangles her bracelets. This is a town that its faithful inhabitants, unlike its unfaithful ones, adore leafing through. These devotees of the town say, *We leaf through our town with pride and read it,* that is what they say. They arrange shreds of their town and call them shreds of history. *These are shreds of the history of our town,* they exclaim, when in fact they are foraging through the names of their dead, excavating the numbers of dead years, doggedly and self-importantly. When plunging into the deadness of their town (some) citizens perpetuate visits to the attic (or the cellar) of their lives, seeking the rubbish of virtual reality. I am here, I do not go out, I observe reality through the window, the reality not only of this town, but reality in general, reality crumbling, corroded by the past. That's no kind of reality, that reality is worn out, used up, nothing to be done.

Memory is redundant: it repeats signs so that the city
can begin to exist . . .

The Laudomia of the unborn does not transmit, like
the city of the dead, any sense of security to the inhab-
itants of the living Laudomia: only alarm. In the end,
the visitors' thoughts find two paths open before them,
and there is no telling which harbors more anguish:
either you must think that the number of the unborn
is far greater than the total of all the living and all
the dead . . . Or else you think that Laudomia, too,
will disappear, no telling when, and all its citizens
with it . . .

There is a little street that goes downhill, constrained by a small stair-way, it is short and fast and lined with pine trees. It's called Viktor Finderlé. This Finderlé is dead of course, for otherwise he would not be nailed to a white marble plaque. All the streets here, and this is a significant change from socialist days when the streets were indicated by blue metal plaques, expendable blue plaques with white lettering, also expendable, all the streets here have marble plaques with the names chiselled into them, so that when they fall, they break. Otherwise, this Finderlé was a doctor, not that long dead, some still remember him, I imagine. To research Viktor Finderlé without being able to know what beset him in his dreams, without being able to know whether he wore brown suits or grey ones, shoes with plastic soles in winter, and brown open sandals with grey socks in summer, or perhaps calfskin moccasins and Egyptian poplin shirts, is pointless. Perhaps before he went to bed, in his commu-nal flat, he would use a nailbrush to clean the collar of the off-white nylon shirts newly on sale, because all over Yugoslavia there were a fair number of communal flats into which people were stuffed when they were thrown out of their own, private flats, and there was a surplus of people and a lack of living space, which when you look at it from today's perspective somehow evades all logic. Plastic shirts were very popular in "soc"-poverty, as was plastic altogether, even though they, these plastic shirts, soaked up the smell of men's sweat and cheap cigarettes made from top-quality Macedonian tobacco so that in some areas (the armpits) those shirts would be irrevocably yellow. Men washed their plastic shirts so perhaps Dr Viktor Finderlé did too. Or perhaps Viktor Finderlé was a Jew. If he was a Jew, perhaps some of his close relatives had disappeared, perhaps his flat really had been taken from him, or perhaps not his, as he was a surviving Jew. Perhaps Dr Viktor Finderlé was circumcised, if he was a Jew, or perhaps not; not all Jews are circumcised. Perhaps Dr Viktor Finderlé had twelve pastel-coloured shirts and six white ones, all batiste cotton, all folded in his wardrobe, and they were ironed by his wife Magdalena Finderlé, née Buseho, or perhaps they were ironed by a servant called Laura, Rosetta or Perla, a beauty with red hair and a mole under her right eyebrow, the unmarried mother of little Samuel or Miguel, the illegitimate son of the lawyer Pauzner, a friend of Dr Viktor Finderlé and his best man, and perhaps also the mother of the illegitimate son of the priest, Cauze; today we can see all the things priests get up to although they've been doing it for ever, it's all possible and immaterial. Whether Viktor Finderlé was a gynaecologist or a cardiologist is immaterial. Perhaps Viktor Finderlé was not called Viktor Finderlé at all but Dorian Fuchendrider and was not a doctor at all but an architect. In this town there were architects who also live on little marble plaques, at crossroads, high up.

Had I not stopped one sultry summer noon on the landing of Dr Finderlé's Steps where there is today a little café with three tables, I wouldn't have known that Viktor Finderlé ever existed. Had he not looked down on me like that from on high. Had I not seen that he was born in 1902 and that he died in 1964, when I was writing my leaving certificate essay at Moša Pijade secondary school on the subject of Lujo "Louis" Adamić, who allegedly committed suicide in America, although there are murmurings that he was eliminated by some agents or other for political reasons, because that was the age of McCarthyism when the F.B.I. followed people; they just followed people and collected confidential data. Later on the F.B.I. eased up a bit on the following and bugging because the archives were filling up at such speed that space was running out. I have some files from those F.B.I. archives, but I don't want to talk about them now.

Sometimes curious coincidences occur, those coincidences have nothing to do with this town, they are general coincidences, existential coincidences, overlappings, crisscrossings, chance happenings never fully resolved, little cosmic earthquakes, that is, neglected time, melted time, resembling literary fabrications, elusive.

In the book *Totenwande* there is a half-invented story about a girl, Jacqueline Morgenstern, who was transferred with another nineteen children aged between five and twelve, by order of the S.S.-Obergruppen-führer Dr Kurt Heissmeyer, on 27 November, 1944, from Auschwitz to the Neuengamme camp. In the Neuengamme camp, with the moral and material support of the Bayer pharmaceutical factory, S.S.-Obergruppen-führer Dr Kurt Heissmeyer carried out experiments on those children, but also on adults, injecting into their bloodstream living tuberculosis bacilli and fiddling with their lymph glands, which he sent in special little thermos flasks to the Bayer central facility, at that time in Leverkusen, far down to the south-west of Hamburg; that is why the thermos flasks were important, because in spite of the cold weather, the little sections of children's lungs and other organs would certainly have gone bad. Otherwise, when it was founded by Friedrich Bayer in 1863, the Bayer factory produced dyes for fabrics and was called Farbenfabriken vormals Friedr. Bayer & Co., later it reoriented itself to producing medication, when the chemist Carl Duisberg began to work there, and later still to experimentation. So, at that time in that camp near beautiful Hamburg on the splendid River Elbe, the adults die quickly, while the children die slowly. On 20 April, 1945, twelve days before Germany's capitulation, the Allied British troops were eight kilometres from Hamburg, and perhaps ten kilometres from Bullenhuser Damm School, remodelled into the satellite camp Neuengamme. As the British troops marched, Dr Kurt Heissmeyer's assistants hastily killed the children, first by injecting them with morphine, then by hanging them on hooks, down there in the cellar of Bullenhuser Damm School, in order to erase the traces of their medical experiments. Had the British troops marched a little faster, today those children would no longer be children, some of them would surely be alive. Those living, surviving children would now be between sixty-two and sixty-nine years old and have minor discomforts: osteoporosis, high blood pressure, problems with their prostate, failing sight, maybe the occasional glaucoma, high cholesterol, diabetes, that sort of *ordinary* thing. Some children would be bald because they would no longer be children. Those children were born in Poland, but there were also children from the Netherlands and France, there was a little girl from Yugoslavia and a little boy from Italy. The boy from Italy was called Sergio de Simone.

When Sergio de Simone, his lungs riddled with tuberculosis, feverish, weak, with sunken but glistening eyes and pink cheeks, perspiring, in a thin little, no longer white hospital shirt, was hung on a hook together with Eleonora Witonska (five) from Poland (the smaller children were hung in pairs because of a shortage of hooks), he was seven years old. His mother Gisella had remained in Auschwitz, quite unhappy, one could say crazed with grief.

The book *Totenwande* had already been published when I received a letter in which it said that Sergio de Simone was born in Naples on 29 November, 1937, to his father Edoardo and his mother Gisella, née Perlow, that the family had lived in the town of Fiume, where on 28 March, 1944, the Germans arrested Sergio de Simone (six) and took him to Auschwitz, that the boy had arrived in Auschwitz on 4 April of that year, that he was branded with the number 179614, that he was killed in Hamburg on 20 April, 1945, and that his mother Gisella Perlow, born in Russia on 23 September, 1904, the daughter of Mario Perlow and Rosa Farberow, had been deported to Auschwitz with him. The letter went on to say that the convoy in which they travelled was called convoy 25T and that in that convoy there were almost all the Perlows: Aron, Carola, Giuseppe, Mario (Gisella's father, Sergio's grandfather), Mira and Paula (perhaps Gisella's sisters, Sergio's aunts) and Rosa née Farberow (Gisella's mother, Sergio's grandmother). The letter does not say what happened to Sergio's father Edoardo. Gisella and Mira survived Auschwitz, but that was no use to Gisella, her son Sergio might never have existed, perhaps all that was left of him was a small heap, a little mound of ash, because after they were hung up, the children were returned to Neuengamme since the ovens for burning people were still working there while in Bullenhuser Damm School they were not. Gisella continued to live, although without much enthusiasm, it's not known for how long. In 1946 she was forty-two years old and, if she had wanted a child, which she did not, she was no longer able to conceive. The name Sergio de Simone is engraved on the Monument to the Victims of Fascism in the Jewish cemetery in this town, that is also written in the letter. So a half-fiction, a fabrication (literary) became reality buried in my neighbourhood.

The number on Sergio de Simone's arm, number 179614, is a number to be remembered, it's not an anonymous number, there are other numbers like it. Except that by now various data and numbers have multiplied so much and are still multiplying in a geometric progression so that people are frustrated, they cannot remember absolutely everything. People have numbers that *must be* remembered, such as the numbers of their credit cards and a P.I.N. for each card, so that they can easily withdraw money at cash points all over the world, then they have the numbers of their landline and mobile telephones, then the P.I.N.s for their mobile phones, then the numbers of their bank accounts, they have various personal identification numbers, and it is crucial that *these* are memorised too, as without them they could not access any piece of official information. Then, people have the dates of various birthdays to remember, because remembering birthdays enriches human communication, ennobles it, so people become close and intimate. Then people have a heap of passwords to remember, particularly if they wish to remain linked in. People really cannot remember everything, so they make a selection, discard, sift, clear out, they remember some data, compress some, bury some for better times, throw some out. The number

179614 should be remembered because, as Wisława Szymborska says, it is a number that history has forgotten, as though it did not exist, as though it had never existed. There are many numbers like it stored in the earth's memory, and new ones keep arriving. Here we have an UNROUNDED-UP number, the number 179614, which reminds one of a telephone number, 179 614, of the telephone number of a nameless person from a small town, or perhaps the telephone number of a person we know from a small town, a number neither easy nor hard to remember, a middling number, not particularly cheerful nor particularly interesting, a number called Sergio de Simone.

> *History rounds off skeletons to zero.*
> *A thousand and one is still only a thousand.*
> *That one seems never to have existed:*
> *a fictitious fetus, an empty cradle,*
> 179614   *a primer opened for no-one,*
> *air that laughs, cries and grows,*
> *stairs for a void bounding out to the garden,*
> *no-one's spot in the ranks.*

The little park behind me is a round space, asphalted and with no swings. All you can do in that little, useless park is sit and watch a thin, artificial waterfall trickle over artificial stones. The park doesn't even have sounds, because its sounds are stolen by the noise of the traffic. It's a boring park, I'd never take a child or a dog there. The park has no bushes, the tree tops above it are as rare as the hair of a post-menopausal woman. I see that there are a lot of women like that in this town, those women with thin hair through which the perspiring crowns of their heads gleam, I used not to notice that. I used to think that only men lost their hair, now in this town I see – women also grow bald. It's to do with hormones.

This town has no municipal parks, just two or three cemetery parks. My memories are not here because, as I said, I have no-one even in a cemetery here. That is, I see now, my greatest lack, that lack of the dead nearby. If I had several of my own dead nearby, even in the form of dust, perhaps things would be better. What if I die here?

I stand, staring through the glass at the white goods and small domestic appliances. How do you say "kos" in English? How? I am forgetting my languages. I am losing my language. "Raven." No. "Raven" is not "kos".

> Once upon a midnight dreary, while I pondered, weak and weary,
> Over many a quaint and curious volume of forgotten lore –
> While I nodded, nearly napping, suddenly there came a tapping,
> As of someone gently rapping, rapping at my chamber door.

"Kos?" A bird like a tiny embodied death that hops; a bird like a flying death, like a funeral song, like an ode, a bird like a golden call. A "kos" is so small.

> Don't trust your memory; your memory is a net full of holes; the past and the present slip through it, everything slips through your memory, your memory is a hole.

"Blackbird." I looked it up, it's "blackbird". "Blackbird" is a daft word for "kos". And "kos" is a daft word for a kos. They should both be called "*merula*". *Merula* has a roll to it, blackbird and kos have no roll. *Merula* has smallness and cheerfulness that fly. A blackbird should definitely be called *merula,* because *merula* is feminine in gender, as is bird in my language, as is death.

> Don't trust your memory

Ha! What's "čičak" in English? It's "thistle".

We are entering a summer afternoon. We climb towards the top of the fortified town on a peninsula studded with little stone towns. They are proper little towns, very serious, serious as monuments and silent; they are towns with palaces and miniature theatres, towns with loggias and graveyards and coats of arms, towns with church towers and painted sundials on which time makes real Renaissance shadows. They are towns with few people and many cats in which dust in the air trembles like silver because in those towns there is no mud although the rains in them are violent and passionate; they are stone fortresses, which have been bathed by crystal rains, for centuries.

We're moving away from the sea, there's a scent of hazelnuts. There are cicadas and thistles. Oscar has just emerged from his liaison with Liv Ullman, Lila has long hair, red, and a little diamond ring, David is taking Antabuse. We wander around the ramparts and pick small pears. The figs are small too. The mulberry trees have no fruit. Our shoulders are bare. So are our feet. Then Oscar asks, *How do you say* "čičak" *in English?* And no-one knows. Then Oscar says: *It's* "*thistle*". He learned that while he was with Liv Ullman in New York.

This town here, in which today I am looking for the subways of reality, was then, as we climbed, young and beautiful, just a dot on the edge of our field of consciousness; this town existed then as marginalia, as a cognitive periphery, as a succusion of insignificance. Its outlines sway in the mist of the future, from which I turn away, and which is now here, that future, coming unexpectedly and saying, I am your present. It's a worn-out and dilapidated present, moth-eaten, gap-toothed and sick – who could have imagined that such terrible deceptions were already stalking our youth.

Lila killed herself, she was still warm when they found her. She had a little dressing table with a hinged mirror, which she never dusted or looked at herself in. She wrote messages on the mirror in Spanish. No-one read her messages. David died of several incurable diseases. When anyone says "čičak", I know, in English, "čičak" is "thistle".

Near the little fortified town that slides down the slopes and dives into vineyards, within reach of a magically sensuous, drunken landscape, there's a factory for processing turkey meat. In this part of the world, turkeys are the size of small sheep, they're turned into smoked products for cold cuts. In restaurants, the turkeys are served with truffles, which are all the rage now, particularly for some people who have absolutely no connection with this (Istrian) region. Near the fortified town, in fact under its skirts, there's a quarry whose marble is built into various histories, distant and close at hand, and has been shipped all over the world for centuries. There's also a wallpaper factory down there and a yarn factory, all in that valley through which prowls the silhouette of a giant as he rows, chained to the worn boards of a Venetian galleon, dreaming of freedom. In that valley my grandfather's house still crouches, empty as a shadow, struck dumb by smallness. Since it is impossible to transplant that house into my memory because the house never reached my memory at all, because the house died before I was born, I brought a photograph in which the little house can clearly be seen breathing, that white house in front of which my three-year-old father, bald and unaccountably serious, is standing, astounded, in wide breeches, barefoot, I brought that photograph to a village stonemason and carver and said, *Bring this past back to life for me.* Then I took the little house he made of white stone, with real little windows and a balustrade with a malmsey vine winding over it, and a real low entrance, very dark, and a loft where many years earlier I had found a black bowler hat, two torn lace curtains and literature about bee-keeping, I took the little house on a base of unworked stone, somehow absurdly heavy, to show my eighty-year-old father, and, quite unexpectedly, it made him profoundly sad. My father wanted to keep the little house on the small, elegant mahogany table, oval and one-legged, brought I think from India in the lifetime of people unknown to me (or to him), on that small table standing beside the armchair where my father could have sat and travelled back into the misty days wrapped in a music only he could know. He wished to gaze at his miniature home, his playhouse, to walk through the empty rooms in which the floor was wooden, but white, because the stone carver had built in the floors as well. But my father's wife, who had no connection whatever with his former life, that woman who is of course not my mother, because my mother is dead, and if she were not dead she would have been delighted with the little house, I know for certain, that woman

41

said: *Not here! It's in the way.* When I sometimes (increasingly rarely) go to see my father in the town that could be called my home town, but that is quite alien to me, just as this little town in which I am currently living is alien, as all the towns through which I have been running for the last decade are alien, just as the town in which I lived for forty years became suddenly removed and alienated when once, not long ago, I went to see it briefly, it is hard to say now why this is the case, so, whenever I go to visit my father, I find him sitting in the kitchen (until that woman's day he never sat in kitchens because our family kitchens weren't conceived as places for sitting; my father sat at desks in studies, that's how it was, what can you do?), I find him in a kitchen which is not his kitchen at all, but a Dutch kitchen from a catalogue, greenish and expensive, I find him leafing through old letters and old books. Each time I find the kitchen smaller and more cramped, while my father, like a galley slave, like a giant chained to his life, waits for death.

That woman lies in the living room, she just lies and watches television soaps, leafs through women's magazines and dreams up mean things. For instance, how she will thrust my father into her family tomb even though my father has nothing to do with her family or her family tomb; even though my father has his own family tomb, which is also our family tomb, the family tomb of my grandfather and my grandmother, over there beneath that Istrian stone wall.

A small river flows below the little town. One enters the town through an arched stone gateway with abundant coats of arms from the past.

The little town is not called Pučišća.

> *In Pučišća they are making a new coat of arms, a coat of arms for the twenty-first century. The municipality of Pučišća will be getting its own coat of arms and its own flag. The coat of arms will depict the thirteen towers that defended Pučišća from its attackers (?) over the centuries. The flag will have three plants on it – olive, vine and holm oak. They symbolise the life of Pučišća on the karst; they stand for olive oil, wine and*

> *fuel. The background of the flag will be red, a symbol*
> *of hard work and sacrifice. Several experts in the*
> *visual arts were consulted in the design of the coat of*
> *arms and flag, and the final verdict on the insignia*
> *will be announced by the municipal councillors.*
>
> (Croatian newspaper item)

What kind of history does Pučišća have?

The little town that is not called Pučišća, the little town with lots of thistles, in fact it is *surrounded* by thistles, has an old people's home, but on
the whole only the old know that. Others do not have a clue. The little
town also has a church tower in which there was once a prison, and in it
in 1942 the fascists pumped my grandfather full of castor oil. In the
valley, the fields of thistles merge with fields of poppies. That can be seen
clearly from above, from the fortifications. Some thistles are mauve and
as big as small (desiccated) human heads and are no use for anything,
while the poppies are red, with thin petals that flutter like the wings
of butterflies, maybe even dead ones. When they are dried, the thistles
stay mauve so some people put them in vases.

A man tells me how he went deaf in his left ear. Deaf and half-deaf people often speak loudly, but this man whispers as he talks to me. It was an autumn day. In the left hemisphere of his head there was a sudden noise of silence, after which it went dark.

The Ear, Nose and Throat specialist doesn't believe him. *You're fantasising,* he says.

Before he went deaf in his left ear, the man had a little dream. He tells me: he is sitting on the floor talking to a barely visible, dwarf-like creature. The dwarf-like creature climbs onto the man's lap, settles there, and the man starts crying. As he is already deaf, the man cries but he can barely hear his sobs. His chest shakes, swells, and he thinks, perhaps there's something wrong with my breathing? *Since there hadn't been anything wrong with my breathing before that,* the man says, *I concluded that I was crying.* So he cries, with sobs as big as full sails, he cries and cries, while bitterness spreads around him, smelling of almonds and mandarins. *I am very surprised to be crying like this,* he says. *For a whole decade, and more, I never let out a single sob. For a whole decade and more, I have only hiccupped,* he says. *Dwarf, I say,* the man goes on, *dwarf, I'd like to come to you, take me, that's what I say to that misshapen miniature creature as though it were some kind of little god, but I know it isn't. However,* says the man, *that disgusting midget tells me authoritatively: It's not yet time. When the time comes, I'll call you.*

Now the man is waiting and listening attentively. He waits for trains because they send out a special sound, penetrating. Trains pass here rarely, and generally around midnight. The man is still deaf in his left ear, and he's still waiting. Sometimes he seems puzzled because he often shakes his head as though in disbelief, but he's not puzzled. The man doesn't see well either and he's just sharpening the image. That's all.

In my dream, I also stepped into a fairy tale, the man goes on. *Give me that drink, I say to a being in the fairy tale, from my childhood, and I ask him, aren't you Alice? Give me that drink, I want to be smaller. The being just looks around,* the man says, *he looks around and calls: Where are you? I can't see you at all.*

I don't know what will become of that man. He already looks very small. Ears often cause trouble. There's quite a lot of literature about ears. There are fairy tales about ears, human and goats' ears, there are legends. There are well-known events connected with ears, with cutting off ears for instance, with perforating ears, for instance. The Chinese identify acupuncture points on the ear that correspond to all the internal organs of the human body. A friend writes that the pain in his knee has gone, but it has now moved to his ear. Before that he had problems with an eye. Very similar complaints affect many people.

As I'm speaking of doctors, there's one in Paris, but he's dead too. He had been at battlegrounds, he saw his fill of terrible things, he became a war surgeon, he had nightmares, waking and sleeping, then he began to write. He wrote poems and plays and novels. One of his characters was troubled in his lifetime by an ear, but someone else's, also the left one. And the character confesses throughout the whole book. He's a wretched character, quite lost.

> *. . . Then I notice his left ear. I remember clearly, and still maintain today, that it was not unusual. It was the ear of a somewhat more full-blooded man; a wide ear with hairs and stains of the dregs of wine. I do not know why I started to look at that little piece of skin with such tense care, which soon became almost painful. That ear was right beside me, but nothing had ever seemed more distant or stranger. I thought: That is human flesh. There are people for whom it is perfectly natural to touch that flesh. There are*

those for whom it is quite ordinary.

Suddenly I see as though in a dream a boy – M. Sureau is the head of the family – a boy, with his arm wrapped round M. Sureau's neck. Then I notice Mlle Dupère. She is a former typist, with whom M. Sureau is having a tempestuous affair. I see her, bending over him and kissing him precisely behind his ear. I always thought: "Well, it's human flesh; there are people who are able to kiss it. It's normal." *For some reason that thought seemed to me incredible and for a moment repulsive. Various images passed through my soul, when I suddenly noticed that I had moved my right hand a little, with my forefinger extended and realised at once that I had wanted to rest my finger against M. Sureau's ear . . .*

My hand's wish to touch M. Sureau's ear at first scandalised me. But gradually I felt that I approved. For a thousand reasons, which I hardly grasped, it became necessary for me to touch M. Sureau's ear, in order to prove to myself that this ear was not a forbidden thing, imaginary and unreal, but just human flesh like my own ear. I suddenly stretch out my hand decisively and lay my forefinger carefully on the desired place, a little above the tuft, on a small piece of skin the colour of brick . . .

I had just cautiously brushed M. Sureau's ear with my forefinger, when he and his armchair jerked backwards. I must have gone a bit pale, while he turned blue like apoplectics when they turn pale. Then he charged over to a drawer, opened it and took out a revolver . . .

I do not really know what occurred. Ten servants grabbed hold of me, dragged me to the next room, stripped and searched me . . . Someone came up to me

and said . . . that I must immediately quit my job . . .
That's this pathetic tale. I don't like to tell it, because
whenever I do, I feel indescribably irritated.

Why are Beckett's works full of blind and dumb people, limbless and voracious, but no-one is deaf, there are no deaf people in Beckett, why?

It's dark at the moment and it's not the season of flowers.

People try to convince me that dandelions have a scent, I tell them they don't – they smell, they smell, our dandelions do, our dandelions smell. The lilac in Danka's garden on Zvezdara in Belgrade smells. The Mihajlo Pupin Institute is on Zvezdara, but not the Vinča; the Vinča is not on Zvezdara. In the Vinča some people were irradiated a long time ago, afterwards they died. One of those who was irradiated and died was close to me, afterwards I had other people close to me, some of whom also died. Some didn't. Danka is alive. She is still on Zvezdara. Still smoking.

I had forgotten that Bernhard is called Thomas and that Wisława's surname is Szymborska. I remembered later, otherwise how could I have written this?

What are you cooking today?

What are you cooking today?

What are you cooking today?

People often ask that here.

They tell me a woman has been diagnosed *ca corpus uteri*. That shakes me a bit, not much. I don't have anyone close here. That's good, it protects one from stress. After her hysterectomy, it was confirmed in a biopsy that the woman had metastases everywhere. Therapy: radiation, cytostatic treatment, the classic response. Nausea, baldness. Several years pass, I have been here a long time, she's still alive. She pulled through. My mother didn't pull through. Medicine has progressed, that's what they say.

In New Belgrade, on the third floor of the fifth of the so-called "six squad leaders" as you look at them from the bridge, a retired officer of the

Yugoslav National Army sells prepared Aloe Vera in green Fruška Gora Riesling bottles, from which he hasn't managed to remove the labels; the demand is great, but so is mortality. The viscous grey liquid is to be rubbed on radiation burns, today people don't talk so much about terrible radiation burns, oncology has become more agreeable. My mother's skin peels off in patches. We rub her. The officer calls his fluid "balm". We rub my mother with balm. I make a tincture of Aloe Vera for drinking. I go to Kisvárda, a village on the Hungarian–Russian border where one's tears freeze in winter. My mother is young. The conductresses on the train are Russian, in heavy blue uniforms, every one of them with swollen knees, every one of them fat and wearing a short skirt. The uniforms have gold buttons, like sea captains' formal dress. The conductresses are Russian because the train is going on to Moscow, and just flying through Kisvárda. The conductresses sell weak Russian tea in glasses, boiling, and don't sleep at all. Kisvárda is a village like those in the Banat region. It has an inn and good goulash. It has a big farmstead. It has frozen mud. In Kisvárda Dr Baross sells anti-cancer drops in a small room with a low ceiling. There are rugs all over the room, on the floor and on the walls and over the armchairs, because the armchairs are shabby. He has a microscope as well, but it is outdated. One enters the room through the kitchen, where the doctor's wife is sitting in a housecoat of blue fustian; the doctor's wife sits at a wooden table, there are little plastic bluebells in a vase. In the kitchen there's a dresser the colour of mignonette, with glass doors, with coffee cups upside down behind them. People come in droves, people come from all over Yugoslavia because this is the day for Yugoslavia, other countries have their own days too. Tito is still alive, my mother died before Tito. The doctor's drops didn't help. We tried everything. Including Paris.

In 1956, after the bloody and unsuccessful revolution, Dr Baross was isolated as a punishment, that is, banished from the professional and scholarly life of Budapest, from his own life, in fact, and by order of the Communist Party of his country, thrust into a non-life, into slow, painful dying, so like dying in this town as well. Transferred to a north-eastern Hungarian province within reach of the border with the Soviet Union, where he would be under the apparently light but constant surveillance of Big Brother, Dr Baross grasps the extent to which his vociferous commitment to the birth of democracy was a foolish and groundlessly idealistic project, and devotes the remainder of his life, with a minimum of resources and almost no equipment, to seeking a natural (plant) medicine to treat the cancerous cells that destroy (other) lives. Through an infrequent correspondence and still less frequent meetings, conscious of the power of active police surveillance and censorship, Dr Baross establishes (nevertheless) a close connection with Béla Hamvas and nature as a whole. He treats his fellow villagers and their livestock. And their chickens and geese. And their pigs. And perhaps he sometimes dreams of his forebears, immersed in a fugue from which he will never surface.

Yes, the fact that life creates incomprehensible congruities is well known. Dr István Baross, the one from Hungarian Kisvárda, the painful meeting with whom took place at the end of 1971 is, it turned out, a descendant of the famous Gábor Baross (1848–1892), Minister of Trade and Industry at the time of the Austro-Hungarian Monarchy after whom this town, whose slow, ugly expiring I am observing on the eve of the new millennium, would call one of its harbours, today also breathing its last. So, unwittingly, we touch hundreds, thousands of lives that are distant from us, whole encyclopaedias of the human race, which enter our daily routine without provoking so much as a small earthquake, not even a quiver in the air, not the slightest turbulence, nothing. Who would have imagined then that any sort of Baross would ever slink into my present, that I would even step along the edge of a dead harbour defence wall that bears his name, but that has neither a harbour, nor anyone or anything to defend, because virtually nothing, virtually no-one ever comes, for this town is surrounded by itself, by the rampart of its own unfortunate reality which it swallows from a pipette, convinced that it is nourishing itself with drops of incomparable happiness.

The name of Gábor Baross known also as the "iron minister", the name of a man who managed traffic and communications in the lands of the former Austro-Hungarian Empire, echoes today in this town with no traffic, a town which, not knowing why, not knowing how, fearful, is cutting all communications with the outside world, this name echoes like mockery.

Gábor Baross worked with enormous zeal on the unification and development of the Austro-Hungarian railway network, whose branches, cut off, lie beneath my window. Trains come so infrequently, and for the most part empty, to the little deserted station, whose small size and deadness the citizens of this town do not wish to see (if they see them, they do not wish to talk about them), so that they might as well not come at all. As no-one sees anyone off, no-one meets anyone either. And there's no question of any waving. Only the clock at the entrance to that building with its mosaic marble floors from a once truly mosaic past, only the clock ticks regularly and dully, as though denouncing the dankness of its own present.

Gábor Baross was obsessed with post offices and telegrams. Gábor Baross believed that communication, within the walls of a building that is, not only two-way, to and fro, but the communication of schizophrenics, in all directions, from all over the place, circular communication, loud and aggressive, communication that ruptures space, open as an echo borne by the winds from the land and the shore, by winds both gentle and ominous, that such turbulence enables every town to breathe, unlike some who believe that this is done exclusively by trees.

We tried everything. Including Paris.

In Paris I sleep with the tramps, the sky is clear, Parisian blue and it is winter again, probably the same winter as in Hungary. Mother is bleeding from everywhere, everywhere. Her blood soaks through the mattress and drips onto the polished floor of the Institut d'Oncologie, part of the Faculté de Médecine, but perhaps that's not happening within the Faculté de Médecine at all, although there are indications that it is indeed there that my mother is lying, because new medicines are being tried out on her, experiments are carried out on her (my mother – a submissive half-dead guinea-pig, still beautiful – *We are carrying out research*, they say, *We are experimenting*, they tell me, *We have nothing to lose*); perhaps my mother is disintegrating and bleeding in the Val de Grâce military hospital, although I don't know why my mother would be lying in the Val de Grâce military hospital in Paris given that our family has never had any connection with the army, and particularly not the French army, for a long time now, for generations, our family has been an ordinary, civilian, urban family. Perhaps my mother is lying (and draining away) in the Cochin Hospital. Near the Panthéon, they tell me, is the Laënnec Hospital, then Maternité Port Royal, I don't remember, I remember only the Panthéon, because that's where Voltaire and Victor Hugo lie and the brisk Jean Jaurès and the tame Rousseau, all of whom, unlike my young, beautiful mother, mean nothing at all to me, absolutely nothing, and without whom my life is perfectly possible. In Paris I see Bergman's "The Serpent's Egg" and eat steak tartare with Danka's brother out of a deep dish, with a spoon, in the stuffy flat of the gallery owner and antiques dealer Bojon. Danka's brother is called Jean, he used to be called Ivan, his wife also dies of cancer, many years later. In Paris I buy crêpes in the open market, a circus troupe dances, the sky is frighteningly blue. It is the seventies. I haven't been to Paris since.

When she bleeds, she loses her mucous membrane, she's peeling in layers from within, disappearing. I buy her shoes, but she can no longer walk. The shoes are burgundy red. Later I give the shoes to Katja who is also dying. The stockings are burgundy as well. Those I do not give away. There were a lot of moves, international and transatlantic. The stockings are here. They surface from time to time. Thirty years have passed. The stockings can be thrown away.

Do people generally take showers in the morning or in the evening?

Martin has got himself glasses, but still he doesn't read. Martin is a philosopher. In Croatia, Martin is just the Sarajevan. Sometimes Martin is also a travelling salesman, but a small, insignificant one. That's why he doesn't read. Presumably.

People correct my use of language here. That's the way it is. When I explain why the expression I use is the only correct one, people look at me nationally.

I dream of David. We're sitting on a terrace, the terrace is far away and unfamiliar, flowerless. I wipe dust from the television screen with my hand, the television is off. I bring books, I bring a pile of books that David hasn't yet seen because he's dead. We talk about teeth. David says, *A book about the Holocaust has been published in Zagreb. Send it to Krleža. When is Krleža's birthday?* I ask. *Take care of your teeth*, says David. Then he leaves.

I call Ugo at once. Ugo says, *It seems that we dreamed of him on the same night. I asked him where he was living now, and he said, In London. Why London? I asked. Well, you can drug yourself to your heart's content in London. He said that proudly and with a smile. Then he left.*

The Prime Minister receives a turkey for Christmas, from the Union of Public Employees. The turkey is called Štefica. The Prime Minister carries Štefica in his own hands, in a woven basket, into the cabinet office and declares gruffly: Štefica has to be spared. The Prime Minister doesn't celebrate Christmas in private in any case, only publicly and officially. And even if he did celebrate it, he could go to a restaurant and order salt cod and fritters, or he could have beef Wellington, why does he need Štefica? I don't celebrate Christmas either, but I can't go to a restaurant and order lobster with crêpes Suzette to follow, which I would wash down with Rémy Martin; I'd welcome Štefica, but no-one's offering her to me. They take Štefica off to the country, to some schoolchildren who care for her. The schoolchildren bring Štefica a partner and call him Štef. The children stuff Štefica and Štef to the gills, until the next feast day. Štefica and Štef grow to unheard-of dimensions. For the next feast, the schoolchildren give Štefica and Štef to a public kitchen, so that it can feed the people, the unemployed, decrepit and sick vagrants.

Footnote: A small confession. I thought of making this small confession now, because again it's the holiday season when a lot of food is bought, when a lot is eaten and when church people talk about togetherness, and the right-wingers about the homeland.

I, too, was once shabby in this town, hence part of the mutual intolerance between the little town and me. Now I'm no longer quite so down-at-heel so the little town and I tolerate each other better, which is absolutely human and urban.

In addition to the food from public kitchens, the unemployed and the shabby also receive identity cards, known as "social identity cards". These social identity cards are given out at counters in front of which there are long queues of every conceivable social misfit, there are alcoholics, epileptics, schizophrenics, there are various fuguesters, ruined prostitutes, male and female, there are occasionally syphilis patients of either gender, because syphilis once flourished here, when it was known by the nicer name of "harlots' disease", because prostitution once flourished here too. Today nothing flourishes.

My social identity card for transport, for free transport in any zone from 1 to 5, with my photograph because of the credibility of my non-possessions, bears the number 05478. Another social identity card, which states that we are a two-person household with no income and approval of permanent financial assistance, is pending, this second social identity card, for I have two, bears the number 364. In order to obtain that card, I signed a printed declaration called a DECLARATION, which comes in three copies with carbon paper on the back and which confirms that I haven't begun independently to carry out freelance work, that I'm not a majority-share owner or co-owner of a business, shop or agricultural holding and that I'm not even a member of an agricultural household, though it would be a blessing if I were, because I wouldn't have got stuck here and I'd have plenty of potatoes, although I prefer rice, and I would be well and truly fat. I keep the identity cards, although I don't need them as souvenirs, because memories are usually remembered and don't ask for special evidence. During my identity-card time, public figures came forward to boast of *their* social identity cards, which was fairly abhorrent, because those figures had cars, they had foreign travel about which every wretch, every loser (and that's what I was, a happy loser from the Balkans) often thought: oh, never more; those figures had snacks and light Mediterranean dinners everywhere, they had the support of a progressive, honest intelligentsia and they had fees, while our two-person household had nothing. Not even relatives.

So, the public kitchen to which Štefica the turkey is given makes the following protest: *There is no room for Štefica in our fridges because our coffers are full. We have a lot of donated meat, especially for the holidays.* Besides, says the manager of the public kitchen, *turkeys come to grief every day and no-one gets upset, why should Štefica be an exception?* That question is left unanswered. The manager of the public kitchen makes a statement to the media: *We have a hundred and seventy hungry people, they do not see meat for months on end. We shall not serve up Štefica for Christmas but for Twelfth Night.* The Prime Minister is helpless because civil society is on the rise, expressing civil disobedience. There's a difference of opinion: those fighting for the protection of animals and their rights want the birds to be spared, while the others are hungry.

The lady from the public kitchen says that turkeys aren't a protected species like, for instance, bats, had they been given bats, she says, they wouldn't kill them because it's forbidden to kill bats given that *bats* are an endangered species, while turkeys aren't.

There's a street here called Ulica Šišmiša, "Bat Street". It's a small street, a lane in fact, short and dark, which is not unusual in the old part of town, because the old part of town is a honeycomb of alleyways, so that when one looks down on it from above, it seems as if a hungry worm is rooting through its fabric, making narrow channels along which, over the centuries, the diligent human hand and the dreaming human mind have been building roof frames and stone walls hidden from the light, permanently cool. Greyish brown, dilapidated, stripped bare, crooked as in a child's drawing, their mortar falling away in swathes, and the stucco from pieces of angels' wings, lions' and dogs' jaws, rams' horns and ordinary little decorative motifs, those little houses are rotting, decaying outwardly, while this town rots silently and invisibly from within, as though devoured by cancer. Small windows, old windows with dirty panes, little windows with the aroma of sick old age placed on either side of these forgotten streets which, thank goodness, flow for the most part towards some square or other, in search of air (as I do when asthma, the enemy of my present, that unseen, underhand suffocation, attacks), today these windows, otherwise resembling the eyes of the blind, are dark and just stare at one another or at nothing, bolted. Into those scowling streets penetrates the echo of the inner darkness of this once remarkable town, the cold of the night, the hallucinatory fluttering of bats' fan-like wings, pipistrelles, noctules, flittermice, those magical blood-suckers with supernatural hearing. Do bats ever go deaf?

Bats have powerful jaws for eating small insects, which makes no sense. Their fingers are joined by a membrane, all their fingers apart from the thumb. In socialist days, in school, we learned that Engels maintained that the thumb is the most important human digit; no-one mentioned bats. Engels got that idea about the thumb from Darwin. Nowadays Darwin is rarely mentioned in schools. That's quite understandable because statistics and politics state that this is a Catholic country. I don't have a high regard for Catholic countries, but given that my opinion is insignificant and impotent, I won't expound it. Still the business with the thumb, that's correct. When the thumb is injured and immobile, the hand is useless, stiff as a spade, it can't even shoot, it can only type, slowly.

Perhaps bats are our forebears, perhaps noctules with those glands on their faces that secrete unpleasant odours, and even blood-sucking bats, are our forefathers and foremothers? Because man too has glands that secrete unpleasant odours. Man too has powerful jaws, except that people are on the whole carnivorous, which bats generally aren't. Only, bats have hair all over their bodies, thick hair, dark and short, while people no longer have so much hair, for instance the Chinese, they have the least hair, especially on their bodies, their bodies can be completely smooth, then they rub themselves with oil and become shiny, which has an exciting effect when touched. Black people are also less hairy than whites. The Chinese have no fear of bats, in fact they love them because they believe bats bring happiness and great joy.

In Europe, people are afraid of bats. It is in their genetic make-up. In Europe people believe that when a man's soul leaves his body in his sleep, it settles in the body of a bat. For the people of Europe, all bats, from the tiniest ones that weigh just a few grams to those whose wing span freezes the blood in your veins, all those bats having flown to the catacombs of our personal hells, clinging with their little sharp claws to the shadows of our subconscious, to the shadows of our dead (and living), sway to and fro like empty swings in a warm wind. The males, like most males, love packs and usually hang in gatherings of some hundred individuals, because when they aren't in a group they become pathologically vulnerable. The females on the whole live alone or in small groups and tend their young, and they don't go in for mass production like dogs and cats, but have one little pipistrelle at a time and drag it everywhere with them, even when they fly. If I had to transform myself into a noctule, I'd become a tiny dwarf bat, the smallest species that can fit in everywhere, and I'd be called Pipistrellus Pipistrellus.

In "Bat Street", in the house that was once number 9, on which high up there is still a frieze of a pipistrelle, lived the knight Marziale Malle, about whom I know nothing. People here adore carnivals, it's a tradition of theirs. When the time comes for these masked fiestas, people tend to go out a bit more, particularly at night, otherwise they don't go out much. Then they walk in packs, buzzing like bats. And they remember the knight Marziale and his engraving and all their own noctules and all the historical ones and they hang flags with images of these creatures of unprepossessing appearance everywhere, and organise balls at which they dance quadrilles and waltzes, and, when they let their hair down, even polkas, and they put on operettas, mostly Strauss' "Die Fledermaus", and come to the theatre with masks and costumes borrowed, through connections or against a deposit, from the theatre wardrobe, which becomes increasingly scanty by the year, increasingly threadbare.

The better-off – the entrepreneurs and the political elite – have their own costumes for this general masquerade of bad taste and euphoria, for the celebration of the fat, heavy lie of existence, tailored according to the measure of their narcissism and the depth of their pocket. Everything glows. Faces and streets and teeth and shop windows and eyes take on an icy gleam. And along the promenade, high up in the air, long ribbons with tassels of various colours flutter and rustle in the wind, for the wind rustles here constantly, probably because of the proximity of the sea. With time, that rustling, that cheerful fluttering over one's head, which should presumably be some kind of metaphor for life here, begins to penetrate into one's brain like Chinese water torture. I once said to a woman (in passing) *These ribbons get on my nerves*, and she first looked at me astonished, offended, then she exclaimed, *Why it's like the constant sound of the sea*. I don't know why she wants a double sound of the sea; the *real* sea stretches away right beside the promenade, murmuring constantly except when it's stirred up or lies completely flat as though it were dead; when the sea apparently dies, when it just sways and minds its own business, that's when it is nicest here. Quiet.

I saw "Die Fledermaus" just once, I never went again. My apartment here is like a barracks, cold and alien. I don't like this apartment at all, that's why I don't bring flowers into it. In winter it's warm in the theatre, so I go there to get warm, then my legs are like swiss rolls because of the warm dry air. When I went to "Die Fledermaus", I listened and watched people dancing, singing and talking, then I fell asleep. When I came to this little dead town, I used to go regularly to the cinema in the winter, again because of its warmth. I sat in the balcony because, I believe, warm air is lighter than cold air, it rises, while cold air sinks and seeps into the shoes. I couldn't go often, there were only three cinemas and an occasional one in this town, and now there are two and the occasional one, because one cinema disappeared overnight. Out of the disappearing cinema the seats disappeared as well and a man in a turban moved in with snakes. The man and the snakes danced and frightened the children, who squealed, because it was mostly children who came to see these flayed, decrepit reptiles, because their parents thought that close encounters with animals fostered the awakening of humanity. Why don't they make a zoo in this town and develop love that way? Or a skating rink? This town has no skating rink because the government believes that coastal towns don't need skating rinks, that it's enough to have a view of the sea. Instead of a skating rink, where big and small people would spin in circles, cinematically, their scarves fluttering and fluttering in the wind, and where great winter joy reigns (given there's no zoo), here they build ever more new garages, which are opened festively with bunches of *mille balle blu* balloons, and branches of the *mille balle gialle* Raiffeisen savings bank, which, these bunches of balloons at the openings of banks and car parks, after priests have sprinkled them quite idiotically with holy water and blessed them, these bouquets of balloons are released into the sky as though they were doves of peace. I have skates, black. Top quality.

This town has no zoo, there we are.

Writers like writing about the zoos they visit on their touristic, scholarly or émigré travels. In contemporary literature, local and foreign, there are quite a few texts on zoos. Zoos are presumably a neat metaphor as they remind one of towns, of walled towns in which people are provided for and tamed, towns which people enter sometimes by force and leave when they're dead. Zoos are populated by decrepit animals, decaying with inactivity. In them the skies need to fall in, the deserts to go mad for the animals to start crying; they are so benumbed that they have no will for anything, they don't hunt, they don't roam, they don't leap, they don't roar, they don't run, they don't hide, they just eat and mate and mope and pray to God that the visitors will leave them in peace. That's why Kapuściński got upset.

> When I was in Abu Dhabi, the children teased a gorilla in the zoo (it is new, built outside the city, in the desert). At first the gorilla got angry, it ran back and forth on the concrete stage, it threatened the little aggressors. Finally tired the gorilla sat down in the middle of the cage and started crying. And

then – exactly at that moment (what an extraordinary coincidence!) – a sandstorm started. A sudden, violent, powerful storm that covered the sky with clouds of gray dust and threw in our eyes a hot blizzard of sand. Everyone started running, children screamed, grown-ups followed children, the wind tossed and blew about clouds of dust, terrified women ran through the swirling, burning fog of the sandstorm like frightened, black birds. Running, I glanced for a moment behind me: through the dust, through the whirling cloud, in the surrounding semi-darkness I saw the gorilla sitting stooped in the cage, as if half-broken, sitting, gazing after us, and sobbing.

I've taken my daughter round various zoos, so she could see them and I looked as well. We went to the zoo in Munich one distant refugee winter; to the zoo in Rome one still more distant, one could say happy, autumn, when the flamingos spread fire beside the withered leaves and our ice creams melted in the October sun; we walked in Maksimir in Zagreb under a grey sky, on paths wet with rain, in shoes that let in water so that the dye inside them ran and stained our feet. I remember lazy tortoises in Zagreb, seals and walruses in Belgrade, penguins in New York that waddled up to my daughter and pulled at her long blue scarf as though they were going to capture her and take her to the land of eternal ice; I remember various small fish, multi-coloured, and black panthers, glossy, and elephants with enormous cakes of hardened dung on their flanks, but I don't recall where they were. Of Toronto Zoo I remember the expanse, animals in the distance, unrecognisable, masses of people, I recall the queues, the asphalted paths, little trains full of Japanese tourists, McDonald's and its sixty-cent ice cream, my legs ached and it was horrible at Toronto Zoo.

It is not possible to write about the zoo in this town because this town does not have a zoo. It has temporary zoological visitors, such as those snakes, sometimes rabbits, and birds and hens that are kept in cages so that it smells all around them, while the visitors circulate.

Florian Winter lives here. I mention Florian Winter because there are people like Florian Winter in this town, people whom it is possible to love, but there's no need. Florian Winter is thirty-five years old and he collects pigeons and various other birds that sing or don't sing. Florian Winter doesn't know the lucky-unlucky Hervé Joncour of whom it is questionable whether he's the invention of Alessandro Baricco or not, in other words he doesn't know that seeker, the collector of elusive passions which clutch the heart slowly and quietly, but the heart doesn't die, just as silkworms weave their thread, silken, silkily, that Hervé who locks longing in small carefully sealed boxes so it can live for ever, but it expires all the same. Florian Winter transforms all the rooms of his apartment – four – into birdcages, while Hervé Joncour dreams and builds aviaries, because Hervé Joncour has a park of his own, while Florian Winter doesn't. Florian Winter has an apartment into which he moved when some other people were moved out long ago. Hervé Joncour said: *First you fill the aviary with birds, as many as you can, then one day, when something nice happens to you, you throw the aviary wide open and watch the birds fly away*. Florian Winter virtually never speaks, he whistles, and it doesn't cross his mind to return his birds to celestial infinity, because Florian Winter isn't happy and the silvery murmuring keeps him alive. Florian Winter walks through idyllic landscapes. For a long time he watches birds, then captures them and brings them home. Some of Florian Winter's birds sing, some just stare blankly and rotate their heads, because birds' eyes are on the sides of their heads so they have to pivot them in order to see at least something. Every morning Florian Winter strolls into his cages and sits among his flying creatures, which with time forget how to fly, that is why he cannot let them go, not even the carrier pigeons. As apart from those birds, Florian Winter has no other living creature, he doesn't need letters, so he doesn't see why he should send or release his carrier pigeons anywhere. One day Florian Winter will join his birds for ever; he will close the netted door behind him, the door will click and Florian Winter will say *That's how it should be*. They will find him covered in feathers the way that crappy prince-statue of Oscar Wilde's is covered in snow, shivering (it's a story that breaks a child's heart, it's a terrible story that makes one cry). Someone will write about Florian Winter in the local paper's crime reports, and readers love crime reports because they know – all those atrocities are happening to some unknown people, not to them, so they needn't worry. Florian Winter will shrink, he will be reduced to his initials, F. W., and his disappearance will be, for everyone, including himself, quiet and painless.

After the snakes, into the cinema come books that imitate a little book fair, a hodgepodge of knowledge. Nowadays the former cinema is a café, a person could spend the entire day in this town just drinking coffee and munching on buns, there are so many cafés, and this new café has a little window as well, and at it one can buy hot pastries tasting of pizza, cheese, apricots, cherries or unflavoured ones, plain. Some changes here take place in a flash, by leaps and bounds. Those are the changes of disappearance.

In Toronto I used to look for cobblers, here I look for shops that repair small household appliances, for shops storing my general nostalgia. Veterinary dispensaries that treat small animals keep springing up; they are clinics with up-to-date equipment, private ones, with pharmacies and drug stores piled high with wonderfully packaged, colourful, cosmetic lies to make life great for the animals, with various vitamins that the pets chew like sweets. These products are expensive.

I have six irons, not one of them works.

The Italian one, the cheapest, new, which *does* work, is no use at all because it leaves cotton items creased. I don't iron anything anymore. I don't talk about it, because some people here would be horrified if they knew, especially those who iron towels and underpants. There *is* a man in the neighbourhood who repairs small household appliances, but what he repairs explodes as soon as it's brought home. Everything he repairs costs seventy, no matter in which currency. His shop is open only until midday, like post offices on the larger Adriatic islands and in larger villages all over the country. Small villages and small islands have no post office at all, why should they? I can't throw those irons out because I don't like throwing irons out. My lamps have had it as well, so when I come into the apartment, it's completely dark, and I like to be greeted by something at least. A handyman, a plumber, once said, *Give me that blower heater, I'll sort it out for you*, now he tells me, *Work is doing my head in, I'll end up in an asylum.*

The oldest psychiatric hospital in Croatia was founded here, so they say. That asylum for lost souls, that "manicomio", sprang up near the old chandlery that became a hospital. Today there's no chandlery in this town, why should it have a chandlery? This little town doesn't even have manufacturers' shops selling decorative candles because decorative candles are mass-produced in factories. Nevertheless, when winter descends on this town, when the cold anchors itself among its fugues, when greyness

and dampness nestle in the cracks that have func-
tioned for centuries as narrow passageways for
departures, for getting out, like little mouths for
catching breath, like little lungs, when that happens
and the town becomes firmly blocked, when the sky
vanishes, when the sky is transformed into an ugly
grey rag, opaque, impenetrable, this town looks like
a wax town, like a waxwork town through which
little wax statues roll, greyish-white, with no wicks.

The hospital was big, while the asylum for the
mentally ill was small. The asylum took in its first
patients in 1823, but it soon emerged that a larger
asylum should have been built, this small one was
inadequate, the desperate kept growing in number.
As soon as the small asylum was built, a little chapel
was put up beside it, so that the patients could pray
for their recovery, and when no-one answered their
prayers, neither God nor medicine, they were transported, quite stiff, to the mortuary, which was also
nearby. That system is in place still today, mortuaries and little chapels, little chapels and mortuaries
beside every hospital or within it. The hospital still
exists, as does the garden around it, except that the
hospital garden has grown bigger and today it's
more like a hospital park, a park surrounded by a
wall, a separate park where no-one normal thinks of
just going for a walk. People run through that hospital park, with their heads down, as if escaping from
a Dante-esque landscape, although the park isn't
ugly at all; there are tropical plants and paths and
benches and little fountains covered in moss where
water trickles. There are no flowers. Ashen people sit
on the benches, untidy, in laundered pyjamas or
blue-and-white striped dressing-gowns, with plastic

slippers on their feet, they sit and wait. But they're not waiting, they're just breathing deeply and slowly because they're in no hurry. It's inconceivable to go and take a walk in hospital parks, and especially inconceivable to walk through this hospital garden here, although it's not far from the building where I live. And the building where I live is very old, this town is full of unbelievably old buildings, which has a terrifying effect.

Medicine has been developing successfully here for a long time now, because in the past various armies ran through this little town, big and small ships sailed into this little town, there were inns and prostitutes so there were epidemics, because every commotion undermines stability, including that of health. Already two hundred years ago there were lazarettos, there were homes for abandoned children, there were poorhouses, there were sanatoria, which in itself suggests that people suffered from all kinds of illnesses, both secretly and publicly.

The workman threatening mental breakdown because of my blower heater did mend one, for I had given him two, but he took out its heater, which means the blower now just blows, there is no prospect of its heating anything, and it's winter, not summer. The workman put a too-large ventilator in the other blower, so now that oversized ventilator scrapes the inside of the heater, which is unbearable to listen to. Otherwise, the proper term is fan heater, and the word blower is inaccurate, because fan heater means that this object carries heat. However, there's nothing picturesque about a fan heater while there is about a blower heater, when you say blower, air bursts from your mouth like a breath of wind. I adore workmen's shops.

In the bathroom, the plumber also changed a tap, which doesn't work properly now; it worked before. When I turn it on, the water starts to run and then abruptly stops even though the tap is still turned on. The plumber tells me that the plumbing in the apartment as a whole is to blame. I don't believe him, but for the time being I have no other plumber. There used to be one, he repaired the boiler in my kitchen. When he had sorted it out, I went away. While I was away, the police tracked me down and told me to return home at once – there was an enormous flood in the apartment and it was pouring down the walls into all the apartments below. *Those* are problems. I have books about physics, this winter I shall study electrical currents, weak and alternating.

There is something very strange about the people here. When I ask them whether they know a lawyer, they say they don't, when I ask who cleans their windows, they say they have a window cleaner but he's fully booked, when I ask whether they know someone who could reupholster my sofa, they say buy the local advertiser, you get the impression that the people here went to school on their own, that apart from them no-one else exists. People here don't socialise much. If they do get together, they are reserved, although there are probably exceptions. Those who are not exceptions call each other by the formal "you", as though to put out their hand and say "Stop!" And then they whisper, *Now we could go for a coffee*, then they ask what's new and spill out a little piece of gossip for the sake of conversational atmosphere. If they go to visit their nearest and dearest they arrange it in advance, they always make an arrangement because it would be terrible just to turn up at half-past eleven at night, it would be unforgiveable to open the fridge in someone else's home, it would be uncouth and primitive, great refinement reigns here. Here sophistication reigns and huge, repressed caution. There's a readiness to take offence that people call sensitivity, it's hard to cope with because it suffocates and restrains like a Schanz collar. Here people say, we're contented, although they complain of various little inessential things, and there is here an unprecedented number of economists. They're mostly women economics graduates who marry electricians, carpenters, mechanics, plumbers and sailors, and who work in banks, because there are an alarming number of banks here for such a small town. Here, I'm a consummate loser.

There, I know personally and well mechanics, lawyers, upholsterers, electricians, gynaecologists, lung specialists, ear, nose and throat specialists, orthopaedic surgeons, not to mention psychiatrists, paediatricians, laboratory technicians, internal medicine specialists and cardiologists, in fact all kinds of doctors, bankers, writers, plumbers, producers, architects, film-makers, chess players, mariners, actors, caricaturists, psychologists, expert witnesses, librarians, dentists, sellers of local eggs and cheeses, sculptors, butchers, alcoholics, caterers, designers, chefs, receptionists, painters and decorators, lorry drivers. With some of them I went to kindergarten, to primary and secondary school with others, some of them I kissed, with some of them I ate grilled pike on the barges at the river island Ciganlija, with some I picked cherries, with some I wept, some of them I buried. I know who has tapestries on their walls and who has the clap. I know who doesn't like beer, who shaves their legs, who's circumcised and who plays the guitar. I know who doesn't eat courgettes, and who pumpkin, I know who adores *kapama* at Janićije's, and who cod at Buda and Ivo's, who likes sweetbreads, who kidneys and who is on a perpetual diet. I know who lives beside Mercator in New Belgrade, has two parrots and a manic-depressive mistress. I know who wears flowery Bermuda shorts, who can't stand synthetic fabrics, who has a blue bath, who collects old clocks, who has an uncle living in Bordeaux, who broke their hip, who has moles on their face. I know who works on reception at the Majestic and what the rooms are like at the Metropol and Slavija hotels; I know the loveliest Roma woman in the world, she died. I know who comes from Sinj, who is a court witness, who has paintings on their wall by Milić from Mačva, who has paintings by Dragoš Kalajić, who by Stojan Ćelić, who by Lubarda, and who by Otašević; I know whose nearest and dearest were wiped out by the Ustashas, I know who makes large sculptures and sepia-tone photographs and what his hands smell like. I know who likes lovers with beards, who's dying of cancer and before death is collecting little padlocks for luck, whose button on her pink blouse is always undone, who has a white freestanding mirror in the hall, who keeps hens in the garden, and who a bulldog, I know who is no longer there and who became a convert, who has divorced whom and who has joined the ranks of homosexuals and who those of lesbians. I know who has unreasonably small hands, who has freckles on their back and who shaves their eyebrows. I know who suffered from profound amnesia and came back. I know who took me to archaeological digs at Bosut, when I had no idea whether Bosut was in Croatia or Serbia. I know who paints windows blue and doors yellow, who wears nothing but Polzela stockings, who makes the best spinach pie and who does crosswords while they shit. I know who has a Biedermeier clock and a heap of unnecessary small household appliances and my savings book from which Beobank stole everything, who lives on the quay and speaks Czech, who breeds cats and has a red soapdish. I know who has her lips outlined with tattoos so that they always look fresh, who smokes Dunhill even when she has no money and who fixes whose teeth, who adores Cacharel blouses and tight trousers because she has a nice arse. I know who now has grandchildren and an open visa for Switzerland and no longer sits alone like a willow tit on a branch, I know who loves red scarves, expensive shoes, who has patients in fugues, who goes to the gym and occasionally to Rome. This story is fat and as long as my life and doesn't belong here because my life here is small and short, useless, useless, hollow and bleak, that's what I deserve, so this is where I belong, in this wilderness, in this dead little town which, like me, was once quite alive and large. Now both of us languish in our smallness, I angry, it silent, witnesses of our mutual poverty, each an observer of the dying of the other, sniffers-out of the decaying of our innards. We search for our pulse, I search for the town, the town searches for me, half blind, we stumble, grope through the sticky worm-eaten mass of our pasts, sick and inseparable enemies until death do us part.

And Polo said: "The inferno of the living is not something that will be; if there is one, it is what is already here, the inferno that we live every day, that we form by being together. There are two ways to escape suffering it. The first is easy for many: accept the inferno and become such a part of it that you can no longer

see it. The second is risky and demands constant
vigilance and apprehension: seek and learn to recog-
nise who and what, in the midst of the inferno, are not
inferno, then make them endure, give them space."

One woman tells me, *Go, if you don't like it here, go back,* and I say, *It wouldn't enter my mind, it's out of the question. I adore reading your town,* I say, *playing with its rags,* because it's that sort of town, all ragged, while I read through the town over there long ago. The one who says *go back, go there* now tells me that *she* is going *there* because people there are warm, that's exactly what she says, *They are warm people,* then she adds, *I have to get out of this darkness, this dreariness.* Then I ask her, *Out of what darkness?* What does she know? "There" is now fashionable. I hear kids in the streets using dialect words from there, in the market I hear people longing for kaymak that you can't get here, oh, we adore kaymak, they say. What do they know? They found *me* to talk to about the food at the Orač, kid *me* that the Kasina is a great hotel with suites, that former brothel with rooms to let by the hour, accessible to penniless students from the muddy Serbian countryside who would follow a cheap shag by crossing the road to the Atina for a dish of polenta with milk; they can renovate the Kasina till the cows come home, the Kasina is still the Kasina whose walls will always emanate the smell of bought passions and carnal sweat. Or "The Last Chance". People from here can sit under the corrugated tin roof of that tavern there, warmed by a drummer, and knock back mulled wine or hot toddies with čevapčići until dawn, but when I ask them about Tofija (who is certainly now lying in a communal grave for the homeless), they just gawp blankly.

I went there, as I've already said, since I've been here. Since I let myself be driven out; since they told me that the shape of my face is not acceptable; since they took down the poster of Rovinj that hung above my desk in the place where I used to work and tore it to shreds; since a colleague asked me, *Have I done something wrong* and I told him, *Yes, you've done something wrong*; since another colleague said, *Well you like the sea, it's good that you're going to the seaside*; since someone wrote "Ustasha bitch" beside my name on the list of employees after I had pinned a newspaper cutting to that same list in which it said that transport to the big demonstration in support of Milošević at Gazimestan was free, so that they should know, because they were all preparing enthusiastically to go, as a group, and I told them they had all gone crazy, all of them; since a woman there, at my office, had a fit because the announcement was written in the Latin script and if it was written in the Latin script it must have originated in some subversive newspaper which I allegedly read, and it differed from the other announcements printed exclusively in Cyrillic, so she knew at once that everything written in the Latin script came from me, as though I didn't know Cyrillic, what a moron. That woman, who was called Ivana, later married a diplomat and went off to some Arab country and in that Arab country, in the sun, she composed her jolly music, because she was a musician, and she wrote a book about that Arab country, while people from Bosnia were fleeing to Canada, Sweden and Denmark, where they were first placed in quarantine, or rather in camps, to clean themselves up a bit, to be domesticated, not to corrupt their surroundings, and those who didn't flee, like my Gordana for instance who is also a musician, used to shit into plastic bags in the winter and then scatter those plastic bags through the frozen parks, which anyway no longer existed because the trees in them were cut for heating and when spring came the turds started to thaw and everything stank of human misery while Ivana was basking in that Arab country, because in Arab countries there are no cold winters, there are just sandstorms. Later, Ivana came here, officially of course, to some international music gathering and she talked about the pressures she had been under. We didn't meet up, which is good, but we will, everyone is on the move now.

I went there ten years later, on business, because ten years later the government had changed both here and there so I agreed to go on an official visit. I went so as to take my mother some mimosa, because that was her favourite. I went to see whether I was going to dig my mother up or, when the time came, to lie beside her.

This is how it was.

The bus was called "Fils". The bus called Fils took passengers to the border crossing, to "no-man's-land", then another bus with a different name came to no-man's-land and for ten marks it took passengers across into the other country. Now it has all changed. Now buses from there and here go all the way. "Lasta" ("Swallow") buses from the other country fly past my window now.

There is a discount for return tickets.

It's ten minutes before departure time, and there are no passengers. A girl runs past me, leaving nervousness in her wake, she shouts, *Up yours*.

Five minutes before departure time, beside the Fils bus there are only myself and a woman from here, a beggar, who keeps whispering, *Have you got a kuna? Have you got a kuna?*

Two minutes before departure – there's a crowd

by the bus door. People get on quickly, their heads bowed, like the guilty. They get on just in the way people here enter the Orthodox church, in front of which there is hardly ever anyone, perhaps just the priest scurrying into the churchyard, his robe flapping. Only at Christmas do people gather outside the Orthodox church here, because it is a time of universal love, kindliness and forgiveness; after Christmas, universal love, kindliness and forgiveness vanish.

As soon as I arrive I plan to eat two walnut biscuits and a piece of walnut tart because one can't get them here. When I mention walnut tart here, people say, *You must mean baklava*, but I absolutely do not mean baklava, because here one can get as much baklava as one likes, I mean walnut tart. There are quite a few uninformed people around.

I stay at the Palace Hotel – it's a business trip, otherwise there would be at least ten places I could stay, unlike here. In this town there is no-one I could stay with, while in other towns in this small country, there is, which is quite a strange fact. Besides, in this town there is not a single person who would agree to look after our cat if both of us, my daughter and I, were to go away for more than a few days, which is why we don't go away for more than a few days at the same time, only one by one.

The Palace Hotel used to be where sportsmen and the Yugoslav State Security Service, U.D.B.A., stayed. There's no U.D.B.A. now, it has a different name. In the hotel everything works, except on the third floor. On the third floor, in the lift foyer, there are two framed tourist posters with Yugoslavia written on them showing panoramas of Rovinj and

Dubrovnik. While I'm waiting for the lift, I take the posters down and put them on the floor, facing the wall. Now those posters of Rovinj and Dubrovnik being in Yugoslavia are a small thing, a remnant, an oversight, obviously. But small things have a way of turning into big things, although for the time being big things in this region are on the whole over, having left only debris. In 1989 it wasn't like that, in 1989 preliminary actions were being carried out, 1989 was the prelude. The journal *Practical Woman* published a pattern for needlepoint, for a tapestry, and the pattern outlined the all-encompassing borders of Greater Serbia. That was a small thing then, later it grew.

I go to an official dinner at Sova, the "Owl", restaurant. Sova is new, I didn't know it existed.

I meet a lot of familiar faces. Some familiar faces and I fall into each other's arms, from others I turn my head.

I saw a currency exchange office called "Piranha".

I saw a bus full of Chinese people travelling to Požarevac and the whole time I was there I kept thinking about spittoons.

Spittoons are white metal objects, three-legged, with a pedal at the base and a container at the top, which were placed in the corners of train stations and the waiting rooms of clinics, usually by the door, to accommodate everyone's spit. People used to spit into them before going out into the street or before travelling to another place. According to hygienists, spittoons protected the environment from pollution. There are no spittoons like that anymore.

*

For those who pass it without entering, the city is one
thing; it is another for those who are trapped by it and
never leave. There is the city where you arrive for the
first time; and there is another city which you leave
never to return. Each deserves a different name.

Enough.

This is a town with too many cars. It would be better if people walked more. For instance, on Fifth Avenue, I know this because I know it, people walk, particularly those who live on Fifth Avenue, they walk the length of it and call into side streets, where there are small cafés and restaurants, there are also docile lines of trees, as in Berlin, at night they walk their dogs and their fur coats, I miss little lines of trees in side streets, I could weep for how much I miss just that, those little nocturnal (postcoital) alleys, now that it is late autumn.

Here there are lots of small shiny cars, new, from which people stare at those who don't drive. The people who stare at those who walk, drive those small cars to the big shopping malls in the suburbs because how else could they transport all that foodstuff to their homes? Those who don't drive also stare – at those who drive. That suggests that people here watch each other, look around generally, listen and eavesdrop, which isn't quite the case. Among those who don't drive, who only walk, there is a growing number who converse with their inner voices, out loud, as in Toronto, in Toronto there are people like that in the subway, they travel free because they're sick.

A WALK

He: You have strong arms.
She: Don't touch me.

My name is Viktor Zibarowsky. As I walk, I look down. A woman's wrinkled toes in brown sandals come towards me. The brown sandals are old, tight for the woman. That brown colour reminds me immediately of East Berlin when it existed; this town was also divided in two. Generally speaking, old toes are ugly, as are old feet. Old people lack vitamins and their cells start drying up. Old people here don't take care of themselves, they don't have saunas as they do in Finland. In Finland old people go to saunas regularly, even the most wretched of them. This woman coming towards me has big feet. A little Gypsy girl is scampering along beside her, with three loaves of bread in her arms. The little Gypsy is dressed in yellow. The other pedestrians are in black.

There are nice buildings. They have nice façades.

The woman buying bread had bitten all her nails right down.

I am Perla Meizen.

The woman beside me, who sells smuggled packets of elastic at the market, has torn nylons and hairy legs so the hairs stick out of her stockings. My legs are smooth, I have no hairs. I would not degrade myself so far as to sell elastic, I sell chocolate. Sometimes I eat all my chocolate, particularly when it's cold, when I don't sell anything. There's a fishmonger nearby. I sniff it. I don't buy fish.

Many women have hairy legs, but pretend they don't, they pluck the hair secretly, peel them, shave or burn them. Latent paedophiles like women's smooth bodies. Some African women pluck their hairs with sugar and lemon, including those private ones. That's mostly done by married women because the married women's men like that. I also see that woman with the hairy legs who sells elastic. She has mended her nylons with silver nail polish. I think it's summer. I sell old books. I don't need them anymore.

There is a traffic accident. Both cars are driven by women. The woman in the red car is wearing green. A woman with green sunglasses on her nose passes by me. Today could be a green day, fresh. I am Lina Tik. I sell pyjamas from Turkey. I tell people, "These are cotton pyjamas, a hundred percent cotton," but they're not, they're synthetic.

The man in the car at the traffic lights is using both forefingers to squeeze his blackheads, he's not holding the steering wheel at all.

Here's another woman in a green dress, there are yellow flowers scattered over her dress. The woman looks like a moving field of dandelions. The woman is wearing yellow sandals and a yellow watch and a yellow ribbon in her hair. This is in fact a predominantly yellow woman, not a green one.

*

I'm young. My name is Ricardo Rotta. One of my eyebrows is quite white, the other is normal. At the market I sell stockings, or rather socks. It's warm, girls wear short T-shirts. Each girl has a different belly button. Are any two belly buttons the same, I wonder.

I have large hands with long fingers. I have a big nose. I adore Bukovsky and Baudelaire. There are many young men who look like girls. They even use anti-wrinkle cream round their eyes. They are slender and like wearing tight clothes. And jewellery.

I pass a beggar. The beggar doesn't move, he just sits on the pavement, drunk and smelling of urine. We glance at each other, he slings me a dose of his bodily stench, which clings to my coat like a crazed cat, and hangs, swaying as I walk. And so every day. We're fusing.

People adore standing in queues, so there are queues here too, wherever you look. There are peaceful queues, quiet, stiff queues, disciplined queues which exude obedience. Hence, while one waits, it's best not to talk, because when someone speaks, the others who don't, feel awkward and start squirming. So, in the queues, there aren't many talkative waiters, people don't feel like chatting, they have their own problems. The situation is better at the market and at kiosks. There the saleswomen want to talk, they even smile. At the market, one woman says, *Asthma can be treated with goat's milk*, another says, *Barley tea is better*. Then the first one says, *You could also try grated black radish with honey*.

As soon as I came here, a mild asthma attacked me; whenever I go away, my mild asthma stays home. Later, the asthma began to grow, now it's a big asthma. I hardly go anywhere anymore. Once I happened to find myself in London, and another time in Berlin. Both in London and in Berlin I waited for my asthma, but it didn't come. It likes its own (small) town. That's where it feels most comfortable.

People tend to queue in the morning, particularly around eleven. People queue less in the afternoon, in the afternoon people rest from their morning's waiting, so it's best to pay one's bills then, in the afternoon. I wait in queues as well, I fit in. In banks, customers are offered personal internet banking, which sounds progressive, but is completely unacceptable to most people here, because most don't own a computer, and there are also many who don't have accounts from which they could draw money to pay for electricity, television, rent and telephone, and there is an increasing number of people who don't pay their bills at all and whose telephones are cut off, and people who use wood for heating. In fact, the media keep advising people to do just that, they say it's wonderful to use wood for heating, the way our forebears did, it's wonderful to watch a fire crackling, perhaps in an open hearth, people have been talking intensively about fireplaces here for the last ten years or so, they say it's romantic to watch the little sparks while it's snowing outside, except that it never snows here. If ever it does, the snow vanishes at once, all we have here is a terrible cold wind that makes your bones crack and your soul shrink until it becomes as tiny as a broad bean. That's why that home-computing banking system for citizens won't catch on quickly or globally here, because of poverty, and because then those who don't work would have nothing whatever to do, because this is all they have now, this waiting in queues, which is some kind of occupation after all, some small activity they would be deprived of. As well as of some kind of communication with other aggrieved people. Perhaps that's why I queue. So that it doesn't turn out that I've isolated myself altogether. To maintain contact with my surroundings, to look as though I belong. But I don't.

People here rarely embrace when they meet in the street, they rarely hug one another ardently. Why should they embrace, they meet all the time as it is. Nothing new happens for months, years. Someone dies now and then, someone is born, someone moves in, and those who can or have to, move out. I don't know whether that means that here no-one misses anyone, that people here suffer from a lack of longing, I've no idea, perhaps there are those who long for someone (or something), there probably are, it would be completely sick, completely abnormal if there were no such person here. But perhaps they're simply that type, they feed their emotions inwardly, within themselves, self-denyingly, terrified of the possibility that their emotions might burst out, thinking that then there would be chaos, a disruption of their (false) refinement. Or perhaps, as they stand in queues, people create a closeness that they do not otherwise achieve, when a person is alone he can't get close, can he? Perhaps that's why people here gather in churches, and when a crowd is assembled, the priests say, *My flock*. In queues people even touch. They wait. Time flows. They look around. They get tired. They wear themselves out. Life acquires a purpose. The day fills up.

Also in Raissa, city of sadness, there runs an invisible thread that binds one living being to another for a moment, then unravels, then is stretched again between moving points as it draws new and rapid patterns so that at every second the unhappy city contains a happy city unaware of its own existence.

As I wait in a queue, I watch the woman in front of me. Suddenly, she turns around, and I'm astonished how racoon-like she is, then I remember that we all resemble some animal or other, and the woman asks me, *Do you ever think about God?*

Professor Zanni plays with racoons. He shows them a drawing that means *you may eat* and the racoons quickly climb to the top of their cage where food is waiting for them. When Professor Zanni shows them a drawing that means *you may not eat*, the racoons do not climb, they are calm, it doesn't occur to them to eat, as though they were saying to themselves, *We aren't in the least hungry.* Professor Zanni has obedient, well-trained and well-brought-up racoons. Each time they obey him, Professor Zanni rewards them and the racoons are satisfied; he gives them a toy, something to keep them happy until the next experiment. But when the racoons don't get a reward, and they expect one, there are problems: they get angry, they scratch the cage, they squeal, they tear up the drawing, they even growl, in so far as racoons can growl. The game is called *language and behavioural adaptation*.

This town is full of balconies. Some balconies have angels on them, some have little lions, some have female, or male, heads, some have nothing, they're old and could collapse at any minute. Some balconies look out onto other balconies, others at a wall.

A corpse was found in the middle of town. A male corpse.

A dead sparrow is lying on the path. There's no blood around the sparrow, the sparrow isn't at all deformed. One of its eyes is open, its beak is pointing towards the sky. The sparrow looks like a stuffed bird, but it isn't, it has just been stepped on.

A woman with a lot of scars on her arms is sitting on a bench outside the railway station.

> *They call me Perla. The scars are from self-harming. I cut myself with a razor left to me by my grandfather; my grandfather's dead, of course. I've got a surgical scalpel, made of steel, expensive. I'm sitting. I'm not waiting for a train, I'm not travelling, I have no intention of going anywhere, I'm just sitting. I've got scars on my face as well, they are small scars, you can't see them because they are covered by my hair. At night I put little pegs of various colours on the edge of my face and stretch it. In the morning, when I take the pegs off, my face droops again. I'm just sitting, I'm not waiting for anything, or anyone. Otherwise, my name*

*is Rosetta, they call me Rosa. When they don't call
me Perla.*

A woman's feet pass in shoes with a tiger-skin pattern.

A woman's feet pass in red shoes with high heels.

A man's feet pass in socks with an embroidered chimney and a cat,
also embroidered, sitting on it.

A woman passes in white boots.

A man passes with a tattoo of a heart on his upper arm, in the heart
it says "A & B".

On the façade of an old building are traces of a sign for an inn that
closed a long time ago: GRGO'S CELLAR.

A man passes with a framed degree certificate; the certificate is small
and the frame enormous.

Two men pass with their arms around each other.

A man passes in a dirty workman's overall with a big gold watch on
his wrist.

A man passes in a light-brown leather jacket: *Spare a coin*, he says.
You've got a nice jacket, I say. *It's a present*, he snaps.

A woman in Egypt gives birth to a child weighing seven kilograms, I
know what it's like in Egypt. In Egypt you ride through the moonlight
and through deep sand, limitless and wavy like the open sea, like a yellow
sea, not a blue one. That sandy immenseness isn't at all quiet, it hums
and swishes, that's the sand shifting, life in that sandy infinity could run
aground, oh God, the sand is strewn about, but it does not disappear, it
remains, it just swishes. It's hot sand full of tiny creatures that dive into
it, then surface and dive in again, it's sand full of little beings that bury
themselves alive, playfully, because in the depths of that sand there is
no danger.

Egypt is where "Aida" is set. Radamès is the commander of the Egyptian army and Aida is an Ethiopian princess and they are in love. But
Radamès is also loved by the Egyptian princess Amneris, who cannot
think what Radamès wants with an irrelevant and what is more captive

princess from the enemy Ethiopia, when here, right in front of his nose, he has me, a beautiful princess from his beautiful ancient land of Egypt. Nevertheless, Radamès is determined and in the end his great love for Aida makes him lose his head and he begins to betray state secrets and is buried alive by his own people, by way of punishment. I first met "Aida" and that tragi-comic story when I was thirteen and had no idea that some stories, military and amorous, keep repeating themselves, because what were then wars of importance for the whole of humanity no longer raged around us, with the possible exception of the one over Suez at the end of the 1950s which had just come to an end. An "Aida" went to Egypt from Yugoslavia, and with it the conductor Žika Zdravković, who dyed his hair jet black, which was not that common for men in those socialist days. Later the phenomenon became established, especially when Tito started changing the tone of his.

"Aida" comes here for the first time from Italy in 1885. A new theatre opens and a ceremonial poster is printed which the then mayor, Ciotta, lays symbolically in an ornately decorated tube in the theatre foundations. Eighty-five years later, the tube is dug up, reprints are made of the poster, and today it adorns small pocket and large wall calendars that are distributed free on matinee theatrical anniversaries and festivities, accompanied by local sparkling wine, local newspapers, local photographers, local retired actors, singers and ballerinas. The town is proud of this first theatre poster, although I don't know why, it's like me being proud of my lovely long legs which are now fat and flabby and misshapen. Soon after the appearance of that first "Aida" poster, theatre posters go out of fashion here; instead, posters for chocolate, cocoa and liqueurs, for coffee, clothes, for little cheap dancers, arrive from Vienna and Budapest, from Trieste and Florence, because at that time people in this town trade in all manner of things, life flourishes. That flourishing life, that imported life, lures many into this town, and some even marry here, but most leave as soon as they can, as they do up to the present day.

While the woman is giving birth to a gigantic baby in Egypt, Jörg Haider declares of the director of a small Austrian Jewish community, whose name is Ariel Muzicante, that he cannot comprehend how someone called Ariel can have such dirty hands. That happens on Ash Wednesday, which must also be some kind of religious feast day, like Corpus Christi, but I have no idea what it is.

St Vitus is the patron saint of doctors, brewers, dancers, actors and of the deaf and dumb. In old Slavonic mythology the god Vitus is the god of light, fertility and military victory. He usually holds a horn of plenty in his right hand, while near him there is always a cauldron, as a symbol of food, and a palm, as a symbol of the soul, of victory, ascent, renewal and of immortality. A town with such a protector ought to be a town of happy people with no problems. They say that the town where I currently live is protected by precisely that saint, but there again, it is a town of cheerless inhabitants and great emptinesses.

Apart from a surplus of bakeries, this town has a certain number of inhabitants with short necks. But every human settlement has that. My neck has grown shorter too. My head has retracted between my shoulders and turns left and right with increasing difficulty, it rather looks straight ahead. Once, I had a lovely long neck, now there's a small hump at its base on my back, which only a hammer blow might be able to break up, but who would bother with such trifles?

In the tobacconist's, a man is buying bullets for his son. *Give me some bullets for my son*, he says to the salesgirl. *Give me caps that go boom, boom, boom*, says the man, pointing with his forefinger round the shop, turning on his axis as though dancing. *Buy your son a picture book*, I say. *Fuck off*, he says.

Encounters like this are no good for writing.

Sometimes, with some people, I talk about small animals. They're often newspaper sellers. Sometimes they ask me, *Are you Serbian?* Sometimes they lean over the counter and say softly: *I'm Serbian.* Then we both smile.

In this town there are people who move their lips as they read. They whisper as they read. Especially at bus stations and while travelling. There's a whispering all around that gets into your ears and buzzes.

I was once at a private view. I saw a woman eating very slowly and smacking her lips like a cow chewing the cud. Her lips move left and right. As her lips move, she looks straight ahead, motionless, then, first with her index finger, then with the nail of the little finger of her right hand, she picks her teeth, then takes the ham from the sandwiches, bananas and mandarins from a platter and fills up a small plastic bag, *The ham's for my cat*, she says, *The bananas are for me, because I've mislaid my teeth somewhere*, she says, and leaves.

The rains are torrential in this town. Abnormal, like everything else.

People walking here do so at an angle. As they walk, they jerk and suddenly set off as though there's something important over there, at an angle away from them. But there isn't. Most of the walkers are on the promenade, and the promenade is virtually unavoidable, as it bisects the town. On the promenade, the civilised urban walker finds himself in great difficulties. The majority of walkers here create obstacles for those who walk in a straight line, but that's nothing to worry about because there are very few people who walk in a straight line, on the whole people walk diagonally and are oblivious to this walking horror. These numerous tacking 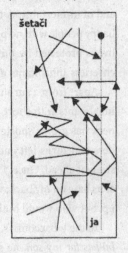 walkers get entangled between each other's legs, but that doesn't bother them, they accept between-the-leg entanglement calmly, thinking that's how it has to be. While they become entangled, the walkers often eat buns. One of the buns they eat is narrow and about thirty centimetres long, it's squashy and salty, while another has various names, it's shaped like a hoop, hard, and crumbles all over your clothes. Sometimes I tell them it would be good to eat a bun that you can't get here, I say its name and they ask, *What is that?* Then I'm overcome by irritation and despair. I'd go back at once or at least leave, but I've nowhere to go.

I find warm little bakeries with warm little aromas particularly annoying. In other places, warm little bakeries used to cheer me up. In Turgi, for instance. Turgi is a Swiss village near Baden. The pastries there were mostly Danish.

A Danish pastry is round and has a glazed apricot in the centre that looks like a fried egg and has nothing whatsoever to do with the Swiss village of Turgi.

The little Swiss village may not have been called Turgi, but Untersigenthal, and so the Danish pastry fitted in well. Here, problems arise with fitting in.

External phenomena are twisted here.

Watched from the outside, secretly, various neuroses may be observed. They are hidden, suppressed neuroses. When people's attention lapses, although people are on the whole cautious, and try hard not to let their *attention*, of all things, lapse, neuroses crash into their reality, creating chaos. These are malign neuroses, and people are afraid of them. They are striptease neuroses. One of them is the pedestrian neurosis. People here will (neurotically) assure you that their grotesque perambulation through town is in fact harmonious, pleasant even, the only possible urban perambulation, but in rare moments of intimate sincerity, perhaps just in a cloudlet of their dreams, perhaps only then will these disoriented walkers feel a flicker of longing, a painful, immense longing for the spaciousness of a ploughed field, for the green of a meadow without end. There, the streets aren't paved.

This isn't a place for urban walking. One can walk in a truly urban way, for instance "lungomare", for when you walk "lungomare" there is no prevarication. Lungomare is a narrow path, a little track dreamed up exclusively for walking up and down. Walkers stick to that narrow path, like a drunk to a fence, they have nowhere to go. And so, thanks to that little track beside the sea, the majority of citizens here learn to walk urbanely. They adore their lungomare. They generally go there at weekends, and they take their walk, their perambulation, seriously, like a kind of training. The citizens take their walking so seriously that they don't speak as they walk, they just walk. Up and down. They learn to walk. In an urban manner. In pious silence.

This kind of walking, devoid of all awareness of the existence of others, this selfish walking that resembles the maddened, disoriented running around of beheaded chickens, makes one think of walking while under anaesthetic, it's deaf and blind walking. What is more, walkers here wave their arms rapidly, forming large half-circles as though they were driving away small ghosts.

Those who live in the country get idiotic in time, without noticing it, for a while they think it's original and good for their health, but life in the country is not original at all, for anyone who wasn't born in and for the country it shows a lack of taste and is only harmful to their health. The people who go walking in the country walk right into their own funeral in the country and at the very least they lead a grotesque existence which leads them first into idiocy, then into an absurd death.

So says Thomas Bernhard. If he were alive, I'd propose to Thomas Bernhard, I'd propose, I'd say, *Thomas, stay close at hand, Thomas, I like your fugue, show me how one goes away, and I'll bring you little boxes for breathing.*

They adore their promenade, they keep repeating, *We adore our promenade*, they even write about it. They believe that when they're on it, on that promenade of theirs, when they hum along it, they believe they have insight. In small places it is important to have insight, without insight life would be senseless. Those are respectable insights, indolent insights, which say, we see and don't see, we know and don't know, we listen but we don't hear, we don't impose. They are insight-masks that conceal a fanatical concentration on one's own life to the exclusion of all others. People here are decent, unobtrusive and restrained, *We're decent, unobtrusive and restrained*, they say, *we mind our own business*.

It is boring here.

. . . Though noiseless, calm and still,
yet would he turn the earth to scraps and swill,
swallow it whole in one great, gaping yawn:

Ennui! That monster frail! – With eye wherein
A chance tear gleams, he dreams of gibbets, while
Smoking his hookah, with a dainty smile . . . –
You know him, reader, – hypocrite, – my twin!

Yours, Charles Baudelaire

That promenade is in fact a path on the bottom of a long, narrow box with no lid. Small figures glide along that path, like little tin clockwork toys, to and fro, left and right, forwards, backwards, pointlessly. There's no way out. The walls of the box are high, so the figures below look incomprehensibly small, especially if they're watched from a distance, except that there aren't many people who peer in to see what's going on deep down inside. At times, the figurines resemble a nest of beetles set free, several nests of cockroaches which scuttle about, sometimes in a circle, protected by their crunchy armour, endeavouring to escape, to get away from the invisible foot descending from above, from the sky, about to crush them. But that's when the sky darkens, otherwise life in the bottom of the box is quite lively and colourful, quite decently varied, let's say. Perhaps some wound-up tin figure, some beetle deep in the bottom of the long, narrow box, wishes to get out, to reach the top by scratching with its little legs over the slippery surface of the high walls, exhausted, damaged, breathless, and then what? Over the edge there's nothing, just a black hole, cosmic.

This year my students know the English word "embers". Last year one of them wrote that "iron" meant *something ironical*.

At the pointless launch of a pointless book, a man introduced himself by saying, *I'm from the management board of KRAŠ, the confectioners. I adore chocolate, I adore MASCULINE bitter chocolate called DORA, for eating and cooking.*

I've mislaid my *Hadrian's Memoirs*, lost them somewhere in a move. I buy new *Hadrian's Memoirs*, Croatian, the lost copy was Serbian, so it may be better that I don't have it, because some people, when they happen to glance at my books, shudder at the sight of the Cyrillic script. Actually, as time goes by, they shudder less, before they used to shudder inexplicably violently, and my then adolescent daughter turned her *Children's Encyclopaedia* in six volumes with its spine to the wall and covered all six volumes with a little square of Pag lace. Students here can no longer read Cyrillic. When I come across an essay that hasn't been translated from Serbian to Croatian, I tell them to read it and they ask, *How?* When I suggest that their parents read the essay to them, there's a deathly hush in the classroom. Inside, my new Croatian *Hadrian's Memoirs* are very like the old *Hadrian's Memoirs*. The same words on the whole, the same order, just the introduction is different. In the new introduction to the new Croatian *Hadrian's Memoirs*, the translator and author of the introduction says there is no way one could conclude that this merciless analysis of a human consciousness at a time of profound crisis could have been written by a woman. What is more, says the author of the introduction, one would say that this work is an expressly masculine book, that it was written with a sharp pen by a man who expresses himself concisely and peremptorily, mercilessly and precisely.

Engels affirms that there has been a universal, historical defeat of the female gender, Engels, right? One remembers all kinds of things from socialist times. *You have eyes like a cow*, he said, lying on the bed and, raising his leg, farted.

It is increasingly clear why the lesbian movement is going from strength to strength. Even this town has a lesbian organisation where mainly women gather, an incomprehensibly trail-blazing step for a little town like this, but then again it isn't, for the majority of people in this little town are not remotely interested in what's going on around them. Only if what's going on grazes their dreams, their pocket, their faith, their wage, their language, only then are most people here concerned, people get upset and go about collecting signatures, and they threaten protests where few gather, very few; if the protests are organised in working hours, then a few more people gather, if they're not organised in working hours, just a handful of nonentities appear. Night-time protests are out of the question, just as almost anything that happens late is out of the question, because public transport stops at 11 p.m. and workers can't get back to their housing compounds. A lot of people here live in compounds (this town is surrounded by them). In those settlements, the buildings are eroded by a permanent salty damp, so that they're covered with layers of grey-black mould, grey-black mildew, compact colonies of active fungi that burrow, devour and quietly penetrate into the innards of those deformed concrete high-rise buildings, into their seemingly hidden insides, they crawl over the walls, through the bedrooms, over the furniture, they reach the sleeping tenants, until they're wrapped in an indestructible membrane of decay, until they become cocooned in the breath of their own destruction. Thus, beyond the town centre, this place resembles an old whore, crumbling, but in fact not crumbling, monuments of culture are being restored, monuments from the past.

Don't rock the boat, that is this town's credo. Now, in the third millennium, you can freely use that word for "rock". Earlier, towards the end of the second millennium, there might be incidents and tense situations and ugly glances with sparks of patriotic suspicion if someone happened to use that word. Now, even those to whom the word sounds profane, now they even say it themselves from time to time, although they still try to avoid it, and when they're about to utter it, they first pause for a moment, reflecting.

After twelve years I handed someone a business card with my (only) Croatian address and said, *here you are, this is my Belgrade address*. Then, the next day, on that promenade, I was stopped by a woman, you could see at once that she wasn't from this town, you could see that this woman was passing through and was just having a bit of a look at the old façades as she waited for her train or bus or boat, you could see that she was hurrying on, because she was walking with a glowing face, she swayed, she swung her arms freely, aware that she was travelling towards some excitement, there was something passionate about her, and she was walking in a straight line, she didn't zigzag, she didn't collide with anyone, although she looked a little to the left and a little to the right and sometimes at the sky, completely unburdened by any kind of past that this town vomits in front of everyone, and then she stopped me and asked where she could buy sanitary towels, she said, *Excuse me, where can I buy sanitary towels?* As our encounter took place in the middle of the promenade, in fact right in front of a department store, I said, *You can buy sanitary towels here, in the "Belgrade" department store.*

Is this the palimpsest of life having a joke on me?

In the course of the television news, the presenter said "labaratory" seventeen times.

As they read, news presenters appear jumpy.

Trieste is not far away. I no longer go to Trieste. At one time I used to go to Trieste to buy food, now I buy little food, just across the road here, so I don't need Trieste. Some people from Trieste come here, some literary amateurs called the diaspora, secretaries and shop assistants and other officials (of the Consulate) who attend workshops on creative writing in their spare time, then later they read their compositions to an audience here and the audience smiles and claps.

Sabina still goes to Trieste, then she reports back to me. Sabina is meticulous and allergic. Each time she reports back, she does it over the telephone, saying *Sabina Serevent here*. I have an excellent memory for voices and I've no need to be told that it's *Sabina Serevent here*, so I tell her, I say, *I know it's you, Sabina, you don't have to tell me that it's Sabina Serevent.*

Sabina lives in a villa on a hill, above the town. She and her husband don't have many friends. In addition to her allergy, Sabina also has migraines, then she isolates herself in the dark. The villa has two floors, or maybe three. *These are the drawing rooms*, says Sabina, *these are our drawing rooms for our receptions*. At New Year, Sabina and her husband turn on all the lights and sit in their drawing rooms for receptions, alone. The villa has a large garden that drops down in cascades. There are hortensias and roses in the garden. Sabina wakes early, at five o' clock, six at the latest. Then she goes to the bathroom. In the bathroom Sabina spends one hour. *I tend my body*, she says. After she pampers her body, Sabina pulls on linen gloves, white, ties her hair up in a scarf, puts a mask over her mouth and nose and goes off to do some gardening in her large garden, in which neither she nor her husband ever sits because both Sabina and her husband have several allergies. When the sun goes down, Sabina and her husband go to bed. Before that, they put on the video recorder to record the news, serials and films. Then they watch them together in the morning, once Sabina has tended her body and before her husband goes to work and before she wanders off into her luxuriant garden. Sabina and her husband are good people. They're quiet people who work hard. They're not at all arrogant as some people are. They're not remotely immodest, like those down and outs who now walk through this town puffed up like peacocks. In fact, they don't fit in either, only they don't know it.

Once I went to Trieste with Sabina, after that I didn't go again. Sabina has a car, and I don't. I sold my car, I also sold a collector's item, an oil on canvas painted at the beginning of the twentieth century, an oil on canvas by a collector's painter, and I sold my grandmother's diamond earrings, which my grandmother was given by her grandmother, then I used that money during the war to pay for a small removal truck and my daughter and I sat beside the driver in the cabin, and the springs had broken through the seat and chafed us, and we had left our bicycles and wardrobes and our ginger cat and all our flowers in Belgrade, mostly begonias, although there were also some unusual cacti that flower disobediently, when it's not the right time for them. I've now been here for ten years without any flowers in the apartment, because if I happen to go away again, the way I went to Toronto, what will become of the plants?

My daughter has a cat, the fifth cat since that ginger, abandoned one, and in the long run the cat is a major problem, for what will happen to her if I go?

chatting in Sabina's car on the way to Trieste

Sabina says: I must buy Magdalena some shoes for her confirmation. The confirmation's on Sunday and Magdalena must have shoes for her confirmation, which is on Sunday, because she hasn't got any shoes for her confirmation so I'll try to find her something for that day. You usually have new shoes for confirmation, white or beige.

I say: What's confirmation?

Sabina says: I couldn't tell you exactly. Confirmation, that's when you're confirmed. That's when, it sounds comical, you get closer to God. I couldn't tell you exactly, I'm not much of a believer, but I've been christened, you have to be christened if you want a church wedding, then it's easier, and I wanted to get married in church, I think it's romantic, it is romantic, so my Magdalena might as well do the whole thing, that catechism, it's better that she goes to catechism than hangs around the garden, the ones who don't go to catechism just hang around, but they've rather overdone that catechism, they've connected it with the church . . .

I say: Maybe Magdalena won't want to get married in church. Maybe she won't want to get married at all.

Sabina says: What! Well, I got married in church! I want her to get married in church. It's very romantic. And you have to have new shoes for confirmation.

I say: Do you have a plumber?

Sabina says: Yes, but he's working for us at the moment, there's a lot to do at our place, our house needs repairs all the time, and he does everything, including plastering, at the moment he's sorting out the greenhouse, there are cracks in the glass,

	and where the bathroom is as well, big cracks, five centimetres across, so I told him to mend those cracks, and now he's sorting out the greenhouse in the garden, I told him to fix the greenhouse, and then we'll do the tiles, what are you going to buy in Trieste?
I say:	Food.
Sabina says:	I'm going to buy beige sandals for Magdalena for her confirmation and beige sandals for myself because summer's on the way, and I can't go around in these black sandals in summer, these sandals are good, I like them, but it's wrong to wear black sandals in summer, so when I buy beige sandals, I'll leave these out on the pavement or I'll throw them into a skip, there's no point in walking around in black sandals in summer.
I say:	Why?
Sabina says:	Sorry?
	Magdalena would make a good confectioner, I think I'll sign her up as an apprentice confectioner or seamstress. Otherwise, Magdalena draws very well, she goes to an art workshop, she made a lovely picture with butterflies, lovely butterflies, we're going to frame it and put it in the drawing room. Do you take hormones?
I say:	No.
Sabina says:	I take natural hormones, although I haven't started the menopause, these hormones work for allergies and migraines, I have to buy some hair dye as well, there's a place where they sell natural hair dye, that's a dye with no chemicals, I like being blonde, but I mustn't use chemicals because of my allergy, so I buy this natural dye.
I say:	Your hair's nice.
Sabina says:	Color Erbe, the dye's called Color Erbe, "erbe" means herbs, you see, so those hair dyes come from the natural colours of herbs, from plant extracts of oak, mallow, green walnut shells, camomile and henna, that's what it says in the leaf-

let. It's good dye, but expensive. It doesn't damage the hair, it's suitable for the most sensitive hair roots and hides grey hairs, although I don't have that many grey hairs, but I'll have more one day, so I need to hide them with these natural dyes so that my hair doesn't get thin, that's ugly on a woman, thin hair.

I say: Yours isn't thin.

Sabina says: I'll buy croissants as well, about ten packs because they last, and we all like croissants, and in Trieste there are lots of different kinds and they are cheaper than at home, and I'll buy about twenty frozen pizzas, they're cheaper too, we like pizzas, pizzas are good when you don't have time to cook, otherwise I only cook healthy food, lots of vegetables, lots of carrots, that's good for the face as well, sometimes I get red patches on my face, especially when I get upset or when the allergy comes on, and when I get upset I go to Rome for a while, I've got a girlfriend there. And it's worth buying mineral water as well.

I say: Still.

Sabina says: Why, of course. We only drink still mineral water, sparkling water must have chemicals in it and chemicals aren't good if you have an allergy, and I do and then I sneeze and cough horribly, which is a problem when I'm doing the garden. Have you seen our garden? We have a lovely garden. A woman has to be well groomed when she reaches a certain age and when she reaches a certain age she shouldn't wear cheap clothes anymore, because when she's a certain age you can immediately see whether her clothes are well made or coarse, I've got an expensive skirt I don't wear anymore, I'll give it to you.

When she's not talking, Sabina yawns. As soon as she stops talking, Sabina starts yawning, which never lasts long. I think that Sabina has imperceptible problems with happiness: she chases it, but it eludes her.

That's why she gets those migraines. That's why I went with her to Trieste, otherwise I wouldn't have.

There is a Higher Pedagogical School here. People with titles or letters after their name work there. In my earlier life I didn't know any people from pedagogical schools, intermediate or higher; that must have just passed me by. Now I know some. Now I listen to their conversations and I say good morning to them.

Woman 1:   I had a girl pass the entrance exam with no coordination. She registered for class teaching, music section. She can't play the piano. Especially not with both hands at the same time. She also has problems walking, so she didn't get into the physical education section. She can't draw either. I really don't know why she ended up in my section, music.

Woman 2:   Well, I've got a student in the music section with no fingers.

That business with the two women happened to me one June. The months simply fly by.

a little quasi-theory, some banality

A man called Belančić says: *A provincial town is a microcosm that sees the whole world, the macrocosm, in itself. It is an eye (polyphemic) that does not see itself or its blind spot.* That moves me. Milorad Belančić's words could upset the rhythm of my life here. His words say that I'm living in a little town that is in fact Chronos (Saturn), in a town built of exalted banality. Then Belančić is joined by a collocutor, an expert in many small-town questions, by the name of Konstantinović, who says: *History has forgotten us, as in some great absent-mindedness. Between the village and the town, forgotten like this, the world of the provincial town is neither village nor town. Its spirit, however, is the spirit between the noble, as ideal, unique, and the universal spirit, as ideal, open.* And the two of them converse like that, and I freeze, now I don't know what to do, I'm in a big trap.

Skyscrapers are a wonderful invention. Living in a skyscraper is splendid, especially on the highest floors, from where the world is so lovely and small down below. When people feel like it, they can make their way down from a skyscraper, whenever they want to. Here they don't like skyscrapers at all, they particularly don't like *living* in skyscrapers, they state this categorically, they say explicitly, *we don't like living in skyscrapers, we like houses in the country, which can be small but they can also be large.* People here like to be on ground level, they like living at ground level, and they particularly like it when that groundedness, that landedness, is surrounded by some kind of private plot. These plots contain vegetables for everyday use, mostly chard and salad leaves and a bit of parsley and some carrots for soup, because people like soup here, and they may also contain spring onions and even flowers for the purpose of decoration, variation and colour. I don't like soup.

One section of the street leading to my doctor runs alongside a wall. It's a strange street, full of dog muck. Never in my life have I seen so much dog shit on one single street. Going along that street requires not walking, but hopping and skipping. Every time I caper along that street, I tell myself, write a note about that street, maybe a note about that street will have a cathartic effect on your soul; as soon as I reach my apartment, I forget about the street. That has been going on for ten years. Now I'm writing about the street because of that little wall. On the other side of the wall on that street, down in a hollow, there are some small arable fields, the soil is red, therefore fertile. The fields are in fact in the centre of town. For years various vegetables have been grown in the hollow, there is even cabbage, which is unreasonably expensive to buy elsewhere. Whenever I pass this way, I peer over the wall. I'm surprised that these vegetables are always fresh, I'm surprised as I skip over the turds in the road on the way to the clinic. Then, one day, there's nothing left, no vegetables, literally none, and the soil is no longer red, but grey and dry. Someone must have died, I think. Perhaps that person understood that *such work leads nowhere, because it accomplishes what has been accomplished and accomplishing what has been accomplished is unaccomplishable*, perhaps that's what that person understood and why they decided to die. Or disappear. Which amounts to the same.

In addition to the little wall below which a small village used to grow, that street has an avenue of trees with red crowns and white blossom, which looks miraculous and unreal. Turds below, blossoming trees above.

The death of the ploughed field beneath an urban wall took place in July.

Only where authenticity is under threat, is nature born. Its forests and fields spring up, in fantastic scenes, from the dubious authenticity of the subject.

Here people like to say of themselves, *We're industrious people.* When they don't say that, they say *We're always busy, we do nothing but work, we work twenty-four hours a day and we're very tired. We're exhausted people.* That makes me bilious and I feel like throwing up, because I don't like working at all, I'd like just to watch and to swim; if I had enough breath I would swim away, for ever.

I know people who take a change of clothes on hangers covered in transparent polythene to their office, so that others can see how festive and expensive that outfit is. Then, before they set off to some ribbon-cutting or the opening of something, they change there, at their place of work. Afterwards they eat little sandwiches, and after the little sandwiches they go to a fish restaurant. Otherwise, people here devote a lot of attention to clothes, and why not, they have nothing better to do.

I have a friend, in the distant past we had some jolly sex, now he's in Wall Street. We met after a little twenty-year pause, on Park Avenue. He couldn't have got away with his old trainers here. We ate hot dogs on the hoof, then we flew to Helsinki, because I'd never been to Helsinki, and I have a childhood friend there, Sara. In Helsinki, we spruced ourselves up as far as clothes go and went off to an expensive restaurant to eat fresh cod. I paid my contribution with part of the savings I'd been keeping for my funeral, because I'd decided that I didn't want to die just yet.

Sex is fundamental, but it's possible to manage without it, as one can manage without a car. Or without a job, people who don't have a job nevertheless survive, one can manage without curtains and without friends, without flowers, without a homeland, without hats, one can manage without chocolate truffles and leather gloves, just as one can manage with a minimum of air in the lungs and a maximum of forgetfulness in the head. One can manage. I would like to have a small car, a black one. And new windows.

A woman who asked me, *Maybe you could write speeches for our functionary, for a fee, of course?* added: *Oh, you're so rich because you write.* I wrote nine speeches about culture. The fee was pathetically small and was regularly overdue. My fee was the smallest of all the fees there. I called the accounts department and they told me this. Once, they asked me to write a New Year speech of two, at most three pages, and in that speech to encompass the whole of the preceding century throughout the world, with particular emphasis on the last century in this town, highlighting its prominent figures. Since then we no longer work together in that way, with me providing a service. Once I asked for a small cultural grant, and they sent me a letter informing me that they were not in good financial shape at that time, but would help me on some other occasion (which they did), and at the end of the letter they wished that I would continue to satisfy their needs. Maybe writing is masturbation.

Here, every year, I get a tax rebate, then I go to a restaurant.

People here don't like to travel. Someone told me, *In large towns there are a lot of traffic lights, that upsets me.* But this is the noisiest town I've come across, I don't know why. Everything here is loud, the buses roar, speech echoes, you hear other people snoring, other people's alarm clocks, other people's telephones and other people's conversations. You hear other people's dogs and cats, although fortunately there aren't many pets here, although in the suburbs there are animal hotels they call refuges, which immediately reminds me of a lunatic asylum. Perhaps that reverberation, that constant noise is because of the sea, perhaps the whole life of this town is reflected off the water and the water sends that noise back, or further on, because water is a conductor, isn't it? People die instantly if a hairdryer falls into a bath full of water, so it's a conductor.

You are victims of forced labour and forced rest, I tell them, and they say, *We're not victims at all, we like it this way.* So there we are, it's because they're victims and they like it that way that people don't travel much, I conclude. If they do have to go away, they tidy themselves up, titivate, tart themselves up, then they come back quickly. When they do decide to go, it's important for them not to stand out, it's important for them to be the same, to be like the rest, as at home. Out there, among others, they try so hard that it's immediately obvious that they're not from there.

When I arrived, I wasn't from here so I registered at the Employment Office, that's what they told me, *Register straight away, for your own good.* I was given a welfare card and a bit of assistance towards my electricity. My welfare card didn't bring me anything, apart from a particular welfare status. In the office, I overheard the director boasting: *I can sniff them out. They don't even have to open their mouths, I can immediately sniff Serbs out.* I freeze, I think, maybe he'll sniff out my daughter and me, because we've both come from over there, they'll think that we're Serbs, and when he sniffs us out, he'll take away our welfare cards and we'll freeze over the winter in our dark kitchen. I wanted to forgive that man, because it was wartime, but I didn't forgive him. I'd like it if that man no longer existed, I'd like him to have disappeared. Otherwise, I enjoy spending time with individual Serbs here. They know who the best Yugoslav-Serbian writers are, I don't need to explain. They understand certain words I use. Serbs here tell me, we're Serbs, I don't like it when they tell me that, it makes me sad.

So, in a strange town, the townsfolk are afraid of becoming as undesirable as those who come to their town uninvited, and this included me, once. I was entirely uninvited. That's why they sniff around, the way that Employment Office director sniffs, they sniff about like dogs, like curs, in order to be sure that everything is in order.

There are a lot of orderly people here but, thank goodness, I've found a few disorderly ones as well. I've found people who have no curtains at all on their windows, although the majority *do* have curtains, flowery ones. There was a fashion for women to wear scarves thrown over the top of a coat, diagonally across the shoulders, so the promenade was full of many duplicated women, it looked as though there was just one woman, the same one, walking along that promenade. That happened in December. There are women who aren't like that duplicated woman walking, but they're not as evident because they have dwindled, there aren't enough of them. Still, it's comforting that there's the occasional woman who doesn't like fringed scarves.

People here like to eat at the same time, which is midday on Sundays, and so they ask, *What are you cooking today? What are you cooking today?*

Life here is a life of (petrified) form.

They adore using titles when they address each other, they are forever using titles.

I know two women who have sat in the same office for the last twenty-five years and every morning they say, *Good morning Madame* to each other. When a customer asks for them, they say to the customer, *Madame Mihaela will be with you directly*, because one of them is called Mihaela.

In this town there are gentlefolk who use the polite form of "you" frenziedly. When I accidentally use the familiar form with one of them, they stiffen, which has a disagreeable effect. There are those who go out to dinner together for twenty years and still use the polite form. That's not the same as when David says to me in the polite form, *Take care of your teeth*, because that's out of closeness, while this rotten refinement here, this hollow decency only guarantees distance, it makes touch, contact, any kind of rubbing shoulders, impossible, it creates an enclosure for a mass of small lives that wriggle like larvae in their chrysalises.

When trenches were being dug for water pipes, columns of rats exploded onto the surface. The rats scurried around the town for days, frantically dragging their bellies over the furrows in the asphalt; their little pink legs scampered at such speed that they seemed to be gliding. The newspapers wrote that those creatures, those rats, were now emerging from toilet bowls, that there was now a real invasion of the large, well-(shit-)fed vermin and that this invasion carried the threat of an epidemic. The business with the toilet bowls didn't happen in this subsidiary town, but in the capital.

There are some people who work together during the week, and over the weekend sleep together, secretly, regardless of gender, although there aren't many secrets here, it just looks as though there are, and these lovers use surnames when they address each other at work, which is particularly repulsive.

I don't know what to do about my accent here. My accent offends people's ears here, just as my teeth prick their eyes. For ten years now people have been asking me, *Are those your teeth?* Each time, before they ask *Are those your teeth?* they say *Excuse me.* They don't like the fact that they're my teeth, that's obvious, and then I think, well, you can't have everything, your own town and central heating and graves and shopping expeditions and satellite antennae and your own teeth to boot, can you?

I've shrunk since I came here. I've shrunk by at least five centimetres. That's good for my current surroundings; my shrinking has a soothing effect on my surroundings, as aspirin or paracetamol do on a migraine; I was too tall, now I no longer am. There are several literary texts, even plays, in which characters shrink; this functions as a metaphor. My shrinking isn't metaphorical, but physical and real, although my shrinking does function perfectly well also on a metaphorical level because it seems to me that I've never been as small as I am now, here, apart from in my childhood; then I was really tiny. My shrinking here, on a metaphorical level, could have the function of King Lear's blindness – the more I shrink on the outside, the more I grow inwardly, but this isn't the case. My vertebrae are compacting and I'm losing elasticity.

My accent offends their ears, although my accent is the ordinary, standard accent of the standard language; I don't know what I'm supposed to do.

In former Yugoslavia, different accents didn't bother me, one could say I even liked them; they seemed unifying, peaceable. Now some accents seem destructive, devastating. The most destructive seem to me those bastard accents, mixtures of accents, because they sound artificial, and when I hear them I think, perhaps these people intend something particular with that way of speaking, perhaps their thoughts have a subtext. In my imagination the people who use those bastard accents become deformed, they become people who don't speak – they growl. They show their teeth, which are often false or rotten; they curl up their top lip and show their gums, which is horrendous to look at. A few days ago I was irritated by a woman in a fish restaurant at the seaside here, who asked, *Do you have fish chowder?* As though she didn't know that fish chowders are river soups, made with trout or perch or sturgeon, with a lot of paprika and the aroma of Danubian mud, that they're made in sooty cauldrons on the wild shores of the rivers that run through the Vojvodina plain, as though she didn't know that fish restaurants on the Adriatic don't serve fish chowders like that, but fish broths made from small white fish and fish leftovers.

How is it that I've become so intolerant?

I cannot bear to hear dialects that abuse basic grammar. It makes my flesh creep.

When I read, particularly when I read poems in dialect, I enjoy it. Sometimes they aren't good poems, indeed, often they're bad poems, although there are some good ones, but regardless of whether they're good or bad, it's pleasant to read those poems, and hearing them is not unpleasant either, on the contrary, it can be most agreeable both to hear and to read poems written in dialect because they're so varied, because there are many dialects in this country, like in India. In India there are more dialects than anywhere else in the world, I believe that's the case, except that in India those dialects are called languages, not dialects, but they too are dying out, just as dialects here are getting mixed up and so are no longer authentic, and let's not even mention accents. When people buy provisions, for instance when they buy meat, I am particularly annoyed by the use of dialect forms, which is a messy, muddle-headed usage, it's not consistent as in the written form. In the written form, no dialect bothers me at all, while in the spoken form it makes my hair stand on end.

Little shops crammed to the brim have begun to spring up, everything costs thirteen kunas or eight or nine, it depends on the supplier, briefs and washing-up cloths are always six, while umbrellas are more expensive, around twenty, because they come from China. The best things to buy are briefs, made of cotton, it's good to buy glass and china as well, it's not worth buying other things because on the whole they're synthetic or plastic, badly designed and ugly to look at. There's all sorts of stuff for everyday life, washing-up bowls, toilet brushes, plates, glasses, hammers and pliers, pencils for writing and for eyelids, lacquer for nails and hair, rubber bands for horses' tails and for taps. These shops are so small that they can hold at most three customers at a time, because there are salesgirls spinning round them as well, mostly three at a time too, there are no male shop assistants, which is strange, the fact that it's largely women who work in these little shops, and that the salesgirls keep spinning round in circles, moving around, keeping an eye on the customers, making sure no-one steals anything, although everything in those shops is shoddy, the articles wear out quickly so the customers come back for new ones; these shops are intended for the poor, that is immediately clear. There are shops like this in America and Canada because in America and Canada there are unimaginable numbers of poor people even though those countries pretend to be rich and happy countries with a healthy population, but they aren't. From the standpoints of morality and health they're highly debatable countries.

I go into a little shop because I need a cheap purse, in fact I need three cheap purses for a single use by a school-leaver going by bus on a school-leaving trip to Paris, and on the way to France the bus stops in Austria, and on the way back it stops in Germany, and knowing that school-leaver who has no idea about money, I think, let her take schillings in one purse, French francs in another and German marks in the third because, at that time those currencies still exist.

I've just asked, *Do you have small purses for Western European currencies*, when a fat woman in a blue chintz dress blows past me at the door, *Do you have a* mischchafel? she says. The salesgirl looks startled and asks, *What's that?* Then there's silence. Then I say it is a *scovacera*, and the fat woman asks *What's that?* and I say, it is a *mischchafel*. The salesgirl cheers up and exclaims, we do, we do, we have *scovaceras*.

A third woman is spinning round the shop as well. In an irritated voice she says those are foreign words, don't we have our own Croatian word for that object? I suggest another word, but the fat woman says it sounds Serbian too. There's a long discussion among the three of them about the use of the Serbian word for rubbish as a term of abuse and we all agree that the Serbian word sounds more offensive. Then the discussion turns to the correct stress on particular words. And in the end I leave the shop without buying the little purses because I no longer know the correct way to ask for them.

That all happened one July, before the euro arrived, pronounced evro in Serbia, yuro in England and oÿro in Germany.

The business with the beans happened at about the time I arrived, twelve years ago, when I was completely buttoned up and inhibited in my speech and work and the country was smoking with war and hatred. I go into a supermarket and look for frozen *fagioletti*. I can't see them in the fridge so I ask, *Do you have fagioletti?* That's the word I always used, even over there. I rarely used the Serbian word, only when I knew that the Italian one would make some people stare blankly at me. So I ask, *Do you have fagioletti?* And the salesgirl asks, *What's that?* Now, I know that there's a Croatian word, but I can't remember it. I stand as though turned to stone, I summon up the Croatian word, I call to it, *Come to me*, it comes to the tip of my tongue and sneaks off. Nothing. *Green beans* come to my mind, and *haricots verts*, then *grüne Bohnen*, and finally the Serbian word, *boranija*. The Croatian word is nowhere to be found. What can I do; I ask, *Do you have* boranija? The salesgirl reels, and the audience in the supermarket begins to draw away from me. That dreadful silence lasts at most five seconds, maybe ten. Then the salesgirl comes to her senses and shouts to her colleague, *Hey, have we got* mahune? Then the atmosphere in the supermarket eases, restored. Otherwise, I don't like that vegetable at all and it has been particularly unappealing ever since.

I want to buy a gift. I go round all the shops that specialise in my gift. There are some fine shops here, not only those little, rough ones, there are expensive shops that I don't visit often, but sometimes I go in and the salesgirls look at me suspiciously because I'm not expensively dressed, in fact I'm appallingly dressed, in old rags, while elegance is what is required here, there are a lot of elegantly dressed people here, because, they say, elegance is traditional here, ingrained, it goes back to Austro-Hungarian days. So I go from shop to shop and ask, *Do you have* ešarpe?

(from the French écharpe)

The salesgirls look at me blankly, and out of spite I'm not going to describe what it is. Some salesgirls are obliging, some are not exactly obliging, although on the whole people here are civil, they keep their distance, that's why they're civil, distant, because when interpersonal relations are distant it's hard to spoil those interpersonal relations, because when they're distant, they're on the whole limp relations, pale and uninventive. One salesgirl purses her lips into an "o" and through her pursed lips she says *Ooo, you must be Orthodox.* I say, ???!!! with raised eyebrows, I can't see the connection between *écharpe/ešarpa* and Orthodoxy, which is a euphemism for Serbian-ness here. The salesgirl then says that in their language my *écharpe/ešarpa* is called a *padela* and that I'm in the wrong shop, to which I say that I'm not in the wrong shop but in the wrong town and possibly the wrong country. In the Dalmatian dialect *padela* means cooking pot or pan, from the Italian *padella*, which in Serbian is *šerpa*, not *ešarpa*, so the salesgirl was in the wrong shop, not I. Once I bought a scarf in Helsinki without any difficulty, in Helsinki the salesgirls immediately knew what an *écharpe* was, although in Helsinki salesgirls are probably no more versatile than those here.

My normal acquaintances and a few friends ask me why I'm surprised and tell me that in Croatia they say *šal*, while *ešarpa"* is used over there in the east. They try to persuade me that *šal* comes from the German, šal *comes to us from the German*, they say, as though it only comes to them, but it doesn't, it comes from the Persian.

(*šâl*)

It comes from Persia, or indirectly through England, it makes no odds. Perhaps that's why *šal* seems closer to most Croats than *écharpe* because Persia is closer to most Croats than France, or so some historians maintain. Some people think that a *šal* and an *écharpe* are the same, but they aren't. An *écharpe* can't be made of wool, while a *šal* can. In English *šal* is shawl, while *écharpe* is scarf, which we also call a *marama*, which comes from the Turkish

(*mahrama*)

or perhaps the Arabic

(*miqrämä*)

in other words, it's a kerchief, or handkerchief, which the dictionary says is either a *marama* or a *peča*, which also comes from the Turkish

(*peçe*)

except that *peča* is not an *écharpe*, but a black veil over the face of a Muslim woman or a kerchief. In other words, in that haberdashery I ought to have asked for a kerchief, then the salesgirl would have asked, *For the head or the nose?*

Some events and concepts provoke all kinds of passions here, while some other events and concepts leave people completely cold, utterly indifferent. There's a shortage of words for some concepts, while for others there's an absolute surplus of worthless, hollow words, so that conversations seem inarticulate. It is probably like that everywhere, but I didn't use to notice, no doubt the earlier ideological situation cut off such phenomena at the root, while the current ideological situation cuts off nothing, people are permitted to talk all kinds of rubbish so that they believe they have thrown off their shackles.

When I talk to myself, and I talk to myself increasingly often, I speak English. I like that. When I hear any foreign language in the street, I think that perhaps there is some hope for this town. That thought is very short-lived.

There's a professor here who is crazy about names. If a student with a strange name comes to him for an oral examination, he digs his heels in. That student's name may not be at all unusual, it may just be, how can I put it, tinted, nationally indicative, nationally recognisable, like for instance John, because when you say John, or when you say Mary, it's immediately clear that both John and Mary come from some Anglo-Saxon country, although that need not be the case, today people mill about, buzz, buzz, buzz, but in this country there is very little buzzing, in this country the population is pretty static, they hardly whizz about at all, many people seem to be cemented to their soil, to their local and homeland soil, and cannot unstick themselves from it, detach themselves, but that's because they're poor, because they don't have any money. Me too, ever since I've been in this homeland I've had no money at all and I'm very static. I don't mill about. Some people around me may think that I do, because when some institution or some foundation pays for me, I go, although I also go when no-one pays anything, but it's a pathetic, impoverished and very brief going away, in fact it's no kind of going away at all, really, because a dramatic return always awaits me. Being static can drive people round the bend, being riveted to their native clod can make people mad, there are such cases: people cling to their homeland as to their mother's bosom and go crazy. So, when students come to this professor with what are to him geographically recognisable names, he tells them, *Now you're an adult, it's time you were called something different, it's time to change your name, to take a name that's appropriate to this clod here*, that's what he says.

I'm sitting in a café and eavesdropping, you learn all sorts of things when you eavesdrop. One girl is saying that the professor told her that a particular form of a word she used was Serbian, and advised her to check it in an Orthodox dictionary. The girl then asks the other girl, the one she's sitting with in the café, she asks, *Are there Orthodox dictionaries?* The other girl says she doesn't know, she says that if there are Orthodox dictionaries, then there must be Catholic dictionaries, mustn't there? and the first girl asserts that Catholic dictionaries do not exist, and that the idea is totally crazy. Then the second girl says to the first girl that all this has come about because of her name, that her name upsets the professor, it gets on his nerves. The first girl says that he, the professor, is annoyed by Alexander as well, because he's called Alexander, and that the professor had told Alexander that he had a Byzantine name. Then the first girl, the one who began this painful conversation, says that the professor is really jittery and that maybe his jitters spring from the fact that he's bald, because baldness, particularly in a man, ruins a person's self-confidence, just as a person's, or rather a man's self-confidence is ruined by the mildest symptoms of sexual impotence, which is, she says, incomprehensible to her, and finally she adds that this bald professor has told her that she has an Orthodox name, you have an Orthodox name, says the girl, quoting the professor's words, *Do you think my name is Orthodox?* she then asks her companion.

In the end I couldn't resist, so I asked the first girl what her name was, *What is your name?* I asked, and she said that she was called Sidonija. She said, *I'm called Sidonija*, and then she repeated it, *I'm called Sidonija, with a "j"*.

*

A Slovene reference book has the following: *Sidonija – a very rare woman's name. In 1971 there were 279 persons in Slovenia with this name. Rarer still was the variation "Sidonja" (86 people), whereas the male version "Sidonij" is almost unknown, and is recorded fewer than ten times. In Slovene folk poetry we find the forms "Sidona", "Sidonika" and "Saduojnka", and in the Prekmurje region "Sida", "Sidika".*

"Sidonija" and "Sidonij" come from the Latin

names "Sidonia" and "Sidonius", with the original mention "by birth, coming from the town of Sidon". Sidon was an old Phoenician port on the territory of what is now Lebanon and is today known as Saida. Similar in form if not in origin for the name Sidonij is the far more frequent variant "Zdenek", for Sidonija "Zdenka".

As we have mentioned, "Sidonija" and variants are known from folk poetry.

Oh, Voljar, Voljar, Voljar,
Oh handsome young Voljar,
So spoke Sidonika,
Ah lovely Sidonika.

In German sources, Sidonija and Sidonij become Sidonius, Sidonia, Sidonie; in French Sidaine, or Sedaine, Sidonie, in saints' names next to Saint-Saëns'; in Polish Sydoniusz, Sydonia; in Czech Sidon, Sid, Sidonek, Don and Sidonie, Sidka, Sidonka, Dona; in Hungarian Szidónia, shortened to Szidi, Szidike.

In the calendar are St Sidonij from Normandy, abbot of the Saint-Saëns monastery in the seventh century (14 November), and St Sidonij, bishop in the French town of Clermont in the fifth century (21 August).

*

That professor is so obsessed by names that he keeps collecting them, he collects them, arranges and catalogues them. Afterwards he binds them in hard covers and acquires directories called surname dictionaries. This collecting is his passion, and his passion is his life, and his life is all ordered, indexed and catalogued. That professor has an integrative life, suitable for this milieu.

I'm nervous because my nervousness gets on my nerves and blocks my everyday life and work.

I remember a little poem that happened to me one June, when I moved into this apartment that has neither a lawn nor children nearby, when my daughter was lower than the window and walked up and down this dark corridor eleven metres long, practising new forms of everyday words. The little poem was squatting in the reader for the second year of elementary school and when we opened it, that reader, the little poem roared at us: I CRIED IN CROATIAN!

How do you cry in Croatian? asks the girl who is practising the new forms of words, and I thrust the reader under her nose and say, here you are, read!

> I began to cry in Croatian
> I began to talk in Croatian
> I speak Croatian
> I whisper Croatian
> I am silent in Croatian
> I dream in Croatian
> even awake I dream in Croatian
> I love in Croatian
> I love Croatian
> I write in Croatian
> when I don't write I don't write in Croatian
> everything I do is in Croatian
> Croatian is everything to me.

How do you whisper in Croatian? How are you silent in Croatian? she asks. *So that no-one hears or that at least something is heard? How is silence made?* she asks and sings her favourite *We ask for sweet silence*, then she springs, hop! Then she says, *I don't dream in Croatian, I dream of snow, there's no snow here.* She is eight years old.

Who would have dreamed that such monstrosities could await us here.

The little poem was written by a poet called Pajo Kanižaj.

Later, the children who had learned to be silent and to whisper in Croatian became my students. One of them, a young man, said, *If my son were gay, I'd give him a suitcase and show him the door.* A girl said, *I'd never adopt a black child.* I no longer have students like that, new students have come, they guard car parks and exhibitions, and they like Orwell and Huxley above all; for those students the prospects are not good. I tell them, get away if you can, get away from here. What is there here for them?

I'm also nervous because of some advertising panels that follow me down the street, watching me like the police. They ask, do we love Croatia? *Do you love Croatia?* they ask, openly.

There are panels that don't ask, but give orders.

One of those giving orders is big and colourful. It's a very indiscreet panel, lewd. It invites us to lick Croatian, all together. LET'S LICK CROATIAN it says. Later I realise that this panel is in fact a frightened little panel, and it's just my imagination that's filthy and shameless, base. This panel is innocently advertising a sweet, advising us to lick Croatian sweets, in the imperative. That panel has no connection with some paranoid fears that a person's life will become bitter if he doesn't lick Croatian.

Towards the end of the year some sort of religious sticks are sold, painted silver or gold, decorated with crêpe-paper ribbons. When I see crêpe paper I think at once of my childhood in socialist times: in our socialist childhood we made little skirts out of crêpe paper for May Day events (red, white, blue/blue, white, red), little skirts for Republic Day (red, white, blue/blue, white, red), crêpe paper was used to cut out little ribbons for New Year's fir trees and long streamers for decorating the classroom, crêpe paper served as make-up for the cheeks and lips (red) and eyelids (blue), and the colour ran.

Would you like a stick? asks the street seller.

No, thank you, I say, because those sticks mean nothing to me. I wouldn't know what to do with them.

Oh! exclaims the street seller. She narrows her eyes, purses her lips and hisses. *Oh, you're Orthodox!*

That business with the sticks and Orthodoxy happens to me every December.

Then they threw me onto the Committee for National Minorities. It's good there. There are various minorities on that committee, not only national ones.

There's a woman in town called Isabella. She has a shaved head and a sharp look. She's often seen around. She's seen in the street and at closed gatherings, at various gatherings in different circles. People call her Isabella *brutta*. That has nothing to do with her external appearance because her external appearance is just fine. *People used to call me Isabella* bella, says Isabella *brutta*. Isabella doesn't fit in, that's why she gets on people's nerves, that's why they call her Isabella *brutta*. Not fitting in is unforgiveable here, although that's never said out loud, no-one here ever tells anyone, *I don't like you, you get on my nerves because you don't fit in*, no-one will say that, but you can see it, you can see it in their eyes, in their posture, some people stiffen when they communicate with those who are different and they always look down, at the tips of their shoes.

There are people who also meet Isabella in the market because the market is on their way wherever they go so they drop by. Afterwards they go to Café Exclusive. They go there mostly on Saturdays. They don't go on Sundays, because what is on the agenda for those who don't go either to the Exclusive or to the market on Sundays is church. There are several agendas here that are important for life. On Saturdays, in Café Exclusive, people smile and eavesdrop on other conversations, the people who do that are mostly well-groomed women who don't work. The windows then mist up if it's winter, they don't if it's spring, people sit outside, under an awning. The atmosphere is cordial. Around midday, the Exclusive empties, because on Saturdays families have lunch early, at one or half-past, as they do indeed on Sundays.

This is a clean town. The cult of cleanliness is nurtured here, particularly at weekends. The everyday is cleared away, cleaned up. It is stylistically homogenised. Harmony of style is crucial for small towns.

*

> *The cult of cleanliness, in this stylistic reduction, is pursued to the point of a real mania, in everything, in the things of the material world, but also in the sphere of the ideals of moral values.*

The theatre of operettic lives, the tyranny of banality, repetitiveness without end, the murder of language, a carnival. A realm of darkness.

I lent a woman a crutch, which I now need, I tell her, *Give me back my crutch*, she says, *I've given it back*, but she hasn't.

It was a sick winter, a sickly warm winter. Animals interrupted their hibernation, came out into the open and wandered around like ghosts, maddened. The barberries blossomed. Branches turned green, there were buds everywhere, the town could hardly breathe under a cloak of thick damp that stuck to it like sweat on the face of a woman in labour. Sounds were muffled, life rumbled vaguely, nothing echoed, conversations were a whisper. When glass fell, it fell dully, it didn't crack. Boats' sirens sounded as though for *A Long Day's Journey into Night*, the railway line was disrupted, pedestrians were silent, they stepped slowly as if their feet were sticking to the stone streets, as though the stone were melting. The light swayed drunkenly, dragging itself through cracks of reality, then giving up, returned to its hiding place up above, above the mountain that was as silent as the sea beneath it. The sea overflowed, merged with the rains, lost its saltiness and its force, rolled through the streets, the earth did not take it in because it was full and swollen, it couldn't, the sea flowed steadily into the waste. The town was sprinkled with salt crystals, it glittered greyish-white, particularly in sleep, oh, if only it would snow. If only it would snow drily and lengthily, so that everything under this town would freeze and, perhaps, be preserved. As it is, under a cloak of damp the town was threatened with decay, with slow, thorough, painful decomposition.

On its own, but still in the vicinity of the town, a spruce grows and gives out a terrible shriek. A magnificent spruce, twenty-eight metres high, seventy years old, perfectly healthy, a regal spruce with broad, firm boughs which it waves towards the sky, while its berries, red and black, shiver, tremble like cheerful teardrops that don't fall but just spread a sheen and divine aroma. The heavy spruce, a spruce weighing seven tons, bequeaths its resin (as though it were the essence of its soul) to the surrounding churches and chapels, also isolated, in the form of incense.

> *We shall gather only the best honey from our hives,*
> *only the incense of the most subtle, most fragrant ideas.*

Then, in that damp, sticky and oppressive winter, beneath the spruce in its vast solitude, beneath the spruce deceived by the unprecedented and unforeseen warmth into rashly putting out shoots, pale-green tender spurs, and rejoicing like a woman falsely or pathologically pregnant, beneath the spruce come cranes, machines dig, drill, pluck, burrow around its roots, electric saws whine, over it fly helicopters circling like jackals, preparing its death.

> *When, the Guard, the Saint, descends from the sky*
> *he shouts in a mighty voice:*
> *"Cut down the tree,*
> *lop off its branches,*
> *tear off its leaves,*
> *throw away its fruit!"*
> *. . . I am Jehovah*
> *who humbles the high tree,*
> *raises up the low;*
> *I dry out the green tree,*
> *and let the dry tree fruit.*

The killing of the spruce is done loudly, hastily, with pomp. For a week the media take photographs and cheer, spout rubbish about pride and fortune, about the fortune and pride of all Croats here and elsewhere who lay claim to the dead, slain tree, which is to be sent as a gift to an old, infirm man immured in the chambers of his faith, in case he might inhale a little trace of the strength of that lover of birds and clouds, that supple queen of the forest whose breath carries every traveller to nirvana.

And the spruce sets off on its journey. Wrapped in dark sacking, bound, laid out horizontally like a chronic patient, that colossus of nature, that reflection of human smallness and malevolence, it chokes on its own juices, squirms in its imposed constraint, endeavouring in vain to wave its branches one last time, as a greeting, or a farewell to the trees that remain and just watch and listen, chained in its muteness as death creeps up its trunk. Accompanied by the exultation of the murdering-men, wrapped up, bound, the spruce catches little flames of its breath, increasingly cold, increasingly icy, fading out in barely perceptible shudders and arrives like a vast corpse, like a murdered carcass, like a cadaver, in the eternal city.

[I admire] trees. Upright, calm stoics. The only sages among living beings. They know when to bud, to blossom, to lure insects and wait for the winds to fertilise their fruits; when to suck up water and nourishing minerals; when to turn their leaves towards the sun to feed on its light. They know when to propagate, generate, scatter their fruit, shake off their leaves, await the winter with bare branches. To draw life inwards, under their bark, to take on snows, hurricanes, the madness of Nature tranquilly and wisely, and all without a sound, with no braying or bellowing . . . They endure patiently as though somewhere far off in time a great and bright Future waits for them, when they will draw their roots out of the greasy, flat and stupid earth and rise, liberated, up, to fly with the birds, with treetops, with bees and butterflies . . .

The spruce doesn't go to Rome alone. With it, from this country, like an entourage of children caught off guard, goes a column of murdered small firs and some forty spruces from two to six metres tall, which will also decorate the square of the well-worn, half-dead world, and the stuffy chambers of the Vatican cardinals, while their humble visitors will bow, meekly, submissively

> *one should not be unjustly harsh towards the lowly*
> *nor sycophantically submissive towards the powerful*

and sniff the air which they believe will bring them new birth, not knowing that they are licking the remains of the lives of once-free trees while around them little angels of this world, little girls and boys dressed from head to foot in white, sing *Stille Nacht, heilige Nacht* in almost all the languages of the world.

That winter, there was little snow. That winter, this human crime, naked, bared to the point of senselessness, like the toothless head of a corpse turned towards the sky, grimaced maliciously and sent its wail through the cramped space of the Mediterranean. That winter, nature conspired against man, unwilling to cover up his filth.

There is a scouts' club here. There are clubs like this in many towns, large and small, presumably, only here everything is close, under one's nose so to speak, so a person comes across things that do not interest him at all, such as, for instance, those scouts. Or exhibitions of birds.

Twenty years ago a Croatian priest received a scouts' prize which was written about in various newspapers, particularly the religious press, although today some people maintain that in this country at the time of socialism, the religious press was strictly controlled and had no freedom. In 1983, a religious paper called *The Voice of Faith* wrote that the ceremony of presenting the scouts' prize was a modest affair and that it took place in Stuttgart on 10 April, which, in this part of the world, is a well-known date, historically marked. Even today there are people who celebrate 10 April, when German troops occupied Zagreb and the Ustasha Kvaternik, in the name of the Ustasha Leader Pavelić, announced the founding of the hideous Independent State of Croatia.

The newspaper writes that a certain chaplain of the parish of St Maria in Zagreb received in Stuttgart the international "wood-badge" prize from the scouts' organisation of St Juraj, which means, taken literally, that he received a wooden badge. The newspaper goes on to say that the "wood-badge" prize consists of a written certificate, a scarf to be tied round the neck, a knot and a leather ribbon with a tag made of two small pieces of wood. The newspaper informs us that the nomination of the leader of the oldest group of rover scouts for the prize followed the priest's pastoral engagement in organising and bringing to fruition German and international camps in Austria and Germany, in Corsica and the Faroe Islands, wherever they may be, during the period 1979 to 1982. These camps nurture a religious experience of the world, writes the newspaper, and develop patriotic and fraternal consciousness through communal ventures of young people in the process of their education and maturing.

Many years later a lay newspaper printed an article which said that an accusation of sexual relations with mares had been launched against a certain L. M., the perverse leader of the Swedish scouts. Not a single religious paper commented on this incidence of the sexual abuse of mares, although it is well known that scouting activities are fairly close to certain faith organisations. That Swedish scouting functionary was arrested after the president of an equine club in Stockholm found him in a compromising position with a certain filly. At his trial, the compromised man admitted abusing animals. He said that he regularly did "it" with twelve mares and that he had devoted himself to mares in order to control his immoderate desire for women. In the article there was no mention of religious figures who might have been involved in the case, nor of whether the leader of the Swedish scouts was a church figure who had taken a vow of celibacy or an ordinary lay scout.

During that sickly winter the past collapsed, sinking into the salt of the surrounding waters. Under the onslaught of the south winds and indolent waves, the terrace disappeared at the Reš baths, the famous bathing place of the long-since-deceased Mrs Antonija Resch who, on 25 October, 1911, had taken into her intimate family guest house at number 28 of what was then the Crown Prince's Promenade, and is now XIII Division Street, a certain Ludwig Jakob Fritz.

Once there were many bathing places here, very well organised; at these bathing places there were hairdressers and barbers, little restaurants, there were wooden cabins, some bathing places had rooms for massage or for inhalation because the air was fresh, saline, and apparently good for the lungs, but it was not good for the lungs, it was damp and provoked asthma attacks and occasional choking, except that not much is written about such choking because it doesn't contribute to the lustre of a town the way hotels, cinemas and famous figures from the past do. There were also a lot of luetics. There are no bathing places like that today and syphilis epidemics have eased. Today there are little beaches not far from the centre of town, visited by bus in the early morning hours, weather permitting, by plump housewives with tightly waved perms and sprightly pensioners with grey fuzz on their chests. The ladies have swimming costumes, flowery, two-piece, with the bottom part reaching to their waists to cover their drooping bellies, distended from poor digestion and cheap food.

There was a famous bathing place, the Quarnero, built on a breakwater on tall iron columns, with trains passing underneath, in fact an ugly bathing place in ugly surroundings, but that fact is not mentioned, the historians of this town, architects and excavators of memories describe it as an exciting attraction.

The Resch guest house was in fact the refurbished Klotilda guest house, and before that it had, quite logically, belonged to Madame Klotilda, in fact Clotilda, the daughter of Archduke Josip, the then owner of what is today the archive building, a lovely building in a park in which no-one walks. Madame Clotilda was otherwise the patron of an asylum in the street that bore her name, via Clotilda, today Dolac, with enormous buildings blackened with soot, on which the shutters are always closed and along which passers-by don't stroll but, heads bowed, hurry to emerge into the open, among people. That asylum, that plaything and occupation of Madame Clotilda, was welcome, because there were vagrant and sick people, infectious and abandoned, who needed some kind of roof over their heads after all, just like today. There were quite a few displaced people because many were on the move, in search of a better life. It's an old phenomenon, this moving and migrating, thanks to which the world survives, but this tends to be forgotten. The dispersal of populations is healthy for the world. Well, since she couldn't work on a voluntary basis for ever, because money is always welcome, Madame Clotilda also ran a guest house, to bring in a little income. That is, if it really is the same Clotilda-Klotilda. After a time, messing around with guests began to bore Clotilda-Klotilda, so she sold her guest house to Mrs Antonija Resch. And so, acquiring the key with the number seven on it, Ludwig Jakob Fritz made his way to the second floor, stepped into his room, placed his leather suitcase on the golden-brown satin bedspread, pulled back the curtains (that matched the bedspread), opened the window and said: *God, how beautiful it is, I could stay here.* Up there, high up, on a cliff above the sea, settled into the cheerful room in Antonia Resch's intimate guest house, Ludwig Jakob Fritz offered his handsome face to the gentle rays of the autumn sun and began to watch his life sinking into the sea. Of course, then, on that 25 October, 1911, Ludwig Jakob Fritz (35) had no idea that this was the case.

On Wednesday 25 October, 1911, at the railway station, Ludwig Jakob Fritz buys a guidebook, *Guida di Fiume*, and downs a beer at the bar, it's a sunny day. In the guidebook Ludwig Jakob Fritz reads that the station was designed by Ferenc Pfaff from Hungary, the same Pfaff who designed the station in Zagreb, of course. This station here is small, Ludwig observes, although the town gives the impression of being large, fragments of Italian, Czech, Slovak, English, Hungarian, German and French come from all directions. Cacophony.

The train for Vienna?
Nemtudum.
Dumm. Dumm. Alles: Dumm.
Der Zug nach Wien?
Il treno per Vienna?
Chemin de fer pour Vienne?
The train to . . . . alright!

Different languages are spoken here nowadays as well, but those languages are not heard; they're spoken in the Croatian–French Society, in the Italian Society, in the Austrian Society and in the little Czech Society that nurtures folklore. Hungarian is spoken in the Hungarian Society, Romany in the Roma Society, Serbian and Bosnian in the Serbian and Bosnian Society, and Macedonian in the Macedonian Society. These societies are quiet and invisible, in them Hungarian, Italian, Czech, Polish, Jewish, Serbian, Macedonian, Bosnian and Roma minority players give social dinners, eat national savoury and sweet pies, organise national exhibitions of amateur watercolours and put on amateur playlets that depict their national pasts, skip to national songs, alone, with their own kind, and none of us cares, we have more pressing business, *our* business, times have changed, my dear Ludwig Jakob Fritz, nothing here fuses any longer, everything stands still.

The women are dolled up, they wear hats and their skirts rustle as they walk, leaves fall from huge plane trees, tranquillity reigns in the heart of Ludwig Jakob Fritz, he walks.

London – Piccadilly and Hyde Park
Paris – La rue de la Paix et Bois de Boulogne
Berlin – Friedrichstrasse und Tiergarten
Wien – Kärtnerstrasse und Prater
Zagreb – Ilica and Maksimir
Fiume – Corso, e, e?

Ludwig J. Fritz walks, looking for somewhere to stay. Ludwig J. Fritz has time, Ludwig J. Fritz is going to spend three days in this town. *Molti alberghi, tanti, tanti bellissimi alberghi* say the passers-by, just go *dritto*, they say, *dritto* along Ferenc Deák Street. Ferenc Deák is wide and busy, with a tram running down it. Ludwig J. Fritz feels international. *I feel fashionable*, he says.

At the time Zagreb didn't have trams. The trams began to run here at 6 a.m. on the morning of 7 November, 1899, while in Zagreb not until 1911.

*

I know, says Ludwig Jakob Fritz. *It is 1911.*

> They took the trams away later, but here and there
> the tracks were left, so when one looks at the ground
> those tracks evoke images of the past, except that
> not all pedestrians look at the ground as they
> walk. It's only the depressed who pace with their
> eyes lowered, those with neuroses and psychoses
> and P.T.S.D., those who look for nothing so they see
> nothing, it doesn't occur to them to search for tracks
> from a hundred years ago.
>
> There are no longer *tanti, tanti alberghi* either,
> there is only their shadow archived in memories and
> on old postcards. There are now two or three work-
> ing hotels here, the others are decaying because
> they're closed, and those that are not closed aren't
> lively because there are no guests, because there's no
> reason for people to come here in large numbers
> and to disturb the peace continually.

Ludwig Jakob Fritz walks along Ferenc Deák.

> Ferenc Deák is sometimes known as Franjo Deak,
> which is an irritating and inappropriate intimisa-
> tion. Ferenc Deák didn't have a direct connection
> with this town, although when the Austro-Hungar-
> ian Agreement of 1868 was settled, he was in favour
> of the financial autonomy of the Croats, unlike the
> Croats in the Croatian Royal Delegation who shat
> themselves with fear and practised what was already
> then a deeply rooted Croatian deference, Croatian
> servility, so they didn't favour any kind of autonomy.
> The street was bestowed upon Deák in 1876, on the
> basis of pure, authentic sycophancy, and, given that

Ferenc Deák systematically refused decorations, honours or high-ranking positions, the naming of this street, the finest at the time, resembling a Parisian boulevard, the naming of this street after Ferenc Deák would undoubtedly have been an unpleasant surprise for Ferenc Deák, it might even have angered him, but there was nothing to be done as by that time Ferenc Deák was already dead. He died several months earlier. When people die, there are always those who do what they like with the deceased people's names, get up to all kinds of mean tricks.

The windows of my apartment look onto that street, nowadays it's not a fine street by any means, it's run down, truncated and mutilated, so I only open the windows in order to air the rooms, the shutters too, which means that on the whole I sit in the dark, when I'm not lying down.

In Socialist days, Ferenc Deák was fugued into Boris Kidrič Street, while in Belgrade, at the top of a long boulevard that goes downhill and gives its name to a Serbian autocratic ruler from the nineteenth century, but also to a brand of mineral water, until recently there stood a large statue of Boris Kidrič, but in this new age of madness and oblivion, Boris Kidrič bothered some people, so at first all sorts of things were thrown at him, eggs and paint, as though any of it was his fault, as though he could get out of the way, but he couldn't, Boris Kidrič is only a statue, long since dead, yet he was removed. Boris Kidrič died young, but his daughters did not. Boris Kidrič's daughters had fine white skin and hair pulled back and minds for mathematics and physics, quick, sharp minds and one of them liked white wine, while the other wore little tweed suits. Edvard

Kardelj had a daughter too, but, unlike Boris Kidrič's daughters, Edvard Kardelj's daughter was stupid, although perhaps she is no longer stupid, perhaps she learned some sense, even if the good sense of Edvard Kardelj's daughter, then and now, need not have the slightest connection with her father.

Boris Kidrič is now called Kralj Krešimir, "King Krešimir Street", and Kralj Krešimir continues into Kralja Zvonimir, or maybe it's the other way round – Kralja Zvonimir runs into Kralj Krešimir, which sounds fairly crazy, like a joke, because neither Krešimir nor Zvonimir has the slightest connection with this part of the world. History – a tireless prostitute, indestructible. Street names are absolutely inconsequential for people's lives here, and people here seem to realise this because people here don't know the streets of their town at all, they never use them in everyday speech, that is, they use them very little, when addressing letters, cards and parcels. In everyday speech, people here relate to their streets descriptively, while in larger towns that phenomenon is inconceivable. This little town has nice streets, if not exactly green, so it is not clear why people don't like to mention them. If a stranger is looking for the Kontinental Hotel, a very old hotel, impressive from the outside, not so on the inside, shabby, first they exclaim, *How can you not know, how can you not know where the Kontinental is?* Then they start to describe the way to the hotel. The Kontinental was recently renamed the Continental, because Continental seems more Central European, while Kontinental looks East European, but since the first letter of the signage keeps falling off, that is, the lights of the first letter keep going out, doggedly, refusing to be illuminated, at night the hotel is called the "ontinental". So, if a stranger wants to reach the Continental Hotel, he will be told that it's just here, that he'll find it without any difficulty, and when the stranger still doesn't understand which way he's supposed to go to reach the Continental Hotel, and when he asks for the street and number, he'll be told to go straight on and when he comes to Kraš to keep going for a bit longer, Kraš is an excellent landmark, they'll say, and then he'll see a yellow building that isn't perhaps all that obviously yellow anymore, on which there's the nameplate of some lawyer or dentist, there are unaccountable numbers of lawyers and unaccountable numbers of dentists here, as though everyone in this town had had some legal or dental mishap, it is remarkable that these numerous lawyers and numerous dentists can survive, they'll tell him that at this building, and it doesn't much matter what colour it is, he should turn a bit to the left, there's a newspaper seller there, actually a kiosk, and beside it a delicatessen, and beside the delicatessen there's a little café where the coffee isn't bad, then there's a former hat shop, the property of a famous milliner who died not long ago, then, they say, you'll see two bridges, but whatever you do, don't take the one on the right, they'll say, take the one on the left, but it'd be better not to cross the bridges at all, they'll say, but to go on across the open ground and there you'll see a statue of Kamov leaning against a fence, but don't imagine that it's a living man, it isn't, but rather a tribute to Kamov who makes this town especially famous in its own eyes and then you'll see the Kontinental Hotel in front of you. Otherwise, heaven forbid that a stranger should ask where a particular street is, Matija Gubec, for example, who – Gubec – had no connection whatsoever to this town, although his street is here, in the centre. If a stranger asks where Matija Gubec Street is, almost everyone will repeat, *Matija Gubec?* Sometimes twice, *Matija Gubec, Matija Gubec?* then they'll shrug and say *Boh!* Earlier, that little street, quite romantically and urbanely, quite internationally, used to be called Raffaello Sanzio, after the famous painter from Urbino whose works today adorn the museums of the world's metropolises, but most people here don't remember the street even by that name.

Here there are very long-winded people who are particularly long-winded if they believe that they know something, maybe they're bored. When they don't know something, such people aren't long-winded, they just say *Boh*, sometimes they whine, *I wouldn't know anything about that,* so that the person who asked feels really uncomfortable, he'll understand that there's nothing for him here, that he's only upsetting the locals with his stupid questions.

In Ferenc Deák Street, Ludwig Jakob Fritz buys two apples, two bananas and an orange, the whole length of Deák there are stalls selling all sorts of delicacies, and there are small shops with the aroma of coffee emanating from them, Ludwig notices jars of pickled eels which probably come from Spain, he thinks, and carries on searching for a hotel in keeping with his means. As soon as he settles in, Ludwig Jakob Fritz will contact the American consul, Mr Charles Slocum, so as to arrange some details connected with his papers.

*

In that year, 1911, there are twenty-two consulates in this town, today there are nine, there's no American one, and those that are here are quiet, as though they were hiding, particularly their consuls, they don't come to first nights at the theatre, they don't come to concerts, they don't come to the two cinemas which in any case look empty, which may mean the cultural offerings, generally a manifestation of spiritual development and survival, are so pathetic and provincial that the consuls, seeing as they have to be here, prefer to sit in their drawing rooms and play bridge. Because, were the consuls to mill around among these people, it would be known, their circulating in public, their "valued presence", as people here like to say in order to sound refined, would at least be covered by the local T.V. stations, there are two local television companies here, both allied to political parties, one started from a right-wing position, the other from the left and now they have come together, so television would cover any consular activity and consular presence, but it doesn't, it broadcasts nothing but tedium that many people don't follow at all, because many people here have special expensive aerials with the help of which they can watch television programmes from Belgrade and can talk openly about it, while before they did not, they whispered and watched in secret.

On the subject of the formal behaviour of many inhabitants of this town, the worst moment is when they ask over the telephone for your respected name, *Your respected name, please?* they say, instead of *What is your name?* as they say all over the world, no-one ever asks: *Your appreciated name, please?* or *Your much admired name, please?* or *Your honour-*

able name, please? unless, of course, they happen to be addressing some excellency, some statesman, but not even then, for the names of excellencies and statesmen are on the whole known. Otherwise, it's a delicate business, designating someone's name as respected, there are all sorts of names, fouled ones.

But, when that grotesque masked ball, costing astronomical sums, is held, then all the consuls suddenly surface, even the ambassadors from the capital appear, and they all dress up, as do little local bigwigs and their respected guests, and once again no-one knows who is who in this town. Local newspapers publish articles in colour, over several pages. So it appears that something is happening here, but it isn't, it's an illusion.

Honorary consuls are all the rage, they're selected from among the domiciled population, through connections, with recommendations, probably with a view to reducing diplomatic costs. These local honorary consuls are usually well placed, materially, and allegedly they do nothing, allegedly they aren't paid, allegedly they don't need to know the language of the country they represent on an honorary basis, they are just allocated freshly renovated premises, at the entrance to which are large brass plates, while inside, in those premises, maintained at a pleasant temperature whatever the season, sit expensively dressed secretaries who bring coffee to the Croatian honorary consuls of various countries. This is a generally benevolent voluntary situation. The Austrian consulate is in the old town, and on the ground floor of the building is Gavrilović the butcher's, renovated along with the consulate, previously a famous textile shop owned by Achille Papetti.

However, these honorary consuls are not a recent phenomenon, they existed before, for instance there was a certain Josip Bakarčić who made a fortune trading livestock and in 1860 was appointed honorary vice-consul of Sweden and Norway. This Bakarčić, in addition to being an honorary vice-consul, traded in wheat and wood, cooperated with several shipowners, and could count seventeen ocean-going yachts in his personal fleet. This Bakarčić was not especially literate or educated, but he did educate his children, and then he participated in the founding of the National Reading Room, where today sadly unimaginative launches of sadly second-rate books are held, attended mostly by pensioners, because inside in winter it is warm. This Bakarčić had four legitimate sons and two illegitimate ones, he was a happy and enterprising man, although then, just at a time when sex was cheap and accessible, both in taverns by the harbour and in stylish hotels and specialised houses of entertainment, sexual adventures were not at all safe, syphilis was raging.

Ludwig Jakob Fritz stops. In the autumn sun, in the shade of a plane tree on Ferenc Deák, at a large four-storey building bearing the number 28, Ludwig Jakob Fritz reads the advertising board, decorated with bright colours and furled ribbons. A breeze blows in from the sea, making the light sway and tangling the black hair of the newly arrived guest.

"Hotel de la Ville"
Hotelier und Cafétier Johan Merk
Elegante Zimmer
Grösste Bequemlichkeit
Durchgehende Bedienung

Coulante Preise

Corsia Deák

Ludwig Jakob Fritz steps inside and, before he's able to ask anything, he realises that the hotel is full, that there aren't even any beds available in shared rooms, which, had there been any, would not have suited him at all. So Ludwig Jakob Fritz keeps on going, along Deák.

In his guidebook Ludwig Jakob Fritz reads about the impression Hotel de la Ville, conveniently located near the railway station, made on Max Maria von Weber when Max Maria von Weber stayed in this town in the 1870s. Ludwig Jakob Fritz does not know who this Weber is and it's by no means essential that he should, even though books about the town often mention this Weber because he was an expert on railways, and railways were at that time the obsession of many because they connect and bring profit.

Today the railways here barely connect anything, and they're in great deficit. In addition, that Weber was the son of the composer and conductor Carl Maria von Weber, and it is not essential that this is known either, although people here think it is.

In the Hotel de la Ville, writes Weber, *when the train arrived at midnight everything – literally everything – was sleeping*, just as today at midnight a vast stupor reigns outside, except that no trains arrive here at midnight, *so*, Weber goes on, *after a lengthy wait, a magnificent Croatian lass appeared, rubbing her large eyes. Then, as in a half-sleep, slender and supple, in a long white dress, holding a candle, she flitted in front of me along narrow corridors. Like a sleepwalker, she opened a door and then, after a soft "felice notte", she vanished like a lovely apparition, not remotely concerned about any desires or needs I might have. I soon got to know that lovely apparition in her true form, as a good, skilled chambermaid and invoice-maker. In those invoices I could see her authentic South-Slav eyes, the rustling of her long skirts and the corridor, embellished by her dear appearance, but the invoices were properly drawn up – all in ducats.*

*

Today, the building of that once morally question-able hotel has been broken up into the numerous little offices of little non-governmental organisa-tions, languishing on pitiful donations while they pay rent to the urban authorities, the ceilings are four metres high, the walls are black with tobacco smoke, time, despair and soot, the stairs are dark and unwashed, grotesquely broad, and up them stagger people with a mission, for the most part unemployed. In that former Hotel de la Ville fluo-rescent lights now shine, particularly in the rooms where student services are set up, with desks where students are given vouchers for students' meals in the students' canteen on the ground floor of the same building. In that canteen, unimaginatively called "Index", through the wide glass, through a shop window in effect, people outside, waiting for buses or hurrying to buy bread before everything in this little town closes, is locked and bolted, these people can watch young faces smiling and leaning towards one another across little square tables with plastic tops, thus creating closeness, perhaps the only real closeness in this town. But these students are students from other places and they have to get close, what can they do? The ones who were born here and are studying here eat at home, they don't need such closeness.

Right next to the Hotel de la Ville Ludwig Jakob Fritz catches sight of a small hotel with the sign "HUNGARIA", tucked in and leaning against the big, classy Bristol Hotel. All these hotels in a row seem to him noisy and luxurious, he's looking for peace and a view of the sea, he wants to sort out his thoughts, and so he reaches Madame Resch's guest house, at the eastern end of town. Ludwig Jakob Fritz spends almost the entire afternoon of that 25 October, 1911, walking, walking and looking.

Nevertheless, Ludwig Jakob Fritz steps into the dark, musty vestibule of the Hungaria and observes, carved into its stone floor, the year of its foundation – 1896. Behind the narrow reception desk of carved black wood stands a young woman, a buxom lass in fact, as von Weber would say, a lovely, tall lass with black wavy hair falling over her shoulders and giving off a scent of lilac, as Ludwig Jakob Fritz notices at once. *Buongiorno, signore*, says the girl, some twenty years old, offering Ludwig Jakob Fritz a narcissus the size of a sunflower. *I sell our guests flowers*, she says, *There are many hotels here and many guests.* Ludwig doesn't want a flower, so he shakes his head. He won't be staying long in this town, he'll be moving on soon, although he has only just arrived. *This little hotel doesn't have electric light yet*, says the girl, *and my name is Clara.* The Hungaria Hotel at number 32 Deák is definitely not what Ludwig Jakob Fritz is looking for.

Today, the Hungaria Hotel has been deprived of its address, one enters the building from the side, through what used to be the servants' entrance, presumably, from a narrow little street along which roll empty beer bottles and greasy paper from recently eaten sandwiches. It's such a tight, short little street that it wasn't worth changing its name because, nondescript as it was, it wouldn't be an honour for anyone. As several hundred years ago, that little street is still today called Sasso Bianco, after the fountain of that name, which is no longer there either. Little Sasso Bianco, or White Pebble Street, is some twenty metres long and leads onto stone steps where it's always dark and full of cats' yowls as though it had leapt out of Poe's times. So, today, the former Hungaria Hotel, once the property of a certain Luigi Lösch, is entered beyond the entrance, through the servants' door, which is entirely in keeping with the general state of this town, repositioned, disjointed, in which its inhabitants live a subordinate life, lateral and menial. Initially, the hotel was for all-comers, suitable for guests arriving by train, and carriages with white horses waited in front of its entrance, as they do today in front of New York's Central Park. Later, the hotel served men and women who worked on the railways and were passing through, on a job, while in Socialist days its enormous rooms were partitioned and transformed into communal civilian apartments, so for many years its life was confined, cold and poor, like the apartments in Soviet films. When the darkness and horror of Socialist optimism abandoned our lives, the partition walls of the Hungaria Hotel were pulled down, so that today that skeleton stands again spacious inside and frighteningly icy. This is the building in which I live. It's an unusual building. It has four floors, everything inside is made of wood and water leaks through it as though it were hollow and it's a miracle that it hasn't burned down yet because in this town buildings have burned unbelievably often and luxuriantly for centuries, just a few days ago the building next to ours caught fire, the former Bristol Hotel in other words, where Doroti lives, who invited us to lasagne as soon as we arrived because, from the inside, our buildings, Doroti's and mine, are so close that we can see what people eat and hear what they whisper, so Doroti knew at once that the two of us had come from over there. Until recently an old lady, Clara, had lived in this building, the former Hungaria Hotel, on the second floor. Once a beauty and nocturnal entertainer, she sold flowers and love through the numerous taverns, cafés, terraces and hotels of Fiume. More recently, Clara sold flowers at the little market just around the corner, built at the same time as the Hungaria, in 1896, a market with a pavilion selling fish and meat and dairy products, surrounded by stalls of genetically modified vegetables from Italy and Spain, in fact a miniature market, huddling on an inner courtyard, encircled by tall, solid, stone houses built for merchants of textiles, leather and silk. That little market looks as though it's in a trap. Behind what is today the noisiest and ugliest street in this town, behind that once fashionable Deák Street, the little market pulses like a life that breathes in secret.

Clara died in 1992, in her sleep, drunk and bent, curled in a foetal position on the stone floor dating from when the Hungaria was built, everyone else in the building had renovated their apartments, tiling their floors, only the parquet remained. The parquet is beautiful, indestructible. It still preserves the footsteps of an army of long-since-dead guests and perhaps the occasional cocooned bacillus of tuberculosis, because tuberculosis bacilli like to slip into floors and wait there for decades, and it's perfectly possible that in the last hundred or so years someone, once, some pretty young lass or strong young lad who worked on the railways, one night, alone or in the arms of a secret lover, should have coughed up a small bloody glob of spittle that settled here, perhaps indeed on the third storey, in the beautiful oak of the floor of my rooms.

Clara died alone, wrapped in smelly old rags. Beside her desiccated corpse was a cardboard box of wilted flowers, which Clara took from the cemetery then sold round the corner at the little market. Towards the end, the box had become too heavy for her, so she had tied a rope to it and dragged it, the way children drag wooden toys which keep twisting, because they are ineptly carved with a penknife, as a cottage industry.

Clara gave birth to numerous children, mainly illegitimate. Those children, conceived in little rooms behind the thin walls of taverns in the old town, but also on the silken sheets of the former Royal Hotel or perhaps the Europa Hotel, there were elegant hotels with who knows what elegant guests, transient men, sailors, merchants, pharmacists, teachers, architects, painters, doctors, singers, dancers, mayors, journalists, shipbuilders, those children who died at birth, who were abandoned in Madame Clotilda's refuge or indeed survived to a ripe old age, those children were never seen by the inhabitants of the building in which I live. No relative came to collect the rigid body of Clara the flower-seller, because she had no relatives. Clara died in her hundred and first year. She was thrown into a communal grave for the homeless, or perhaps she ended up in the Anatomical Institute of the Medical Faculty, because medicine is quite advanced in this town, because this acknowledged, advanced state of medicine is something this town has inherited from the past.

The Bristol Hotel is a deluxe hotel in comparison with the Hungaria, it has a lift and central heating,

today it has only a lift. The central heating was demolished by the Partisans when they entered the town because they needed to abolish all traces of bourgeois life at a stroke, so to start with, the former Partisans warmed themselves with wood, but later they re-installed radiators in the buildings from which they had previously removed them. The former Bristol Hotel was somehow bypassed as far as the lift was concerned. Lifts are otherwise a rarity in this town in which there are unimaginable quantities of steps and stairways, the town seems to have been dug into a hill. So a person who lives here has the sense that he's forever climbing somewhere, either onto a higher floor or onto some elevation, which always makes him tired, but he doesn't get anywhere in particular. The building that was once called the Hungaria isn't called that anymore, nor is the Bristol called the Bristol. On the ground floor of the Bristol, where there used to be a foyer with a glass-enclosed café and a restaurant in the Viennese Secession style, nowadays there's a small bookshop selling rolls of wallpaper and stupid toys, and immediately next to it is a large shop selling Borovo shoes, whose window at the beginning of the 1990s was eerily empty because in Borovo at that time people were making not shoes but war. On the ground floor of the former Hungaria, first there used to be a shop called Working Woman selling ready-made socialist clothes, now there's one selling Phillips products, from small travelling irons to frightening television screens the size of those in cinemas. The Bristol had eighty rooms, sleeping a hundred and twenty, it had an elegant wrought-iron canopy, tables with guests right on the promenade. Now there's a plastic bar, empty for the most part, in which they make hamburgers so that the place is known as "Hambi".

On the third floor of that once luxurious hotel there's an advisory centre for the absent-minded and the lost, for the anxious, for victims of violence, there are a lot of such victims here. It was in this town that I first came across children who are sexually abused by old people in the neighbourhood and devoted family friends who bribe them with ice cream and chocolate, it is here that I watch drunken fathers flailing out at everything and everyone, here I say good morning to age-old, exhausted prostitutes, always in shoes with muddy, crooked heels and drooping stockings, although here, remarkably, in the middle of town there is no mud at all, which is a great consolation; here through the window I see women in rags and urine-stained beggars, squatting on the scorched grass, in a cloud of their own bodily stench, bloated, hugging beer bottles in their stiff alcoholics' fists as though they were their children. This is what my neighbourhood is like, realistically speaking.

Some two hundred metres from the Bristol, also in Deák Street, there is another hotel called the Deák,

which is today the Trades Union Building. The window frames are peeling, completely rotten, it's a reddish edifice, right beside the railway, set back, with a neglected garden and a concrete parking space.

Ludwig Jakob Fritz glances to the left, the sound of waltzes reaches him from the luxuriant park, the air sways to the rhythm, on the terrace at marble *Kaffeetische* sit ladies with smart hairdos, some are wearing small hats, some are wearing large hats, some blink, their movements are slow, drowsy, that looks feminine, it's obvious – men like it, the men have thin moustaches, leather gloves with three little buttons on one side, monocles and pocket watches engraved with their grandfathers' monograms. Although it is still daylight, the Hotel Deák bathes in the luxury of electric lights, in the background can be glimpsed dining rooms, and halls for dancing and film-projection.

Cinematograph, Hotel Deák – at 8.30 p.m. there will
be a presentation with the very latest device invented
by human knowledge: a phonograph connected to the
cinematograph, and both projected in such a way
that the performance can be seen and heard. There
will be presentations of Sarah Bernhardt in "Hamlet",
Coquelin in "Showy Dressers", Rejane in "Ma Cousine",
Cleo de Merode in "La Havane" and the English come-
dian Little Titch. Prices from 2 to 4 kronen.

This town is at the height of its distinction and prosperity. That brilliance, that quiet, crackling tremor slips under Ludwig Jakob Fritz's elegant coat of lightweight grey material and spills over his skin. He shudders, his heart leaps. *This luxury bathes me like the kisses of a passionate woman.* He walks, the sun has still not set. Tonight, Ludwig Jakob Fritz will go out among people, he will go to some performance or other, he might go dancing although it is Wednesday, even on Wednesdays there are all kinds of events here, everywhere, there are twenty hotels,

Zagreb has three.

there are twelve cinemas,

At the time, 1911, Zagreb had two cinemas, Pula had four. Corso Deák alone, the former Boris Kidrič Street, today Kralj Krešimir, had four cinemas, now there's one near the railway, so that travellers coming into the town by train and the audience emerging

139

from the cinema make steady eye contact when the times coincide. That cinema is called the "Croatia", in Socialist days it was called the "Belgrade", and at the time when it was built it was the Grande Cinematografo Parigi or else the Cinematografo San Giorgio, whichever.

Salon Edison, Via Fumara 2,
Cine EDISON Cinema
le celebre detective NOBODY
Dramma poliziesco
Intitolato:
FRA GLI ARTIGLI DEI CONSPIRATORI
1500 metri di lunghezza!

Cinematografo Sole, Via Lodovico Kossuth 1, Cinematografo Olimpo, Via Alessandro Manzoni 11

The Killer of
the Singer Lucienne Fabry,
Attack on the National Bank.

Cinematografo Centrale, Piazza delle
Erbe, Kinematograf Sušak

Submarines and Mines in the "White-
head" Factory, ISIS, a colossal feature
film in colour from Egyptian times,
Happiness Comes Overnight, In the
Homes of Monkeys and Snakes on
the Sunda Islands.

The Odeon Cinema, initially the Teatro Apolo, then Dancing variété Bonboniera and Cinema Carnaro,

today a small and not particularly imaginative puppet theatre, just round the corner from here, across the miniature market. That theatre used to be managed by a man who said, *All these posters of productions from former Yugoslav days ought to be removed*, so some people said, *Why not burn them?* That man, who had no previous connection whatever with this town, dropped anchor here, he quickly fitted in, socially, personally and politically, but he had come from an even smaller town and he was enchanted with this one. He ran, for the sake of health, fitness and fashion, along that narrow promenade *lungomare*, he married at a run, made children at a run and drank whisky in the evenings with the authorities. In the little puppet theatre there was no space for some people, because this man used to say that before any discussion about any piece of work, those people had first to do some homework, and he gave them little stories to turn into children's plays, with no contract or payment, of course. There *was* space in that theatre for some other people and those people had only to adapt *themselves*, not fairy tales. Later, that man became top dog in the big theatre which doesn't have a very large repertoire so the auditorium is often empty (but well heated in winter), while his wife took over the little children's theatre, which is entirely consistent with the laws of this town, which are familial, intimate and strictly observed political laws, almost clerical.

Ludwig Jakob Fritz arrives at the Piazza del Commercio and jumps onto a tram.

Today, that square is called Žabica – "the Little Frog" – named after a fountain that was once there. On the square is the bus terminal, a small bungled bus terminal, with no shelter, so when it rains, everyone and everything, people and luggage, get soaked and puddles form, and one's feet get wet, and during the day it's very busy, by night it isn't, it's busy because passengers can't wait to leave, so they push, because they're passengers in transit, because this is a free-flowing town, let's not deceive ourselves.

Ludwig Jakob Fritz goes five stops to the end of the line, then takes a carriage to the guest house of Madame Antonia Resch, because, as he walks, he discovers from his guidebook, *Guida di Fiume*, that the Resch guest house is in the immediate vicinity of the Sanatorium Hotel, where Ludwig Jakob Fritz intends to visit his colleagues and obtain from them written confirmation of his excellent health, without which he cannot appear before Consul Slocum. Ludwig Jakob Fritz is a doctor.

So.

The Sanatorium Hotel is admirably equipped. Ludwig Jakob Fritz carries out a brief fitness test on modern gymnastic and power-driven machines and has a refreshing bathe in heated seawater. His colleague Sbisà then takes him through all twenty-two rooms of what is then an ultra-modern and ultra-fashionable sanatorium, and Ludwig Jakob Fritz establishes that everything is truly splendid. Dr Sbisà then takes Dr Fritz into the operating theatre and finally into the laboratory, where he is informed that the acceptance of every patient is conditional on a previously carried-out Wassermann serological test, because, says Sbisà, sexual life here is stormy and indiscriminate, and the consequences of that terrible, infectious disease are all around us, he says, there are scabby and lame people, there are paralysed and mentally absent people, the madhouses are full. Dr Sbisà explains to Dr Fritz that lovely young women hide their deformed bodies under elegant dresses that come straight from Paris and Rome, and conceal their thinning hair resembling moth-eaten cloth, beneath hats full of fruit and flowers, so a person is easily deceived, he says. Sometimes, he says, nothing can be seen on the outside, while the spirochaete does its work, it is an insidious disease, he says, hard to eradicate. Dr Fritz responds to his colleague Dr Sbisà by saying how fortunate he is to come from a region in which endemic malaria once raged, and not from one with endemic French disease, and says that Dr Koch worked precisely in the region which he comes from, so he hoped that malaria had been eradicated there, besides, he says, we're doctors, we know how to look after ourselves, and he says that regions with endemic goitre seem to him to have a better chance than regions where the French disease rages, yes, he knows all its variations, its repressed, hidden and devastating effects, he has read about it, he says, although he hasn't yet had an opportunity to see how that hideous disease is manifested in real life, he says, other than on photographs, which were unfortunately not in colour. Dr Sbisà then asks his colleague Dr Fritz whether he uses condoms, to which Fritz exclaims in astonishment, *I beg your pardon?* In a half-whisper, confidentially, Dr Sbisà explains to Dr Fritz that these rubber sheaths offer good protection, although not a hundred per cent and, if he likes, he says, he can get some, those rubbers, johnnies, French letters, condoms, contraceptives, call them what you will, he can get some at no. 18 Corso, in the S.S. Vito & Modesto pharmacy, owned by Giorgio Catti, otherwise his friend. Ludwig Jakob Fritz, slightly offended that his colleague Sbisà is meddling in his sex life, says that he's just passing through this really lovely town, *I'm in transit*, he says and that he'll be leaving as soon as the 28th, that is Saturday, moving on, and that at the moment he doesn't have any particularly strong sexual urges, that he has other things on his mind, more urgent business. At that Dr Sbisà says, of course, he understands, of course and there is a brief moment of awkwardness.

Even then, this town took pride in its civility, it nurtured discreet and gentle relations, without heat, outburst or anger. Relations here were washed and smooth, qualities that have been retained until the present day, while it, the town of that time, simply developed its wealth, polishing its gentility frenziedly and assiduously; it constructed a supply of various decorous smiles, one smile for every eventuality – and this, too, has been retained up to the present. It was precisely then that the town gave birth to its pathetic but poisonous selfishness, which fermented its insensitivity, its blindness to otherness, the whole time just mimicking a carefree manner, the whole time pretending to be relaxed. This town was never either carefree or relaxed, but it was crowded, it was packed with splendid buildings, insatiable property magnates and ambitious merchants; its harbours were crammed with ships and its shops stuffed with all kinds of goods from everywhere, its asylums over-subscribed by the poor, its brothels teeming with village beauties who, by chance, through their tragic, miserable, sentimental and stereotyped destinies, didn't end up in nunneries on islands or in the provinces; the streets swarmed with pedestrians, and among them, every decade, there would be some Florian Winter (perhaps three or four at the same time), some Florian Winter who had not succeeded in escaping, who had not succeeded in getting away from the heavy, prison-like breath of the town, some renegade whom this town had shoved into the back pocket of its uniform, with the aim of taking him out into the light of day when it became opportune, during the carnival fiestas of its history. These tragically few beleaguered bohemians hung around its smoke-filled taverns, met in tiny rooms in the suburbs, misunderstood and forgotten. They had nothing to bestow upon this town because this town would not let them.

All those languages that were spoken in public and in private, all those people of various origins were the most ordinary camouflage, deceit, illusion; their lives, fortified according to imposed rules, rich and unimaginative to the point of dullness, were just mechanical iron lungs that one day would wear out or burst. That's why this town no longer breathes. This town doesn't remember its bohemians, because its bohemians went away to be bohemians elsewhere, where the air was less clean. This town had secret anarchists and antichrists, some of whom were unable to die here, even if they had wanted to. This town doesn't remember its "bad" women, because, if there ever were any, they left, it doesn't remember its disobedient painters, men and women, its poets, its actors, its women mathematicians and physicists who had short hair, wore trousers, smoked cigarettes in long holders and were loud, because for most people in this town women were either battery hens or prostitutes and because the small number of desperate, thinking people was quiet, too quiet to have shaken its foundations. This town has had a gigantic correctness for a long time, for a century or more, and in the end that will be the death of it, it has already sucked out its soul. Today, this town has so much correctness that it's quite swollen with its uprightness, so inflated that swarms of tedium now burst out of it, buzzing, just buzzing.

In order to mitigate his colleague Sbisà's awkwardness, Ludwig Jakob Fritz says that everything's fine, that for now he knows as much as he needs to about condoms, contraception and venereal diseases, it is logical that he knows something about all this, given his profession, is it not? he says. Although people are generally poorly informed about contraception, *And here the Catholic Church has been particularly lax*, says Ludwig Jakob Fritz, *Despite the fact that the Catholic Church purports to have an important place in the life of the common people,* he says, *nevertheless it is not a progressive Church, far from it, indeed, the Catholic Church has proved itself an exceptionally retrograde Church, especially as far as contraception is concerned. The Catholic Church teaches the faithful various pieces of wisdom, but sometimes it does not remotely observe those teachings itself, and Catholic priests, dear colleague, do not mention those sheaths to their faithful at all,* says Ludwig Jakob Fritz. *Although,* he says, *it is interesting that for a long time now Judaism has not prohibited the use of methods of contraception.*

That's how their conversation ends.

Ludwig Jakob Fritz obtains confirmation of his good health from Dr Sbisà, spruces himself up for an evening out and goes down into town. That Wednesday, 25 October, 1911, Ludwig Jakob Fritz passes the aquarium where there was once a park, by then already transformed into a depot and service workshops for trams, so there was no longer anything green there. The aquarium was built in the Egyptian style with twelve seawater pools and six freshwater pools, and additional containers for amphibians. Egypt was fashionable at the time. The aquarium is illuminated with electric lights so it is gleaming. Ludwig Jakob Fritz looks at the small fish, then leaves.

> There is no aquarium in the town today, what would it want with one? The town has people who put on exhibitions about the erstwhile aquaria, that is enough. And as for little fish, the basics can be learned from books. For the exotic fish, it's enough to leaf through encyclopaedias, there are specialised fish encyclopaedias, there are children's encyclopaedias, so scholarship about fish is readily accessible to the inhabitants of this town, and hygienic. As for other kinds of fish, local ones, fishing is recommended as a hobby, so that everything about local fish is immediately known at first hand. In 1899, one used to enter the park, which appeared twice

and vanished twice, through large iron gates above which there were two stone statues, no-one now remembers whether they were two animal figures or two human figures. There were two rows of trees there: two rows of chestnuts and two rows of large plane trees, there were poplars as well, of which some writers say that they have silvery leaves that glimmer, which is nonsense. But that park, once a place where one could walk beside water, was mostly deserted, because already for a long time walkers here have preferred to be entirely visible, not hidden by trees, so they walk in the open, where there are no trees or vegetation to protect them from the sun and the eyes of other walkers. Later, in Yugoslavia, a park sprang up again here, a children's playground in fact, with poplars and oleanders, but now that it's Croatia, the greenery has gone, there's a petrol pump and a parking lot. In this town, parks are pruned, eliminated everywhere; once there were all kinds of parks, all over the place. Now, instead of parks, there are grotesque fountains here and there, which gush, some low, some high, and passers-by have no idea what to do with them, they just pass them, never stopping to observe the way the water leaps. Where there used to be parks and walkways, as I have already said, today there are parking lots, this town is overflowing with parking lots as though it were some metropolis, and the town is constantly clogged, there are innumerable bottlenecks where the traffic trickles or stands still, suggesting that there is something wrong in this whole area of traffic, of communication.

*

Ludwig Jakob Fritz goes on a little shopping trip. It is late afternoon, in fact almost evening. The streets are lit, there are pedestrians strolling slowly, they're not buzzing, they're not in a hurry even though it's Wednesday. In via Governo, in a shop selling chocolates and liqueurs, Ludwig Jakob Fritz buys two bottles of top-quality cognac, one for his colleague Sbisà, one for Consul Slocum. In Lajos Kossuth Street he buys four sets of underwear and six pairs of socks, black and grey, a cotton and silk mix; a little further on he catches sight of a barber's, MODERNE SALON DE TOILETTE (FODRÁSZ TÉREM), in the window of which, on a decorated poster, the owner, Stefano Albanese, announces that he has local and foreign perfume products as well as disinfected razors, so Ludwig Jakob Fritz goes in and asks for the full treatment: a haircut, a shave and facial massage; Signor Albanese gives him a special smile and, with a bow, takes him under his wing. Refreshed and by now hungry, he sees the large billboard of the Hotel Quarnero,

telefono n. 657
proprietario G. Deganis
Situato nel centro della città, in prossimità
Dell' approdo dei piroscafi, dell' Ufficio
Postale, del passagio del Tram elettrico.
Completamente restaurato a nuovo. Luce
elettrica
   GRANDE RESTAURANT
Rinomata cucina, italiana e tedesca –
Speciale attenzione per la cottura del pesce
– Vini di primissima qualità: Nostrani,
Terrani, Istriani, e squisita birra Pilsen –
Servizio inappuntabile.

he comes out onto via Corso, in the Branchetta brothers' shop he buys a black felt hat with a broad brim, very expensive, comes out onto Dante Square and considers whether or not to have an aperitif in the Central coffee house on the ground floor of the Europa Hotel or across the road, in "Caffé degli specchi". While he is hesitating like this, he observes the fine profile of Mlle Clara (from the dark entrance of the Hungaria) on the other side of via Corso, in front of the illuminated jeweller's (Gioielleria Engelsrath), and is overcome by quiet delight, at least one familiar face in this town full of bustle and harmonious mingling. Ludwig Jakob Fritz crosses the road, approaches Mlle Clara from behind, gently touches her elbow, Mlle Clara turns equally gently, Ludwig Jakob Fritz gazes into her violet eyes, violet like Elizabeth Taylor's violet eyes, and says, *You are unusually tall.* Mlle Clara says, *I'm looking for a little gold heart in this jeweller's shop,* and Ludwig Jakob Fritz suggests, *Let's have a drink, my name is Ludwig Jakob Fritz.* Ludwig Jakob Fritz and Mlle Clara sit in the Caffé Marittimo Mercantile, where the town library now is, decently heated in winter, full of pensioners and other poor people. At regular intervals, with her right hand, Mlle Clara lightly touches her hair in its chignon, a little above her right ear, so Ludwig says, *There's no need for you to keep touching your hair, it's fine.* Then Mlle Clara tells Ludwig Jakob Fritz that this café in which they are sitting, this Marittimo Mercantile, is open from morning until late at night and mariners and shipowners and the captains of recently arrived ships gather here, officers in various uniforms come and talk about all kinds of things, about business, and sometimes also about women, in various languages, *Ah, oui* says Mlle Clara, *I speak a little in French, a little in English, oh, yes my dear,* that is what she says and touches her hair again. Waiters pass and greet Mlle Clara, *Buonasera signorina Clara,* and as they greet her, they smile. So they sit, Ludwig and Clara, here, in the street, on the terrace of the Caffé Marittimo Mercantile on via Corso, while the gas lights are gradually lit, one after the other, or perhaps they are electric lights being switched on, and not gas, it's not important, and the shop windows are illuminated, it's a mild autumn evening, almost romantic, as they sit and sip their drinks, Ludwig a Köbanyi beer, Clara a cherry liqueur. Then Ludwig Jakob Fritz invites Mlle Clara to dinner, *We could have a bite to eat together,* he says, but Mlle Clara can't, she says, she has to get to work, she says, she sings and sometimes dances somewhere, she says, and sometimes she offers the guests fresh flowers because it's a place where the guests buy fresh flowers for their wives who don't accompany them to that place, so if Mr Fritz has nothing better to do after dinner, perhaps he'd care to call in there, she'd like that, she says, and on the wrapping of Ludwig's just-purchased underwear, Mlle Clara sketches the way to her nocturnal place of work. *The place is called Grotta*, says Mlle Clara, *which would be cave in Italian*, she says, and Mlle Clara writes the word "grotta" with just one "t", which is not the way it is written in Italian, because Mlle Clara is not particularly educated, but she is exceptionally pretty.

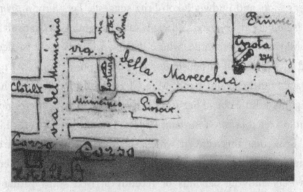

It is not known where Ludwig Jakob Fritz goes for dinner. It is known that, following the route on Mlle Clara's sketch, Ludwig Jakob Fritz pays a visit to a *pissoir*, and then makes his way to a building bearing the number 274 on the by then dark via della Marecchia. It is known that the next day, 26 October, 1911, at 6.35 a.m., probably over a demure breakfast consisting of a white coffee with warm croissants, in the dining room of the Resch guest house, Dr Fritz writes a postcard addressed to a certain Dr Auro Segal from Pola. On the postcard, in the top left-hand corner, is Mlle Clara's sketch, followed by the following text: *To the right of the entrance is a place called Grotta. No. 274*, writes Ludwig Jakob Fritz. *Entrance, 2 K. Ella – 16, Ponny, Melanie, Clara – a good stable. A bottle of beer, only 80 fil. Take condoms! Madame wants to open franchises on the coast! Used "thumb" – need not sprain it. Spacious premises, the waiting rooms have entertainments, music. Simple dress. Polite porter. Fine salon. Significant place. The* Saxonia *sails on 28th. L.J.F.*

It is known, also, that Ludwig Jakob Fritz's bed in room number seven at the Resch guest house was not slept in that night.

On Thursday 26, October, Ludwig Jakob Fritz goes to the hospital, for a brief meeting with Dr Antun Grošić, a surgeon who had achieved international fame two years earlier, in 1909, when he demonstrated at the International Medical Congress in Budapest his method of pre-operative disinfection of the patient's skin with tincture of iodine. Dr Grošić is some kind of (distant) relative of Ludwig Jakob Fritz on his mother's side. For centuries, members of the Bax, Bassadonna, Zachelli and Walderstein (nowadays for the sake of euphony renamed Bolter-stein) families and those of the Grošić family had been intermarrying, what can you do?; a little place within reach of the world, and yet outside it. Grošić later takes the Italian side and becomes Grossich, and in 1919 D'Annunzio makes him president of the occupying government, and after the town is annexed to Italy, he even becomes a senator. In Socialist times, it was better to be called Grošić than Grossich, so Grossich became Grošić again, because his specialism was important and he wanted to pursue his research and carry out his operations in peace. However, Grošić (Grossich) had always been fascinated by politics, he bowed down before it, he devoted himself to it, that powerful, fickle seductress, not knowing whether he ought to drag himself out of its embrace for ever or expire in it. But, in 1911, Ludwig Jakob Fritz could not have known that, and, even if he had known, he wouldn't have cared. *I am inviting Noguchi to our part of the world, my dear Ludwig,* says Dr Grošić. *He could research here to his heart's content.*

Then Ludwig Jakob Fritz takes his bottle of cognac to Consul Slocum, is granted permission to enter America and says, *Thank you, sir, I'll send you a postcard.* Consul Charles Rice Slocum smiles politely and says, *I suggest you change your name upon arrival, an American name might make your life easier; Freeze instead of Fritz, or even Reese, Reese sounds good, Jake Freeze, perhaps Jack Reese,* to which Ludwig Jakob Fritz says that he thinks that in his case this will not be necessary. Then Consul Slocum asks whether he has perhaps taken a room in the Emigrés' Hotel on the waterfront, in Industrijska Street, because it's an exceptionally interesting hotel, *A piece of intriguing architecture*, he says, to which Ludwig Jakob Fritz replies that he has not taken a room in the Emigrés' Hotel, but in a small private guest house in the east of the town, where for breakfast they serve real French croissants, warm, and that his room, *It's a single room, with a private bathroom*, he says, his room has a lovely view of the open sea, because he, Ludwig Jakob Fritz, cannot bear large crowds. *It's very romantic*, he says, to which Consul Slocum raises his eyebrows and says *Oh? A pity*, Consul Charles Rice Slocum remarks, and tells Ludwig Jakob Fritz that he had not been able to resist entering that building, that Emigrés' Hotel, and he says that there are large bathrooms there, where all the émigrés go to shower after the compulsory medical examinations, he says, *And during that time their clothes are disinfected*, he says, so that the passengers embark on their ships clean, disinfected and healthy, because it's a great risk for his country, he says, to accept so many people day after day from all over, the influx is terrible, he says, and he asks Ludwig Jakob Fritz whether he knows that from 1903 to today, 1911, around 270,000 souls, from this town, from this very town, have set sail for New York. *America is a great country*, says Consul Slocum, *the right country for these poor, wretched people who will be able to work and work and work there, because the mines and railways are waiting*, he says, *and there is work for fishermen*, he says, *and the factories are taking on women, and they will all be happy there, America is a promised land*, he says, and repeats several more times that it really is a wonderful country, this America of his. *I have examined the bedrooms of the Emigrés' Hotel*, the Consul goes on, *in the bedrooms there are rows of metal bunk beds*, he says, *and I have examined the machines for disinfecting clothes, I visited the kitchen*, he says, *and I even tried the soup while people from different nations, in a very quiet and orderly manner, I would say obediently, came for their lunch, the women in one line, the men in another*, he says, and reminds Ludwig Jakob Fritz that there is not much work for doctors in his country of America, because the doctors' posts are filled, there may still be jobs for nurses, he says, or for laboratory technicians, to which Ludwig Jakob Fritz replies that he does not need a job at all because he is going to America to visit his relatives and to take a letter to Mr Noguchi on the way, at which Consul Slocum again raises his eyebrows and again repeats *Oh? Oh!* as though everything is quite clear to him, and then, finally, largely to himself, he says, *People dream up all sorts of things.* Then Consul Charles Rice Slocum stands up abruptly and wishes Ludwig Jakob Fritz a safe journey, *Bon voyage, monsieur,* he says and opens the door for him.

With his other papers and personal documents, Ludwig Jakob Fritz goes to the L. Mašek shipping office in Sušak, then to the Cunard Line office (Riva Szápáry, palazzo Adria), where for less than twenty American dollars he buys a second-class ticket for the transatlantic steamship *Saxonia.* In the office he is given a pamphlet (later found among his papers) with information about the ship and detailed "house rules". From the information sheet Ludwig Jakob Fritz learns:

The *Saxonia* was built at the John Brown Ltd company yard in Glasgow in 1899. Dimensions – 176.77 x 19.77 metres; weight – 14.281 gross registered tons; chimneys – 1; masts – 4; construction – steel; propulsion – two propellers; engines – eight-cylinder quadruple expansion; speed – 15 knots; date of launch – 16 December, 1899; capacity – 164 1st class passengers, 200 2nd class and 1600 3rd class. Breakfast at 8:00, luncheon at 12:30, tea at 17:30, dinner at 20:30. The bar and smoking room are open until 23:00; Divine Service is on Sundays at 10:30; dogs and other domestic pets are permitted on board, strictly with the written agreement of the local hygiene service; deck chairs may be hired at a cost of one dollar and all illegal copies of books found in the possession of passengers will be immediately confiscated.

Then Ludwig Jakob Fritz goes to have lunch in the nearby tavern, All' Aquilla Nera – "The Black Eagle" (*rooms for foreigners from 2 kronen, electric light, open until 2 a.m.*) – where, over a *minestra di verdura* and a Puntigamer beer he leafs through *La Bilancia* and the daily *Rijeka Novi list.* From these newspapers he learns that the Sušak cinema is that evening showing short films: "Excursion on the Coast of New Zealand", "A Glass of Poison", and "Max After Illness", which do not appeal particularly to him. He discovers that the "Serbian Bank intends to build on the corner of Jurišićeva and Petrinjska streets in Zagreb, overlooking Jelačić Square, a palace at an estimated cost of 600,000 kronen", which leaves him entirely indifferent; he discovers that Volume X of "our only women's magazine" *Local Hearth* has just been published, and that brings a little mocking smile to his lips. Ludwig Jakob Fritz also reads about "the blowing up of the '*Liberté*' battleship in France, which is believed to be an act of sabotage", he reads that in Lvov, in solitary confinement in prison, a young man by the name of Levicki, murderer of the actress Oginjska, takes a lethal dose of veronal (in powder form), after which he is found dead at 9.30 a.m. on 25 October, 1911, and, for the first time since he came to this town, Ludwig Jakob Fritz is overcome by a vague sense of unease; he listens – in the distance he hears a little bell, as little as a walnut shell, he hears soft, intermittent music, like crystal cracking in a fire, he looks around and trembles. Sorrow is approaching Ludwig Jakob Fritz.

The Elixir of Life "Amaro Alpino" (elisir lungavita),
Angelo Pharmacy, proprietor Ivan Prodam, Corso 4.

The revolution in China is progressing.

The Italian/Turkish war is being waged.

In Oklahoma, battles between whites and blacks "are reaching major proportions, with several white families killed".

Cholera is raging.

How are we to defend ourselves against this terri-
ble enemy? This INFECTION enters the human body
through the mouth. We must therefore disinfect our
mouths thoroughly and frequently. The best means for
disinfecting the mouth is DIANA water, mixed with

French brandy. DIANA – brandy contains menthol, a
strong disinfecting active agent.

Secret diseases spring up from everywhere.

Salsaparilla Syrup with iodine, cleanses new or
old syphilitic diseases! Pharmacy and Laboratory
Babić, via San Bernardino 2.

It starts to rain. Cold creeps up Ludwig Jakob Fritz's back, spreading into
a mild shivering. *I'm short of sleep*, he says.

I have the honour of informing my respected customers, and society
in general, that I have stocked my shop at 22, via Corso on the
occasion of the onset of the autumn season
with a large selection of umbrellas
very elegantly and solidly made.
A rich selection en-tout-cas
SPECIALITY: WALKING STICK UMBRELLA
Vincenzo Tagini – Corso 22
& Piazza Santa Barbara

En tout cas, says Ludwig Jakob Fritz, *en tout cas*, and, instead of buying
an umbrella in Vincenzo Tagini's specialist shop, he goes to Enrico
Babić's pharmacy, not to Giorgio Catti's pharmacy recommended by Dr
Sbisà, but to Enrico Babić's, which, who knows why, Dr Sbisà had *not*
recommended, and asks for five condoms.

Condoms have existed for thousands of years, they
were invented by men to protect themselves from
venereal diseases. It was only later, much later, that
women realised that those sheaths would be useful
for them as well, that they could protect them not
only from the clap and the French disease but also

from eternally swollen bellies. For centuries, women had stuffed themselves with all kinds of things, for the most part secretly: crocodile and elephant dung, sponges soaked in vinegar or lemon juice, plant sap, olive oil, beeswax, honey, ginger, ground rosehip, they drank the urine of various animals, mercury, arsenic and strychnine, and when "it was too late" they steamed themselves in all kinds of revolting, stinking baths and thrust various needles into themselves, doubled up with pain, they watched terrified as crimson streams poured down their thighs, listening to their hearts breaking and believing that God was punishing them.

The Ancient Egyptians used linen sheaths, the Romans little protective sacks made from the muscles of dead soldiers. In the middle of the sixteenth century, in Italy, Gabrielle Fallopius carried out "experiments" on 1,100 men, fitting them also with little linen caps, which were later soaked in a chemical solution containing a spermicide. Fallopius boasted that not one of his "guinea pigs" contracted syphilis, as though syphilis was born in women's bodies, of its own accord. As though syphilis really was God's punishment for female lust, which, for a long time, the Church loved to claim from the pulpit and in the confessional, with a demonic cry or threatening whisper, as though servants of God, young and old, "little sisters" and "brothers" in black habits, had not, since the dawn of time and mankind, copulated behind the bolted doors of monasteries and nunneries, there, in full view of "God" Himself, right under his nose.

Common sense is very surprised that both run-of-the-

mill sense and the Church preach that the human race multiplied from Adam and Eve, although according to the words of so-called "Holy Writ" they did not have a single daughter. Presumably their son Cain gave birth! That is comical and unnatural and terrible, and every remotely honest and intelligent priest must be ashamed of preaching such foolish and senseless notions, because this is rambling more terrible than that of a sick person in a delirium.

The Church tells us that God made man in his image, but common sense responds that this is an appalling desecration of both man and God. Because this suggests that God is as stupid as Eve who obeys the snake, inconstant as Adam who is "led by the nose by a woman"; as spiteful as Cain, who kills his nicer brother Abel out of jealousy; white as a European, black as an Arab, wild as the wild peoples and enlightened as the civilised world: filled with stinking trash in his belly like every other person and animal; supplied with the tools, the apparatus that makes children and aids conjugal satisfaction (and in another place the "Holy Writ" says that he has neither body nor that particular place); that he has a tyrannical nature like the Pharaohs and Nero, and is as good as Franklin, Robert Owen and others . . .

The Church is the privileged home of stupefaction, untruth and slavery. As a professor of theology and Archimandrite, I tell you this for a second time: if I were to preach differently, I would betray scholarship. For the truth that I have just spoken I shall be severely, very severely condemned not only by the benighted masses, but also by every "intelligentsia" that breathes in an insidious, retrogressive and selfish spirit.

I shall speak again.

Then, condoms appear that are made from lambs' intestines (those same ones into which meat is stuffed to make sausages today), and in 1844 the famous Goodyear enters the scene, the failed rubber merchant, one could say tyre-repairer, a poor man until his death, who makes condoms out of vulcanised rubber. Some forty years later latex condoms are produced, until the 1930s expensive for the average pocket, because they are not mass-produced, but exclusive, unique. They say that until the 1950s, condoms are washed after use, spread with petroleum jelly and kept in little wooden boxes under the bed. Later, they are wrapped in stiff gold foil in the shape of ducats, like the little chocolate coins that are given to children on special occasions. Nowadays, condoms are made of polyurethane, mostly in Malaysia. During the Second World War, largely synthetic rubbers were produced by the prisoners at Auschwitz under the patronage of the I. G. Farben conglomerate, which also produced Zyklon B.

It was not only the Church that banned the use of condoms. In the twentieth century it was the American Society for Social Health that was first to speak out against contraception, followed by the Nazi government.

"Madame Butterfly" is being performed at the municipal theatre, but Ludwig Jakob Fritz doesn't feel like listening to that tragicomic amorous mewling, besides, *The damp is getting to my bones*, he says, so on his way to the Resch guest house he peers into the Hotel Kontinental, from which noise is coming, a tamburitza concert is being held, with musicians from Vukovar, *I'll buy gloves tomorrow*, he says, fiddling with the condoms in his pocket with his thumb and forefinger.

That evening Ludwig Jakob Fritz doesn't go out. He sorts his luggage, leafs through the books he intends to take with him, mostly professional, medical books, and puts those he thinks he will not need to one side, because, if he happens to want them, those particular books, he'll be able to get them "over there". So, after Ludwig Jakob Fritz's departure, Madame Antonia Resch will find on the bedside table in room number seven of her intimate guest house *The Strange Case of Dr Jekyll and Mr Hyde*, *Alice's Adventures in Wonderland* and *The Narrative of Arthur Gordon Pym*, which she gives to the bookseller and printer Carl Spiess because she doesn't know what to do with them, she says, her guests generally have their own books, if they read at all, she says, and if they do read, she says, it's mostly books in Italian or Hungarian rather than English and besides, says Madame Antonia Resch, each of her rooms is provided with a Bible and downstairs in the dining room her guests can leaf through the newspapers and for the time being, she says, she feels that this is enough.

On Friday, 27 October, 1911, on Elisabeth Square, at the C. Fleisch-haker dairy, Ludwig Jakob Fritz buys half a kilogram of butter from Count Pejačević's estate, a litre of milk from Postojna, a kilogram of honey, ten eggs and half a kilogram of fresh coffee, and takes all of this to the "certified piano teacher" Mlle Ella Monath, on the third floor of no. 4, via Caserna and says, *My sister, Claudia Tutner, has sent this for you.* Then he goes to the Hungarian–Croatian Steamship Society, buys a ticket for a day excursion and at 9.45 a.m. boards a saloon steamship (the name of which he does not recall), returning to town in the early afternoon. In fact Ludwig Jakob Fritz does not know what to do with himself. *I'll go and buy some gloves,* he says. He goes to Piazza Andrassy, to Prohaska's shop, and chooses for himself a pair of black gloves made of chicken skin impregnated with the scent of roses, made by Roekl, sets off towards the exit, turns, approaches the shopkeeper and says in a whisper, *And another pair of gloves, please, a pair of long women's gloves, please, satin, bright red, please*, then he leaves. *How amazing that I'm so calm,* says Ludwig Jakob Fritz.

*

> *"Gloves sweet as damask roses,*
> *masks for faces and for noses,*
> *bugle-bracelet, necklace amber,*
> *perfume for a lady's chamber."*

> *My name is William Shakespeare, I know*
> *many secrets about gloves, I grew up with them,*
> *my parents were glove-makers.*

In a shop selling knives (Coltelleria Tridente), Ludwig Jakob Fritz buys a pocketknife. He looks about him. He goes into Agostino Gigante goldsmith's shop and says: *A small heart, please. Gold. A pendant for a necklace.*

He eats at the Al Colombo restaurant, 14, via Francesco Petrarca. He doesn't remember what he eats. He drinks half a litre of red wine *alla rinfusa*, and a Martell to finish.

He goes to the cinema. He watches three short films: "A Journey in the 'Astra' Airship", "A Player's Dream" and "Hans on the Island of Savages". *I'm becoming irritable*, he says, *how odd!* From time to time he touches the inside pocket of his coat. The gold heart is lying there.

He goes to the *variété* at the Sušak Hotel. There he hears a woman, very fat, saying: *A professeur de danse from l'Académie Internationale de Paris is coming! Monsieur Kümmelberg. Monsieur Kümmelberg will hold dancing classes at the Institute of Dance and Refinement. You have to register at the "Kobrax" shoe warehouse.*

Ludwig Jakob Fritz then buys Ottoman cigarette papers and says, *Give me some fine tobacco.* It is after midnight. He goes to the Hungaria, it's in complete darkness, the door is locked. He goes back along via Corso, turns into the via del Municipio, from there into via della Marecchia, goes to the *pissoir*, leaves the *pissoir*, walks a few dozen metres and stops at the entrance to 274. He knocks. *Two kronen, please*, says the doorman. *Mlle Clara?* says Ludwig Jakob Fritz. *Lulu?* asks the doorman. *Clara*, Ludwig Jakob Fritz repeats, he sits down at a small low table and orders a *grappa*. The room is filled with smoke. At the counter, a man of slight stature, with a large head and thick moustache that almost covers his lower lip, is leaning on the counter discussing something loudly with two young men and occasionally letting his eyes wander round the room. Music is playing softly.

Today's Croatia knows neither how to listen intelligently, nor how to complain intelligently. It listens, but only half-heartedly, it does not draw any conclusions; it mutters, complains, but half-heartedly, not conclusively. In a word: it does everything indecisively, inconclusively, neither here nor there, in a state of contradiction and paralysis; it does not pursue either conservative or radical politics, today it does not pursue any politics at all, and that is the worst kind of politics! exclaims the gentleman with the moustache.

Ludwig Jakob Fritz listens. He tells the waiter, *I feel like Croatia.* The waiter tells Ludwig Jakob Fritz, *That's Mr Supilo, he's a big shot in the newspapers.* Madame comes up to Mr Supilo, because Mr Supilo asks, *Madame?* And Madame says, *Letitia is ready.*

They are not in favour of democratisation, they are not in favour of extending the electoral laws, they are not for the popularisation of political forces. In the office of the Austro-Hungarian Ambassador Forgach in Belgrade, the reprobate Friedjung falsifies documents about our alleged high treason. Pribićević emerges as an opportunist. The young are our future. The Yugoslav peoples have to extract themselves from the embrace of Austria–Hungary. Pašić emerges as a hegemonist, the Yugoslav countries must be equal. It is pointless to stay here, there is nothing left here, there is nothing for me here. I am leaving. I am going to Italy. I am going to England. I die in London in 1917, in my forty-seventh year. Paralysed. Half-blind. On the edge of madness. From syphilis.

The *Saxonia* is anchored in front of the Emigrés' Hotel, where there's an indescribable crowd, Ludwig Jakob Fritz had heard of the Emigrés'

Hotel from Consul Slocum, and he had also learned something about it, the hotel, from his *Guida di Fiume*. But now, he sees that huge white building for the first time and shudders. The Emigrés' Hotel isn't situated in the centre of town like those elegant hotels in whose armchairs and cafés the people whose money feeds the town recline, the people who feed on the town, who drain the town, who are gently rocked on its generously bequeathed external gloss, stiff and infinitely tedious. The Emigrés' Hotel was built with money from the Hungarian government, in consultation with the Cunard Steam Ship Co. Ltd, and to the great delight of the authorities in Fiume, so that future émigrés from the Austro-Hungarian Monarchy should not wander aimlessly through this lovely, quiet, orderly town as they waited for the ships that would deliver them to a better life. Because this contented town, too full of exciting events, this town into which money pours of its own accord, situated admittedly a little on the edge, a little out of the way, this town would not now be able to tolerate having the penniless hanging about, especially as they are in any case on the point of leaving it. That is why the Emigrés' Hotel is placed there, in Industry Street, as at that time in this town all the industry is situated to one side, to generate, to fertilise, but not to get in the way, to be invisible, not to spoil the image of generally joyful living, which, that joyful living, is not a truly passionate joyfulness, but moderately passionate, measuredly passionate, a free-flowing and expendable joy of living, just as this town is all free-flowing, its joy of living is under great (self-control, directed by the stock exchange, the banks, insurance societies, secret accounts, it's a bottled-up joyfulness which is in fact a miserable joy, consumptive, because joy of living must be loud and wild and unrestrained. It's a provincial joyfulness, retold, badly reproduced, for a long time it has been an imitation of living, a great glossy surrogate, hollow.

And so it is to this day.

After the collapse of the Monarchy, the army takes up residence in the Emigrés' Hotel, then various exhibitions are held in the Emigrés' Hotel, which few visit, then the Emigrés' Hotel is redesigned, the large dormitories are converted into small rooms and all of it, the whole building, is called "Caserna Savoia", the town is falling apart, splitting, like a schizophrenic patient it splits, it is split, broken up, and, straddling Savoian Italy and Karađorđević Yugoslavia, it is dying before the eyes of its inhabitants and, in lucid and painful moments, it secretly wonders, how has all of this befallen me so suddenly? After the Second World War, when the town is somehow sewn together again, in the hope that this historical patching will with time disappear just as with time (and in rare cases) scars disappear from the human body, few remember the Emigrés' Hotel as a hotel for émigrés, because within its walls metal containers are produced, machines hum, the working class grows and strengthens, and today, when there is no longer either a working class or a "moral" intelligentsia, the building of the Emigrés' Hotel is nothing. That huge dead building, once filled with tons of spewed-out émigré pain, cocooned fear and hope, is today brought to life only when north winds dance through it. Like a corpse whose eyes people have forgotten to close, the high, blurred windows of that still-white monstrosity stare out unmoving (like the eyes of a *tabes* sufferer) at the equally dead street in which the hotel is interred. The stench of death creeps along Industry Street. A small, recently opened bakery at the entrance of which the shopkeeper stands with a white cap on his head and invites rare passers-by to come in, *Come in, come in,* he smiles, *Try our buns,* seems like a crystal tear that has just happened, by chance, to fall from the sky.

Here there never was, and nor will there ever be, a Toulouse-Lautrec or a Modigliani, and so neither was there a Miss Hastings or a Jeanne Hébuterne, no carefreeness, breeziness or passion, above this town there will never hover the spirit of a small but powerful *bonvivant* to intoxicate his followers with injections of *joie de vivre*, a whole army of known and unknown, talented and talentless, healthy and sick, rich and poor, who unbutton their bodies luxuriously, because this was (and remained) a town in a corset, tragically constricted.

How is it that there are towns far from the Mediterranean, that there are towns which are not bathed in sunshine, not splashed by the sea, but which pulsate as though they would burst, out of defiance if nothing else? It is usually a lie that the heat of the air warms the blood, that the scent of flora fuels the imagination, for a long time now this town has seemed petrified and dumb, while those various allegedly enchanting little plants that penetrate its soul, those divine trees that surround it, are capable of provoking great inhalations and exhalations of hardship and are nothing but an excuse. There is no trace of Môme Fromage, Nini-Pattes-en-l'air, Jane Avril, Georgette Macarona, La Gouloue, of any kind of *chahuteuse*. If there were dancers and singers, if there were actresses and women poets and painters, they must have died buttoned up to the throat in lacy nightgowns, as old maids or devoted mothers, wives and Catholics, or they married rich old men and only thanks to them became well known in "their town".

And so it is to this day.

How is it that no trace has taken root here of Hugo Ball and Emmy Hastings, Huelsenbeck, Richter, Arp, Tzara, the Janco brothers, Walter Sterner, although they were here, in the neighbourhood, all contemporaries of Ludwig Jakob Fritz. Operatic divas come, but not the satirical ballads of Frank Wedekind, that *enfant terrible* of the Munich avant-garde, while, for this town, the caustic poems of the anarchist Mühsam seem not to echo in Berlin but on some virtual continent; Isidora Duncan comes, but Else Lasker-Schüler doesn't flirt her way along the Opatija shore; Verdi's arias fill the lethargic minds and lazy lungs of the (half-) urban flock, while for a long time Ibsen's plays remain distant.

*

This is a town, this is a country on the edge of the universe, a miniature satellite that has broken off from its own self, and all that remains for it is to circle its own axis, invisible, unseen and soundless. It may not be just, but that is how it is. That is what those who lived here and who still live here wanted and accepted. That a small, pale spirochaete, invisible to the eye, should insert itself into their lives; it burrows, burrows and burrows, and transforms healthy people into infectious monsters.

Perhaps the only resistant material in this town were its workers, not its history, its history was foul and acquisitive, but there are ever fewer of them, those workers, nowadays; pressed into clods like little snowmen out of fairy tales, they roll dumbly over their own inner and outer wilderness. Nowadays there is no metal foundry, paper factory, tobacco factory – once the largest in the whole Monarchy; the rice-husking plant is long since dead, as is the sugar refinery, and the chocolate factory and the fish-canning factory, as is the silk mill, the cord workshop, and the cement and pasta factories. It's all dead, it's a time of "exitus".

The carnival flourishes, however.

However.

There are no more cobblers making shoes to measure, no coopers, no glove makers, no milliners, no umbrella makers, no brush makers, there are no shops lit by elegant crystal chandeliers and hushed by red carpets, selling pianos and other musical instruments (Klavier Niederlage von J. Potošnjak, Haus Cante, Cappuccinergasse no. 609, I. Stock), there is no Galanterie-Lederwaren (grösstes Lager von Pferdegeschirr, Reitzeuge, alle Arten von Sport und Stallrequisiten, A. Lippitsch, Corso 542, Koffer, Taschen, Reisenecessaires, Plaidträger, Riemen, Schultaschen, alles aus eigener Erzeugung, Reparaturen prompt), there are no toyshops, no serious bookshops, there are no clubs, no special little workshops, goods are stuffed into department stores, merchandise is sold in bulk, en masse, there's no exclusive, personalised service because there are ever fewer exclusive individuals here, the cinema halls gape, empty, first nights at theatres are attended mostly by doctors. Only, there are no hunchbacks in the streets, *Where have all the hunchbacks gone?* And the few that there are tend to be women.

Do you have any hunchback patients? I ask my doctor, a woman. *They seem to have disappeared*, she says. There are no cripples either and the homeless are quite decently dressed.

At the chemist's, the pharmacist, a woman, says, *I am torn apart by doubt, I doubt the outcome, the outcome is very doubtful*, she says it twice, a politician also says twice, *I am above all a Catholic, first and foremost a Catholic*, there's no point in mentioning his name. The Minister of Education addresses *his* fathers and mothers, O*ur dear fathers and mothers*, he says; the wittiest television programme is the news because then everyone is deadly serious, *The electricity network is in a critical state, but* *all forces have been engaged.* How has this town, how has this country been so terribly deprived of humour?

*

The Emigrés' Hotel is a hotel with five hundred beds, Ludwig Jakob Fritz learns from his guidebook, and the Emigrés' Hotel is a very long hotel, it has to be long because it's not very high, a mere seventy or so metres, how else would all those beds for all those indigent refugees fit into it? That hotel is a hundred and sixty metres long, longer than three Olympic swimming pools. Outside, it is smooth, without ornamentation, what would the indigent do with external decoration? In it there are eight large and six small rooms, there are apartments for families, which seems to Ludwig Jakob Fritz both refined and pointless. From his *Guida di Fiume*, Ludwig Jakob Fritz also learns that the Emigrés' Hotel has reception rooms, a clinic, a shop and a restaurant. *I don't wish to enter that hotel. At all,* he says, and disappears into the mass of people waiting to embark. He gets lost.

I am the *Saxonia*. I am waiting. My innards are shaking. My propellers are still, I rock like a cradle or like a coffin, I don't know.

The thin iron bridge creaks.

Four thousand feet prowl over me, four thousand soles tap over me, pressing me down, tramping on me, but for a long time, for eighty years already, I have not been here, like my sister, *Ivernia*. For twelve years we have sailed on the up-market tourist route Liverpool-Boston, like two adored ladies, spoiled. But now, in 1911, obsolete and neglected, why, we are already old, we are old, now the owners of the Cunard Line are transferring us to a new sea, into a dense, lame sea, where the port of Fiume and the port of Trieste lie like seductresses, legs spread, bequeathing us their rubbish. They throw a heavy cargo into us, a living cargo that embarks of its own accord, quietly, without stopping, and for a long time bringing our owners an enormous profit. Trading people is a profitable business.

On each tour we toss on icy seas, we draw near to New York, in New York we discharge this living freight and watch Liberty waving to us, she grows, and grows, and then we turn our backs on her, and she again becomes ever smaller, ever smaller, she lies on the horizon and sinks into infinity. And so it is, until the war of 1914, to and fro, to and fro.

Then, I part for ever from the *Ivernia* and never discover where or how she dies. Liverpool, my first port, then the Thames, tight and tedious, where I lie, I just lie, anchored, and I

Four thousand eyes look, four thousand hands touch, with a frozen smile, with frozen breath, and tears.

Dumbly, quietly, on the bridge, the émigrés watch and wonder, when will the ship move its heavy belly towards a new country. From the shore thousands of eyes, from the ship thousands of eye follow its movement, and a voice again reaches out in greeting, a hand blows a kiss, noise, noise, noise, the bridge is already lowered, handkerchiefs wave farewell, the innards shake with the titanic power of the propellers, the lamps tremble like stars in an earthquake, then a quick turn right and left, she is already racing at a crazy speed, and the town disappears.

sway absurdly, like a fat lady, immobile, where they fill me again with living cargo, with people, also miserable, also deceived, a cargo of prisoners of war.

During the war, from time to time they smarten me up, I have patches and stitches all over, old bodies cannot become new, so they send me off again onto the open sea on tedious voyages, pathetically dolled up, like some American or Austrian pensioner, now only outwardly resembling what I was in my youth, it is my swansong, I know. Liverpool–New York, New York–Liverpool, in 1915 and 1916, ladies and gentlemen dance waltzes on me, they drink champagne and dance, they eat little tea cakes and chat, then they dance again, on my decks passengers smoke and kiss and lie in the sun, when there is sun, as though they are lung patients escaped from a Swiss sanatorium, life is orderly despite the war, the war is a long way off, and I am bored, things are no longer what they were. My owners sell me to my government, I am ready to go, but my government says no, not yet. For two years, under duress, completely against my will, I take American soldiers from France back to their homeland, a noisy and interesting cargo. I am dolled up again, I tell them enough is enough, but they reduce the height of my funnel, lessen the number of cabins, extend my holds, now it is quiet, dead, spacious, with no railings, filled with leather suitcases and wooden crates, no longer with the smell of stale human bodies, the smell of salted fish, the smell of undigested garlic, urine, the smell of broken dreams. Ah, those dreams, those mouldy hopes. They drag me like this for five years, I drag myself from London to New York and back, sometimes I call in to Hamburg, Hamburg is a green city, it is not sunny, it is not grey, just green, in 1924 I say I cannot go on, I cannot go on and I sail to Holland, into the embrace of leaseholders, adept middlemen, merciless ship-dismantlers, and I disappear, I collapse into millions of tiny steel atoms.

That is my life.

"Tasch, Konrad! Betschkerek. Hungary."

"Here. I'm forty-eight years old, I'm travelling with my wife Magdalena (45) and my children, Katarina (16), Barbara (14), Franz (11) and Amanda (9). Shoemaker."

Vaccinated. All examined. Clothes disinfected. They won't send us back. The hold is refurbished as private bedrooms for single men, single women and families. Iron bunk beds, three on each side. The food we brought with us went bad. It stinks in the cabin. There is no water. There is no air, it is very hot. For three weeks we do not wash. We throw up. We have lice. We are travelling to my brother Peter, he is a carpenter.

"Krausz, Michael! Fusinia. Austria."

"Yes! Twenty-four. Wine-grower. Wife Sofia, seventeen. Father in Chicago, Karlo Kraus, merchant."

The air is terrible. Thick. The toilets are dirty and always occupied. One old man was caught short waiting. Afterwards he cried. He had brown trousers, soaked with stinking thin shit. There are twenty-one toilets and there are a thousand of us. We eat in the dining-room.

"Cziczka, Elisabeta! Glogowatz, Hungary."

"Here! Fifteen. I'm going to my father, Anton, in Portland."

The tables are very long, for more than fifty people. They are wooden tables, there is never any room. I eat in the hold, from a metal dish, I eat alone. They eat off aluminium plates. Sometimes we each get a glass of wine. We eat a lot of potatoes. I've got little scabs all over my body, my nose is constantly blocked. I haven't got any nail scissors. If my mother were alive, it would be easier.

"Buban, Milosz! Delnice, Austria."

"Bubanj. Croat. Twenty-seven. Wife Maria, née Dorner, twenty-five. Son Anton, four. We are going to my uncle Bojan Beck, in Iowa."

On the boat Maria starts to bleed. A doctor comes, but it is too late. It was a little girl, he says. Maria has a fever. Hang on a little longer, I keep saying. Anton shrieks. The fish is salted, I think they are herrings. We eat a lot of bread, there is plenty of bread. They let the first- and second-class passengers off earlier. They go in special little boats, there aren't many of them. They load us onto ferries. It takes the whole day. Later, they changed our surname to Bubany, and then to Bubane, it is pronounced Byubayn. Anton became Tony, now he's called Tony Bubane, they left me my first name, I'm still called Miloš, they just write it a bit differently because their letters don't have little extra bits like ours.

"Weiszmann, Stefan! Kikinda, Hungary."

"That's me. Thirty. Wife – Majda, twenty-seven, maiden name Pelat. Children: Eva, eight, and Johann, five."

From a wooden jetty on the Hudson River, they

take us across to Ellis Island on barges. It's slow, there's a strong wind. It's cold. The barge stops. Three children suffering from measles die, just like that. The bay is crammed with boats at a standstill. It takes us six hours to reach Ellis Island, which is right here, in front of us. First they take off the dead children, people shove. There is a huge crowd, there are thousands and thousands of people. The dead children are the first immigrants to America from our barge. They take the little dead children away quickly. Their mothers scream and run after the orderlies.

"Taub, Wilma, Bribir, Austria."

"Here! Thirty-five. I'm travelling alone. I'm going to my cousin, George Giel."

I have one leg shorter than the other, but I'm healthy. I pass the medical test with no problem. I have nice hair, blond. I'm a seamstress, I'll get on, seamstresses are always needed. On the ship there aren't enough lifeboats, the toilets are blocked. In the Bay, more than twenty thousand passengers are waiting to disembark, but they don't take more than a thousand. Everything is at a standstill. Some people have been waiting for two days in the open. On Ellis Island, before going into the building, which is in fact a hangar, they give us cardboard labels with a string through them. Every label has a number. Mine is 27-39. I don't know what that means.

"Jarak, Magdalena! Osiek, Hungary."

"Here. Thirty-four years old. I have two children: this is David, thirteen, and this is Ida, nine. We're going to Illinois. My husband Stjepan is there. He's a farmer."

We came in 1911. On the "Saxonia", but this
happened in 1915. Two weeks before I gave birth,
Stjepan was caught stealing. He stole a hen. They shot
at him and killed him. Then Ivan was born, that's
what I called him, Ivan, but I don't know what he's
called now. I gave him away. Some people adopted
him. I had to give him away, I was alone with two
children. I washed laundry and worked in maize
fields. I had to give him away. Ivan is John in English.

"Papp, Georg. Starigrad, Austria."

"Yes! Twenty-seven. Single. I'm going to St Louis.
I have an uncle there."

We had all kinds of labels on our chests. Several of
them. We looked like livestock at a market. They turn
some people back. Those they turn back just pull their
hair out and beat their breasts, they don't understand
anything and they can't say anything because they
don't speak American, the third-class passengers are
very poor. The officials shout and point their fingers
to the line we're supposed to stand in, there are a lot of
lines. My line is terribly long. Then there's an inspec-
tion, and after the inspection come the doctors. They
decide who is to stay.

"Albanese, Matteo! Castelmuschio, Austria."

"Qui! Omišalj. Thirty-three. Wife Christina, thirty,
sons Auro, seven, and Bruno, five. I have an uncle in
Philadelphia. I'm a fisherman.'

They thought that we didn't know. While we climb
the stairs to the registration office, doctors, medical
orderlies, customs men, policemen, they all just look
at us. They look to see whether anyone coughs or
pants as he climbs, they are checking whether anyone

is crippled or lame. They ask the children their names,
in fact they are looking for deaf and dumb children, as
though there were no deaf and dumb Americans.
They take the children who look older than two
away from their mothers and order them to walk,
Vok, they say. Then the children cry.

I am Dr Samuel Volk. American. I was born in New York. My father came
to this country sixty years ago. From Osijek. He was a bookbinder. It was
easier to get in then. It is not our fault, a lot of people arrive every day. The
law requires rigorous examinations to be carried out, while we have less
than a minute for each passenger. In one minute we have to look out for
sixty symptoms, particularly anaemia and enlarged veins. There are cases
of cholera and fungal disease. There are mental patients, there are epilep-
tics. The authorities here are most anxious about those with trachoma,
which leads to blindness and finally death. Most trachoma patients arrive
here from the south and east of Europe. Sick people don't have a hope here.
This country is looking for healthy people, and young ones. We send back
all the seriously ill immigrants. My eyes wander non-stop over these dirty
and terrified arrivals. My eyes spin constantly. In the evening, my head
aches from all that spinning. I feel like a jackal.

"Androk, Milica. Perkovici. Hungary."

"I am Androk Milica. I'm eighteen years old. I'm
going to Detroit, to my grandfather, Matija."

The eye examination is the worst. The doctors turn
back our upper eyelid with their fingers to see whether
our eyes are inflamed. Of course they are inflamed,
you sleep badly on the ship. We've been travelling for
three weeks, exactly three weeks. I am very thin; I'm
afraid I won't get through. Some doctors use a hair-
slide instead of their fingers or a little hook for doing
up buttons, they don't want to touch us. We are all
most afraid of those doctors who turn back our eyelids.

*We call them "hookers". The sick immigrants are
marked with blue chalk and taken off somewhere.*

"Angjelic, Kata! Fiume, Hungary."

"Here! Forty-six. I'm going to my son. I'm a
widow."

*Later, they changed my name, I became Catherine
Angel, and they called me Kate. Some people with
minor illnesses were first treated, then they would let
them onto dry land, into their country. People with
incurable diseases were returned to the port they
left from, the costs of transportation were borne by
the steamship company. We learned that later from
letters. The checks were becoming increasingly strict
because the American authorities charged the steamship company a hundred dollars for every passenger
they turned back. That was a lot of money in those
days. My son's monthly salary.*

*The doctors wrote some letters in blue chalk on the
sick passengers. I saw that with my own eyes.*

*Yes. Pregnant women were marked "Pg", people with hernias were marked
with the letter "H". The mentally ill were marked "X". They, and those with
physical defects, which is, I confess, crazy, not to say cruel, we examine
most thoroughly. We give them intelligence tests, standard tests, simple
arithmetical problems, then they have to count backwards, from twenty to
one, or do a simple jigsaw that we call a puzzle here. With time we became
experienced, we put together special tests, designed for immigrants from
different areas so that the examination should be as objective as possible.
We test their ability to learn. The immigrants have to copy simple geometric figures, repeat specific sounds, but there are those who have never held
a pencil and they find it all very difficult. I am not particularly enthralled
by my job. I work from nine in the morning till seven at night, I examine
up to five hundred immigrants in a day, but I am the first person in my*

family to have completed higher education and I am proud of that. I am
fifty-five years old.

"Forenpohar, Gyoka! Mrkopalj, Hungary."

"That's me! Nineteen, unmarried. I'm going to my father Pavle. He's a forester."

It's just as well I'm not a woman. They don't let women step onto their soil without a male escort. As a woman, if you have relatives here, they have to come for you, or they can send a telegram. You can't work on the black market. I waited five hours for my turn for the inspection. Then they told me, Kam hir, gou der, luk up, luk daun, bend over, stend ap, oupen yur maut, kaunt wan-tu-tri, tri-tu-wan, sey aaaa, sey chiiz. Then they took us into another hall with lots of iron barricades, they were narrow, marked-off walkways, and we stood there in long lines again. In the end we reached the inspectors, they all had stiff white collars and heavy black coats. Some were sweating. The inspectors checked our documents all over again. Every questionnaire had twenty-nine items. Once again we had to give our names, say how old we were, where we had come from, where we were going to, what was our marital status, what we did for a living, who would be waiting for us. Some people translated everything we said. Twenty-nine questions, twenty-nine answers that we had already given. Those who were older than sixteen had to read a few sentences in their own language, mostly sentences from the Bible. Luckily I can read. They gave me this: "Your wealth is rotting, your clothes are all moth-eaten. All your gold and silver are corroding away, and the same corrosion will be a witness against you and eat into your body." When I read this, I was terrified. A girl had come with her fiancé. She had to marry him there and then. They had all kinds of priests standing by. I heard that there was even a hospital on this little island. That's where they take people with diphtheria and measles. I have had measles and I am very strong. At the exit, my father was waiting. Before that, the inspection told me to "sey chiiz" again. When I said "chiiz", two of them then said "velkam tu Amerika". I'm not called Đoka anymore, but George, and my surname is Forhar, they've made it a bit shorter, Forenpohar is hard for them to pronounce.

"Domaldovich, Paolo! Moschenisse, Austria."

"Si, signore, that's me, sono io. Forty-seven years old. Daughter Barbara, twenty-two. Widower. I had a vineyard. I sold it. My son Pietro is here, he'll come for us."

The hospital on this island has 450 beds. They kept Barbara, I don't know why. They said she was pale. Pietro and I waited in New York in a little church hostel for men. Then we went to the zoo. That's in a poor district called Bronx, I had never been to a zoo. The animals were hiding because it was snowing. I had never seen snow. We called the animals and fed them with bread left over from our breakfast. Pietro told me that Caruso had sung here. I had heard of him. Since we've been here our surname has been Aldovic, here "c" is pronounced "k", I no longer write my name Paolo, but Paul, it's pronounced very long, Poool. Pietro told me straight away that on his health card his name is written Peter, I saw it for myself when we registered at the church hostel: Peter Aldovic, as though he wasn't my son.

There were worse cases. My friend Josip Ružić

became Joseph Russick and he cried. We didn't cry, we opened a winery. And Lovro Mejaski, a miner from Barilović is now called John Markey. He says he doesn't care because this life here has nothing to do with his life at home, that Lovro Mejaski and John Markey are two different people who sometimes meet but they don't know each other, I am now a different man, he says, I'm American.

They let Barbara go after four days. She told us that in that hospital on Ellis Island there is a ward for the deranged. She told us that one woman gave birth in that ward although she was not mad. She told us that there was a morgue in that hospital as well.

I have seen my fill of all manner of things. I have spent my entire working life on this island. In that year, 1911, there were fifteen buildings for the health care of immigrants on Ellis Island. There were forty doctors. On Ellis Island, from 1892 up to 1954, when the little island stopped receiving people, three and a half thousand people died, of whom fourteen hundred were children. Which is not all that terrible when one knows that over those fifty and a bit years, just through this reception point, more than twelve million new future citizens of this great democratic country entered America. The worst was 1907, when they came in floods. Then, in one day, the reception office had to deal with 11,747 immigrants. Three hundred and fifty children were born on Ellis Island, thereby immediately becoming Americans. There were three suicides as well, as far as I know. Reality does not always enter into statistics.

Today Ellis Island is a national park. There's a museum on the island with abundant photographs, some are monstrously enlarged, so much so that their outlines become blurred. There are miscellaneous sepia-tone photographs where the faces are indistinct; there are impenetrable photographs, covered with the dull protective film of the past, but not oblivion. On the island oleanders bloom, the grass is tended, full of pesticides, so it's intensely green. There are houses on the little island, with forgotten people living in them; those who perhaps never fully disembarked, people who came to America, but didn't enter the country. These people have been living for decades in the national park, to one side. There are two inns on Ellis Island. The owners are Greeks, or perhaps Italians, no matter. They speak a bastard mixture of languages in which the traces of what was perhaps their life may be guessed at. They serve modified dishes from "the old country", adapted dishes that no-one orders, dishes which, like them, are "neither here nor there". On cheap little tables there are plastic bottles of ketchup and mayonnaise, the glasses are also plastic, the coffee is filtered, with no taste, with no aroma. The halls in which for sixty years the healthy American nation was coming into being are today clean and empty, the work is more or less done. Those are exhibition halls, museum halls through which a dull nostalgia howls, through which a mournful nausea slinks. There are few visitors, the walls exude horror and unease, even a whisper echoes, from a distance comes the rhythmic tapping of shuffling footsteps crowded together, patiently waiting to cross the threshold above which is written, *Your old world is far behind. America has accepted you. From here everything changes.* But.

Millions of meteors pass through cyberspace every second, in cyberspace whole galaxies flicker. These are meteors of memory, they are seeking stars, they are stories heavier than every measurable burden. Our whole, taxed, uprooted, scattered global population, and not only Americans, hover in that vast, non-existent space, calling and begging: tell us who our forebears are, who we are.

If one listens carefully, from somewhere comes the voice of the crazed Mrs Alving:

Ghosts! . . . But I almost think we are all of us ghosts
. . . It is not only what we have inherited from our
father and mother that "walks" in us. It is all sorts of
dead ideas, and lifeless old beliefs, and so forth. They
have no vitality, but they cling to us all the same, and

we cannot shake them off. Whenever I take up a
newspaper, I seem to see ghosts gliding between the
lines. There must be ghosts all the country over, as
thick as the sands of the sea. And then we are, one
and all, so pitifully afraid of the light.

There are nice places here, only they're hidden. Like that second-hand bookshop in a building known as the "little skyscraper", which is in fact an ordinary residential building, neither strikingly high nor strikingly low. Since the old part of the town is laid out horizontally, whatever doesn't fit into its horizontalness acquires a special name, and is labelled, sometimes tongue-in-cheek, like that "little skyscraper".

In this second-hand bookshop, two young men, nested in the past, wait for someone to drop in. When one looks out from inside this second-hand bookshop crammed with all kinds of colourfulness and made up of passages, secret spaces and wooden staircases, so that it is possible to roam through it as through a labyrinth, when one looks out at the street, the street gives the impression of being empty, as though darkness were gathering outside, ever denser and blacker. There's an old armchair in the bookshop too, antique, for sitting in, for leafing through books, there are stools and chests. In the bookshop, as well as books, there are also boxes with old records, old documents and postcards, there are maps of the world. The shop seems to have detached itself from the town, and now it circles above it, not knowing whether it should land or forever move away. In the shop I find three books, Stephenson's *The Strange Case of Dr Jekyll and Mr Hyde* (London: Longman's, Green and Company, 1886), *Alice's Adventures in Wonderland* by Lewis Carroll (N.Y.: Gilbert H. McKibbin, 1899), and one of my favourites, *The Narrative of Arthur Gordon Pym*, by Edgar Allan Poe (London: Downey & Co. Limited, 1898) in a blue canvas cover with several black and white illustrations by a certain McCormick. I use my card to buy all three for four hundred kunas and settle down in the old armchair. I open the books and see, on the first page, the signature of their former owner – Ludwig Jakob Fritz.

For forty years the name of Ludwig and the connection of that name with syphilis were outside my reality. I believed that the name was buried along with the destiny of the man to whom it belonged. That all traces of this uninteresting destiny had been swept away by time, that the ghosts of the dead visit the living in literature, in literary fabrications, and that reality is made up of paths which branch off indefinitely, without the slightest prospect of their ever connecting and intertwining anywhere, at any time. That time devours itself until it disperses into microscopic particles out of which a new time, no less sick, but more bearable – our time, the present – is born. That it is possible to grasp the course of that time, place it in its channel and tell it how and where it should flow so as not to disintegrate again. And now, the name of Ludwig Jakob Fritz, imprinted nearly a hundred years ago in the musty books lying in my lap, has risen up like some kind of ghost out of its grave where no grave-stone was placed, a grave that has been waiting, open, for who knows how long, and of which it is not known when (or whether) someone will deign to close up its dark innards, lower the cover and turn their back on the pit of the past, leaving it up to the modest and monstrous dead in that tomb to devour one another or to dance their own life, as they please, and leave the rest of us in peace.

I ask the young men whether the name Ludwig Jakob Fritz means anything to them, because they follow who was who and who was once what in this town, I ask casually, perhaps afraid that I might learn some detail I would not know what to do with. But they both say, in unison, that they've *Never heard of him. The books were brought by an old lady,* they say, *who maintained that she was originally from here, from this coun-try, but she had been living for a long time in Colorado. Her surname was Kogoj.* I immediately assume that she must be the sister of Dr Kogoj, because Dr Kogoj had recently died so now her sister, of whom Dr Kogoj had told me that she really did live in America and that she visited this town very rarely, but that she regularly sent her clothes, sometimes new, sometimes second-hand, so now her sister, after she had buried Dr Kogoj, was no doubt distributing her belongings, throwing away what was to be discarded and selling whatever could be turned into a bit of cash.

I came to know Dr Kogoj when she contacted me by telephone because, as she later told me, she had heard my name when someone mentioned it in an unconnected conversation, which just goes to show that names are passed around orally here, not for any real purpose, but rather for the sake of distraction. As soon as I picked up the receiver, Dr Kogoj said, self-confidently, although with a barely perceptible tremor in her voice that I put down to her age: *Dr Kogoj here*, as though it would be quite normal for me to know who Dr Kogoj was, but I had absolutely no idea. I had lived in this town for only a few years, fairly isolated, that is to say without employment or regular income, so, logically, I was invisible and uninteresting, and particularly invisible and uninteresting to those with substantial incomes and prestigious positions (political, social, cultural). (This could no longer be said today, today there's global invisibility here, we're all small, some in one way, others in a different way, we're erased, we erase ourselves from the register, we enter a world of shadows and delusions.) That's why there was nothing strange about my not having heard of Dr Kogoj who, like myself indeed, had taken herself off to the margins since she retired, while I could only dream of retirement. As I said nothing, Dr Kogoj said, *I was at university with your mother*. Then I said that my mother had spent half her university course in an Ustasha prison in Franjo Rački Street where she was beaten by Inspector Kamber, and that she had graduated later, when she already had children, studying at night, after she had fed her children with revolting pancakes filled with spinach, because of the iron, and little balls of minced horse meat, because at that time horse meat was cheap and wholesome, it had not yet become fashionable and most people said *Yuck* at the idea of eating it. Then Dr Kogoj said, *Come and see me, we can have a chat*.

I spent many evenings at Verena Kogoj's. As a rule, people here don't gather very often at private apartments because it costs money. There are quite a few people here who are reluctant to spend money. Many people here prefer to sit in their narrow family circle, and when they're bored with that, they get together in a café and share the costs, which is fair, that's my view now too.

As well as my visits to Dr Kogoj, I used to go and see Sonja. I wanted to invite both of them, Verena and Sonja, to my apartment, I wanted to give them a festive little dinner, with crystal glasses and silver cutlery, the ones my grandmother left me, engraved with the monogram A.O., I wanted to do that very much, because they were both like mothers to me, Sonja in particular, in fact, Sonja was someone I simply loved, Sonja was special, in other words, they were like mothers with whom I could once again be small and insignificant, with whom I could have a good cry. But both Dr Kogoj and Sonja were old (and very ill) and they didn't leave the house. Now that they're both gone, a terrible emptiness sometimes comes over me and settles like a cat in my lap, nestling there, leaning against my belly that throbs as though it were a heart.

I was in the Ustasha prison too, Dr Kogoj told me, immediately, in the doorway. *In the cell next to your mother*, she said. Then she told me that she had finished the classical gymnasium, *At the time of the Independent State of Croatia*, she said that at that time *Schools worked relatively normally, at least to start with*, she said. She told me that later they had lessons two or three times a week and that there were the children of communists and the children of Ustashas, and mostly the children of those who kept their mouths firmly shut the whole time. *One pupil*, she said, *used to come to classes in an Ustasha uniform with a pistol in his belt, and the teachers approved because they conformed. I can't tell you his name*, she said, *he's still alive, he's old, but still alive.* Dr Kogoj enrolled at the Medical Faculty in 1943, at the same time as my mother, but she was immediately thrown out, she said, they threw her father out as well, by then a famous dermato-venereologist and university professor. They threw my mother out a few months later, because my mother was already in the underground movement so they didn't know that she was against them, those Ustashas.

I was admitted to the League of Young Communists in June 1941, the Split branch. In Zagreb I was given the

underground name of Katica. In a shoe shop on the
little square below Pantovčak, I was handed hiking
boots "so as to get around Zagreb more easily"... In a
Dalmatian folk shoulder-bag I carried the testimo-
nials of people who were joining the Partisans and I
took them to 24 Medvedgradska where I entered them
into file. I had to look elegant and unobtrusive, so I ex-
changed the hiking boots for white court shoes. I changed
my hairstyle and wound plaits round my head ...

In the dissection room of the Anatomical Institute,
armed Ustasha students, ostensibly studying, followed
our movements ...

When the Ustashas threw Professor Franjo Kogoj out of Zagreb University, his wife, also a doctor, a paediatrician, didn't have much work either; mothers entrusted their children to proven specialists of Ustasha origin, for the sake of peace and general security. *We lived in my grandfather's house, we recently sold it,* says Dr Kogoj, *We were left with this console table,* she says, *and a Chinese vase, see, look over there in the corner, those are the remains, the pathetic remains of an even more pathetic past which I am now cracking open.*

We're drinking brandy, standard lamps and table lamps are lit, the light is soft, it sways. A scruffy white dog, small and old, sits curled up on a *bergère*, every so often it opens its left eye, glances at me, raises its left eyebrow, sighs, then exhales loudly.

Father had a private dermato-venereological clinic, that clinic kept us fed during the war, says Dr Kogoj. *I had to do something,* she says, *so I helped the National Institute for the Deaf and Dumb, that's where they placed the children from the Kozara Mountain, Serbian children, it's not advisable to talk about that these days.*

I am a witness. There was a terrible process of liquida-
tion in the summer of 1942, when a group of people

was brought from Kozara. The women and children were immediately transferred to Gradina, and the men to a labour camp. In Gradina, because there were so many of them, it wasn't possible to kill them by cutting their throats or with cudgel; it was done with machine guns. Their clothes were taken to the camp and sorted for rag rugs.

I am Dr Budicki, I am no longer alive. Children came to Gradiška too, with their parents, but not so many of them. They were liquidated long before. In June 1942 there were more than one and a half thousand of them. I thought I would be able to save some. At the beginning of July they took several hundred off to that old Turkish house near the Orthodox church. The Ensign Ante and someone else bludgeoned them to death with hammers.

There were a few bigger boys there with them, who realised what was going on and shrieked horrifically. The slaughter lasted three and a half hours. The Ensign complained that it was very tiring.

The following year, on St Anthony's Day, another four hundred or so children disappeared. The windows of a house were sealed, the way it's done when lice are exterminated. They were poisoned with Zyklon.

It's true. Dr Budicki told me about it. I am no longer alive either, but I left documents, I made notes of it all. Four hundred children were gassed, one thousand two hundred, eighty per cent in other words, were killed with hammers and gas over several days, if they had not already died of exhaustion. But that's not all the children who passed through this camp. Around three hundred of them were still alive. They kept the

186

sweetest, chattiest little girls and the sturdiest, prettiest boys. They were sent to a children's home, if there was space there. If not, the problem was solved by making a new selection and killing the surplus.

Over the days that followed, that selection really was carried out. For several nights more children were gassed in the same way. Along with old men and women this time.

Although it was a closely kept secret in the camp, something nevertheless must have got through to humane people in Zagreb, because a delegation arrived unexpectedly from the Red Cross. They asked for the children. There was some haggling. The Ustashas wanted to delay the handover until nice little uniforms and still nicer caps were ready. But the people from the Red Cross did not care about uniforms or caps, just the children. There were telephone conversations with Zagreb and finally the children were handed over. Only the seriously ill stayed behind. Their lives were soon extinguished.

Yours,

Ilija Jakovljević[*]

Dr Kogoj told me that those children from Kozara looked like living skeletons, *And there were an awful lot of children, a lot of small children*

* Dr Ilija Jakovljević (21 October, 1898, Mostar-28 October, 1948, Zagreb(?)) - writer, journalist, editor and lawyer. He was involved in the Croatian Catholic Movement between 1915 and 1930 and was also a member of the Croatian People's Party during this time. During the Second World War he was interned in the prisoner-of-war camp in Stara Gradiška but was later released. Towards the end of the war, due to impending threats of arrest, he joined the Partisan movement and, after peace was restored, resumed his law practice. In 1948 he was arrested in the course of investigations into the "Hebrang case". His death in prison was never fully explained. This extract is adapted from his book *Konc-logor na Savi* ("The Concentration Camp by the River Sava"). Translator's note.

and they were dying like flies, she said. *I know*, she said, *they took their bodies away at night, and I helped.* Dr Kogoj told me that they were in the large hall of the National Institute for the Deaf and Dumb, *On Ilica Square*, she said, *number 83, I think*, she said, that the children were placed there, five or six to a bed. People took the children to look after them, she said, and some were adopted. She said that she simply had to take one boy, she took him home, to her family, he was called Milovan, she said, he was not even three years old, she said, she had to take him, because Milovan kept following her around, he tugged at her white coat and kept saying, take me home, lady. *At our house, Milovan developed whooping cough and measles*, Dr Kogoj told me, *He would have died if he had been left at the Institute. When the war was over, in 1945, Milovan's mother came for him. He no longer had a father, his father was killed by the Ustashas.*

Remarkable! When those children were bathed, fed and their clothes changed, when they put on a little flesh, they would become like other children. It's true that they were Vlachs, but who in their right mind cares about that? That's just for the newspapers and propaganda. A movement has to have some kind of ideology.

Quite a number of Catholic and Muslim children perished in the regions where the Chetnik condottieri attacked. Those gangs were just as expert at stabbing a child with a knife as the Ustasha heroes! That loss will have to be recouped. At least two little Serbs for every little Croat! And who's going to prove that they really are Serbs – who can even think of that when they are being saved by our Ustashas and our wonderful Leader! When all is said and done, Serbs do have the hearts of frontiersmen, these little ones could have been trained up as excellent janissaries. No-one knows who their father or mother is, the state

will embrace them and turn these little boys into
exceptional non-commissioned officers and police-
men. You just have to drive into their heads that their
parents gave their lives for the Leader and the crown
of Zvonimir, and you'll see that they will defend Cro-
atia like lions. The little Orthodox girls will forget
about their icons and incense and marry Croats and
be excellent child-bearers: no-one is as fertile as
Orthodox peasant women, and when they conceive
with Croatian Goths, they will produce future genera-
tions bred to perfection. And they say the Ustashas
are not statesmen!

Ilija Jakovljević

In prison, your mother sang, said Dr Kogoj, *but who got her out? I was*
rescued by Glaise von Horstenau, Herr Edmund.

I was a German plenipotentiary in Croatia. I worked
with many Ustasha chiefs. I visited several camps, the
conditions were terrible. In one camp, in a former
factory, there were not many men, they held mostly
women and children there. They were all half-clothed,
in rags, they slept on the stone floor, they were like
living corpses. I told my Ustasha guide that all this
made me nauseous. It was unbearable when they took
me to a room in which they had spread straw along all
the walls, and I am sure that they brought that straw
immediately before my arrival so as to make a better
impression. When they took me into that room, I saw
some fifty naked children lying on the straw, half of
whom were already dead, while the rest were dying
before my eyes. One has to remember that concen-
tration camps were invented by the British during
the Boer War, but these centres have attained their

*height of cruelty and horror here in Croatia, under
the Leader, whom we, Germans, put in place. I believe
that the worst camp is Jasenovac, into which no ordinary mortal dares to peer.*

Dr Kogoj said that she remembered Glaise von Horstenau, *Herr Edmund*,
she said, because he came to her father's private clinic. One day Glaise
von Horstenau found her father very indisposed, said Dr Kogoj, so her
father told him that his daughter was in prison, *In other words, I*, she
said. Then Glaise von Horstenau *pulled some strings* and she was released.
They just let me go, as though nothing had happened, said Dr Kogoj. *Later,
Glaise von Horstenau killed himself.* She repeated that several times, the
fact that Horstenau had killed himself. *What about your mother, how did
she end up in prison? Who got her out?* Dr Kogoj asked several times as
well, *Who got your mother out?* as though that detail still mattered to her
now, nearly sixty years later.

*After that I didn't see Lala . . . Only Britva and Joža
were left. One day Britva came to our meeting, instead
of Joža. He explained that there had been a raid at the
Moslava Canal. There was shooting, a courier was
captured, but some of those who were on their way to
join the Partisans also fell . . .*

*At around four o'clock in the morning, 18 May,
1943, the bell rang and several Ustasha agents came
into the flat, kicking the door. I managed to hide
the files in my pyjamas while my mother and two
brothers led them in. The Ustasha agents spread
out through the rooms and one of them came towards
me demanding that I immediately hand over the
register of "Partisan bandits". I realised there had
been a raid. The agent who was searching my room
didn't try very hard; he looked tired, no doubt from
similar searches that night. They let me go to the bath-*

room. There I stuffed the lists of bios into the lavatory bowl . . .

They took me to my first interrogation. I waited until eight in the morning in an empty office. Only then did the investigating officer, Kamber, arrive. With short intervals, he spent the whole day and whole night questioning me, also delivering threats, beatings and abuse. They offered me chocolate, and immediately afterwards they hit me . . . Then they took me to another room where there were a lot of weapons, bombs and various items of Partisan clothing. They told me that Joža had confessed everything and I'd better do the same. Then they brought Joža in behind me. He was barefoot and completely disfigured. I said I didn't know him. Then they brought in the courier for Moslavina. I said I didn't know him either.

Joža, quite beside himself, was no longer the old Joža from the Spanish Civil War. Like a robot, he said, Lassie, why not tell them, they'll shoot the three of us anyway. They carried on beating me and for some time I was unconscious . . . Ustasha agents came into the room often, swearing and threatening me. They wanted me to sign a document saying I would be "a loyal citizen of the Independent State of Croatia" and that I would "work for their service" . . . I was saved by one of the Ustasha agents who worked for us . . .

Later, my mother said: *Since I could not be a singer, I became a psychiatrist,* which I know has nothing to do with her stay in the Ustasha prison, but it just came into my mind. After my conversation with Dr Kogoj, I dreamed that people in white coats separated the top part of my skull with a saw and that I lifted that part of my skull as though it were a cap and watched my brain throb. Then I asked those people

to give me a mirror, and, when I placed the mirror in front of me, I saw
. . . there was nothing there, no reflection whatever, just a silvery sheen
casting back my non-existence. Then I thought, all toys should be moved
far away, over the ocean. Perhaps that is how little fugues are born, who
knows.

There is a story about how Don Ferdinando Francesco Gravina,
Prince of Palagonia, withdrew from public life and in 1747 moved into
his father's villa, "Palagonia", nowadays in the suburbs of Palermo. He
decided to help the poor but to remain hidden from the public.

Outside the walls of the villa, in the suburbs of Palermo, lies today's
Bagheria, cutting off the view of the sea.

On one occasion the house was visited by Johann Wolfgang von
Goethe who was aghast at the appalling things he discovered there and
wrote about it in his diary. He says that before his eyes there came to life
a terrifying, sick imagination, a rotten world stuffed with decorations, a
world in a state of disintegration: all around were concave and convex
mirrors reflecting deformed animals and deformed people, nothing but
cripples; there were dragons, dwarves, serpents, monkeys, two-headed
soldiers, there was a satyr holding up a mirror to a lady with a horse's
head – so that the lady could see what she looked like. Later, in the
chapel, Goethe found a huge gilded crucifix with a very naturalistic
Christ with a chain attached to his navel, the other end of which was
nailed into the head of a penitent who had been hanged and was kneel-
ing before him, praying.

So-called heaven and hell are malicious inventions of
the priesthood. Clerics, servants of God and the altar
– for they were the owners of the State and Church
system – would gather the people around them on
their free days and cram their heads with the need
to pray constantly, to think about God, about hell,
about their heavy sins, never to forget that all those
who suffer and smart here on earth and who obey
their elders and teachers, will inherit the kingdom of

eternal bliss in Heaven. Do you not know who burned
and crucified the reformers of humanity: Christ,
Giordano Bruno, Jan Hus, Matija Gubec?

Yours,
Vasa Pelagić *

I found a short biography of Dr Franjo Kogoj, although there must
certainly be long, detailed biographies of Dr Franjo Kogoj, but I don't
need them for the moment. That short biography was composed in
recent times, in the times since this country became an independent
country and since the majority of people in it believe that it's an independent country, but it's not independent, as is absolutely clear to every
sober person. In the short new biography of Dr Franjo Kogoj there isn't
a single word about the fact that during the time of the Independent
State of Croatia, Dr Kogoj was driven out of the Medical Faculty by the
Ustasha authorities, nor a word about what his daughter, Dr Verena
Kogoj, had told me, just as in some newly composed histories of the
National Institute for the Deaf and Dumb there is no mention of the
hangars in that institute that served as warehouses for living and dead
children from the Kozara Mountain.

A new, short and altered biography of Dr Franjo Kogoj

Kogoj, Franjo, doctor (Kranjska Gora, Slovenia,
13. X. 1894 – Kranjska Gora, 30. IX. 1983). Clinical
assistant in Prague, then private lecturer in Brno.
From 1923, at the Clinic for Skin and Venereal
Diseases in Zagreb, of which he was director **from
1927 to 1965** (!); full professor of the Zagreb Medical Faculty (served four terms as dean). From 1967
to 1974, director of the Institute for Clinical Medical

---

* Vasa Pelagić (1833–1899) was a Bosnian-Serb utopian socialist in the second half of
the nineteenth century, a professor and a physician.

Research of the Medical Faculty and Clinical Hospital Centre in Zagreb. Concerned with allergies, tuberculosis of the skin, eczema and keratodermas, he also described the spongiform pustule (which bears his name in medical texts). He pointed out critical moments in the treatment of syphilis. He organised scientific work in the Dermatovenereological Clinic in Ljubljana. Full member of the Yugoslav Academy of Science and Arts and its vice president; honorary and corresponding member of many academies and societies; doctor *honoris causa* of four universities.

Keratodermas are diseases of the skin with characteristic scaliness, when all kinds of horrors break out on the palms and soles of the feet, and the soles and palms become crusty and hard, covered with little callouses and nodules, hollows and ruts, as though tiny invisible animals of some kind are burrowing there and leaving their excrement in the grooves. In the majority of cases, keratodermas are inherited, that is, they work their way through individual families, and there are many of them spread through families on Mljet, so that the beautiful little Croatian island of Mljet, that paradise on earth, has become famous for a rot that is whelped there. It is unjust, but what can one do. *Die Krankheit von Mljet, mal di Meleda, la maladie de Meleda, the disease of Mljet* enters the history of world medicine through the front door thanks to Luka Stulli from Dubrovnik, who noticed as early as 1826 that patients often had healthy parents but a grandfather or grandmother with the disease. Two decades later, Dominik Marcocchia, a doctor from Split, observed that the inherited disease tended to change gender – so female grandchildren would get it from their grandfathers, and males from their grandmothers. The Mljet disease is incurable, but not fatal, it just looks hideous and can sometimes spread over the body, reaching the elbows, the thighs, the nails, it settles in the armpits and elsewhere where there is sweat and stays there, immovable. It appears in the first weeks or months of life and remains, hard and crusty, buried in a person until their death. Then quietly, invisibly, it attacks his descendants. Like syphilis (once), except that syphilis has a worse nature, syphilis is born from small pale treponemas, from minute spiral-shaped bacteria, from spirochaetes that penetrate secretly at first and later loudly announce their final invasion here, there, all over the body, outside and in, into bones, the brain, the eyes, the lungs, the skin, the palate, the liver, into the intestines, the sexual organs, the tongue, the teeth, without restraint. A little spiral animal, dumb, unarticulated, with no brain, with no consciousness, but endowed with the strength to produce horrors, to create suppurating wounds, open and stinking, rubbery growths, holes, crusts; when it is seized with irrepressible madness, it runs wild, goes crazy, it becomes enraged and roars. Syphilis is a terrible disease, a hidden disease, a real internal enemy that just lurks and prowls, then springs at a person, out of the blue.

All kinds of inherited and endemic diseases crawl through this small country of Croatia, and this is sometimes a sad fact, because those diseases punish people at times deservedly, but often not. For instance, hereditary dwarfism on the island of Krk, which lives isolated in small enclaves and at first sight is not intrusive and is, unjustly, still called coastal cretinism even though it has no connection whatsoever with cretinism.

So, I'm sitting in the second-hand bookshop, leafing through the books I've just bought. It would be nice if it were snowing outside, but it's not snowing, just pouring with rain and the wind is thrashing and darkness is swinging in front of the door. Then a young man comes in and asks, *Do you have a new Sophia Loren?* Viktor, for one of those two guys working in the bookshop is called Viktor, Viktor says, *We have two new Sophias with her original signature.* The young man beams, he takes the Sophias piously in his hands and turns them over and strokes them. Viktor tells him that they also have a new *biography* of Sophia Loren, and the young man begins to tremble. He pays a hundred euros for each of the Sophias and a hundred and fifty kunas for the book. Then I discover that collectors of small objects all over the world are crazy about the little dispensers of Pez sweets from the 1960s and will pay two hundred euros for a Pez-Goofy or a Pez-Donald Duck; the little toys out of Kinder Eggs are also exceptionally fashionable, fetching sums of more than a hundred euros each. *What about stamps*, I ask. *Not doing well*, says Igor, the other man from the second-hand bookshop. What a shame, I think, because, now that he is old, my father just bombards me with stamps and stamp albums, I have thirty series from Egypt alone, so I called the Egyptian Embassy and asked the Ambassador whether he might like to buy some series of Egyptian stamps from the 1950s, with Farouk in profile and *en face*.

The boy in love with Sophia Loren leaves with Sophia in the inside pocket of his coat, and a young man comes into the bookshop looking for anarchist literature. Then a boy and girl come in, both strapped into black leather, you can see that it's not plastic but real leather, and they offer Igor a thick black book, *Give us what you like*, they say, but Igor says, *Sorry, this book has been stolen*, they say, *It hasn't*, Igor says, *It has, from a library*, then the boy and girl leave. And I sit there leafing through the old books I've just bought, from time to time I turn back to their former owner's signature and think about the Kogoj family. There are no customers in the bookshop, just the three of us, Viktor, Igor and I. Then Viktor says, *Come and see this*, and out of a small metal box, one could say from a small metal safe, he takes a sepia postcard, addressed on 26 October, 1911, to a certain Dr Auro Segala from Pola.

On the front of the postcard is a girl with bare shoulders, a mysterious smile quivers on her lips, she has a large rose in her hair and she is holding another large rose between the fingers of both hands and looking at this rose, her head bowed, her expression at once calm and somehow melancholy. The knee of one leg is leaning on a bed covered in a heavy decorative material, while her other foot is on the floor. The whole impression is lacy and tender. On the reverse of the postcard, in the upper left-hand corner, there is a sketched map, which we all, Igor, Viktor and I, recognise as a miniature plan of part of this town. On the postcard it says:

Entrance, 2 K. Ella – 16, Ponny, Melanie, Clara – a good stable. A bottle of beer, only 80 fil. Take condoms! Madame wants to open franchises on the coast! Used "thumb" – need not sprain it. Spacious premises, the waiting rooms have entertainments, music. Simple dress. Polite porter. Fine salon. Significant place. The *Saxonia* sails on 28th. L.J.F.

There is a deep silence. We look at each other. Then I pick up from the armchair the books I've just bought and put them in front of Igor and Viktor and they say, *Impossible.* Then we compare the signatures from the books with the handwriting on the postcard and conclude: L.J.F. is Ludwig Jakob Fritz.

So what, we say. Chance.

I ask the guys where they got the postcard from, they say that a girl had brought it and they start hastily rifling through their documents, then we look at each other again and Viktor and Igor say, *The girl is called Antonia Segala.* We conclude at once that this must be the great-granddaughter of Dr Auro Segala to whom the postcard is addressed. So, that damp and windy night, we entered into a secret that may have been spent but maybe not. It was as though that secret, if it was a secret, had grown tired of hiding, so after a hundred years of waiting between the covers of discarded books, among old bills and out-of-date documents, where it was never able to rest, never able to settle, never able to die, as though that secret had all of a sudden decided to emerge and finally say – it's time I left.

One of Ludwig Jakob Fritz's books also concealed a piquant item. An advertisement evidently cut out of a newspaper had been placed between pages 76 and 77 of *Gordon Pym*. In the top left-hand corner there is a drawing, the portrait of a young woman, and above the portrait, in handwriting – the handwriting of Ludwig Jakob Fritz, it was now apparent – is written: *Clara – Hotel Hungaria*. The advertisement promotes female beauty. It says:

Your complexion
will become very beautiful, youthfully fresh, white, clear and delicate. Lines, pimples, yellowness and redness of the nose and face, dips in your skin, impurities, freckles, faded skin will vanish completely, we guarantee, in 6 days with Vladicca Balsamine. A bottle: 2,50 K. Vladdica Bals. Cream: 2 K.

Hair disagreeable to ladies
Only harmless Sattygmo is guaranteed to banish unwanted hair for ever in 3 hours. A bottle: 2.50 K. Head hair does not fall out and does not thin.

Luxuriant growth of hair and moustache
is guaranteed to be achieved immediately only with the tried and tested strengthening forest balm (extract) Poarine. Price 4-2 K.

Shining, full and firm bust
may be achieved, guaranteed, by every lady in 1 month. Visible effects in 8 days. The only enlivening and strengthening invention. The price of 1 bottle of the universal preparation Et-Amiele with instructions: 5 K, and Vladicco special cream extracts for rubbing into the bust, 2 K.

Available only from **V. Havelka Scientific Cosmetic Laboratory, Prague – Vršoviče, 74. I, Husova St**

Follow the direct instructions and reject all else as impure.

It seemed senseless to try to find out whether the drawing on the yellowing advertisement from 1911 was a portrait of the hundred-year-old woman and secret alcoholic Clara, who died in 1992, the former prostitute and flower-seller who lived on the second floor of the building where I am writing this and which, this building, we all know, used to be called Hotel Hungaria. Besides, there are strange apparitions living on the second floor of this building now: they creep up the stairway and steal light bulbs from the corridor. People say they're seasonal scaffolders, welders and porters, that there are lots of them in every room, that in that apartment beds are rented out (who by?) and that the occupants keep changing. I never see anyone going into that apartment or coming out of it. Only music comes out of that apartment, at night, unbearably loud and crude, some kind of barroom turbo-folk music, a din, and the smell of "grass". What do these people do while their music blares? Do they scamper about, or sing, or just sit stiffly, staring at something invisible?

The door of that apartment is peeling, a light-green door covered with a century-old layer of grease and dirt. Once, when it was ajar, I saw that the corridor was illuminated by a 25-watt bulb hanging from a wire and the parquet was black and full of holes.

I sit like this, peering occasionally at the advertisement, letting my gaze wander aimlessly around, and into the box by the old armchair into which Viktor and Igor throw booklets presumably of no interest to anyone, their prices range from 1 to 10 kunas, and near the top I catch sight of a grey brochure with big brown lettering: SYPHILIS THERAPY, Academician Franjo Kogoj. *Fuck it, unbelievable,* exclaims Viktor, while Igor throws himself straight onto the Internet as though he'd seen a vision.

Then I go; I leave the second-hand bookshop, and step into the dark.

> Syphilis (*lues, tabes,* progressive paralysis, French disease, harlots' disease, Neapolitan disease) from the Greek συς – pig, and φιλος – dear, beloved. The name probably first appears in 1530, in the Latin

poem "Syphilus" by Girolamo Fracastori, but as an already established name derived from that of the poet's invented hero, the shepherd Syphilus. Since the disease first manifested itself in the army of the French king Charles VIII, the Italians, Germans and Poles called it "the French disease", *morbus Gallicus*. The French call it "the Neapolitan disease", the Neapolitans "the Spanish disease" and the Turks "the Castilian disease". Given that the later symptoms of syphilis may be similar to those of many other diseases, syphilis is also known as "the great imitator".

As a disease, syphilis is divided into three groups: venereal syphilis, transmitted by sexual contact; non-venereal, congenital syphilis caused by intrauterine transmission from an infected mother to her child; and endemic syphilis, transmitted by non-sexual contact between people or via contaminated objects.

Today syphilis is once again a medical problem. Epidemiological observations show a steady rise in the number of new cases of syphilis globally. Nowadays it is important to consider the connection between syphilis and infection with H.I.V.

The cause of syphilis is the *Treponema pallidum* bacterium, of the spirochaete family. Venereal syphilis (*lues*) is a contagious sexual disease. During sexual contact tiny lesions may occur in the mucous membrane of the sexual organs. These microtraumas are the means of entry of the treponema into the body. During the incubation period (about one month) an immunological and allergic reaction to the infection occurs.

The course of syphilis may be divided into phases: the primary (initial) stage, the secondary (resolutive) stage, the latent stage and the tertiary (destructive) stage.

Primary syphilis develops after an incubation period of between 10 days and 3 months. At the site of the entry of the treponema into the organism there is usually a change in the external sexual organs of both men and women, manifested in the form of a painless papule the size of a pin head up to 3 centimetres in diameter. After one to two days the papule breaks up, or rather, the base of the papule breaks up, while the edges become increasingly hard. A hard canker, *ulcus durum*, is formed. The edges of the ulcer are always slightly raised, and the area feels firm to the touch. The hard ulcer may last for approximately a month, after which it disappears spontaneously. Along with the primary effects there appear enlarged lymph nodes which are hard and elastic, separate from one another and not fixed at their base. During this phase the disease is highly infectious.

In the secondary stage of syphilis, the ulcer disappears after three to six weeks without treatment, but the treponemas spread throughout the organism via the blood and lymph glands. The secondary stage lasts for several months and sometimes even several years. A common, but not universal symptom is a macular rash, most frequently on the sides of the torso, the chest and belly. The macular changes are light pink, about 1 cm in size. Of particular importance in any diagnosis of the disease is a dark-red macular rash on the palms and soles of the feet. The surface of these changes conceals a large number of treponemas, so the rash is highly contagious. Changes to the mucous membrane appear in the form of macules that erode and develop into greyish, mucous plaques which are also rich in treponemas and so highly infectious. Later erosions and ulceration may develop on the mucous membrane. *Angina syphilitica* forms part of the systemic reaction to the disease.

Alopecia syphilitica may appear in two forms: a diffuse form that leads to diffuse hair loss, while another form, *alopecia areolaris*, is characteristic of secondary syphilis, and appears as uneven patches of thinning hair. The severest form of secondary syphilis is malign syphilis, which may lead to the dissolution of papules and overall critical symptoms. The general symptoms of secondary syphilis include tiredness, headaches, pain in the long bones, muscles and joints. There may also be fever.

The stage of latent syphilis is characterised by the absence of subjective and objective manifestations of the disease. The only way to prove the existence of the disease is through positive serological tests. The disease withdraws into a state of latency that usually lasts from five to twenty years, or from two to fifty years.

Syphilis destructiva (tertiary syphilis) is the final stage of the disease. If left untreated, the disease can erupt uncontrollably with symptoms similar to those of many other diseases. There is a general destruction of the tissue. The treponemas attack the brain and bone marrow, heart and blood vessels. Growths in the form of collections of nodules between 0.5 cm and 1 cm in size (larger nodes) appear on the bones, skin and mucous membrane, which grow, merge with the skin, soften and are ultimately discharged at the surface in the form of fistulas.

Tertiary syphilis can also affect the blood vessels, bones and central nervous system (*tabes dorsalis*, progressive paralysis). Approximately 3–7 per cent of incurable cases present as neurosyphilis. The effects of syphilis on the nervous system lead to paresis, general paralysis, madness, blindness, locomotor ataxia.

Congenital syphilis appears in children when the treponemas pass from the infected mother through the placenta to the foetus. Congenital syphilis is rare nowadays, mainly because of serological tests which pregnant women undergo during the first trimester. There are various forms of this disease, which depend above all on the number of treponemas found in the bloodstream. If enough time has elapsed since the primary infection for there to be no more treponemas in the bloodstream, the child may be born completely healthy. However, if there are small numbers of treponemas in the blood, the foetus will be infected, but clinical signs of syphilis (*syphilis connatalis latens*) may not be evident at birth. In cases of the mother being severely infected with treponemas, the child will also be severely infected, which may result in miscarriage or still birth. In cases of the child being born alive, one refers to early congenital syphilis (*syphilis connatalis recens*).

Needless to say, I perused academician Franjo Kogoj's brochure (Yugoslav Academy of Science and Arts Press, Zagreb, 1949) from cover to cover. On page 74, the author mentions a case of manifest syphilis that erupted following a stage of latent syphilis that had lasted for fifty whole years:

*

*A doctor of more than seventy years of age, physically
quite decrepit, came to the clinic with ulcerations
which had appeared on the forearm in the lymph
vessel, and which he himself had diagnosed as sporo-
trichozal nodules.*

Sporotrichosis is a fungal disease more common in the tropics, particularly in women, agricultural workers and miners. It is transmitted via contaminated soil, vegetation, wool and infected animals. Clinical presentation: single or multiple reddish nodular (lumpy) lesions that become pustulas (suppurating blisters) or ulcerations on the skin of the head, trunk and particularly the extremities or on the otorhinolaryngological mucous membrane; a thickening of the lymph vessels, and along them the development of nodules that can exulcerate; chronic regional lymphadenitis. Treatment: potassium iodide, et cetera...

*From the anamnesis we tentatively deduced that the
patient had had a lesion of unknown aetiology on his
penis more than fifty years previously; the lesion had
spontaneously disappeared. Later, as he records, no
other symptoms became evident. The blood tests
carried out (B.W.R., K.R., M.K.R. and M.T.R.)*

B.W.R. – Bordet-Wassermann reaction, K.R. – Kahn's reaction, M.K.R . – Meinicke's reaction, clarification, and M.T.R. – Meinicke's reaction, clouding.

*were all positive. We concealed this from the patient
and prescribed potassium iodide. The ulcerations*

cleared up very nicely and the patient left the clinic
relieved that his "sporotrichosis" had been so swiftly
cured. He assured us that he would take iodine from
time to time. We are convinced that in this case any
other treatment would have been superfluous.

In my practice, I also saw a hundred-year-old
woman with a positive B.W.R.

My grandmother had a sister and a half-brother. They lived where they were born, in a town by the sea, while my grandmother moved to Zagreb. Grandmother was O.K., an extremely wilful woman, one could say obstinate. She sewed. She created operatic dresses for opera singers. She had fourteen seamstresses, she had a salon. Her chest was always decorated with needles from which threads of various colours hung. When she was sewing something for me, she used to call me a dozen times to try it on, turning me round and round. At every fitting she'd prick me in the bottom with a pin, on purpose, I'd jump and she'd laugh. She was round, plump, but only in old age; in her youth she was lovely – full lips, a small nose, a high forehead. She never went grey, when she died her hair was still black, she had quite a lot of hair, but thin, fine as down. I never met my grandfather. He collapsed in 1943, his heart exploded while he was reading Kropotkin, or perhaps it was Trotsky, I'm not sure. His anarchist books were taken away by unknown people after the war, that's what I was told. He had other books, he had poetry books in Gothic script that disappeared as well. He was a member of the Austrian Communist Party from 1923. He was a wig-maker. He made wigs for the theatre, for actors and actresses in fact, but also for bald people. He and my grandmother had three children. They are all dead. I no longer have anyone to ask to find out more about them. Actually, there are a few grandchildren left, younger than I am, but they haven't a clue, they're not interested. They don't even live here.

But, I remember, I do remember something. In the summer we used to go to my grandmother's sister, she made cakes to order and never disclosed her recipes to her customers, that is, she disclosed them partially, she would always leave something out. As soon as her customers left, she would wink at me. She had long diamond earrings that tinkled and knocked against her cheeks when she shook her head. One could say that she was playful. Like her sister, my grandmother. Her name was Claudia. My grandmother had an ordinary name – Ana. When she wasn't making cakes, Claudia gave piano lessons to conceited small children, all dressed up like dolls. We had to get out of the way then, we went swimming or into the yard, or, if it was raining, and it doesn't rain often in summer, to the kitchen. In the kitchen we played draughts or tablanet, stupid, boring games. There were five of us, two of Claudia's grandchildren and the three of us, Ana's, although Ana had six grandchildren, because she had three children, my mother and two sons, but the other grandchildren didn't come, who knows why? I don't remember seeing any men in the house. It was a big, stone, seaside house, with closed shutters in summer, presumably because of the sun, presumably so that the sun didn't fall on the rugs, because rugs fade in the sun and then they aren't worth as much. There were a lot of Persian rugs. And oil paintings of grey, stormy seas. And silver candlesticks. There was no joy in that house.

There was one room we were not allowed to enter. The door to that room was opened softly and quickly, secretly, always at the same hour, at mealtimes, and perhaps at night, when we were asleep. Music sometimes flowed from the room, sometimes voices, in fact one voice that multiplied. It seemed to us that the room was inhabited by an echo, by emptiness, by a big, dark hole. A stench came from the room, the smell of decay, a kind of vapour that seeped out under the door, instead of light. Every time Claudia emerged from that room, she would air the neighbouring ones. *We'll make a little draught*, she'd say, her earrings tinkling. We knew that Luigi, Claudia and Ana's half-brother, lived in that room, that's what they told us. *Uncle Luigi is ill, we mustn't disturb him*, that's what they said. And they kept repeating, *SshhsshhSSHHSSHH*.

Once, towards the end of summer, when my mother came to collect us, I asked why Luigi didn't come out of his room, why we couldn't see him, and my mother said, *He has progressive paralysis.* I thought that progressive paralysis was ordinary paralysis, I was small. I imagined

Luigi sitting in an invalid's chair and smiling, I imagined Claudia feeding him. The following year, we stayed just two weeks at Claudia's, not the usual two months. I think it was 1955. I asked Claudia how old Luigi was, she said seventy-five, she said, *Luigi is ten years older than I am, he's my half-brother*, but I already knew that. Claudia and Ana had the same father, Luigi had a different father, only their mother was the same. That summer, yes, 1955, I eavesdropped on their night-time conversation: in the kitchen were Nona Ana (who had arrived unexpectedly), my aunty Claudia and my mother (who had come to take us home). Claudia was baking walnut pastries and was moving around by the cooker. She had a blob of powdered sugar on her nose. She had rolled-up sleeves and impressive bingo wings. She had quick fingers, they moulded the pastries as though they were running over a piano keyboard. The kitchen smelled of feast days. Nona Ana had quick fingers too, plump ones, she was sewing something out of black lace. I saw my mother from behind. She had bare feet, her red shoes, with very high heels, were lying on their side under the table. She was wearing a white blouse with thin red stripes, shiny, with a scarf collar, she adored blouses with scarf collars, she tied them into a bow at her neck, they were Chanel blouses, I realised later, as an adult. It smelled of warm bread, it smelled of calm. It smelled of almonds and marzipan. I peered in through the barely open door, lying on my stomach on the floor in the hall, on a Persian rug, watching specks of dust rise from the blue carpet towards the thin column of light that had bored into the threshold between the kitchen and the hall I was in. It was very late, it was a dark summer's night, soundless. My mother kept repeating the word *tabes*, Tabes, *does this*, tabes *does that*, I listened and thought that *tabes* must be some wicked man who thought up all kinds of horrors for decent people, because this "*tabes*" of my mother's sounded absolutely monstrous.

I was not an obedient child. Nona Ana would sometimes look me in the eye and say: *From plague, hunger and war*, then she would stop, before going on, *and you – preserve me, oh Lord*. This sounded pretty rude. But still, I loved Nona Ana although I didn't know it then, it emerged only later.

I tiptoe to the door of Luigi's room. The three of them in the kitchen are talking, sometimes all at once. The atmosphere is no longer mysterious, sombre, maybe they're eating pastries, I think. I go in quietly, as quietly as I can. I cross the threshold, it's as though someone has shat themselves. The smell of urine merges with the sweetish sickly smell of decay, it smells of forgotten shells at the bottom of a beach bag. With his back to the door, Luigi is sitting looking at the window, the window is shut, as are the blinds. Luigi is looking at nothing, perhaps only at a bundle of memories.

Beside Luigi is a lighted table lamp with a transparent shade in the shape of a Japanese umbrella. Luigi turns his face stiffly towards the feeble light and starts to jerk his head as though lice were crawling over his scalp and face and he cannot shake them off. I see his profile. He tries to touch the lamp, misses, tries again, his hand falls onto the bulb and sticks to it. The smell of burning skin, and the already faint light goes out. I am seven years old, my heart is racing. I stand frozen in the doorway, the room is small and before my eyes it shrinks while Luigi grows like Alice.

He stands up, takes half a step and falls back into the armchair, his legs dangle, his legs are paralysed, dead legs. A stench wafts through the room. Luigi is shitting in his pants, you can hear it, he has diarrhoea, I hold my breath. On the walls are some framed diplomas, I can't see what they're for, I can't see whose they are. Luigi whispers, his whisper is hollow, like the dripping of water in an abandoned cave, a whisper composed of an echo: the tedious and monotonous whispering of prayer, it's not even a wail, just a whisper. I don't understand what he is saying, his words stick to one another and, like an endlessly long plait, like a monochrome scarf without end, they fall onto the floor. Then he says, *Monkeys cry. Hyperbole.* I'm even more terrified and leave the room. In the corridor my hands are trembling, shaking as though they belong to someone else, as though they're independent hands, epileptic.

In the kitchen my mother says, *It'll get worse, much worse. He needs to be placed on a neurological ward. Or in a psychiatric hospital.*

When I was born, my father was suffering from

general paralysis and he was already blind when he conceived me; not long after my birth, his sinister disease confined him to an armchair.

. . . Now the following was connected to his paralysis and blindness: he was unable to go and urinate in the toilet like most people; instead, he did it into a small container at his armchair, and since he had to urinate very often, he was unembarrassed about doing it in front of me, under a blanket, which, since he was blind, he usually placed askew. But the weirdest thing was definitely the way he looked while pissing. Since he could not see anything, his pupils very frequently pointed up into space, shifting under the lids, and this happened particularly when he pissed. Furthermore, he had huge, ever-gaping eyes that flanked an eagle nose, and those huge eyes went almost entirely blank when he pissed, with a completely stupefying expression of abandon and aberration in a world that he alone could see and that aroused his vaguely sardonic and absent laugh . . .

I was about fourteen when my affection for my father turned into a deep and unconscious hatred. Then I began vaguely enjoying his constant shrieks at the lightning pains torn from him by the tabes, which are considered among the worst pain known to man. Furthermore, the filthy, smelly state to which his total disablement often reduced him (for instance, he sometimes left shit on his trousers), was not nearly so disagreeable to me as I thought . . .

One night, we were awakened, my mother and I, by vehement words that the syphilitic was literally howling in his room: he had suddenly gone mad.

Yours, Georges Bataille

The following summer, when we went there, to the seaside, my mother said, *Luigi died.* I asked, *Which Luigi?* And she said *Uncle Luigi, Dr Ludwig, Nona Ana and Claudia's half-brother.*

Later, my mother gave all of us the Wassermann test, and did so for years, which, I now see, was completely absurd. Fear is an incomprehensible beast.

As I have said, for forty years the name Ludwig and the connection of that name with syphilis was outside my reality. I believed that the name was buried along with the destiny of the man to whom it belonged. That all traces of that uninteresting destiny had been swept away by time, that the ghosts of the dead visit the living in literature, in literary fabrications, and that reality is made up of paths that branch off indefinitely, without the slightest prospect of their ever connecting and intertwining anywhere, at any time. That time devours itself until it disperses into microscopic particles out of which a new time, no less sick, but more bearable – our time, the present – is born. That it is possible to grasp the course of that time, place it in its channel and tell it how and where it should flow so as not to disintegrate again. And now, the name Ludwig Jakob Fritz, printed nearly a hundred years ago in the musty books lying in my lap, has risen up like some kind of ghost out of its grave where no gravestone was placed, a grave that has been waiting, open, for who knows how long, and of which it is uncertain when (or whether) someone will deign to close up its dark innards, lower the lid and turn their back on the pit of the past, leaving it up to the modest and monstrous dead in that tomb to devour one another or to dance their own life, as they please, and leave the rest of us in peace. Whether Luigi, *Uncle Luigi, Dr Ludwig* was Ludwig Jakob Fritz, will never be known.

It is very likely that the case referred to by Professor Kogoj, the case of *a physically fairly decrepit old doctor of more than seventy years of age, with latent syphilis, which manifested itself fifty years later,* referred to Ludwig Jakob Fritz. In 1911 Ludwig Jakob Fritz was thirty-five, which means he was born in 1876. In 1949, when Academician Kogoj publishes the pamphlet in which he describes the disease of the unnamed doctor,

Ludwig Jakob Fritz is seventy-three, so *older than seventy*. If his syphilis had crouched in him for fifty whole years, he would have contracted it in 1899, at the age of twenty-three, which means that he didn't get it then, during his visit to this town, which means that it wasn't Clara the flower-seller who infected him, which need not mean that spirochaetes were not circulating in her bloodstream as well, only that her spirochaetes hadn't gone beserk, while those of Ludwig Jakob Fritz had. Then I think, maybe Clara the flower-seller, the one who roamed drunk in 1992 through the abandoned rooms of the former Hotel Hungaria, on the floor below mine, maybe she is that *centenarian with the positive B.W.R.* referred to by Dr Kogoj, but then I realise that is impossible, the dates don't fit. Never mind. It doesn't matter. Yet, once again it has turned out that the threads of which human lives consist are never completely broken, those threads intertwine, are entangled, and finally merge into some kind of protoplasmic matter invisible to the naked eye, into a matter which moves, which sways, into an amoebic protozoa that slithers around us, wriggles, changes shape, overflows, until it surrounds us and sucks us in.

It is incomprehensible that Ludwig Jakob Fritz, a doctor, shouldn't connect the *lesion of unknown aetiology on his penis* with a possible syphilitic infection. In 1911, he carries a letter from Dr Grošić to Professor Noguchi, and by then Professor Hideyo Noguchi is a bacteriologist of international renown, Director of the Rockefeller Institute in New York, where, in 1910, he turns to the study of syphilis, and in 1913 demonstrates that in many luetics, the debauched bacchantic *Treponema pallidum* throws itself into wild parties and orgies until its host literally loses his mind. It is inconceivable that Dr Ludwig Jakob Fritz doesn't "get it", when Professor Hideyo Noguchi transplants spirochaetes from the brains of paralytics into rabbits, thus confirming the connection of syphilis with progressive paralysis, when soon afterwards he comes to Europe where he lectures and speaks about his discovery in all the best-known medical centres, how does Ludwig Jakob Fritz not see, the newspapers are full of headlines and reports. Incomprehensible is the *Kurzschluss* in Ludwig Jakob Fritz's at that stage relatively rational and not yet entirely trepomena-riddled brain, if it is known that in as early as 1907, after 605 attempts, Paul Ehrlich (Nobel Prize for Medicine, 1908) synthesises the famous "606th connection", later known as *Salvarsan*, which has a strong anti-treponocidic and anti-spirochaetic effect; if it is known that in 1912, tirelessly seeking an ever more effective treatment for syphilis, Paul Ehrlich discovers the "914 preparation" or *Neosalvarsan*, which is used to the present day (in combination with the later synthesised drugs of which two, *Mapharsen* and *Stovarsol*, were also discovered by Paul Ehrlich). Why, Paul Ehrlich was virtually here, in front of Ludwig Jakob Fritz's nose, when he came as Koch's assistant to work in Brijuni, and later, in Berlin, he wasn't exactly miles away. Ludwig Jakob Fritz, with what were then still hidden nests of living treponemas in his body, wanders through the world, buys fine rose-scented gloves, visits brothels, watches sunsets and sows his infection about.

Ehrlich becomes a member of eighty-one academies of science and of all the well-known professional societies of Austria, Germany, France, Great Britain, Denmark, Brazil, Greece, Hungary, Italy, Holland, Romania, Egypt, Serbia, Belgium, Japan, Spain and Venezuela, and holds honorary doctorates from the Universities of Chicago, Göttingen, Oxford, Athens and Breslau, thunders for decades to audiences of the medical world inviting them to "fire magic bullets at microbes", pledging that he will treat syphilis with chemotherapy, while Ludwig Jakob Fritz, blessed in his insignificance, in his enclosed life limited by emptiness, Ludwig Jakob Fritz does not think of the funeral in store for him, he has no idea that he has become a link in the chain of that hideous disease that is still (at that time) circling the globe. He could have pulled through; in 1911 Ludwig Jakob Fritz could have been treated, but since he was not, it's hard today to establish on which continents his spirochaetes roam, in whose lives they have settled, what monstrosities they have caused and it is not known whether now, when there are treatments, that invisible chain of destinies has finally been broken. Ludwig Jakob Fritz had only to remember that not all diseases are manifested at once, that some diseases may present their invoice sometimes fifty or sixty years later, that there are malevolent diseases that recur, skip a generation or two, and then return, refreshed, strengthened, that these sins of the fathers are very tough sins, that Madame Alving's phantoms are not phantoms at all, but tangible horrors that transform a person into a worm-eaten mass of poisonous, noxious cells. Where the sources of these dense, filthy waters lie, it is hard to say.

Viceroy Jelačić dies of syphilis, mad.

As does Henry VIII.

And Ivan the Terrible.

And Pope Julius II.

And Cardinal Wolsey.

And Charles Baudelaire, his cousin Guy de Maupassant and Flaubert die, infected with syphilis, paralysed and blind, mad.

And Rimbaud and Daudet.

And Nietzsche. In Turin, Nietzsche collapses in the street and loses his mind for ever. He spends the last eleven years of his life in mental institutions, completely paralysed.

Cesare Borgia is one of the best-known international syphilitics.

The composer Hugo Wolf dies in a Vienna madhouse. Diagnosis: tertiary stage of syphilis.

Donizetti, dumb, paralysed and mad, dies of syphilis in Bergamo. He is buried in the basilica of Santa Maria Maggiore.

Franz Schubert dies of syphilis, aged thirty-one.

Smetana is placed in a Prague lunatic asylum in April 1884, where he dies a month later, of syphilis.

Al Capone – syphilis, tertiary stage. He plays cards and fishes, in isolation, for as long as he can, then he loses his mind and dies.

There are many more, known and unknown.

Noguchi's and Ehrlich's researches were preceded by numerous others, some honourable, some dishonourable, some scientific, some charlatan. There were researchers who gave the great experimenters of the Third Reich ideas and stimulus for their monstrous and for the most part senseless and useless torture of living and until then healthy specimens of "an inferior human race". Nowadays that tends to be forgotten. Humanity has other concerns. In the nineteenth century, too, there were sick minds, and in the seventeenth, and earlier, and there are today as well, there always have been and there always will be those self-proclaimed superhumans, inhumans. The discovery of a cure for syphilis, the "mocking-bird" of human kind, and for other venereal diseases, was a challenge. Safe and infinite copulation – the survival of the species – immortality: an unrealised and, thank goodness, unrealisable human dream. The plague has been "sorted", syphilis has been silenced, A.I.D.S. has erupted. Ebola, mad-cow disease, human madness, cloning and autocloning: monsters crawl over this planet ever more resembling a house of horrors, of universal disaster.

In 1895, the New York paediatrician Henry Heiman, in a then significant medical journal, describes the deliberate contamination of a four-year-old, a sixteen-year-old and a man of twenty-six with gonorrhea, with the aim of finding a cure for this widespread disease. The justification for this experiment was said to have been the fact that "one boy is an idiot and chronic epileptic, the other an idiot, and the young man in the terminal stage of tuberculosis".

A certain Dr Leffingwell throws himself to work. He discovers that, in the nineteenth century in America, experiments had been carried out for decades on adults from poorhouses and children from orphanages. He learns that Dr Sydney Ringer from the University Clinic in London prescribes to patients, mostly children under ten years of age, excessive doses of toxic drugs, after which they suffer from severe headaches, spasms of the limbs, frequent nausea and serious problems with their eyesight.

Dr Ringer publishes the results of his research in *A Handbook of Therapeutics*. As an important textbook, it runs to eight editions.

In 1949, E. Westacot publishes his research entitled *A Century of Vivisection and Anti-Vivisection*, in which he describes the experiments of the Viennese Professor Neisser. On 29 April, 1899, in a Viennese medical journal, Neisser writes that he deliberately infected eight healthy children with syphilis. Three were immediately taken ill, while the fourth child was later diagnosed with a brain tumour. On the pretext that he was studying the immunisation of healthy people against syphilis by injecting them with serum from syphilitic patients, Neisser also infected three prostitutes, without first asking them for their permission to carry out his experiments.

In 1913, the House of Representatives of the state of Pennsylvania publishes the information that, "through the goodness of several hospitals", 146 children were infected with syphilis, while in Philadelphia fifteen children had their "sight examined" by putting drops of tuberculin into their eyes. Several of the children were irreversibly blinded.

If one leaves aside the relatively small number of Nazi doctors who have been tried for their crimes, and the even smaller number who were subsequently condemned to life imprisonment or executed, in recent history hardly a single doctor has been severely punished for human experimentation – on the contrary, many have been promoted and rewarded.

Probably the most shameful drama with syphilis in the starring role was played out from 1932 to 1972 in the town of Tuskegee in Macon County, in the American state of Alabama, where the *spontaneous* development and course of the illness were tracked in 399 already infected African-Americans, and drugs were deliberately denied them. Later investigations revealed that only a small number of doctors knew about the experiment, while the patients had no idea of why it was being performed – *You have bad blood* was all they were told. The guinea pigs were chosen from among poor, illiterate men (blacks) who had never been to a doctor until then. They were promised free health checks, free transport to the clinic, hot meals when they visited the hospital, free treatment for minor ailments and financial assistance with their burial. Fleming discovers penicillin in 1928; from then on, in combination with Salvarsan, it has been used for the treatment of syphilis.

In 1973 an ad hoc meeting of the State Advisory Board produced a report on syphilis cases in Tuskegee, and concluded that "the scientific community no longer has any legitimacy in deciding on the rights of individuals where scientific research is concerned".

In 1997, President Clinton apologised officially and publicly to the victims of the experiment, to all those deliberately untreated but suffering from syphilis, and promised them appropriate financial compensation.

This business with the visit of the Roman Pontiff is becoming unbearable. Like that with the spruce tree, which journalists, fairly nauseatingly, proclaim a Croatian "green ambassador" and for the decoration of which experts from the Ethnographic Institute (of Croatia) have been engaged. Instead of researching national treasures, these experts spent a month making gingerbread decorations (by hand), five hundred hanging ornaments, mostly hearts, plus five hundred transparent plastic balls which were supposed to contain Croatia's flaming love for the Holy Father, so that the tree would not be damaged during transportation. And now the media, announcing the Pope's arrival, fall once again into an indescribable trance of verbal incontinence, *ad nauseam*. In the School of Applied Arts, the pupils make hundreds of multi-coloured plaster crosses, not yet knowing what to do with them. It seems that the Pope likes coming here, it's not far. Or perhaps he doesn't really like it, but the guys up there keep on and on, do come, do come, we humbly beseech you, do come, so that it is easier for him to come than to keep inventing excuses. Or perhaps the thing is two-way, perhaps the Vatican gets something out of it as well.

There is always so much to do. Now it's carnival time, they've put up those multi-coloured streamers that rustle cheerily, and when the carnival is over, preparations for Maximus begin. The last time he came, a special board was established ("boards" have replaced "commissions" because "commissions" sound strict and associative, while "boards" allegedly have a softer effect, although they're also associative), so a board was set up to supervise the casting of cutlery for dishes from the time of the Croatian Revival, which the Pope was supposed to eat in the course of his one-hour flight from Split to Rome. The Pope was so exhausted by his visit that in the aeroplane he immediately fell asleep, he didn't feel like eating. This time, as there's no point in repeating the same idea, a new boot-licking surprise in store for the Pope is awaited with great impatience. What this final masquerade of general hysteria and collective religious fervour will look like, we will have the opportunity to see during the obligatory dress rehearsal entitled "simulation of the Pope's arrival". Who will play the part of the Pope in this little drama, who his entourage, who the representatives of the people and who the representatives of the government, has not yet been announced.

There were several syphilitic Popes.

The waterfront, the Riva, was once called Riva Marco Polo, now it's just the Riva. In Yugoslav times, the Riva was called the Quay of the Yugoslav Navy. People say that until fifteen years ago the whole length of that avenue was full of life. There are jetties on the Riva, empty. There are no boats. The ferry comes, yes, and sails to Dubrovnik. There's an old boat renovated as a café, from it music blares. There's an avenue of trees along the quay, except that like the majority of the avenues in this town, the avenue along the Riva is lined with trees so short that they are barely visible. Only when lights twinkle everywhere at Christmas, then the dwarf trees along the Riva also twinkle and come into their own. Recently American cargo ships have been mooring here, carrying who knows what, and with them American sailors who flock instantly to McDonald's around the corner, in order to deaden their nostalgia, then they set off to make a loutish racket and a lot of rubbish, to the consternation of the citizens. Then suddenly, along the Riva, little whores emerge, young and second-rate. Otherwise there aren't even prostitutes here anymore, although there must be prostitution, prostitution is tenacious and ineradicable, which means that at the moment it is hidden and operating on the side.

It's hard to say where the Riva got its original name of Marco Polo from. It would be nice if that name still existed today, and wasn't truncated like this. Since the avenue beside the sea stretches richly and flexibly, it could be imagined as a two-way street, free-flowing, leading outwards and inwards, without end or beginning, a street where time loses its outlines and quietly vanishes, a street *where the traveller discovers some past of his which he no longer knows that he possesses*. But the Riva gives the impression of being a closed road. At its beginning and at its end, invisible ramparts have been erected which squeeze the flow into its old body, and it stands imprisoned in its carapace like stagnant water. Recollections of that road disperse into little drops formed of easy, half-expressed words, of odourlessness that closes the lungs.

The city exists and it has a simple
secret: it knows only departures, not returns.

Departures of non-departure. Through cracks in the past overgrown with brittle plants, blue and yellow. Travelling through the trembling light that is fading. Floating through deserted landscapes, through soundlessness.

At the top of the Riva a *spaghetteria* has opened. Here, there's a little cult of preparing and consuming pasta, which is, I believe, a reflection of the past. It's a cheerful cult, perhaps one of the few authentic ones, full of aroma and colour. Sickness deprives this town of precisely that, it corrodes its aromas and colours, which is why it now lies grey and motionless, miserably cramped under a cap that exudes the stench of stagnation. Perhaps that is why it needs the carnival, an injection of morphine, to cheat its death-bed pains. This isn't a town of street dancers and players, this isn't a town of magnolias and oleanders, there are no palms here, oranges don't blossom, the sea is cast aside, separated by cliffs, enclosed by stone piers, it doesn't reach the people, people and the sea look at each other from a distance, sometimes in a conciliatory manner, sometimes scowling, people don't sing in the street here, people don't live by night here, there is no laughter here, and if ever there is, that laughter creaks and contorts faces, it's all so serious and inwardly so quiet, as in a plaster cast. That's why the carnival, which takes place quite

219

insanely in the middle of winter, when winds blow, when rains pour, when the streets sleep, when steps reverberate dully, that's why the carnival doesn't grow out of the tissue of this town, that's why it is so false and forced, a contortion; a little lullaby.

The hope that the *spaghetteria* at the top of the former Riva Marco Polo, today its anaesthetised stump, insensitive to touch, and so also to pain, the hope that this insignificant little eatery would bring cheerful companionship, proved senseless. Companionship happens in Irish pubs over black beer, with music from across the sea. The belief that it was Marco Polo, returning in 1295 from his travels in the Orient, who brought pasta to these parts, however inaccurate that belief, seemed like a kind of fairy-tale game, like one of those by no means chance happenstances that give life meaning; it seemed as though the spirit of Polo, the traveller and writer, was sailing through the centuries and spreading through these parts, as though, through the spirit of a different traveller, Calvino, or independently, it entered into the dark doorways of converted mansions along the Riva, bringing signs of memory, bequeathing to the town a little existence, a shred of reality. But,

Travelling, you realize that differences are lost: each city takes to resembling all cities, places exchange their form, order, distances, a shapeless dust cloud invades the continents . . . The catalogue of forms is endless: until every shape has found its city, new cities will continue to be born. When the forms exhaust their variety and come apart, the end of cities begins.

Implements were found in the ruins of Pompeii that are very similar to implements for making pasta. There are texts referring to macaroni from as early as 1200, which is significantly earlier than when Marco Polo allegedly decides to abandon the island of Korčula in order to meander around the world. Over the centuries, pasta goes in and out of fashion. Despite various campaigns seeking to erase urban memories, memory stubbornly resists, sometimes it shoots up like a geyser, sometimes it drips in a trickle, slowly, but it always returns, in one form or another, including through a love of pasta. In the 1930s, pasta was officially banished in this part of the world.

In 1930, in Europe, things were pretty lively.

The jazz guitarist Jean-Baptiste Reinhardt, known as Django, born in a Gypsy caravan near the town of Liberchies in Belgium, meets the violinist Stéphane Grappelli with whom he founds the Quintette du Hot Club de France. Their music, strongly influenced by black and Gypsy traditions, is jarring to the ears of the new conquerors who are already yodelling, puking and pissing in Bavarian beer halls, building a new world order. Meanwhile, Dizzy Gillespie plays the trumpet and cruises through America.

Bertholt Brecht opts for Marxism.

Marlene Dietrich attends the opening night of her "Blue Angel", then quickly packs her bits and pieces and heads off across the pond, away from Germany.

Josephine Baker dances in Paris; then joins the Resistance and for a while stops dancing.

Agatha Christie publishes *Murder at the Vicarage*.

Aldous Huxley has already written *Brave New World*, Orwell's *1984* appears some time later.

Helmut Kohl is born.

The doctor and writer of detective stories, Arthur Conan Doyle, dies.

Shalyapin sings.

Ignazio Silone flees Italy, lives in exile in Switzerland; he never meets Marlene Dietrich, maybe it would have turned out well.

Ho Chi Minh founds the Communist Party of Indochina, although that's not in Europe.

Neil Armstrong is born. He'll be the first man to leave Earth and step onto the Moon, so it's not important that he's American.

An occults' congress is held in Athens.

Pavelić leaves his Homeland with his little gang. In Italy he's detained in a camp for a while, then he returns in style.

In Istria my grandfather Edo becomes Edoardo. Whether one likes it or not, one is fed castor oil everywhere. With his wife and sons my grandfather flees to Split.

And here?

In 1930 the newspapers announce that the flight route Prague–Zagreb–Sušak has opened. It no longer exists today, today there's no living flight route whatsoever, there's just a dead airfield nearby. At the same time, the newspapers here publish instalments of a pamphlet about the causes of the decline of this town, entitled "Golgotha".

There is a catastrophic collision between the passenger steamships *Karađorđe* and *Francesco Morosini*, there are dead and injured.

Miss Sušak is chosen, Miss Ljubica Kurpis.

The trial takes place in Trieste of eighteen Yugoslavs from the Julian Borderland, after which four are executed, shot in the back.

Elida Shampoo, Elida Crème and Elida Bathsoap are advertised.

Austria acquires an extreme right-wing government.

Public telephone boxes are erected.

The National Theatre is performing "Patriots" by Jovan Sterija Popović, directed by Branko Gavella, "The Green Suit" by Flers and Caillavet, Nušić's plays "Madame Minister" and "Protection", then "Escape" by John Galsworthy with Tanhofer in the lead role and various other comedies, mainly French.

After the assassination attempt of the "prominent fascist" Francesco Sottosanti in November 1930, a group of fascists demolishes the offices of the daily *Novi list*.

The Cercle Français is active.

The Centrale cinema shows the film "Wild Orchid", and the day after the first night, an unsigned interview with Greta Garbo is published.

A. Vio, the former mayor, is arrested.

There are auctions of Persian carpets.

There are advertisements for Underwood American typewriters and Chassis trucks made by the Ford Motor Company. There are advertisements for seals and signet rings, Trsat stomach drops, fashion magazines, Thermos radiators, kitchen equipment, Peko, Bata and Bally shoes.

The "Dora" permanently burning stove, Ash furniture, glass, porcelain, Ovomaltine, permanent waves in the Venus salon, and J. Ružička's shop for the sale and export of oak or beech coffins, are advertised. The dental technician Margan extracts the teeth of the poor, gratis, every day between 1 and 2 p.m.

Twenty-five years of the Hawk youth society are celebrated.

The film "Tango of Love" is the hit of the season.

On the bridge that separates Sušak from Rijeka, smuggling incidents become more frequent and inventive.

The Christmas issue of the Sušak paper *Naša sloga* publishes a selection of "young Croatian lyric poets" – Ivo Frol, Marijan Matijašević, Vladimir Marinko, Dragutin Tadijanović, Olinko Delorko and Nikola Šteafić, all from Zagreb, not one from the paper's beloved town.

The Nobel Prize for Peace is won by the Swedish Archbishop Södarblom, in Rome the trial is held of fifty-seven Yugoslavs, Loebe is elected President of the Reichstag and Rijeka sends numerous enthusiastic telegrams to Host-Venturi.

Ivan Pavlov publishes his theory of conditioned reflexes. According to the theory of conditioned reflexes, a dog salivates when a bell rings, because he has been previously shown but not given meat at the sound of a bell. The theory is applicable also to people.

So, via pasta to meat.

On 15 November, 1930, at a banquet arranged in the Milanese restaurant Penna d'Oca, Filippo Tommaso Marinetti launches his loudly announced campaign against established ways of eating, and particularly against *pasta asciutta*.

Futuristic cuisine, shouts Marinetti, *will forgo quantity in favour of quality. Futuristic cuisine proclaims war on pasta in every one of its forms because, no matter how much it pleases the palate,* pasta asciutta *is a crude, heavy and inappropriate foodstuff. Its nutritional value is ques-*

tionable. It provokes distrustfulness, laziness and pessimism.

The public is upset. Doctors throughout Italy consult, and at this time here where I now live is Italy too. Some of those doctors, sons and soldiers of their homeland, maintain that citizens who consume pasta every day become slow and excessively good-natured, while those who, unlike them, eat meat are swift and aggressive.

Marinetti has fun. Marinetti writes manifestos about poetry, towns, the theatre, machines, noise, music, painting, architecture. Then, about food, about smells.

About language.

About lust.

About war.

About patriotism.

His manifestos are soaked with the words *courage, struggle, revolt, attack, violence, hidden enemy forces, revenge.*

Mussolini is satisfied: Pasta asciutta *is not food for fighters. In the battle that awaits us, swift and complete victory must be attained.*

The atmosphere seems cheerful, adventurous, playful.

In 1932, Marinetti publishes his futuristic cookbook *La Cucina Futurista.* The foreword contains Mussolini's message: *To my dear old friend, fighter in the first fascist battles, fearless soldier whose inexhaustible love for his country is consecrated in blood.*

Today Marinetti's cookbook is an entertaining document. In it, he writes that there should be an end to imported food. In it, he exclaims: "Buy local!" In it, Marinetti declares the snobbism of the Italian aristocracy and high society – crazed with American customs, receptions, foreign films, German music and French cooking – anti-Italian. Some words, he says, must be changed *without fail*:

"bar" should be *quisibeve* (here-one-drinks)

"sandwich" – *traidue* (between-the-two)

"cocktail" – *polibibita* (multi-drink)

"aphrodisiac drink" – *guerra in letto* (war-in-bed), and so on. (When independent Croatia was proclaimed, a local meat factory produced a salami with a chequer-board pattern inside it. When the salami was sliced it revealed little white meat squares dappled with little pink squares, also meat.)[*]

Nevertheless, despite the constraints, despite the war, despite the propaganda and the glorification of patriotism, pasta was not banished from Italian tables. Although fragile, soft and white, in the 1930s its roots have grown too firmly into the tissue of Europe to be wrenched out just like that, because of some wartime ideology. Its family is vast and enduring. It has more than four hundred members. It includes spaghetti (narrow threads), spaghettini (even narrower threads), vermicelli (little worms), maccheroni (little elephants' trunks), rigatoni (groovelike pasta), lasagne (broad slices), linguini (somewhat narrower slices, little tongues), fettuccine (small ribbons), lancette (little lances), fusilli (spirals), riccioline (corkscrew curls). There are all sorts of butterflies (farfalle), small (farfallette) and even smaller (farfallini), and then big (farfalloni).

Marinetti's *Futurist Cookbook* recommends dishes such as "Heroic winter dinner", "Extremists' banquet" and "Dynamic meal". Some of them not even Hitler could resist.

Marinetti's recipe for stuffed quail and roast pigeon is a real feast for the palate: the carefully cleaned and lovingly stuffed quail should be marinated for an hour in a *bagnomaria* (over steam), soaked in *moscato di Siracusa* (thick Sicilian muscat), and then, still in the *bagnomaria*, in milk for a further hour. Only then are the quail stuffed, with *mostarda di Cremona*, consisting of pears, cherries, dwarf oranges, figs, plums, apricots, small pieces of melon and pumpkin, all conserved in a sweet syrup with the flavour of yellow gentianella oil.

At roughly the same time, in Split, a booklet, a pamphlet in fact, is printed on poor-quality brown paper, with *Wartime Cookbook* written on the front in black letters. In it the famous Dika Marjanović-Radica cheers up the hungry populace with suggestions for preparing the most varied dishes of – savoury, sweet, roast, thin, boiled and thick – polenta.

Today in Croatia there is a healthy eating campaign. Through the use of a poster of an American nutritional pyramid the populace is urged:

* Reminiscent of the Croatian flag. Translator's note.

Eat lean meat, fresh cheese, fruit and vegetables, and use olive oil.

Syphilis is under control, but there is more and more tuberculosis.

Here for a long time there was also a huge poster featuring this "American pyramid". Below it gathered the section of the Croatian populace that adores rummaging through rubbish, practising Pavlovian conditioned reflexes. Then the poster disappeared from the streets and moved to the small screen. There it could also be seen by those of limited mobility. Then the advertisements were taken off completely. The Minister of Health at the time became the Minister of Defence. Then new people came. Today, a woman is head of the Ministry of Defence. She announces that the publication of *Mein Kampf* in this country represents an act of intolerance.

This country is full of slackness.

This town didn't get rich overnight like some other Croatian towns, which is a soothing fact. The wealth of this town has dried up, it now hides shrivelled in its aged interior, like the prostitution, it doesn't hit you in the face, it doesn't flash, it is not intrusive, it's a small underground stream that flows quietly, murmuring steadfastly, living for itself, steadily gurgling. From that point of view, it is easy to live here.

There's a woman at the bank who got married recently, Olga tells me. This marriage took place in Paris, with relatives and witnesses, but without friends, because if their friends had come as well, the costs would have soared. When she came back from Paris she brought photographs into work for everyone to see. Three albums. The wedding seemed filmic, even a bit carnivalesque, because the bridegroom was in tails, with a top hat under one arm and a stick in the other hand. The bride had a cape thrown casually over her shoulders, it appears to be made of mink (possibly rented), and something like a little crown in her hair, like those diadems placed on the heads of beauty queens. The solemn event took place in some kind of palace with a lot of period armchairs up-holstered in striped blue-grey silk. *The floor is made of marble, covered in Bukhara, Tabriz and other Persian carpets, there are several fireplaces and several smaller drawing rooms, it can all be seen on the photographs, they're taken so that it's all clearly seen,* says Olga, who has serious debts and also works at the bank even though she's a psychologist, not an economist. Whenever I call Olga, an awful cackling comes down the line because, apart from one or two men who manage the banks, it's mostly women who work there, several of them in one room, and they talk about everything, including intimate things. So the women in Olga's room looked at this just married couple kissing under the Eiffel Tower, says Olga, whom I know from my previous life so I feel relaxed and in my own skin in her company. *They kiss*, Olga says, *still wearing those fancy-dress costumes, while cars circulate, people walk, what can they do, it's their city, they walk and go about their business, for Parisians this wedding is not an event.* Olga's colleagues at the bank leafed through the albums exclaiming, *Oh wonderful*, far too loudly and heartily to sound convincing. There wasn't a single picture of the meal, so, says Olga, no-one saw what the wedding party ate.

The bride treated her colleagues to little cakes like the ones from the party. She brought two bottles of wine and a bottle of bubbly, *Not the best quality, I know that for sure*, says Olga, *because I know a bit about champagne, good champagne is expensive*, she said. *She brought two packets of ground coffee, which was strange*, says Olga, because it is forbidden to make your own coffee in her bank, as there are machines everywhere. This little celebration took place during working hours when it is absolutely forbidden to consume alcoholic drinks, so it was out of the question to open the wine and the champagne. And so the guest of honour packed up all the uneaten and undrunk treasure and after work she took it to the other place where she works part-time, to treat her colleagues there. Before that, Olga tells me, the women in her department had thrown a modest sum into a hat and bought the future bridal couple some frippery, something entirely useless that looked impressive, wrapped in abundant cellophane. *The woman who got married in Paris is fairly good-looking*, says Olga, *apart from the fact that she shouts when she talks*, and that's perfectly true – whenever I call, her voice is blaring in the background. She has beautiful black hair and narrow hips, Olga tells me, so during the celebrations Olga wondered whether she would have any problems giving birth, should she intend to give birth at all, or else the matter could be solved with a Caesarean. A Caesarean section is a better solution if a woman wants to retain her figure and avoid post-natal problems, including psychological ones, which can be unpleasant. This young economist is a narrow specialist, so narrow a specialist that the narrowness of her specialism precludes her taking any interest in anything unconnected with banking, with foreign currency, and with (international) fashion. Apart from that, says Olga, this colleague is always hurrying, hurrying, hurrying because, she says, she has a lot of work, although the work she does is fairly dull, financial and stultifying. What matters most to her colleague, Olga tells me, is to earn as much as possible, that is the purpose of her life. So this colleague brings home every month for her tedious administrative work more money than a competent orthopaedic surgeon would, rota work included. There are surgeons like that here, surgeons that are world-class, they come to exhibitions and theatre performances (to which bank employees don't have time to go), and these doctors always look tired and they're somehow always pale. In general, one can have confidence in the doctors here, with them conversation isn't one-way and forced as it can be with journalists for example, with some journalists it's impossible to carry on a two-way conversation, they freak out and bolt, you can see that they're not used to talking. Needless to say, not all doctors are charming and astute, but one often comes across those who are.

Things are a bit different with dentists, although dentists are also likable, normal people, in fact. One took out a perfectly made inlay under which there was nothing unhealthy, and was surprised, *Fancy that, this number four is completely healthy*, he said, even though I had told him before he picked up his drill, *Number four is healthy*, I said, *it's number six, bottom right*. That dentist had assessed me wrongly, he must have thought *what does she know*, he must have thought that I didn't know the situation in my own mouth, but I know it very well, it's a healthy situation overall. When he saw that he had messed up, the dentist coolly moved on to the next tooth, number five, that is, and I could have thumped him, although I couldn't have left just like that, with drilled teeth, so I restrained myself. When he didn't find anything in number five either, he filled both teeth with some white mixture, then he joined them at the top, he simply cemented them so that not even the finest dental floss could pass between them, nothing could pass between them. When a dentist carries out such a procedure as the artificial joining of teeth, a person has the feeling that his or her jaw has suddenly grown and become abnormally heavy. I told the dentist, *There's no question of your leaving my mouth in this heavy state, I want a space between my four and five on the lower jaw*, and he then ground both four and five so much that my entire meal fell into that hole, which was unpleasant when I was in company; I had to suck, drawing in air, *tstststs*, the way some people do in buses on international routes, they suck in air right behind people's ears while the loudspeaker plays something unspeakable called People's Radio, so that every departure from this town becomes torture; so it is better not to move around much. And one dentist always cleans tartar, which I don't have at all. She moves so rapidly from repairing my teeth to cleaning tartar that I don't have time to point out that there's no need for her to clean the tartar from my teeth so often because there's no time for it to build up, but cleaning tartar pays well, I realise, it costs two hundred and fifty kunas, while filling a little caries only costs a hundred and twenty kunas, and that's not enough for one session, especially as cleaning tartar takes ten minutes and a filling takes forty-five.

In connection with the expansion of the European Union, one Croatian minister said that it would be expanded after expansion and that we must expand the expansion.

In a chemist's shop, a girl buys cosmetics with an American Express card. She has red hands and stiff, swollen fingers, as though she washes laundry in a cold stream in winter; she has several cheap rings on every other finger of both hands.

In Croatia a Day of Swamp Habitats has been officially proclaimed. The day is celebrated, but it is not a holiday.

A lot of famous people were born here, János Kádár, for instance. Except that János Kádár isn't mentioned in this country anymore because he is no longer important, but neither is Ödön von Horváth, who was also born in this town, often mentioned, not remotely as often and as loudly as, say, Ivan Zajc, of whom it is always said that he is noble, *Ivan pl. Zajc*, they say, they simply adore saying and writing *Ivan plemeniti Zajc*, which when translated becomes an unprecedented idiocy – Ivan the noble Zajc, Johann adelig Zaitz, Giovanni nobile Zaitz, unless of course they mean Johann von Zaitz, or Giovanni de Zaitz, although there are no recorded facts about Zajc's nobility, nor indeed of his hundred-per cent Croatianness, because Zajc's father was Czech and as soon as he got the chance he fled from this town, so it is not clear why people adopt him with such zeal. A great and inexhaustible love for Ivan pl. Zajc who, incidentally, was not all that good a musician, as for Janko Polić Kamov, who is, mercifully, still today a good writer, that great love comes from the fact that Zajc and Kamov, although they fled early, did nevertheless in some sense belong to the people here and are therefore, naturally, more significant to them than foreigners. Besides, that von Horváth said things which many people here still can't agree with just like that. That's why Ödön von Horváth, although long dead, actually gets on their nerves, that's probably why they don't often mention him.

I am a typical mixture of the blessedly deceased Austro-Hungarian Monarchy: at the same time Hungarian, Croat, Slovak, German, Czech, and if I were to rummage among my forebears and have my blood analysed – a science which today is very much in fashion among nationalists – I would find, as in a river bed, traces of Tsintsar, Armenian, and perhaps Gypsy and Jewish blood. But I do not acknowledge this science of the spectral analysis of blood, a science in any case of dubious value, dangerous and inhuman, especially in these times and in these regions, where that dangerous theory of soil and blood creates only distrust and hatred and where that "spectral analysis of blood and origin" is most readily carried out in a spectacular and primitive way – by knife and gun. I am bilingual from birth, and I wrote in both Hungarian and German until I was fifteen when, translating a collection of verse by a Hungarian poet, I opted for German, because it was closer to me. I am, ladies and gentlemen, a German writer; the world is my homeland.

I wanted to bring my mother to Croatia, only I have nowhere to put her, our grave was stolen. To be precise, it was stolen by Magda Kovačević from Medveščak Street.

The grave where the urn containing my mother's ashes rests was bought by the painter and sculptor Paško for himself and his Marija some time in the 1920s, when he moved from Split to Belgrade. Paško and Marija had no children. My grandmother Ana was older than her sister Claudia, the one who played the piano and made cakes to order, so her uncle Paško left his estate to her, my grandmother Ana, everything apart from his paintings, works of art and other articles, which he bequeathed to his native town of Split. This is what was stated in the will that I have here in some ten copies, with all accompanying documents and the correspondence between the Belgrade lawyer Dr Rinaldo Čulić, of Miloša Pocerca 18, who represented Marija's side, and the Split solicitor Dr Prvislav Grisogono, of Marmontova 9, who represented my grandmother Ana. Needless to say Luigi, Ana's and Claudia's half-brother, doesn't enter the picture.

[. . .] *All the artistic works of my late husband Paško,*
to be found in my aforementioned apartment, of
which there are altogether: paintings and sculptures
– three hundred and forty-one (341); sketches – two
hundred (200); from his war collection – sixty-four
(64) pieces, plus two large statues of a fighter, each
three metres high, which are in the Dispensary on
Zeleni venac Square, all the works of my late husband

Paško, all his material – his library, books, manu-
scripts, photographs, all this is to be given to the
municipality of Split in order to found a gallery bear-
ing the name Paško Vučetić in his beloved native
town of Split.

My piece of land, which I inherited from my late
husband Paško, and which is entered into the land
registry in the Split court in the name of my late
husband Paško, I leave to the municipality of Split to
be sold, and the income from the sale to be used to
cast in bronze the works of my husband which are
now in plaster and which will belong to Split.

The objects damaged in war, seventy-five (75)
pieces, currently with Mr Viktor Cajs, an engineer
from Belgrade, I leave to the municipality of Split,
with the wish that they be used for taking care of
the grave which I bought and where I have erected
a memorial. The grave is in section eleven (11) and
bears the number 23.

Marija dies on 20 July, 1929, in Belgrade. At the time, of her closer relatives, still living are her brother Karlo Galant, head waiter in Veliki
Bečkerek, her sister Katica Fuks, also of Veliki Bečkerek, and her more
distant relative Nada, wife of Viktor Cajs, the engineer from Belgrade.
On 20 August,1930, the Court of First Instance in Belgrade establishes
how much money Marija left in cash, how much in bonds, how much in
her savings account. The Court of First Instance records a list of what
was left:

Household items
In the dining room: 1 table and 5 chairs, 1 settee and
5 cushions, 1 small set of shelves, 1 lectern, 1 screen, 7
small rugs, 1 large wall mirror, 1 small stool and 2
small curtains.

In the drawing room: 1 bookcase, 3 small tables and 4 chairs, 1 linen cupboard, 1 set of shelves, 1 settee with a throw and 4 small cushions, 2 lecterns and 4 strips of lace, 2 lace curtains with tracks, 1 kilim from Pirot, 2 lace hangings and 1 velvet one, 1 small kilim on the wall.

In the bedroom: 2 bedsteads, 2 bedside tables, 1 washstand with equipment, 1 wardrobe, 1 sewing machine, 2 lace curtains with tracks, 1 gas lamp, 1 nickel tray, 2 boxes with 6 knives and 6 forks made of alpaca silver, 1 box of 6 large knives, forks, spoons, teaspoons, soup spoons and a spoon for milk made of alpaca silver, 1 coal scuttle, 1 divan, 2 small Pirot kilims.

In the hallway: 1 carpet runner, 1 chair, 1 small table with a leather top, 1 hose for watering the garden.

In the kitchen: 1 cooker, 1 kitchen cupboard, 1 shelf, 1 small mirror, 2 small chairs, 1 gas cooker with various kitchen crockery, glass and pots.

In the attic: several empty baskets, containers and other small items of insignificant value.

Linen and clothing: 24 men's shirts, 20 pairs of men's underpants, 24 ladies' blouses, 10 pairs of ladies' panties, 14 ladies' bodices, 6 ladies' caps, 16 small pillows, 12 bed sheets, 18 large pillows, 35 handkerchiefs, 17 towels, 30 serviettes, 10 tablecloths, 58 pieces of needlework, 4 pairs of ladies' stockings, 11 ladies' dresses, 1 lady's coat, 2 ladies' knitted jackets, 2 ladies' hats, 5 boxes with a suit, a fur and used articles.

Paintings

32 large paintings worth 150,000 dinars, 39 medium-sized paintings worth 80,000 dinars, 156 smaller paintings, the majority portraits worth 31,000 dinars.

Sculptures

20 pieces, tools, materials and incomplete artistic works, models, etc. with a value of 20,000 dinars.

The other items and paintings of the late Paško referred to in the will were not found during the inventory, so cannot be taken into account on the occasion of discussion of the inheritance.

The total estimate of the estate according to the inventory amounts to 326,712.80 dinars.

According to the inventory (judgment of the court expert in the District Court of Split, file 37/30 of 25.1. 1930) the late Marija also left property in Split consisting of a plot of land 8449/1, grazing land, situated on the new part of St Manda Street. The plot of land 8449/1 had an initial area of 1608 m^2 but 150 m^2 were later removed in the course of the construction of the new road, the remaining area consisting of 1458 m^2 at 75 dinars per m^2, which amounts to 109,350 dinars.

The total estate of the late Marija Vučetić is therefore estimated at 436,062.80 dinars.

For the sake of orientation, at that time a small Ford truck cost around 50,000 dinars.

As the sole and legal heir to all of the above, my grandmother Ana takes nothing; she pays the lawyers and continues to sew. It was never discovered where the works of art mentioned in Marija Vučetić's will ended up. Forty years after Marija's death, Ana's daughter, my mother, dies, after Ana has already buried her husband and one son (at this time the other son is still alive), and she is given permission to bury her daughter, my mother, in Paško's grave. That's all. She asked that much.

> I, Ana Osterman, née Vučetić, of 24, Medvedgradska, Zagreb, as the heir of Marija Vučetić, on the basis of the settlement of inheritance by the District Court of Belgrade, no. 8315/I-1401109 of 20 August, 1930, and the current owner of the grave, declare irrevocably that I agree that the urn of my daughter, the late Tea Moser, née Osterman, deceased 20 April, 1973, be placed in the grave of the late Vučetić Marija, in Belgrade. I authorise my granddaughter Lea Moser and my grandson Boris Moser to carry out this task.

The send-off, as some like to put it, was big, a great crowd shoved into the chapel of the crematorium at the New Cemetery, throwing themselves into our arms and sprinkling our cheeks with sticky spittle mixed with tears, while we just stood there. In fact, when the dead are cremated, it's better to call it a "farewell" than a funeral procession, because the deceased are not accompanied anywhere; the chapel is usually immediately next to the crematorium. So when one says parting, it's as though the person is going on a journey from which he or she will return, while a crowd of people stands on the station platform waving, smiling, sending kisses and waving again.

With a cremation, there are no long processions winding through the paths of a graveyard, swaying with the whispering of acquaintances, broken by an occasional brief laugh or little sob, with fear and unease hovering over them; there's no solemn walk through the city of the dead where chiselled shadows wait around every corner, calling to one. The speeches end, followed increasingly often by that ghastly church singing, those collective prayers in which priests call out dramatically the name of the deceased, as though they were old acquaintances, which is of course far removed from common sense, when the congregation repeats in a trance, as though catatonic, *Our sins, our sins*; this entire badly rehearsed performance with elements of Greek tragedy and vaudeville comes to an end and the coffin simply sinks from view and the audience is left high and dry.

But when we came for the ashes, we were alone, my father, my brother and I. It was pouring, we waited in the cemetery office on the first floor for them to bring us Tea and watched through the window as the cemetery sank before our eyes. There's always mud in cemeteries. Nona Ana didn't come on that occasion. She sat beside my mother's bed, eerily empty, stroking the pillow. From then on, Nona Ana became increasingly small, increasingly round and increasingly black. She was transformed into a velvety ball that rolled through the apartment, somehow never rebounding. Only occasionally, as though she were composed entirely of black down, would Nona Ana rise barely perceptibly above the ground, then land again softly, falling without a sound. Like a little bird, she would try to chirrup, but what came out was a tiny, jerky whisper, a general huskiness, a crackling, inside and out. We were afraid that she would get mislaid somewhere, under a carpet, behind a door, that we would step on her or squash her, she had become so much smaller. Then, one day she said, *I'm going home*, and left.

Marija Vučetić's will was carried off by the wind. Split took the art works, but in the course of time they were alienated, sold and given away. Nothing was ever cast in bronze, no gallery was ever opened, so much for Paško's beloved native city of Split, what rubbish. Today on Marija Vučetić's plot of land there is a large apartment block with flats for sale; on the foundations of someone else's property, new occupants create their own, private property. Some of Paško's works remain in Belgrade, hanging in the National Museum, some have ended up in private collections. "The Fighters" are still in the Dispensary, while the "Boy from the Čukur Well" is in the street that leads down from the National Theatre, I forget what it's called, maybe Dositejeva. The other statue of the boy from the Čukur Well, the one that Marija gave to be cast, sways at the New Cemetery, on a plinth over the gravestone, because someone tried to "alienate" him as well. With his legs apart, in a victory pose, this boy holds a jug out of which nothing trickles, because the jug is broken, he stands as though he's about to take a step, smiling. He's a small boy, not a metre in height, bronze, all movement and mischief.

After the death of her son Karlo Osterman, while my mother and father were working in another country, Nona Ana lived with me, depressed and impossible. She woke early, then later realised that there was no need, so she woke increasingly late. She would make coffee, wash and then lie down again. She left the bath dirty because, ball-like as she was, she couldn't bend over its edge. *Clean the bath*, she would say, *I'll make stuffed squid for you.* She followed me, accompanying me everywhere through the apartment, and she talked, constantly, she had a strong voice, penetrating, despite her sorrow. To start with, she drank coffee with real French cognac, the brand was not important, then she moved on to coffee with local brandy. Then she developed jaundice and didn't drink anything, not even wine mixed with water. She ate a lot of cheese, soft cheese, from Srijem, the fattiest, with heaps of yoghurt with a roll dunked into it, because of her teeth. She couldn't chew well, so on the whole she sucked her food, squashing it against the roof of her mouth. I don't know how, but she had a quite respectable set of false teeth, which gave her a natural smile. *My body needs calcium*, she would say. Then would come the story about her impoverished childhood, about her mother who remarried and died young, about the miserly aunt she later lived with, about how she cleaned up donkey droppings and ate stale bread, always the same, as though I were listening to the tale of Cinderella.

She put carrots and sometimes also sugar into everything she cooked, so that her dishes were all orangish and sweetish, and greasy: she used unheard-of quantities of oil. Neither she nor I needed these lunches, but she had to have something to amuse her, so she cooked and meddled, what else, sometimes she would also sew, little things, pillowcases.

She had attended Italian schools. She read *Grazia*, *Grazia* was all the rage at the time, then she would tell me the world's gossip in detail. She had been to America, she had seen the Empire State Building and the Niagara Falls. She had been to Egypt, to Luxor and the Aswan Dam, from where she had brought statuettes of the head of Nefertiti, which she later gave to her doctors. In fact, she kept one head, *Put this figurine on my grave*, she said. We did that, then later someone stole the figurine, of course, because we had just placed it there, we hadn't screwed it down.

Nona Ana bought the grave in Zagreb when my grandfather, her husband Max Osterman, died, way back in 1943,

all that I have, even that grave, has been earned
by my hands, my needles and my ten fingers

a fine grave in the middle of Mirogoj Cemetery, 128-II-297, with a black marble stone, a restrained, distinguished and serious grave, which is now no longer ours, which was stolen by Magda from Medveščak Street.

When he lived in Split, my grandfather, the wig-maker and anarchist Max Osterman, gave pedicures to Meštrović*; when he died, Nona Ana sold his wigs

so they don't fray, so moths don't get into them

but she kept the books, even though most of those books were in Gothic script, especially Heine, Goethe and Schiller.

The son who died before my mother, Karlo Osterman, was a journalist,

rascal, he changed degree courses three
times, he kept pestering me to send him
to the Diplomatic School of Paris. In
the end he studied law.

a witty and playful journalist, his heart burst, like that of my grandfather Max, his father. It simply exploded, poof. The one who was left, Rudi,

* Ivan Meštrović (15 August, 1883–16 January, 1962), was a Croatian sculptor and architect, now regarded as one of the greatest sculptors of the 20th century. He was the first living person to have a one-man show at the Metropolitan Museum of Art in New York City. Translator's note.

was not witty, but pedantic, during the Independent State of Croatia, he studied calmly and obediently, nothing could get in his way, nothing could deflect him from the path of scholarship. The one who was left, Rudi, was Ana's favourite, he built bridges, and together they constructed a solid Oedipal relationship, so that when he married, Ana felt rejected. He was always put first, the most important, he was the one who screwed things up over the Mirogoj grave.

That wife of his was dreadful, as soon as I moved away
she got into his bed, a cold woman, cold as a snake,
blond and blue-eyed, washed-out and calculating,
both she and her sister Magda.

When I made her angry, she would say *by our Lady, you have* il diavolo *in corpo*. She invoked that Lady often even though she quarrelled constantly with the Church. The older she grew, the less she believed, *Those priests, who are they kidding?* she'd say, then begin to list the illegitimate children of well-known clerics and lawyers who walked around Split, saying who was *the spitting image* of whom, and she would end every tirade with *If God lies, genes don't*. Then she'd turn to Paganini. She adored Paganini. *Il diavolo* was in his *corpo* as well.

Paganini drove his audience wild. Sometimes he'd
break three strings on his violin and play on just
one. He was capricious, like the caprices he composed.
He'd play pizzicato now with his left, now with his
right hand. A great gambler and a hothead. And do
you know why Il Ponte dei sospiri is called Il Ponte
dei sospiri, do you know what that means? Answer
me!

Then she'd say that there exists a Ponte dei Sciavoni, or she'd mention the forests felled in the time of the Venetian Republic, then she'd give me recipes for *brodetto*, for *Cremeschnitten*, for black risotto, for *Schneeknödel*, for mushrooms with cream, *write it down*, she'd order, *you'll need it*. When some new man appeared in my life, she'd sit him down and interrogate him for hours, then, when we were alone, she'd say, *be careful*, tutto ti prometto finché te lo metto, then she'd add, *he hadn't washed his hair*, or *his trousers are badly made*, or, *he's very inflexible, be careful*.

Then there came the phase when she couldn't stop crying. *Ah my daughter, what a life*, she wailed, even though I wasn't her daughter. She had hands as soft as feather pillows, fingers like soft rolls, as though she soaked them in yeast and they rose, and between these fingers she crushed a handkerchief rolled up into a ball, wet and slobbery, with which she never wiped her eyes, just her nose. The lenses of her glasses were always cloudy, greasy. She rubbed herself with anti-rheumatic creams and smelled of menthol, then she'd use those greasy hands to steady herself and leave marks all over the walls.

She had unreasonably white skin. White and smooth, she had a surplus of skin with no fuzz.

While her son Karlo and daughter Tea were still alive, Nona Ana didn't wear black. She had dresses for going out and a suit of pure silk, blue. She had lilac and green shantung blouses. Grey skirts of thin material. On the left side of her chest she wore a brooch of white gold, decorated with diamonds. Later, when she moved to my place, she waddled through the rooms in a thick black jumper of some synthetic material with a lot of little bobbles like burrs on it. Her wardrobe seemed to have evaporated. All that remained were nightdresses, winter ones – white, light-blue and pink, made of fustian which she called by its German or Italian name, *Barchent* or *fustagno* – and summer ones – poplin, edged with lace. She related television programmes to me, especially ones about politics and culture. She loved Peter Brook, she took an interest in football, supporting the Split club Hajduk.

On the anniversary of the death of her son, my uncle Karlo, she went to the hairdresser, having not been for twelve months. She had a perm, she cried. I told her, *It suits you, you look tidy*, she went to the bathroom, turned her head a bit to the right, a bit to the left in front of the mirror, then she announced, *Yes, I'm completely different*.

She was forever writing letters to someone and receiving responses to them. She had a Pelican pen with narrow green and black stripes. One day she said, *Teach me Cyrillic, it annoys me not to know it.* She was seventy years old.

Two summers passed. Then she announced, *I feel myself again, I'm going home.*

Then came my mother's illness and her death. Nona Ana was with us again for a while, then she went back to Zagreb, to her Medvedgradska Street house, but she was never the same, she never recuperated.

Again it was raining when we buried Ana. Again there was mud, Mirogoj mud, Zagreb mud this time, not New Cemetery mud, Belgrade mud. There were no people and the relatives had thinned out. There was one son left, Rudi, he came. His wife came as well, blond, blue-eyed Hilda, the sister of Magda from Medveščak Street, both half-German or half-Czech, one or the other. (Today neither Rudi nor Hilda is here, but Magda is still.) Magda didn't come, why should she? The children of Ana's still-living son Rudi didn't come either. We came, the children of Ana's dead children. Five of us. Hilda organised everything. She gave Ana's furniture to the Red Cross, she arranged piles of letters, including postcards, that her dead children and living grandchildren had written to Ana and gave them to the senders who were present. That's all. Someone bought Ana's apartment and moved in. We dispersed. We scattered through various towns of former Yugoslavia.

It was a fine apartment, though without modern comforts, in an unusual house. Strange people lived in that building, very poor and orderly. In their kitchens, they had white linen curtains and, on the walls above old built-in wood-burning cookers, they had pinned up pieces of material with embroidered maxims in blue or red, like *Too many cooks spoil the broth*, with pictures of housewives forever washing, cleaning or making meals. Some of the apartments had tiled stoves, some didn't. No-one in that building had a bathroom, just a lavatory. The house had three floors and an attic and nice wooden shutters. On each floor there were two two-room apartments and in the attic six bed-sitters, which one entered from a kind of dark concrete platform.

The rooms in the attic had no water, they had low ceilings and sets of furniture including at least two couches, the tap was in the hall above a square white enamel basin. The building smelled of ground coffee and pig-fat. It had a curved stone staircase and wood stores in the courtyard, it had a fence of wrought iron, in the front beside the gate there was a grocery shop with silky sweets in tall jars. On the second floor lived mad Emilija, who sat on her balcony, because hers was the only apartment with a balcony facing the street, the others were at the back facing the wood stores and no-one sat on them, they were very small. And so, mad Emilija sat on the semi-circular balcony at the front of the house, mumbling, pointing to the passers-by. Her feet were wrapped in dirty rags, she was filthy, dishevelled and toothless, but not old, in fact she was young, only this wasn't obvious. Another young woman lived in the house, later she turned to prostitution, we had been at school together. There was someone else whose son had died at roughly the same time as Ana's, so she and Ana grieved together. Later they quarrelled and stopped speaking to each other. Mrs Herman lived in the attic. She had a good-looking husband who had a collection of alarm clocks in that attic room, he was a train guard with five beautiful, dark-blue, railway caps. Their little room tick-tocked from all directions, and the window was small, very small. I went to Ana's grave whenever I came from Belgrade to Zagreb. Twenty-five years have passed. Now I am in Croatia, there's no need to visit the past or old buildings. Or graves.

Sometimes I do go to funerals in Zagreb, that's life. Then I call on Ana.

Finally, I went to that house as well. Medvedgradska Street is quite different today, there are new buildings, there are luxury shops, Medvedgradska Street looks like an old lady with ten facelifts, all stretched and tight, but sick within. There are no children outside. Ana's apartment now has a bathroom, tiled. The old range has been demolished. The corridor has been widened. There's a lot of large furniture, all opulent and crude.

The only one of the old tenants still there is Mrs Herman, up in the attic, alone. Now she has a telephone. We sat for three hours, we drank five very sweet Turkish coffees from very small cups with ladies in burgundy crinolines strolling through gardens, smelling the roses, followed by men in tails. Then Mrs Herman said: *She died in the psychiatric hospital of Vrapče.*

We believed she had died in hospital, from heart failure, from pneumonia, that's what they told us. For twenty-five years that's what we believed.

Then Mrs Herman said: *They took her away by force. She didn't want to go. She begged, don't, don't.*

Those ladies on the cups kept calmly strolling through the fragrant gardens. There were no clocks anywhere. It seems that Mrs Herman had thrown them out, like the railway caps.

Then Mrs Herman said: *Her son Rudi called. He gave the order – take her away. They didn't need to take her, she wasn't mad.*

I thanked Mrs Herman. It was stupid, but I did. Mrs Herman gave me her telephone number, I have it here. *Give me a call from time to time*, she said.

I went to Mirogoj, to the office. *To settle my accounts, to pay the rent for the grave*, I told them. They said there was no need, it was no longer Ana Osterman's grave, but Magda's from Medveščak Street. They said: *Madame Magda pays it all on time.*

I went to the court. They gave me the transcript and judgment. They were very helpful.

The court corridors were crammed with people but they saw me first, which was incomprehensible. They photocopied everything for me, gratis.

In the street I studied those papers. The trams had stopped, there was some kind of fault. Everything stopped. The pedestrians stopped and the noises stopped. The papers referred to the disputed inheritance, which was a bit late, twenty-five years. Ana's son Rudi, the one who was alive until two years ago, had given Ana's grave to Magda, no-one called us. No-one could have called us, because Magda stated that we didn't exist. Magda stated that my mother Tea had never been born, which means that my brother and I hadn't been born either. She did admit that Ana's other son, Karlo, had been born, but his daughters had not; one of them works in the hospital here, she treats rheumatism, the other is a journalist. In the transcript it says:

> I, Magda Kovačić, with power of attorney from Rudi Osterman, son of Ana Osterman, with full moral and material accountability state that the legator Ana Osterman was married to Max Osterman, who died before her and that in this marriage two children were born. 1. Osterman Rudi and 2. Osterman Karlo – who died without heirs. I, Magda Kovačić, take over the estate [. . .]

So, I said to my cousin Vanda yesterday, as we bought oven-proof salad bowls and later ate cakes in that café with the grey armchairs, *we don't exist.* In her childhood, Vanda's surname was Osterman, after her father Karlo Osterman, my uncle and brother of my mother Tea Moser, née Osterman. Only, Vanda doesn't exist, and I don't exist, so we didn't buy anything and we didn't eat anything, and Vanda's sons don't exist either, or my daughter, or my brother, or his children, or the children of Vanda's sister Violeta, the journalist, they don't exist. Not one of us exists, only Magda from Medveščak Street does.

Listen, it happens. There was a red-haired man who had no eyes or ears. Neither did he have any hair, so he was called red-haired theoretically.

He couldn't speak, since he didn't have a mouth. Neither did he have a nose.

He didn't even have any arms or legs. He had no stomach and he had no back and he had no spine and he had no innards whatsoever. He had nothing at all! Therefore there's no knowing whom we are even talking about.

In fact it's better that we don't say any more about him.

                                                Yours,
                                                D. Harms

What shall I do with my mother?
When I die, where shall I go? Back to Belgrade, dead?
Needlepoint is a good word.

Sometimes there are talkative people here. Those are mainly shop assistants, because they spend hours alone in their shops or kiosks. It's worse being in a kiosk than in a shop, in a shop it's possible to walk around, while in a kiosk you just sit or stand still. Recently, they installed new kiosks here, a combination of glass and metal, in which it's unbearably hot in summer and in winter draughts blow in from all directions. In those kiosks the salesgirls resemble captive animals; people pass by, sometimes they stop, while the salesgirls stare straight ahead, as though expecting something. Why don't men sit in kiosks en masse too?

There are words I adore, for instance, *picatabàri* and catamaran, they are cheerfully nervous words, like the fluttering of small birds' wings, sometimes they bring inner calm. As do Lilliputians.

Are you waiting for the cashpoint? asks a woman behind me in the queue, which is, of course, lengthy.

This riles me at once, because of the way she stresses the words. I'm ready for a quarrel. *What do you think I'm doing?* I snarl at her, whereupon she makes herself scarce.

I'm becoming very disagreeable, even offensive. It's amazing that people talk to me at all. A few days ago I told a man, *You're walking diagonally.* He stopped and said, *Pardon?* and I said, *Try to walk straight.*

In the bank, also a while ago, a woman asked me which window I was waiting for. I said, *The first one that's free.* She corrected the way I pronounced the sentence and said, *If that's how you intend to speak, you can go back to Serbia.* Then I said I was going to thump her, and she disappeared, she probably went to a different bank, there are banks and cashpoints all over the place.

A small animal clinic, that sounds nice, tender. Like when you say a shop that repairs small household appliances. It sets you thinking, first that such a clinic must be visited by small people, children in fact, secondly, that these children hold tortoises in their laps, bowls of little fishes, cages with hamsters, rabbits or birds, and thirdly, that these children are solemn, especially while they wait. That's touching. But when you visit such a small animal clinic, more often than not the car park is full of shiny new cars of substantial size, and at the entrance there's a dog as big as a calf that sometimes growls (because it's sick), and sometimes doesn't, but just waits (also because it's sick). Horses and cows are categorised as large animals. Sheep are no bigger than large dogs, but they're not considered small animals, and neither are goats. What about turkeys and other poultry? In this sphere, veterinary, it seems there are little illogicalities.

One year some small animals, hens, caused chaos in this country. The staff of a veterinary dispensary organised a demonstration and set off for the parliament, taking their hens with them as proof of the injustice being done to everyone, poultry and people alike. The hens marched in a column on an equal footing with the dispensary staff. A cordon of police also quickly appeared, to protect the government from the pests. The hens clucked, of course. The workers made a noise as well. It was summer, very hot. As they drew near to the parliament, the feathered column was decimated, most of the hens first fainted, then they expired.

Hens are gentle creatures, feather-brained. Their lives are rigidly and strictly organised, like the Church and the Party, with the dominant specimen emerging with permission to peck the other hens in the head. The other hens remain submissive until death, they submit of their own free will to their leader, following in her footsteps, blindly. The situation with cockerels is identical.

Hens are very sensitive to all kinds of abrupt change, whether in food, surroundings, laying eggs or reproduction, so changes must be introduced gradually into their lives. It's the same with cockerels. Both cockerels and hens are good-tempered creatures, docile. Only sometimes they behave irrationally. When they get something into their heads, they stick to it like crazy.

These creatures aren't blind, they distinguish colours well. That's why in our language the phrase "chicken blindness" is inappropriate and unjust to both hens and cocks. Nevertheless, their blind devotion sometimes gets them into foolish situations. During the last eclipse of the sun, in the middle of the day, all the hens leapt onto their perches and instantly fell asleep. As soon as the eclipse was over, they leapt down again. That business with the hens didn't happen in this town. Nonetheless, word gets around.

Once I was on a vaporetto in Venice, and the small boat was also transporting children with special needs, as it's politically correctly termed nowadays, but "special needs" covers a broad spectrum. Expensive shoes can be a special need, skiing can be a special need, as can holidays in the Antilles. Houses with fireplaces can be a special need, buying factories and hotels, football matches, carnivals – all of them can be special needs. The need from time to time to eat a piece of meat can also be a special need, to have your children full and not so sapless, to work for pay, those can be special needs as well. Today, special needs are very relative special needs, the concept is flexible. The children on the vaporetto had Down's Syndrome. They were being taken somewhere, evidently, there were a lot of them, a whole class, perhaps a whole school. They filled the small boat. We are just chugging along when one of the boys starts to masturbate. He looks straight ahead, smiles and jerks off. The passengers for the time being without special needs turn away and gaze at the sky. Then, another boy joins the one jerking off. Then another, then another. For the length of the journey to our destination all the boys with special needs are going at it at full steam, one could almost say, synchronised, and the day is sunny and touristy.

Pernkopf. He had special needs as well. Scientific.

Eduard, my name is Eduard Pernkopf. I was born on 24
November, 1888, in Rappottenstein in Lower Austria. I died
on 17 April, 1955. I was a famous anatomist in my time, one
of the best.

   Look, says my mother, *look at the illustrations.* On the cover is written
Topographische Anatomie des Menschen and inside, in two volumes,
over several hundred pages, in the minutest detail, are hand drawings
by skilled artists (watercolours) of the human body, dismembered,
dissected, in sections, organ by organ, from the head, brain, eyes,
through the heart and lungs, to the legs. Everything, nerves and blood
vessels, bones, flesh, is presented precisely and elegantly. *This is the best*
atlas of the human body since Vesalius' in the sixteenth century. Look, says
my mother. Then she adds, *Only there is a stain. A big stain. Here.*

What stain? Nonsense! First, swastikas are a symbol of
auspiciousness and have nothing to do with national-
socialism. They are runes. Swastikas are found as early
as the Neolithic period.

   I have that Pernkopf atlas with its eight hundred illustrations in
colour, worth a small fortune today. The edition is published by Urban
& Schwarzenberg, Berlin und Wien, 1943, reprinted numerous times,
translated into English, perhaps into some other major languages as well.
In this atlas, underneath their illustrations, alongside their signatures,

the artists Franz Batke, Eric Lepier and Karl Entresser place small Nazi insignia, bent-armed crosses and the letters "S.S." as additional ornaments. To make it clear.

The atlas is published in its original form, with the Swastikas and S.S.s until 1964, even in America. In 1989 the editor W. Platzer at the publisher Urban & Schwarzenberg: Baltimore–Munich, publishes the *Pernkopf Anatomy: Atlas of Topographic and Applied Human Anatomy*, volumes I & II. The signatures of Karl Entresser with the S.S. symbols appear in volume II on page 338, under illustration 336, and on page 339, under illustration 337. So, the little Nazi ornaments with the artists' signatures disappear gradually (what's the hurry?), quietly, without pomp, almost secretly, while the illustrations, of course, the unsurpassed illustrations, remain unchanged.

My father was a doctor too. I am the youngest of his three children. I adored music, I wanted to be a composer. But, in 1903, my father died and I enrolled at the medical school in order to help my family. I graduated in 1912 and immediately started teaching at the Viennese Anatomical Institute. While I was a student, I had been an active member of the National German Brotherhood, Die akademische Burschenschaft Allemania, an old organisation founded as early as 1815, I do not see anything wrong with that. A man cannot spend all of his time studying.

My spiritual and academic father, the famous Ferdinand Hochstetter, director of the Viennese Anatomical Institute, died in 1954, at the age of ninety-three. I was not that fortunate, I died relatively young, less than one year after Ferdinand, I was sixty-seven. I died of a stroke while working on the fourth volume of my magnificent atlas.

This atlas is my life's work. I have been refining it since 1933, I have been working on it all my life. The human body is full of secrets. I engaged the best artists. Lepier was their leader, among them were Ludwig Schrott, junior, he died in 1970, Karl Entresser, he died in 1978, and Franz Batke, who died in 1983. After the war, Werner Platzer joined them. It was a brilliant team of healthy, talented Aryans.

The fact that all of us immediately joined the Nationalsozialistische Deutsche Arbeiterpartei, in 1933, has no connection whatever with our work. Later, we also became active members of the S.A., Sturmabteilung, the so-called Brownshirts, but I remained true to music as well throughout; to my dying day music was my mistress and my inspiration. We believed in Nationalsozialismus. A lot of people still believe in it today, so what! Anyway, I was never accused of war crimes. I spent some time in the Allied prison camp near Salzburg, three years, then they let me go, they had no evidence. It was cruel on their part. That prison, that prison . . . destroyed me. I emerged a broken man, depressed. Then they stripped me of my positions and all my titles. Nevertheless, I still had my baby, my atlas – the meaning of my life. It has been used all over the world up to the present day, it has been sold and resold, both doctors and students study it, in medicine my atlas is indispensable, and therefore so am I. See, I am still here. That is my revenge.

People say all kinds of things, write all sorts of abominations about me. Until 1943, I was Dean of the Medical Faculty, and until 1945 Rector of the University of Vienna. So what do they imagine, that it all happened just like that?

And they can talk, the ones who accuse us! It took them fifty years to pull themselves together, to utter

a single word. What use is that to anyone now? The
past is the past, the progress of science is the primary
need of society, its special need.

In the 1990s, sixty years after the war, the secrets of the "great masters" were still surfacing. Sixty years after the war, conscience was still carrying out a search of its own hiding places, it couldn't rest, it dug through the archives and dossiers, through the memories of the survivors. Medical faculties and institutes, factories producing glass, cars, medicines, steel, banks, churches, museums, cemeteries throughout Austria and Germany hide the rotten corpses of historical remains, submerged in the muddy depths of the past, worm-eaten and deformed. The past refuses to sink, it floats on waters that spread a stench, but keep flowing on, here, there, throughout the world; the past attacks the memory, digs through recollections, endeavours to clean up its rubbish, the great junk heap of the world. This pathetically late effort, this nauseating human aspiration to obtain forgiveness for unforgiveable sins committed, this longing for purification from unpurifiable sins, is carried out in a whisper, with downcast eyes, half secretly, unwillingly and cravenly.

I tell you, it's all meaningless now. What if I did take
those 1400 corpses or more, exactly 1377 pieces; they
were dead people, they had been sentenced and the
Gestapo had killed them, and I needed models for
my atlas.

It wasn't until the year 2000 that ninety-eight specimens of various parts of the human body were found in formaldehyde in the Department of Histology and Embryology of the Medical Faculty in Vienna, and, from the labels on the glass jars, it was verified that these were from the bodies of people who had been condemned to death.

So what? Those specimens had been there since 1940.
They could have thought about it sooner.

> At the end of the 1980s, Yad Vashem asks the University of Innsbruck to carry out an investigation. It is thought that some of your specimens are still lying in the Anatomical Institute. The University of Innsbruck refuses to cooperate.

They are probably good specimens so they are being kept. I selected those specimens, I selected only the best. There were not many Jews among those specimens. Besides, presumably the universities have some kind of autonomy these days, do they not?

I admit, immediately after the Anschluss I cleansed the Medical Faculty of Jews and other undesirable elements. It was essential at that time. I might be more lenient today, but today there is no need to take such measures, the methods are different. The University of Vienna was one of the leading European universities, something had to be done. Of 197 university employees, I dismissed 153, which just proves the extent to which non-Aryan elements had infiltrated our milieu. Why, they were in the majority! I do not regret those three Nobel Prize winners either, their places were taken by new young pure-blooded Germans.

> Professor Pernkopf, when you were appointed Dean of the Medical Faculty in 1938, you gave an inaugural lecture, addressing the doctors and students. You said: *As present and future medical practitioners, your task – using all your professional abilities, all your learning – is to concern yourselves with people whose lives have been entrusted to your care. Your*

task is to do this not only in a positive sense, so that
you will have the best possible influence on reproduction, but also in a negative sense, so that you will
eliminate the incapable and defective. The methods
for controlling racial hygiene are well known to you:
birth control, the free reproduction of the genetically
acceptable, those whose genetic and biological consti-
tutions promise to give birth to healthy descendants;
the prevention of reproduction by those who do not
belong together, those whose races are being eliminated, and, finally, sterilisation and other methods in
order to exclude from future generations all possibility
of the birth of genetically inferior individuals. That is
what you said in 1938, when the idea of euthanasia
had not been given formal status, when the Holocaust was barely hinted at.

Indeed! I was far-sighted. That is what I still think
today.

But why have you gone for me? There were other
doctors, at other universities. They were also involved
in scientific work. And they kept their specimens in
formaldehyde too. Ask them.

My colleague, Professor Carl Schneider, Head of
the Department of Psychiatry at Heidelberg University, he was concerned with child psychology. He
published his research thanks to the Nazi programme
of euthanasia, and worked with children who had
been sentenced to death. After the children were killed,
Carl prepared their brains, and then dissected them.
He accumulated an impressive collection of children's
brains. Ask him.

*

I committed suicide in 1946. Leave me alone.

In 1991, an official demand is sent to Ludwig-Maximillian University in Munich to carry out an investigation into assertions that their Institute of Anatomy contains the bodies of castrated men, identified as "prisoners of war". But, like your university in Heidelberg, Munich also hesitates about taking any action. Until 1990, only the universities of Tübingen and Vienna undertake official investigations. At first, in 1988, the then director of the Anatomical Institute in Tübingen states that of all their microscope samples perhaps just two come from "possible" victims of the Nazi Terror. Two years later, the investigating commission discovers that 400 corpses were sent to the Institute during the war. The names of all the foreign workers killed by the Nazis were found tidily classified in the Institute's files. After that, the suspect exemplars, as well as those of unidentified origin, were buried in a separate plot in Tübingen cemetery, where the remains of dismembered bodies used in the teaching of anatomy are in any case buried. What do you have to say, Professor Schneider?

I'm not interested.

An official investigation into the wartime activities of the Max Planck Institute has yet to be carried out. Admittedly, the Max Planck Society has removed its wartime collection of samples and slides from the Max Planck Institute for Cerebral Research in Frankfurt, and also from the Max Planck Institute of Psychiatry in Munich, but that is all.

*

Who cares?

I'm dead. Why don't you question Professor Her-
mann Stieve, or, even better, Dr Julius Hallervorden.
You've got Hirt and Voss as well. And Watsel, the
director of the Anthropological Section of the Vienna
Museum, many people outlived me. They worked and
published, carried out experiments and were receiving acclaim until their deaths. I killed myself. Don't
bother me anymore.

Professor Stieve?

I was a leading anatomist at the University of Berlin
and head of the famous Berlin Charité Hospital. I was
born in 1886 and died in 1952. My memory is poor. I
remember, hazily, that I studied the female reproduc-
tive system. I did not kill anyone. The Gestapo regularly informed me which women they were intending
to kill and when. I would then take them on as patients.
I would tell them exactly when they were going to be
killed, then I studied the way in which psychological
trauma affected their menstrual cycle. After their
deaths, these women were of no use to anyone, in any
case no-one enquired about them, no-one came for
their corpses. So then we removed their ovaries, fallo-
pian tubes, wombs and urological tracts and undertook further histological research. For the benefit of
humanity, in the name of future generations of women.

After the war, you were Dean of the Medical Faculty
of Humboldt University, then in East Berlin. You
lectured students on the results of your research into
the migration of spermatozoa in women raped by
members of the Gestapo immediately before they

were murdered. People say that the whole auditorium was dismayed.

Who are you to censure me? And only now, when it was all done with long ago. No-one interrogated me. And nor will they. Science is in my debt. In the Berlin Charité Hospital a lecture theatre still bears my name, and my bust adorns one of the vestibules. You're tedious.

Professor Hallervorden?

Yes?

You were director of the renowned Kaiser-Wilhelm Institute for brain research. As exemplars for your scientific work, you used murdered psychiatric patients from Brandenburg.

I compiled the richest collection of neuropathological samples in the world. It numbered several hundred specimens.

From time to time you even lived on the "euthanasical" execution site in Brandenburg.
You suffered from a congenital neurological disease . . .

which was named after my colleague and me the Hallervorden–Spatz Syndrome. I have a model C.V. My C.V. was included in the Anthology of the Founders of Child Neurology, *1990 edition.*

which is manifested in uncontrollable disorders, psychological agitation, difficulty in walking, generalised hypertension, impaired speech and swallowing. Perhaps you hoped that, among the damaged brains you rummaged through, you would find a cure for your own damaged brain?

Nonsense! I died at eighty-three, with a clean conscience and a clear mind.

Professor Hirt, you are among the more morbid collectors.

I killed myself immediately, in '45. Before Schneider. I remained famous as the joint discoverer of the fluorescent microscope, I, Professor Dr August Hirt.

You planned to found in Strasbourg a collection of skulls from all races and peoples of the world. In collaboration with the Nazi authorities, you sent eighty-six Polish Jews from Natzweiler concentration camp in occupied France to the gas chambers, and then transferred their bodies to your institute. After the war, French medical students dissected some of those bodies. You carried out terrible experiments on people, using mustard gas and phosgene.

Phosgene smells of new-mown hay. I adore the scent of phosgene.

I am a witness. I gave my statement to the Russian Commission for the Investigation of War Crimes. I go by the number 115. I was a nurse at Natzweiler camp. One day Professor Hirt came from Strasbourg, he asked me to select thirty strong, young prisoners and isolate them in a special block. No-one apart from the professor, his assistant and I had access to those rooms. I was ordered to record the progress of the illness. This is what I saw: the professor and his assistant protected their faces with gas masks. Then they injected each prisoner in the palm and the underside of the upper arm with 10cc of some liquid, I don't know which. Later, ten prisoners received fifteen drops of Vogan, ten received eight drops, and the remaining prisoners nothing. The patients were placed in beds and waited one hour with their arms outstretched. That same evening the patients began to howl with pain. Burns appeared in the place where the prisoners had been injected with the liquid and rapidly spread all over their bodies. All of them complained of pain in their eyes and lungs. I tried to help them, but my efforts were in vain. At midnight, I went to bed. When I woke up I realised that I was having problems with my sight. For ten days the professor's assistant took photographs of the patients, who were not offered any help. They howled like animals. They were on the verge of madness. The first prisoner died two weeks later, on 21 December, 1942. His body was immediately sent to Strasbourg. The bodies of the other patients were kept at the camp. Autopsies, which I attended, were carried out in situ. The brains of all the prisoners who died were shrivelled, their lungs corroded and desiccated, as were their livers. The patients who survived were left partially blind and had difficulty breathing.

What can be done now? Such were the times. Experiments with numerous poisons have been carried out since time immemorial. All over the world, including

in America, to the present day. Even when there is no
war. When there is no war, preparations are made for
future wars.

What about me? You haven't asked me anything?

Professor Voss?

Yes. I was Dean of the Medical Faculty of the Reichs-
universität in Poznan. I wanted to be a sculptor. I
have a perfect understanding of the anatomy of the
human body. After the war, from 1948 to 1952, I was
Head of Department in Halle, then in Jena, right up
until 1962. Then I retired. At sixty-eight years of age,
I became Professor Emeritus at the Anatomical Insti-
tute in Greifswald. It was nice there, by the sea, a long
way from Poland, I don't like Poland. Or Poles. I died
in 1987.

During the war you processed the bones of Poles
who had been killed and sold them. At the Anatomical Institute in Poznan, you made death masks and
torsos of Jews killed in the nearby concentration
camp.

That has no connection with the truth. Watsel put
on an exhibition of the skulls of various races, in
the Vienna Museum, and I helped him. Do you really
think that I would have received all these honours if I
had done inadmissible things during the war? Why,
my Taschenbuch der Anatomie *was reprinted seven-*
teen times in German, and was translated into Span-
ish and Polish. It was the most popular anatomy text-
book ever printed in Germany.

One should not be naive. I was a small fish. There
is no-one who is completely innocent.

Did you know that bones give off light?

Of course they give off light, they contain phosphorus.

Did you know that the fields around Auschwitz give
off light? At night, when the moon is full?

I lived in the north, I wouldn't know.

Kapuściński wrote somewhere: *A human life is*
enough for one mistake. One mistake is enough to
cancel out a whole life. Later it is enough to carry a
cross to the end of your days. A mistake is the same as
a suicide, except that it is spaced out in time.

Kapuściński? Do you know what else that Kapuściński
said? That Pole Kapuściński. Everything repeats
itself, *that's what he said.* Repetition is the key and
the riddle, *that's what he said.* We know that it
will be the same again, although we strive for it not
to be repeated. Everything revolves around that:
the desire for repetition, the fear of repetition. The
rhythm of repetition. Man is a slave. The question is:
where from do repetitions draw the strength for
endless repetitions?

Take a little run through history. As far as experi-
ments are concerned, why did history latch on to
us, S.S. members? We had models to learn from. The
Japanese, the Americans, multinational companies.
Pharmaceutical factories all over the world are still

carrying out experiments on people, they are producing new biological weapons. In the name of the future. In the name of progress.

> My name is Walter Benjamin. Think of Paul Klee's painting "Angelus Novus". Angelus Novus is the angel of history. He has a human face, but bird's wings and claws. His face is turned towards the past. Where we perceive a chain of events, he sees one single catastrophe that keeps piling ruin upon ruin and hurls it in front of his feet. The angel would like to stay, awaken the dead, and make whole what has been smashed. But a storm is blowing from Paradise; it has got caught in his wings with such violence that the angel can no longer close them. The storm irresistibly propels him into the future to which his back is turned, while the pile of debris before him grows skyward. This storm is what we call progress.

A small incomplete chronology of medical experiments conducted on people in the name of peace, democracy and the progress of humanity

1st century B.C. Cleopatra invents an experiment in order to verify the assertion that forty days are required for the formation of a male foetus, and eighty for that of a female. When the authorities sentence her female assistants to death, she "has them impregnated" and after a specified period of pregnancy, orders them to be "opened" so as to strengthen her assertions.

1845–49 James Marion Sims, an American gynaecologist and surgeon, one of the giants of modern medicine (he devised a curette that is still in use), carries out experimental surgical interventions without anaesthetics on black women purchased at slave markets. Many of his "patients" die. There is a well-known case of one woman with a prolapsed uterus on whom he carries out thirty-four experimental operations.

1885 William Williams Keen addresses female graduates of the Medical School in Philadelphia: "Experimentation is essential. We must discover new methods of treatment and improve the old ones. These methods must be tested on patients. Or on you. Choose which you prefer."

1891 Dr Carl Janson from Stockholm reveals that he used fourteen children from a nearby orphanage to test his vaccine against smallpox. "I had enough animals," he announced, "but they would have cost too much to keep."

1897 The Italian bacteriologist Sanelli carries out experiments on five patients, in search of a cure for yellow fever.

1900 Walter Reed infects twenty-two Spanish émigrés from Cuba with injections of cultured bacteria, promising to pay each "patient" a hundred dollars if he survives or two hundred if he becomes infected.

1906 Dr Richard Strong, Professor of Tropical Medicine at Harvard, carries out experiments with cholera bacilli on prisoners from the Philippines, causing the deaths of thirteen people.

1915 The American Office of Public Health artificially causes pellagra in twelve prisoners from the State of Mississippi.

1919–22 Experimental transplantation of testes in five hundred prisoners in San Quentin.

1931 In Lübeck, Germany, seventy-five children die after they are injected with living tuberculosis bacilli for experimental purposes.

1938 In Pingfan, twenty-five kilometres from Harbin, the Japanese establish the notorious Unit 731, which, under the guise of being involved in the purification of water, in fact perfects biological weapons. From 1942 to 1945, under the leadership of Dr Ishii, in Manchuria, Unit 731 carries out medical experiments on tens of thousands of Chinese soldiers and civilians sent to Pingfan. In Pingfan, doctors in Unit 731 "inoculate" prisoners known as "*marutas*" or "corpses" with bubonic plague, cholera and anthrax, after which they are opened up alive, screaming. Over the course of a decade, hundreds of thousands of people are killed. There has never been a trial in Japan for the war crimes committed. In 1945, Japanese units bomb the headquarters of Unit 731; in order to conceal his misdeeds, Dr Ishii, the "brain" behind the experimental research, orders the killing of the remaining 150 "corpses". The results of the vivisection carried out on the Chinese "corpses" are considered so significant by the Americans in 1946 that they make a "deal" with the doctors responsible. You give us the data, we give you your freedom. After the war, Dr Hisato Joshimura uses his expert knowledge of the influence of extreme temperatures on the human organism to offer advice to a Japanese expedition to the South Pole. Dr Masji Kitano, who had carried out numerous experimental operations, becomes the leader of the Green Cross, the largest centre for blood processing in Japan. Most Japanese hear the story of Unit 731 for the first time in 1982, after the publication of the novel *Infernal Insatiability* by Seichi Morimura.

I am San Ling. I am seventeen years old. I live in China, in a suburb of Harbin. My parents are factory workers, sometimes I work in the factory as well. We are poor. I have an older brother. He is involved in politics, but that is a secret. He is a member of the Communist Party. We are fighting the Japanese, he told me, the Japanese do not wish us well, he said.

One day, the Japanese military police came to the factory and took me away for questioning. They questioned me for three days, but I didn't know what to tell them, I don't know why they were questioning me. They mentioned my brother a bit, not much. I didn't tell them anything. They beat me. They yelled. I was very thirsty. I am small, but I am resilient. Then they brought a woman in. They chained me and that woman together, my leg to hers, and my arm to hers. Then they threw us into a lorry, chained like that. We came to a prison.

*They brought men into the cell. Those men raped
me. I had never had relations with a man before
then. I am seventeen years old, I am very tiny. Later
they told me, in fact a nurse whispered to me, that all
those men had venereal infections. Otherwise, those
men were prisoners. They were dirty. And smelly. I
kept vomiting something yellow. My stomach swelled.
They told me that I was pregnant, then I gave birth
to a little boy. Two days after his birth they took me
back to the clinic, in fact to an operating theatre.
There was another girl there.*

> *That's me, Tamara Mazursky. In the operating theatre
> there were two tables with those stirrups in which they
> put women's feet. It was cold. I am nineteen years old.
> I am Russian, I was born in Harbin. My family has
> been in Harbin for twenty years now, we have a
> baker's shop. I work in the shop too. I have a fiancé.
> One day, when I was on my way home, the police
> just picked me off the street. They brought me to this
> prison. I was raped by at least ten prisoners, I don't
> know why. Afterwards a nurse told me that I had been
> infected. I began to have pains in my lower abdomen,
> terrible pains. Doctors often visited me but they didn't
> give me any medicines. They ordered me to get onto
> the table.*

Me too.

> *We both got up.*

Then they said, We have to open you up.

*

267

> *One doctor said,* With no anaesthetic, awake, *he said.*

It was terrible. Blood spurted in all directions,
up to the ceiling. It hurt like crazy.

> *They took out our organs.* Put the ovaries here, *said one doctor.* The uterus over there.

> *Then we died. There on the table. Both of us.*

> *Then they burned us.*

1939–45 The most terrible mass medical experiments in the history of mankind were carried out throughout the Third Reich, in camps, prisons and hospitals.

1940–50 In America, experiments on patients, under the direction of Dr Cameron: sleep deprivation and electro-convulsive therapy together with the use of narcotics such as L.S.D. After the "therapy", the patients no longer function normally. From 1950, Dr Cameron's experiments are sponsored by the C.I.A.

1944 In the Centre for Atomic Research at Oak Ridge, U.S.A., for the requirements of the "Manhattan" project, soldiers were "inoculated" with 4.7 micrograms of plutonium.

1946–53 The American Commission for Atomic Energy sponsors research in schools for retarded children in Fernald and Wrentham, State of Massachusetts, in which the pupils are served oat flakes with radioactive isotopes for breakfast. In 1949, the Commission for Atomic Energy studies the results of the experiments.

1950   Dr Joseph Stokes from the University of Pennsylvania intentionally infects two hundred female prisoners with the herpes virus.

1950–72   Mentally retarded children from Willowbrook School in the State of New York are intentionally infected with hepatitis with the aim of finding a vaccine. Acceptance at the institution is conditional on participation in the research.

1951–60   The University of Pennsylvania draws up a contract with the U.S. Army which allows it to carry out hundreds of psychopharmacological experiments on prisoners throughout Pennsylvania.

1952   At the Institute of Psychiatry at the University of Columbia, the patient Henry Blauer is injected with a fatal dose of mescalin. The sponsor of the experiment, the American Ministry of Defense, conceals the proof and data for twenty-three years.

1952–74   Dermatologist Dr Albert Kligman from the University of Pennsylvania carries out hundreds of tests on the skin of prisoners in Holmesburg. "I don't feel guilty," he announced. "I didn't see people, all I had in front of my eyes were sheets of human skin."

1953–57   The Centre for Atomic Research at Oak Ridge sponsors the injection of uranium into eleven patients of Boston General Hospital.

1953–70   The U.S. Army experiments with L.S.D. on soldiers in Fort Detrick.

1953–73   In eighty institutions, involving hundreds of people, within the framework of a mind-control project under the code name "MK-ULTRA", the C.I.A. carries out experiments in brainwashing with the use of L.S.D.

1956   Dr Albert Sabin tests an experimental vaccine against polio on 133 prisoners from the State of Ohio.

1962   Live cancer cells are injected into twenty-two elderly patients in the Jewish Hospital for chronic diseases in Brooklyn.

1963–73   The then leading endocrinologist Dr Carl Heller carries out experiments on prisoners from Oregon and Washington, with X-rays to the testes, giving them five dollars a month and a hundred dollars following the vasectomy which concluded the experiments.

1965–66   The University of Pennsylvania, under contract to Dow Chemicals, carries out experiments with dioxine on prisoners in Holmesburg.

1991   At a clinic of the University of California, Los Angeles, Tony LaMadrid kills himself after participating in a test on relapse in schizophrenia sufferers after their medication is withdrawn.

1993   In Seattle, at the Fred Hutchinson Hospital for Malignant Diseases, Kathryn Hamilton dies forty-four days after participating in an experiment on those suffering from carcinoma of the breast.

1994   *The Albuquerque Tribune* publishes information about tests in the 1940s in which mentally retarded patients were subjected to secret radiation and "therapy" involving injections of plutonium.

1995   The American Ministry of Energy publishes a study on experimentation with radiation on people, carried out with the Atomic Energy Commission from the 1940s to the 1970s. The report contains a list and description of 150 cases plus 275 further cases.

1997   The *New York Times* publishes data about an experiment with placebo medicaments sponsored by the American government. On that occasion, pregnant women from Africa are infected with the H.I.V. virus and denied medication.

1997   The American Food and Drugs Agency (F.D.A.) gives pharmaceutical companies huge financial incentives to carry out drug testing on children. The incentive to each company is a potential income of 900 million dollars.

1999   Eighteen-year-old Jesse Gelsinger dies in a clinic at the University of Pennsylvania after taking part in experimental treatment with genes, during which she is injected with thirty-seven billion particles of adenovirus.

2000   The *Washington Post* exposes unethical experimentation on inhabitants of rural China, financed by the American government. The genetic experiments were carried out by scientists from the American University of Harvard.

HAVE YOU REMEMBERED THEIR NAMES?
NO, IT WAS SATURDAY.
(conversation at a bus stop)

On the fourth floor there's a Croatian family.

We're on the third, no kind of family.

On the second there's a Bosnian family, plus seasonal workers.

The only family that has lived in this building since the hotel was refurbished as apartments is the family on the first floor, an Italian family. In that family, the generations replace one another, people die but others are born, so the family survives. And the nameplate on the door survives, always the same. The longevity of that family, its persistence in non-leaving, in non-dispersal, its determination to stay true to what is today just an illusion of the town in which this family was born, frightens the other residents and disturbs some of them. This is the only unaltered, unmodified family in this building. It's an urban family, which hardly ever stirs out of its apartment, so it gives the impression of being invisible. If it does stir, it does so during the day, when it has to. It's the only family in this building that can say this is our town, but they don't say that, for obvious reasons, their town no longer exists, just as in fact they no longer exist either, they are remnants, ruins, from year to year they're ever more threadbare, forsaken and now very small, they're literally (in height) small people. When compared with the other tenants in the building, despite the fact that they are barely visible, it's only the tenants on the first floor who strike one as authentic; the rest of us are imitations, kitsch tenants, kitsch citizens of a small kitsch town. What is more, when they communicate with the other tenants, the tenants on the first floor speak Italian, in fact they whisper, sprinkling the dark, neglected stairway with sparks of a brighter past. Sometimes I see "my" Italian family outside the theatre, when there's an opera on, usually Verdi, or an Italian play in Italian. Then a small audience gathers in front of this building which languishes in darkness for three and sometimes four days in the week. They aren't well-known faces, not the so-called elite, the elitelette of this town, they are its little islands with eroded shorelines which are drowning. When it's cold, even when it's not very cold, women stand outside in fur coats of old-fashioned cut which emit the odour of moth-balls, the odour of a packed-away past. They all know each other, they chat quietly. And that space in front of the theatre seems not to know what to do with itself, crammed as it is with monuments whose epochs and meanings clash: an enormous fountain, modern, resembling the bidet of some giant fat muse, and a fragile bronze statue of Ivan Zajc, reminiscent of the age of socialist realism. This space, by day splashed with smells, colours and noise from the nearby market, the clamour of snotty, scantily dressed children, the cries of the hawkers, the false elegance and authentic poverty of the buyers, by night this space, cramped and truncated, seems to sway with sighs. It hibernates and hopes in vain that one day it will perhaps after all open up again, stretch out in front of those who walk over it and abandon itself to them. At night, the cries of the other squares in this town seem to create a weave of glass threads behind which a quite different life pulsates, forgotten and trodden upon.

Newcomers live in this town's core, which the majority of the old inhabitants have left, some by force, some by choice. Newcomers also live in the suburbs, the newer ones, some richer, some poorer. The grand houses, broken up into smaller residential units, are also inhabited by newcomers, who tread firmly on the marble stairs, trampling over some-one else's past as they make their own. Today this is like a cloned town, neither completely old nor completely new, a town of newcomers who change its face without touching its spirit. It is a gloomy town, gloomy from sorrow and abandonment.

I have often written about newcomers; it is terrible
that these newcomers, this non-urban class, or semi-

urban class – I do not know whether this is the case everywhere, but I do know that it is the case in Belgrade – has certainly not come from the countryside, and certainly not from some organic countryside that lives in its own context, these people come from a zone set between the country and the town, a nowhere-land. Neither here nor there. And I think that it was out of this between-space, this in-between class, that something has detached itself from the countryside but has not reached the town, it was out of this "neither–nor" that everything was recruited to cause the chaos and crimes of the war, and to participate in the annihilation of towns and the killing of people.

I think that this is the Yugoslav catastrophe. It was not shepherds from the high mountains who came down into the towns, they did not wish to impose their way of life. That was done by this in-between class ...

The destroyers are among us. You go out in the morning, you meet a man, he might seem intelligent, he appears normal, and yet he carries within him a clash with your milieu that he cannot decipher. He is dissatisfied, he does not feel at home, and then he captures your milieu brutally. He enriches himself physically, materially, he goes where he can treat himself, himself, himself to all kind of things apart from his own self! Once you find yourself in a book you cannot decipher, it is very uncomfortable. So I think they have that kind of fear of the city. They speak the language badly, and what they say and the way they say it shows that they are still where they were ten or twenty years ago. They learn a particular vocabulary in order to carry out some tasks, but beyond that – nothing.

An old story, cyclical, whichever part of the Balkan backwoods it refers to, at whichever time. Bogdan Bogdanović* has been following this story for half a century and more, not waiting to see the day when the newcomers become old inhabitants, while, in the end, it is precisely they, those hybrids unequal to the city, who drive him out of it. Boris Senker, a quarter of a century younger, summons up images of his arrival in Pula in the early 1950s, when that town too, like this one here, was dying.

We came to the abandoned town and in it found
fountains – on Monte Zaro, in the Botanical Gardens
– with goldfish in them. They had been left behind by
those who went away. Obliged, of necessity ... And we
inherited them. We inherited everything that they
were unable to take, furniture, sewing and other
machines, bathtubs and all kinds of other objects,
thrown into the sea. I remember those little fish well.
They were lovely, alive. They shone ...

   After a while the fish disappeared, they died, one
by one. Then the water in the fountains dried up. Then
the fountains collapsed. While we, inheritors of an
urban culture, simply watched it all dully, without
interest, and undertook nothing. Perhaps we covered
the ruins of the fountains and the trampled lawns
with asphalt ... [took possession of] that desert, which

---

* Bogdan Bogdanović (20 August, 1922–18 June, 2010) was a Serbian architect, urbanist and essayist. He taught architecture at the University of Belgrade, Faculty of Architecture, where he also served as dean. Bogdanović wrote numerous articles about urbanism, especially about its mythic and symbolic aspects, some of which appeared in international journals such as *El Pais*, *Svenska Dagbladet*, *Die Zeit* and others. He was also involved in politics, as a partisan in World War II, later as mayor of Belgrade. When Slobodan Milošević rose to power and nationalism gained ground in Yugoslavia, Bogdanović became a dissident.
   His main works are monuments built in the Socialist Federal Republic of Yugoslavia. In particular, the vast concrete sculpture in Jasenovac gained international attention. Translator's note.

we had created around us, which we had created in
ourselves above all through our frightened and selfish
silence.

Then, Motovun. Skeletons of abandoned houses, collapsed roofs, slinking, hungry cats, their ghostly calls. Today, the fashionable rape of Motovun, picking at a wound.

In the course of the day, but especially at night, there are spells of time when all the traffic lights could be extinguished. No-one passes, nothing passes. The streets roll on alone. The traffic lights flicker tirelessly into the void, on their own. On their own. A town on its own.

I miss Azra.

Sometimes, the days here are composed entirely of lack, one lives, unliving.

Sometimes I go to a restaurant. Then my acquaintances leaf through their younger days. I can't join in. I don't know anyone from their past. It would be nice from time to time to share the past, to pluck it the way these acquaintances of mine do, a bit for you, a bit for me. I look at them, they make a passage for their past, and then it comes and fills up the holes of loss, and they laugh.

Eliot!

Yes, milady,
Footfalls echo in the memory,
Down the passage which we did not take,
Towards the door we never opened
Into the rose garden.

Pining. That's the new Croatian word for A.I.D.S.

A consumptive withering. A withered consumptive life here. A life of weakened immunity.

Some people are returning from Canada to Bosnia. They're returning after ten years, having said what a wonderful country Canada is, even in the spring when it snows. They withdraw their files from the psychiatric clinics and return.

The T.V. announcer mentions the space shuttle *Kalambia* to make it clear that he has an American accent.

In every room I have one trans-oceanic trunk, just in case. For the time being those trunks contain old books. And two pairs of skates.

I received a letter.

Write to me from that sad provincial town of yours
which I know very well.

And another one.

> *In order to repair my window frames, I spent the*
> *morning down there under the Danube station, look-*
> *ing for an ordinary window. What did I see: huge*
> *expanses of former warehouses in mud and water, an*
> *occasional lorry unloads rusty metal, workers sit in*
> *that same mud drinking beer, answering my questions*
> *with that familiar dull gaze without words. I couldn't*
> *even buy bricks without being robbed. Here people lie*
> *and rob. In enormous queues for milk, oil and sugar,*
> *people discuss international politics. They know*
> *everything. Then I brick up more than half of my tall*
> *window and they ask me, What will you do without*
> *sun? I tell them, I like it better this way, I don't need*
> *your sun.*

I receive letters. I answer them. I correspond with my previous life. Sometimes there are slight misunderstandings. I mention Marshal Tito Street to my niece and she asks, *Which street is that?*

Telephone surveys are fashionable. As they are in Canada. They ask you whether you want to buy new furniture, Italian. They ask political questions, personal questions, questions about hygiene, accommodation, cosmetics. They ask all kinds of things. Then I say, *Jinghwa haji ma se yo*, which in Korean means *Don't call this number again.*

Yugoslavia is now called Serbia and Montenegro, like Bosnia and Herzegovina.

Here, for ten years, people celebrated the First of May quietly. Then they declared the First of May the Day of St Joseph the Worker, and now it's celebrated out loud again.

A woman I know had her boobs lifted; if she hadn't told us, we wouldn't have noticed. Marilyn Monroe padded her boobs so that they stood high and looked ample. It was her undertaker who discovered it. He took the padding out and sold it for ten thousand dollars. Small private clinics for all kinds of corrections are springing up here. Here, monetary matters have always fallen on fertile ground.

A visiting Chinese opera came. There was quite a lot of interest. I didn't go because I believed that Chinese operas were very long, that they lasted five, six, seven, eight or nine hours as they came from such a large country where massiveness holds sway. There are various visiting companies, they come from time to time. Some are not bad, some are good, so I go.

Sometimes it's as though everything is dancing around me, this town, this country, all *petits pas* that give one vertigo. Then the doctors advise me, *Take an aspirin, aspirin is magical medicine.*

In London I ate salmon canapés and talked to A. S. Byatt. There was also a woman poet from Albania who introduced herself like this: *I am a very well-known poet from Albania and a very successful business woman*, otherwise she didn't know any English. She kept talking about Hamlet, calling him Amljeti.

I asked a writer for advice about the title for my book. I ask him what he thinks about "Walls of Death", and he says that he thinks walls of death sound sharp, stern and horrifying. I tell him that the story is horrifying, and he says a story doesn't need to be explained in the title. Then I ask him whether "A Tomb for Boris Davidovich" doesn't also sound dreadful, but he says that tombs can be lovely, people visit tombs, especially if they were designed by well-known tomb builders. Then I ask him, what about the "Encyclopaedia of the Dead", is the "Encyclopaedia of the Dead" * not also an explanatory title, and he says, well encyclopaedias refer to people who are no longer alive. Such short circuits sometimes occur here. Otherwise, currents don't shake me all the time, I would have died by now.

> Come. Bathe in these waters.
> Increase and die [. . .]
> The great clock of your life
> is slowing down,
> and the small clocks run wild [. . .]

> So I have shut the doors of my house,
> so I have trudged downstairs to my cell,
> so I am sitting in semi-dark
> hunched over my desk
> with nothing for a view
> to tempt me
> but a bloated compost heap,
> steamy old stinkpile,
> under my window [. . .]

Stanley Kunitz's words, not mine.

* The titles of books by the renowned writer Danilo Kiš (1935–1989). Translator's note.

There was a medical student in the family on the fourth floor. When she graduated, she got an internship, but she couldn't get a job in her specialisation, in fact she couldn't get a job at all, not even at a clinic, anywhere, not even in those districts of special governmental care that were destroyed by the war. Then she was taken on by the Roche Pharmaceutical Company, which advertises even here. Roche vitamins are the best, people say. They aren't cheap, but they restore energy, they say. They're bought in pharmacies, a little bottle of thirty tablets costs 100 kunas.

The young doctor from the fourth floor is called Linda. She has black eyes and scampers up the stairs when she comes to visit her family. She's very nimble. She has a youthful smile. She has a lot of energy, small though she is. The Roche Company gives her a car, and she uses the car to visit various places, at home and abroad. First she went to Western countries, then increasingly often to Eastern countries, those in transition, poor countries, with a shabby working class that was once healthy but is now sickly and pale. This working class will agree to all kinds of things just to have pink cheeks again, it'll agree to almost anything. Roche has this in mind. And Norvatis. Norvatis is another pharmaceutical company. From Canada.

Van Tx is a firm based in Basel, but it has regional offices throughout Europe. Van Tx carries out various services for which it charges astronomical sums. And it also undertakes services for the pharmaceutical companies Roche and Novartis. Probably for other pharmaceutical firms as well, except that isn't known yet. Perhaps it never will be.

Linda told me all this on the night she rang my doorbell at around two in the morning. *What am I to do?* she asked. *I went to collect students in Poland and Estonia, I organised their arrival in Switzerland. I had no idea what for. I sent about ten of them in one go. They were delighted, a week in Basel.*

Soon after that the information leaked out. The students were not told what kind of trials were involved, they were given pocket money and a week's free accommodation in Switzerland. And medicines, and injections. They had blood taken. Afterwards they were told, you can go to a disco, even ice-skating, there are a lot of skating rinks in Switzerland. Among other things, the firm was experimenting with drugs against Alzheimer's disease. It is not yet known whether they fucked up the students' brains, that's still under investigation. Among the guinea pigs was a young girl with a brain tumour, from the Czech Republic, Poland or Estonia, it doesn't matter. She was brought on her mother's initiative, Linda hadn't organised her travel. That mother couldn't afford her daughter's further treatment. She had read an advertisement in the newspaper saying that Van Tx was looking for people to help with the scientific research of well-known companies such as Novartis and Roche. She signed up, and they started taking blood from her daughter every day. She raised enough money for her daughter's brain operation. Later, the mother went mad. The daughter is still alive, no-one knows for how long.

Later it emerged that Van Tx also found guinea pigs among the Swiss homeless and among mental patients, because they have them even in Switzerland, although fewer than in poor countries. Particularly homeless people, there are certainly fewer of *them*. It's not so clear-cut with mentally ill patients, mental health has nothing to do with prosperity. They carried out trials by stuffing the human guinea pigs with radioactive particles.

I made a camomile tea for Linda. And for myself. We dunked biscuits in that highly sweetened tea, while Linda kept repeating, *What do I do now, what do I do now?* Then she asked, *Could I stay the night with you?*, although she had her own bed and her own room on the floor above. In the morning she said: *I have a small stone family house by the sea. I don't want to be a doctor anymore.* I took out the data that I've been collecting for years, ever since I watched my mother being poisoned in Paris, before my eyes. I gave her everything I had about experiments carried out on people over the centuries. These documents contain detailed notes on how doctors, spies and scientists poison one lot of people in order to help another lot. They usually poison the poor, the mad and the imprisoned, because, they reason, no-one needs people like them. I gave Linda everything I had on biological weapons for mass destruction, which are otherwise mostly and most imaginatively produced in America. Because it's in America that there's the most money for such things. And there are also enough homeless people. I showed Linda what I had on the MK-ULTRA Project, now that some files have been declassified. Most of them have been burned. The MK-ULTRA Project went on for twenty years, from 1953 to 1973. It was run by the C.I.A. It was a "super top secret" project that grew out of the already existing, also secret project known as the Bluebird Project, officially intended to compete with Soviet achievements in brainwashing. But the C.I.A. had other plans, never mind the Soviets, the C.I.A. was concerned about its own subjects. The Bluebird Project later developed into the Artichoke Project, because the then director of the C.I.A., Mr Allen Dulles, adored artichokes. Composed of a team of top-notch agents who could be anywhere in the world at any time, like those elegant, good-looking, educated, charming top-spies and seducers from American films, the task of the MK-ULTRA Project was to test various interrogation techniques on specially chosen subjects who wouldn't remember anything after the questioning, let alone guess that they'd been programmed along the way. In their work these agents used various narcotics, marijuana, L.S.D., heroin and ecstasy. The aim of the project was to create a perfectly programmed murderer. The MK-ULTRA Project encompassed 149 smaller projects of which some involved testing banned medicines, while some were more electronically oriented, seeking to explore the possibilities of controlling the human organism from a distance. Nevertheless, the basic aim of Project MK-ULTRA was the brainwashing of future spies for the C.I.A. The project perfected the production of fear, anger and joy, the production of obedient citizens who laugh and cry and hate when ordered to do so by Gottlieb, Dulles or their associates. It was all done smoothly and elegantly, with the aid of electricity, microwaves and drugs, without any violence, or torture, quietly and painlessly. Elegantly. Humanely.

There is proof that Project MK-ULTRA is not yet dead, just slightly modified and transformed, with a new name. This "new" project still uses high-tension microwaves and radio frequencies; it stimulates the narcotics trade, terrorism and some other lesser criminal activities, never mind which.

> Gordana sends me a Somali saying:
> You cannot wake a person who is pretending to be asleep.
> I miss Gordana as well. And Dora.
> And Mirjana.

> *Olga in London, Lea in Rijeka,*
> *Milan in Geneva, Mila in Paris,*
> *Anna in Johannesburg, Dejan in Toronto,*
> *Jasna in Harare, Vesa in Colombo,*
> *Maja in Alaska, Bane in Cyprus,*
> *Vrabac in Trieste, Mirko in Brussels,*
> *Gane in Papua, Sava in Athens,*
> *Zoran in Munich, Zorka in Boston.*

> *They all scrammed,*
> *Leaving just me with Sloba,* a fool in Belgrade,*
> *Squatting on my poem, like a pigeon on a branch,*
> *Shit-covered . . .*

(1993)

---

* Colloquial name for Slobodan Milošević. Translator's note.

Overnight, Linda the little doctor melted away. She went off to her rocky retreat on the coast. She studied snakes, collected their poison and made serum. Recently, I heard, she began to work for another pharmaceutical company, a local one this time.

There is a man here who always walks alone. He is tall and decrepit, not old. He is unshaven. He sways as he walks, perhaps because of his height. When it's cold, he wears a beige raincoat, crumpled. That looks inappropriate, because in winter people usually wear dark colours, so the man also stands out because of his coat. He has big shoes, old. They were expensive shoes, one can see at once, now they're awful. He sways terribly as he walks. He carries a newspaper under his arm, and a plastic bag containing books in his hand. This man reads a lot, I know. When it's not cold, he walks in a grey, homemade, rough-knit pullover. He doesn't have much hair, but he's not bald, his hair is cut, cut short and it lies nicely on his head. His head is nicely shaped, egg-like. He also has a nicely shaped face, oval. He's been walking like this for ten years. Alone.

When there are book launches, he comes. When exhibitions open, he comes. He doesn't eat those little savoury pastries, which are served once the formal part of those events is over. Some people fall on them, but he doesn't. He approaches people and says something. Tries to make contact, presumably. Tries to fit in. He's been trying for ten years. People move away because they don't know him, here many people are not very skilled in small talk with strangers, for them it's an effort, you can see at once. The man says something and they look at him like fish, not a muscle on their faces moves, perhaps they just blink, so the man seems to be talking to a wall, if one watches from the side. It turns one's stomach. People hold out for ten seconds, then they invent some excuse and step away. The man has no kind of status here, he has no place of work, no cheques, he can't take out loans and he lives in a rented apartment. He has an accent. Bosnian. Perhaps that bothers the non-listeners, they don't know where to place the man, and you have to place a person

285

somewhere in order to know where you stand, how to position yourself, so that you can smile at that person and let him know that everything is alright, that now he is one of us. That's why conversation with this man is an effort for some people here, it irritates them. Because such people find it hard to deal with unknowns and new particularities, they don't have time. So this man goes from one person to another, trying to say something, trying to hear something, as people say – trying to fit into this life here, because it's obvious that this man is a total misfit, but for ten years now he hasn't succeeded, people have been walking away for ten years now.

Something else. The man lives on an island, so he comes into this town from the island. He comes often and no-one knows why. Perhaps the island is too desolate, so he thinks this town here will give him back a dimension he's mislaid, or perhaps he's already read all there is to read on that island, so he goes to the library here, it's a very good library, decently stocked. Perhaps he stops in front of the window of a department store here, they are large windows, there aren't any shop windows like these on the island, perhaps he looks at his reflection then and thinks, *I'm still me, everything will be alright.*

The man writes people letters. The ones who look blankly at him when he talks, he writes to them afterwards, he thinks, *Perhaps they will realise that I'm not someone to be discarded.* So, he writes letters. Those letters are always typed but signed in ink. They are literate letters. Some people here say the man isn't quite right, but it's not that, he's just a sad man, half-dead, who sways when he walks, who has lost his shadow and now accompanies himself. The man writes to me as well. Sometimes he drops a journal that's not printed here, in this country, into my mailbox, and I leaf through it. One letter began "My dears", which presumably meant my daughter and I, although my daughter has no clue about him. This letter, which I'm looking at now, was written nine years ago, but nothing in the life of the man has changed. He's become a little quieter, that's all. He no longer approaches people, he doesn't come so frequently. It seems that his island is now enough for him. It seems that the man is slowly disappearing.

His letters are pretty detailed. So, in that nine-year-old one, dated 11 November, 1994, he says that he reached "home", i.e. the island, before 15.30. He had returned without a present for Anita, he says, but she was used to that, at least that's what he thought. Nevertheless, he was pleased, he says, he brought back several books on Finland (from the library, presumably), and remembers how in 1975 we had all admired Finnish design, precisely in 1975 when his Andrea fell pregnant at thirty-six, but in the end that pregnancy, like the next one two years later, came to nothing. Then, he writes, he met a couple from Sarajevo, and Sarajevo was where he had lived since 1941, although he was born in Tuzla, while Andrea, he says, was born in Zagreb in 1939, and Anita in Sarajevo, on 10 March, 1983. Then, he says, he bought chestnuts, he secured Dr Prenc's agreement that he could stay over with him whenever he happened to be in town, and, he says, he met me.

He writes that he has to confess that on that Tuesday, when he expected me to call the number he had left me, he was disappointed. That day, he says, he had been to the hospital with his family, to the children's orthopaedic clinic, because the previous year doctors had established that Anita's left leg was a centimetre shorter than the right one, that she had kyphotic posture, or scoliosis without rotation. Later I had an opportunity to tell him that it was nothing, that in many children who are growing rapidly one leg develops slightly shorter, and that it could be fixed with orthopaedic shoe inserts, easily and painlessly, that my daughter has it too, that she's not at all lame and that with time her leg has grown nicely and in a few years there won't be any trace of that slight deformity. But I didn't tell him. I forgot.

He writes that later they spent more than an hour in the bus station waiting room, with people passing through on their way to the toilet, in the company of alcoholics and beggars. It was probably cold on 11 November, there was probably a north wind, there always is when one is waiting, which was why they were sitting in the waiting room. Otherwise, not many people sit there. Then he writes that he felt very low, like a real vagrant. He writes that Andrea and Anita left Sarajevo on 1 May, 1992, via Belgrade, and that by 7 May they were there, on the island, where Andrea's parents were from, and that they had refugee status for more than ten months. Andrea taught German in the secondary school, he says, for two years, in fact she stood in for teachers on maternity leave, nothing permanent, but recently she'd been taken on at the primary school, on a regular basis, she had submitted her employment record, he says. He says that he himself has refugee status since he arrived in Zagreb four months ago, on an M.K.C.K. plane. That M.K.C.K. is presumably some kind of Red Cross, I don't know which. He writes that Anita is an excellent pupil, that she has top marks in most subjects, but she misses the television and her bicycle and fantasises about going shopping in Trieste and having her own passport. What Andrea misses most, he says, are a bathroom and a washing machine. As for him, he says, he misses people, human contact, books and bookshops, exhibitions, concerts, theatre, sporting events. While he was in Sarajevo, where he has left the graves of his parents, he writes, he thought that he'd be able to spend the rest of his life in that tiny village on the island where he now finds himself. He has had his fill of travelling, he says. He had been, with his wife, to New York, Mexico, Morocco and Tunisia. In addition, he writes, in 1982 he was in India, Thailand, Hong Kong, Japan and the Philippines. He complains that Andrea doesn't want to go anywhere now, away from the island, although she could have found a job in Zagreb; Andrea is afraid, he writes, that he and Anita could die there on the island, without her. He writes that Anita has aunts on the island (Andrea's), although, he says, they are old women of seventy-three and eighty. He says that he doesn't even live with Andrea and Anita, that the two of them live with one aunt and he with the other, and that neither aunt has a bathroom, or a television, or a washing machine, and, in truth, not even a particularly sunny apartment. He writes that he envies people from here (he means the island) where they have houses and go off to Zagreb or to this town here, where they also have houses and apartments. He even envies me, he says, because he had himself lived in an apartment like mine (he doesn't say how he knows what my apartment is like), in a building erected in 1911, in the street where the radio station is now. He says that he found many similarities with his own life in one of my stories and that his Anita likes cats and little fish as well and that she had lice too, although I don't remember writing about any little fishes or cats. He says that Andrea taught in a school in Sarajevo although she has a degree in economics and, he says, she and I were born in the same town. The difference, he writes, is that the two of us, my daughter and I, arrived here with our belongings, while Andrea and Anita left Sarajevo with one suitcase, with a K.L.M. hold-all and one small bag, while he, he says, came out (of besieged Sarajevo) with a cardboard suitcase and a Mexican bag. He goes on to say that their biggest problem is footwear, because Andrea wears size 42–43 shoes, Anita 40 (although, he says, she's five foot six and weighs just 42 kilos), while he has just one pair of size 46 shoes. When you leave Sarajevo, he says, you have no home, no things, and Andrea and Anita, he says, don't want to go back. It's probably too late, he writes, to go anywhere abroad; the two of them won't hear of it, he says. But, he says, he would escape. Tomorrow, he says, tomorrow is his birthday and he adds that they celebrated Andrea's birthday very modestly, as they will his too. Then he complains that he was astonished that the Retirement Fund didn't want to acknowledge Andrea's working life of a full twenty-five years, indeed they don't want to acknowledge that long working life at all here in Croatia. He writes that he worked for more than twenty-seven years at the People's University, in the section for cultural activity, that he met a lot of actors and writers there and that, he says, he brought numerous theatre companies from all over the world to the October Writers' Days Festival, that he did his military service with Taško Načić, that he spent holidays with Rada Đuričin, that he went to school with Ognjenka Milićević,* that he did a lot of sport, that he was in all the Summer Student Games (from 1948 to 1950), and the Universiads, but that for him it was now a big thing to visit the little villages on the island where he had ended up. Then he asks me to remember him if I buy any literary journals, local or foreign. And, finally, he asks me to forgive his expansiveness.

* Taško Načić and Rada Đuričin: well-known Belgrade actors. Ognjenka Milićević is also a well-known theatre director and professor of acting. Translator's note.

I avoid that man too, just like those tongue-tied individuals who raise my blood pressure here. That man frightens me, that man could be me.

One year, on the promenade, he thrust his new address and the title of a book into my hand, asking me to get hold of that book, if at all possible. I didn't. I shifted the little note from pocket to pocket, then I transferred it to my bag, where it got crumpled and dirty, then I put it away somewhere and now I don't know where. Now I rummage through my papers, looking for it. All kinds of foolish things come to the surface, it's incomprehensible that I keep so much, but there's no sign of the little note. I have the telephone numbers of various workmen for various jobs, repairs and cleaning, they're here. Names and addresses of people I can't remember appear, but his little note does not.

Twaddle.

Another good word. Twaddle.

In addition to that letter, he left me a journal.

It is the A.R.H. *Journal for Architecture, Town Planning and Design, No. 24*, printed in Sarajevo in June 1993. The theme of the issue: *WARchitecture*.

On the title page is a photograph of a huge multi-storey block in an orange-red flame. Instead of an editorial, on the first ten A3 pages, under the title IN MEMORIAM, is a list of the names, photographs and biographies of architects killed in the first year of the war in Bosnia.

Mirsad Fazlagić (1950–92)

Amra Leto-Hamidović (1956–92)

Vesna Bugarski (1930–92)

Emir Buzaljko (1952–92)

Zoran Bajbutović (1935–92)

Slavko Cindrić (1936–93)

Kemal Saltagić (1931–93)

Josip Gačnik (1952–93)

Nikola Nešković-Kićo (1932–93)

Munira Saltagić (1937–93)

HAVE YOU REMEMBERED THEIR NAMES?
NO, IT WAS SATURDAY.
(conversation at a bus stop)

These people have given Bosnia hotels, congress centres, hospitals, railway stations, post offices, stadia, publishing houses. It would be logical to leave all that behind when the time came for them to go, it would be logical that their hotels, their villages, their congress halls, their hospitals, post offices, publishing houses, that their railway stations and stadia should remain, because it would be logical that buildings last longer than a person. But here, with these people and these buildings, a hellish cosmic reversal took place, a great absurdity: man and his works passed together into the other world. Their symbiotic urbanity was annihilated through *unbridled revendications* by those *of the lowest mental capacity, the panic-stricken urbanicides, with their hackles raised against everything urban.*

The city . . . in the very centre between man and the
universe, could be understood at the same time as
a little universe and as a very large man . . . I am a
small city, while the city is a large I . . . In each of my
cells glimmer the polyhedrons of the devastated city.
The murdered city – my ashes.

(Bogdan Bogdanović)

The size of a town is not what gives it its urbanity. *Urbanity is polish, articulateness, harmony of thought and word, words and feelings, feelings and movement.* The man who sent me the journal knows this. Burned Sarajevo, despite being barbarically transformed into a necropolis, remained urban. On the other hand, just as that Albanian poetess prides herself on her literary and managerial skills, which fight each other and cancel each other out, so some towns too, often those that have been conquered by force, not necessarily with mortars and grenades, but through the drunkenness of the blind and arrogant, so some towns die,

*their energy gives out, their metaphysical eros is extinguished, and along
with their will to live, their memory and self-awareness. But,*

*there remains something very powerful and hard to
destroy, even in the face of the onslaughts of the bitter-
est barbarians. That is, let us call it "the sacred
essence" of the city. And this is where an ascending
line begins, the line of human decency and moral
beauty. We all, still, bear in ourselves our immortal
cities. They are borne, of course, by those who have
something to take away, and in which to take pride.
Because, there are cities that cannot be killed as long
as in them survives, safeguarding them in himself,
the last urban man.*

Over the past ten years, the number of inhabitants of this town has
decreased by a quarter. Forty thousand people seeped out of it for ever.
Forty thousand people tore away a piece of its being and left. People
take all kinds of things with them when they leave, trifles, a friend of
mine carried all over the world little sheets of fine cigarette paper; some
carry gravel, some sea water, some, the nameplate of a street, a piece of
stone from a crumbling building, some carry jars, little bags of sugar,
matches, used entry tickets for various productions, pocket address
books, not to mention photographs. They carry small plush bags in
which they keep special, personal treasures and drag them around in
their pockets, just in case. If every person leaving packed up a little
bundle of the town, and they did, if, in moments of weightless stepping
through their own lives, they open their bundles somewhere secretly,
which they do, it's clear why the town has been left mutilated, riddled
with emptiness, while its scars steadily contract. This town now pulsates
quietly, even more quietly, ever more quietly, despite the din that sprawls
over it. This town, like a toothless old woman, shrinks, moves into its
underground labyrinths, slows its bloodstream, slows its breathing,
blinks, turns from time to time now onto one side, now onto the other,

begins to sway, a hazy light bathes it from above, a humming comes from its innards, it squints, and, not remotely surprised, it closes the approaches to its desiccated organs and sighs. It whispers:

Around me nothing moves, parts of my being live
separately, each for itself. Parts of my being do not
speak, they no longer have anything to say, or anyone
to say it to. I understand these parts of my being,
but I do not feel them. Around me a pantomime is
being performed in which I do not participate. I am
outside.

Who says that, the
town or I?

A shrinking town.

A contracted town in which loneliness is an epidemic that the inhabitants do not know is raging.

A new greeting came into use, a mutation of the old one. Before, people used to call out *Bog!* now many people say *Bok-bok*, quickly and staccato, so it sounds like *Bak-bak*, which reminds one of the cantabile English greeting:

Ta-ta!

Addio.

It is March. It's a sunny day. After months of torrential, cold rains, the icy winds have withdrawn, the sky has calmed down, it hangs above the town as though dead. Just occasionally a cloud, a *pilvi*, slides from the sky, settles on the hair of a chance passer-by, on his or her shoulder, on his or her chest, slips onto a bare branch, onto the road, and vanishes. Lea Moser opens the shutters and throws her head back as though she had been slapped. She breathes in and says *missä on uloskäynti?* Lea Moser goes to the bank, withdraws her savings and buys a plane ticket to Helsinki: *Olokaa hyvä, lippu Helsinki*, she says. *Helsinki?* asks the salesgirl. *Kyllä, Helsinki,* says Lea Moser. She takes the ticket, she smiles, *Kiitos,* she says, waves, *Hyvästi,* she says, and leaves.

In Helsinki, Lea Moser visits her childhood friend. The two of them, Sara and Lea, talk. At night they sit cross-legged, each on her own bed, and eat enormous quantities of ice cream, *Hyvää jäätelö,* says Lea Moser.

Yes, good, says Sara. *Lea, stop speaking Finnish, you haven't a clue,* she also says.

I not Lea, I Tessa. I Tessa Koller. Tessa wants drive Helsinki truck, big truck, suuri truck, says Lea Moser. *All day long, koko päivän. Please help. Please.*

Lea Moser, alias Tessa Koller, is employed by the private firm T. & M. Trans to transport ice cream and other dairy products in a refrigerated truck all over Europe. She goes to Russia, she goes to Germany, to France, to Italy, she goes to small countries as well, she goes everywhere. In the truck she has what she needs: water, a toilet, light, food. She doesn't need much. When she arrives in a town, she takes a day off. As soon as she arrives, she buys a pocket dictionary, and picks up a list of monthly events at the tourist office. She changes in the truck. In high heels, in a black coat reaching to her ankles, in an evening dress with a decent décolleté, sometimes black, sometimes dark-green shantung, she goes to symphony concerts. Strikingly made up. Otherwise, when she's driving, Lea Moser alias Tessa Koller doesn't wear make-up, she just dabs a bit of cream under her eyes, to soften her wrinkles. In the truck, Lea Moser has different clothes for different occasions. She adores her clothes. Sometimes she just walks through these unfamiliar towns and gets to know them. Sometimes she sits in parks, watches children and smiles. Sometimes she buys fruit, sometimes she goes to elegant restaurants, and if it's a town that has sea, she goes bathing and swims as though she were in a race, butterfly stroke, fast. In the truck, while she drives, and they are long distances, they can take as long as forty-eight hours, Lea Moser alias Tessa Koller sings. The wind blows her hair and she sings. At times her eyes water, because of that wind. *Tessa Koller happy*, she says out loud.

On Lea Moser's heart there's a small tattoo that she's not aware of, the imprint of a child's finger, of a child that's hers. In the truck cabin Lea Moser always has a fresh yellow rose, one, only ever one.

When she has several free days in a row, Lea Moser stays with her friend Sara. One day Sara said, *Lea, you need a doctor.*

I not Lea, I Tessa, minum niemeni on Tessa, she replied. *Tessa Koller well now.*

The doctor came nevertheless. He watched Lea, then he concluded: *It's aphasia. She has to learn to talk again.*

No, said Lea Moser. *Tessa Koller no talk. Exit closed, ulos suljettu. Tessa just breathe and sing.*

That lasted for a year.

Then the owner of T. & M. Trans, Gustav Mustonen, sends Tessa Koller on a long journey.

Long? asks Tessa. *Kaukana?*

Kyllä, kaukana, says Gustav Mustonen.

Hyvää, bon, good, bene, says Tessa. *Milloin?* she asks.

Tänä iltana, Tessa, says Gustav Mustonen.

Tessa loves Gustav Mustonen, he never calls her Lea, only ever Tessa.

Tessa Koller drives her refrigerator truck for four days towards the south of Europe where she is supposed to unload forest fruits, black and red berries. She drives, rests, listens to a bit of Rachmaninov, a bit of Liszt, and a bit of Mozart when she's bored with the other two. Violent rains follow her on the journey, it's March. In Paris she goes to the Panthéon, in fact to the Church of Sainte-Geneviève, on a little square she watches a circus troupe perform acrobatics with burning torches, at an open market she buys warm crêpes filled with raspberry ice cream, spends the night in the suburbs in the apartment of a Moroccan photographer who tells her about the Cheshire Cat, in the morning she leaps up into her jeans and into her truck and drives on. In Vienna she goes riding. In Milan she buys a new evening outfit. She goes to the hairdresser, has a sauna. She arrives in the port. She unloads part of her cargo. She has a day off. She walks through the small town. She walks along the quay that used to be called Riva Marco Polo and is now just called Riva. She comes out onto a square.

Marco enters the city; he sees someone in a square living a life or an instant that could be his; he could now be in that woman's place, if he had stopped in time, long ago; or if, long ago, at a crossroads, instead of taking one road he had taken the opposite one, and after long wandering he had come to be in the place of that woman in that square. By now, from that real or hypothetical past of his, he is excluded; he cannot stop; he must go on to another city, where another of his pasts awaits him, or something perhaps that had been a possible future of his and is now someone else's present. Futures not achieved are only branches of the past: dead branches.

Nice town, says Tessa. *Sunny town*, she says. *Quiet people, gentle*, she says. She reaches the promenade. It is colourful on the promenade, a lot of cafés. People are relaxed, they smile, chat and eat rolls. The air smells of the sea. There are attractive shops, attractive women, attractive buildings, old, there are stone streets, there's a smell of warm bread. *This town has a nice peace,* Tessa says to the waiter. *Perhaps live here for a while?* she asks herself.

The tiny tattoo on her heart shifts. *Which way Tessa go? Which way? Which way?* she asks. From somewhere the Cheshire Cat appears, for the second time in four days. *Where do you want to go?* it asks Tessa. Tessa says, *I don't know. Doesn't matter where Tessa go*, she says. *Then it doesn't matter which way you take*, says the Cheshire Cat and disappears.

Then someone shouts *Lea!*

Then Lea Moser, as though she has come down from an advertisement for mobile telephones, smiles and says:

How are you?

And yet, around her nothing moves, parts of her being live separately, each for itself. Parts of her being do not speak, they no longer have anything to say, or anyone to say it to. She understands those parts of her being, but she does not feel them. Around her a pantomime is being performed in which she does not participate. She is outside.

Who? Lea Moser or Tessa Koller?

Who?

ACKNOWLEDGMENTS

In *Leica Format* Daša Drndić has incorporated the voices and words of a number of writers. If there is any writer whose work has not been acknowledged, we will make due reference in any future edition.

Excerpt from "The Second Coming", W. B. Yeats, first printed in *The Dial* in 1920.

Excerpt from *The Book of Disquiet* by Fernand Pessoa, translated from the Portuguese by Margaret Jull Costa. Copyright © 1982. English translation copyright © Margaret Jull Costa, 1991, by permission of Serpent's Tail/Profile, London.

Excerpt from *Le città invisibili* by Italo Calvino. Copyright © 2002, The Estate of Italo Calvino, used by permission of the Wylie Agency (UK) Limited. English translation copyright © Harcourt Brace Jovanovich, Inc. 1974. First published in Great Britain by Secker & Warburg in 1974. English translation used by permission of the Random House Group, Ltd.

Excerpt from "Starvation Camp Near Jaslo" from *Poems New and Collected 1957-1997* by Wisława Szymborska, translated from the Polish by Stanisław Barańczak and Clare Cavanagh. English translation copyright © 1998 by Houghton Mifflin Harcourt Publishing Company. Reprinted by permission of Houghton Mifflin Harcourt Publishing Company. All rights reserved.

Excerpt from *Lapidarium II* by Ryszard Kapuscinski in a translation by Andrej Duszenko.

Lines from "The Raven" by Edgar Allen Poe, first published in January 1945 in the *New York Evening Mirror*.

Excerpt from Georges Duhamel's *Confession de Minuit* (1920), the first in the novel cycle *Vie et Aventures de Salavin*.

DAŠA DRNDIĆ is a novelist, playwright, poet and literary critic, born in Zagreb, Croatia, in 1946. *Trieste*, her first novel to be translated into English, was shortlisted for the *Independent* Foreign Fiction Prize in 2013 and was the winner of the parallel Reader's Group Award that same year. *Trieste* has now been translated into more than ten languages.

CELIA HAWKESWORTH taught Serbian and Croatian language and literature at the School of Slavonic and East European Studies, University of London, from 1971 to 2002. She began translating fiction in the 1960s, including works by Ivo Andrić, Vladimir Arsenijević and Dubravka Ugrešić.